I0823957

THE BALLAD OF SONGBIRDS AND SNAKES

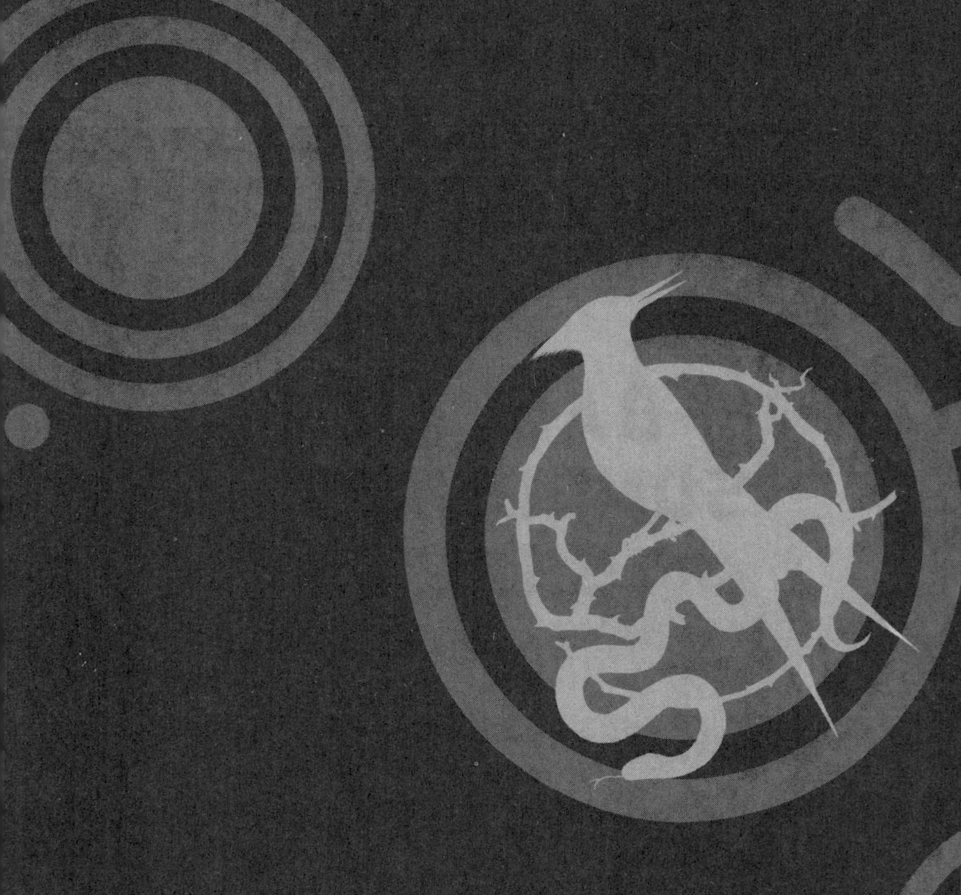

SCHOLASTIC PRESS / NEW YORK

SUZANNE
COLLINS

THE BALLAD OF SONGBIRDS AND SNAKES

Library of Congress Cataloging-in-Publication Data available

ISBN 978-1-338-63517-1

10 9 8 7 6 5 4 3 2 1 25 26 27 28 29

Printed in Italy 208

First edition, May 2020

Book design by Elizabeth B. Parisi

For Norton and Jeanne Juster

"Hereby it is manifest, that during the time men live without a common Power to keep them all in awe, they are in that condition which is called Warre; and such a warre, as is of every man, against every man."
— Thomas Hobbes, *Leviathan*, 1651

"The state of nature has a law of nature to govern it, which obliges every one: and reason, which is that law, teaches all mankind, who will but consult it, that being all equal and independent, no one ought to harm another in his life, health, liberty, or possessions. . . ."
— John Locke, *Second Treatise of Government*, 1689

"Man is born free; and everywhere he is in chains."
— Jean-Jacques Rousseau, *The Social Contract*, 1762

"Sweet is the lore which Nature brings;
Our meddling intellect
Misshapes the beauteous forms of things;
— We murder to dissect."
— William Wordsworth, "The Tables Turned,"
Lyrical Ballads, 1798

"I thought of the promise of virtues which he had displayed on the opening of his existence, and the subsequent blight of all kindly feeling by the loathing and scorn which his protectors had manifested towards him."
— Mary Shelley, *Frankenstein*, 1818

PART I

"THE MENTOR"

Coriolanus released the fistful of cabbage into the pot of boiling water and swore that one day it would never pass his lips again. But this was not that day. He needed to eat a large bowl of the anemic stuff, and drink every drop of broth, to prevent his stomach from growling during the reaping ceremony. It was one of a long list of precautions he took to mask the fact that his family, despite residing in the penthouse of the Capitol's most opulent apartment building, was as poor as district scum. That at eighteen, the heir to the once-great house of Snow had nothing to live on but his wits.

His shirt for the reaping was worrying him. He had an acceptable pair of dark dress pants bought on the black market last year, but the shirt was what people looked at. Fortunately, the Academy provided the uniforms it required for daily use. For today's ceremony, however, students were instructed to be dressed fashionably but with the solemnity the occasion dictated. Tigris had said to trust her, and he did. Only his cousin's cleverness with a needle had saved him so far. Still, he couldn't expect miracles.

The shirt they'd dug from the back of the wardrobe — his father's, from better days — was stained and yellowed with age, half the buttons missing, a cigarette burn on one cuff. Too damaged to sell in even the worst of times, and this was to be his reaping shirt? This morning he had gone to her room at daybreak, only to find both his cousin and the shirt missing. Not a good sign. Had Tigris given up on the old thing and braved the black market in some last-ditch effort to find him proper clothing? And what on earth would she possess worth trading for it? Only one thing — herself — and the house of Snow had not yet fallen that far. Or was it falling now as he salted the cabbage?

He thought of people putting a price on her. With her long, pointed nose and skinny body, Tigris was no great beauty, but she had a sweetness, a vulnerability that invited abuse. She would find takers, if she had a mind to. The idea made him feel sick and helpless and, consequently, disgusted with himself.

From deep in the apartment he heard the recording of the Capitol anthem, "Gem of Panem," kick on. His grandmother's tremulous soprano voice joined in, bouncing off the walls.

Gem of Panem,
Mighty city,
Through the ages, you shine anew.

As always, she was painfully off-key and slightly behind tempo. The first year of the war, she'd played the recording on national holidays for five-year-old Coriolanus and eight-year-old Tigris in order to build their sense of patriotism. The daily recital hadn't begun until that black day when the district rebels had surrounded the Capitol, cutting it off from supplies for the remaining two years of the war. "Remember, children," she'd say, "we are but besieged — we have not surrendered!" Then she would warble the anthem out of the penthouse window as the bombs rained down. Her small act of defiance.

We humbly kneel
To your ideal,

And the notes she could never quite hit . . .

And pledge our love to you!

Coriolanus winced a little. For a decade now, though the rebels had been silent, his grandmother had not. There were still two verses to go.

Gem of Panem,
Heart of justice,
Wisdom crowns your marble brow.

He wondered if more furniture might absorb some of the sound, but the question was academic. At present, their penthouse apartment was a microcosm of the Capitol itself, bearing the scars of the relentless rebel attacks. The twenty-foot-high walls were veined with cracks, the molded ceiling was dotted with holes from missing chunks of plaster, and ugly black strips of electrical tape held in place the broken glass of the arched windows that looked out over the city. Throughout the war and the decade that followed, the family had been forced to sell or trade many of its possessions, so that some rooms were entirely empty and closed off and the others sparsely furnished at best. Even worse, during the bitter cold of the siege's final winter, several elegant, carved wooden pieces and innumerable volumes of books had been sacrificed to the fireplace to keep the family from freezing to death. Watching the bright pages of his picture books — the very ones he'd pored over with his mother — reduced to ashes had never failed to bring him to tears. But better off sad than dead.

Having been in his friends' apartments, Coriolanus knew that most families had begun to repair their homes, but the Snows could not even afford a few yards of linen for a new shirt. He thought of his classmates, riffling through their closets or slipping into their newly tailored suits, and wondered just how long he could keep up appearances.

You give us light.
You reunite.
To you we make our vow.

If Tigris's revamped shirt was unwearable, what was he to do? Fake the flu and call in sick? *Spineless.* Soldier through in his uniform shirt? *Disrespectful.* Squeeze into the red button-down that he had outgrown two years ago? *Poor.* Acceptable option? *None of the above.*

Perhaps Tigris had gone to ask help from her employer, Fabricia Whatnot, a woman as ridiculous as her name but with a certain talent for derivative fashion. Whether the trend was feathers or leathers, plastics or plush, she could find a way to incorporate it at a reasonable rate. Not much of a student, Tigris had forgone university when she'd graduated from the Academy to pursue her dream of becoming a designer. She was supposed to be an apprentice, although Fabricia used her more as slave labor, requiring her to give foot massages and clean clumps of her long magenta hair from the drains. But Tigris never complained and would hear no criticism of her boss, so pleased and grateful was she to have a position in fashion.

Gem of Panem,
Seat of power,
Strength in peacetime, shield in strife.

Coriolanus opened the refrigerator, hoping for something to liven up the cabbage soup. The sole occupant was a metal saucepan. When he removed the lid, a mush of congealed, shredded potatoes stared back at him. Had his grandmother finally made good her threat of learning to cook? Was the stuff even edible? He replaced the lid until he had more information to work with. What a luxury it would be to toss it in the trash without a second thought. What a luxury trash would be. He remembered, or thought he did, being very small and watching garbage trucks operated by Avoxes — tongueless workers made the best workers, or so his grandmother said — humming down the streets, emptying large bags of discarded food, containers, worn household items. Then came the time when nothing was disposable, no calorie unwanted, and no item unable to be traded, or burned for heat, or tucked against a wall for insulation. Everyone had learned to despise waste. It was creeping back into fashion, though. A sign of prosperity, like a decent shirt.

Protect our land
With armored hand,

The shirt. The shirt. His mind could fixate on a problem like that — anything, really — and not let go. As if controlling one element of his world would keep him from ruin. It was a bad habit that blinded him to other things that could harm him. A tendency toward obsession was hardwired into his brain and would likely be his undoing if he couldn't learn to outsmart it.

His grandmother's voice squeaked out the final crescendo.

Our Capitol, our life!

Crazy old woman, still clinging to the prewar days. He loved her, but she'd lost touch with reality years ago. Every meal, she'd rattle on about the Snows' legendary grandeur, even when their fare consisted of watery bean soup and stale crackers. And to hear her tell it, it was a given that his future would be glorious. "When Coriolanus is president . . ." she often began. "When Coriolanus is president . . ." everything from the rickety Capitol air force to the exorbitant price of pork chops would be magically corrected. Thank goodness the broken elevator and her arthritic knees prevented her from going out much, and her infrequent visitors were as fossilized as she.

The cabbage began to boil, filling the kitchen with the smell of poverty. Coriolanus jabbed at it with a wooden spoon. Still no Tigris. Soon it would be too late to call and make an excuse. Everyone would have assembled at the Academy's Heavensbee Hall. There would be anger to deal with as well as disappointment from his communications professor, Satyria Click, who had campaigned for him to receive one of the twenty-four coveted mentorships in the Hunger Games. Besides being Satyria's favorite, he was her teaching aide, and doubtless she would need him for something today. She could be unpredictable, especially when she'd been drinking, and that was a given on the day of the reaping. He'd better call and warn her, say he couldn't stop vomiting or something but would do his best to recover. He steeled himself and picked up the phone to plead dire illness when another thought hit him: If he failed to show, would she allow them to replace him as a mentor? And if she did, would that weaken his chance for one of the Academy prizes presented at graduation? Without such a prize, he had no way to afford to go to university, which meant no career, which meant no future, not for him, and who knew what would happen to the family, and—

The front door, warped and complaining, scraped open.

"Coryo!" Tigris cried out, and he slammed the phone down. The nickname she'd given him when he was a newborn had stuck. He flew out of the kitchen, almost knocking her over, but she was too excited to reproach him. "I did it! I did it! Well, I did something." Her feet did a rapid little run in place as she held up a hanger draped in an old dress bag. "Look, look, look!"

Coriolanus unzipped the bag and stripped it from the shirt.

It was gorgeous. No, even better, it was classy. The thick linen was neither the original white nor the yellow of age, but a delicious cream. The cuffs and collar had been replaced with black velvet, and the buttons were gold and ebony cubes. Tesserae. Each had two tiny holes drilled through it for the thread.

"You're brilliant," he said earnestly. "And the best cousin ever." Careful to hold the shirt out of harm's way, he hugged her with his free arm. "Snow lands on top!"

"Snow lands on top!" Tigris crowed. It was the saying that had gotten them through the war, when it was a constant struggle not to be ground into the earth.

"Tell me everything," he said, knowing she would want to. She so loved to talk clothes.

Tigris threw up her hands and gave a breathy laugh. "Where to begin?"

She began with the bleach. Tigris had suggested the white curtains in Fabricia's bedroom looked dingy and, while soaking them in bleach water, had slipped in the shirt. It had responded beautifully, but no amount of soaking could entirely erase the stains. So she'd boiled the shirt with dead marigolds she'd found in the bin outside Fabricia's neighbor's, and the blossoms had dyed the linen just enough to conceal the stains. The velvet for the cuffs was from a large drawstring pouch that had held some now-meaningless plaque of their grandfather's. The tesserae she had pried from the interior of a cabinet in the maid's bathroom. She'd gotten the building maintenance man to drill the holes in exchange for mending his coveralls.

"Was that this morning?" he asked.

"Oh, no, yesterday. Sunday. This morning, I — Did you find my potatoes?" He followed her into the kitchen, where she opened the refrigerator and pulled out the pan. "I was up until all hours making starch from them. Then I ran down to the Dolittles' so I could have a proper iron. Saved these for the soup!" Tigris upended the mess into the boiling cabbage and stirred it around.

He noticed the lilac circles under her golden brown eyes and couldn't help feeling a pang of guilt. "When was the last time you slept?" he asked.

"Oh, I'm fine. I ate the potato skins. They say that's where the vitamins are anyway. And today's the reaping, so it's practically a holiday!" she said cheerfully.

"Not at Fabricia's," he said. Not anywhere, really. Reaping day was terrible in the districts, but not much of a celebration in the Capitol either. Like him, most people took no pleasure in remembering the war. Tigris would spend the day waiting hand and foot on her employer and her motley crew of guests while they exchanged morose tales of the deprivation they'd experienced during the siege and drank themselves senseless. Tomorrow, nursing them through hangovers, would be worse.

"Stop worrying. Here, you better hurry up and eat!" Tigris ladled some soup into a bowl and set it on the table.

Coriolanus glanced at the clock, gulped down the soup without caring that it burned his mouth, and ran to his room with the shirt. He had already showered and shaved, and his fair skin was, thankfully, blemish-free today. The school-issued underwear and black socks were fine. He pulled on the dress pants, which were more than acceptable, and crammed his feet into a pair of laced leather boots. They were too small, but he could bear it. Then he pulled the shirt on gingerly, tucked in the tails, and turned to the mirror. He was not as tall as he should have been. As for so many of his generation, a poor diet had likely compromised his growth. But he was athletically trim, with excellent posture, and the shirt emphasized the finer points of his physique. Not since he was little, when his grandmother would parade him through the streets in a purple velvet suit, had he looked so regal. He smoothed back his blond curls as he mockingly whispered to his image, "Coriolanus Snow, future president of Panem, I salute you."

For Tigris's sake, he made a grand entrance into the living room, extending his arms and turning in a full circle to show off the shirt.

She squealed in delight and applauded. "You look amazing! So handsome and fashionable! Come see, Grandma'am!" It was another nickname coined by little Tigris, who'd found "Grandma," and certainly "Nana," insufficient for someone so imperial.

Their grandmother appeared, a fresh-cut red rose cupped lovingly in her tremorous hands. She wore a long, black, flowing tunic, the kind so popular before the war and so outdated as to be laughable now, and a pair of embroidered slippers with curled toes that had once been part of a costume. Strands of her thin, white hair poked from the bottom of a rusty velvet turban. This was the tail end of a once-lavish wardrobe — her few decent items were saved for company or the rare foray into the city.

"Here, here, boy. Put this on. Fresh from my roof garden," she ordered.

He reached for the rose, but a thorn pierced his palm in the shaky exchange. Blood welled from the wound, and he held his hand out to keep it from staining his precious shirt. His grandmother seemed perplexed.

"I only wanted you to look elegant," she told him.

"Of course, you did, Grandma'am," said Tigris. "And so he shall."

As she led Coriolanus into the kitchen, he reminded himself that self-control was an essential skill, and he should be grateful his grandmother provided daily opportunities to practice it.

"Puncture wounds never bleed long," Tigris promised him as she quickly cleaned and bandaged his hand. She snipped away at the rose, preserving a bit of greenery, and pinned it to his shirt. "It does look elegant. You know what her roses mean to her. Thank her."

So he did. He thanked them both and sped out the door, down the twelve ornate flights of stairs, through the lobby, and out into the Capitol.

His front door opened onto the Corso, an avenue so wide that eight chariots had comfortably ridden side by side on it in the old days when the Capitol had put on displays of military pomp for the crowds. Coriolanus could remember hanging out the apartment windows as a young child, party guests bragging that they had front-row seats to the parades. Then the bombers arrived, and for a long time his block was impassable. Now, though the streets were finally clear, rubble still lay in piles on the sidewalks, and whole buildings were as gutted as the day they'd been struck. Ten years after the victory, and he was dodging between chunks of marble and granite as he wove his way to the Academy. Sometimes Coriolanus wondered if the debris had been left there to remind the citizens of what they had endured. People had short memories. They needed to navigate the rubble, peel off the grubby ration coupons, and witness the Hunger Games to keep the war fresh in their minds. Forgetting could lead to complacency, and then they'd all be back at square one.

As he turned onto Scholars Road, he tried to measure his pace. He wanted to arrive on time, but cool and composed, not a sweaty mess. This reaping day, like most, was shaping up to be a scorcher. But what else could you expect on July 4th? He felt grateful for the perfume of his grandmother's rose, as his warming shirt was giving off a faint scent of potatoes and dead marigolds.

As the finest secondary school in the Capitol, the Academy educated the offspring of the prominent, wealthy, and influential. With over four hundred students in each class, it had been possible for Tigris and Coriolanus, given their family's long history at the school, to gain acceptance without much difficulty. Unlike the University, it was tuition-free and provided lunch and school supplies along with uniforms. Anyone who was anyone attended the Academy, and Coriolanus would need those connections as a foundation for his future.

The grand staircase up to the Academy could hold the entire student body, so it easily accommodated the stream of officials, professors, and students headed for the reaping day festivities. Coriolanus climbed it slowly, attempting a casual dignity in case he caught anyone's eye. People knew him — or at least they had known his parents and grandparents — and there was a certain standard expected of a Snow. This year, beginning this very day, he was hoping to achieve personal recognition as well. Mentoring in the Hunger Games was his final project before graduating from the Academy in midsummer. If he gave an impressive performance as a mentor, with his outstanding academic record, Coriolanus should be awarded a monetary prize substantial enough to cover his tuition at the University.

There would be twenty-four tributes, one boy and one girl from each of the twelve defeated districts, drawn by lottery to be thrown into an arena to fight to the death in the Hunger Games. It was all laid out in the Treaty of Treason that had ended the Dark Days of the districts' rebellion, one of the many punishments borne by the rebels. As in the past, the tributes would be dumped into the Capitol Arena, a now-dilapidated amphitheater that had been used for sports and entertainment events before the war, along with some weapons to murder one another. Viewing was encouraged in the Capitol, but a lot of people avoided it. How to make it more engaging was the challenge.

With this in mind, for the first time the tributes were to be assigned mentors. Twenty-four of the Academy's best and brightest seniors had been tapped for the job. The specifics of what this entailed were still being worked out. There was talk of preparing each tribute for a personal interview, maybe some grooming for the cameras. Everyone agreed that if the Hunger Games were to continue, they needed to evolve into a more meaningful experience, and the pairing of the Capitol youth with the district tributes had people intrigued.

Coriolanus made his way through an entry draped in black banners, down a vaulted passage, and into cavernous Heavensbee Hall, where they would watch the broadcast of the reaping ceremony. He was by no means late, but the hall was already humming with faculty and students and a number of Games officials who were not required for the opening day's broadcast.

Avoxes wove through the crowd with trays of posca, a concoction of watery wine laced with honey and herbs. It was an intoxicating version of the sour stuff that had sustained the Capitol through the war, supposedly fending off illness. Coriolanus took a goblet and swished a little of the posca around his mouth, hopefully rinsing away any trace of cabbage breath. But he only allowed himself one swallow. It was stronger than most people thought, and in previous years he had seen upperclassmen make complete fools of themselves by imbibing too deeply.

The world still thought Coriolanus rich, but his only real currency was charm, which he spread liberally as he made his way through the crowd. Faces lit up as he gave friendly hellos to students and teachers alike, asking about family members, dropping compliments here and there.

"Your lecture on district retaliation haunts me."

"Love the bangs!"

"How did your mother's back surgery go? Well, tell her she's my hero."

He traveled past the hundreds of cushioned chairs set up for the occasion and onto the dais, where Satyria was regaling a mix of Academy professors and Games officials with some wild story. Although he only caught the last line — "Well, I said, 'I'm sorry about your wig, but you were the one who insisted on bringing a monkey!'" — he dutifully joined in the laughter that followed.

"Oh, Coriolanus," Satyria drawled as she waved him over. "Here's my star pupil." He gave her the expected kiss on the cheek and registered that she was several glasses of posca ahead of him. Really, she needed to get her drinking under control, although the same thing could be said for half the adults he knew. Self-medication was a citywide epidemic. Still, she was amusing and not overly uptight, one of the few professors who allowed students to call them by their first names. She drew back a bit and surveyed him. "Beautiful shirt. Where did you get such a thing?"

He looked at the shirt as if surprised by its existence and gave the shrug of a young man of limitless options.

"The Snows have deep closets," he said airily. "I was trying for respectful yet celebratory."

"And so it is. What are these cunning buttons?" Satyria asked, fingering one of the cubes on his cuff. "Tesserae?"

"Are they? Well, that explains why they remind me of the maid's bathroom," Coriolanus responded, drawing a chuckle from her friends. This was the impression he fought to sustain. A reminder that he was the rare person who had a maid's bathroom — let alone one tiled with tesserae — tempered with a self-deprecating joke about his shirt.

He nodded at Satyria. "Lovely gown. It's new, isn't it?" He could tell at a glance that it was the same dress she always wore to the reaping ceremony, refurbished with tufts of black feathers. But she had validated his shirt, and he needed to return the favor.

"I had it done especially for today," she said, embracing the question. "Tenth anniversary and all that."

"Elegant," he said. All in all, they were not a bad team.

His pleasure drained as he spotted the gymnasium mistress, Professor Agrippina Sickle, using her muscular shoulders to maneuver her way through the crowd. Behind her was her aide, Sejanus Plinth, who was carrying the ornamental shield Professor Sickle insisted on holding for the group photo each year. It had been awarded to her at the end of the war for successfully overseeing Academy safety drills during the bombings.

It was not the shield that caught Coriolanus's attention but Sejanus's outfit, a soft charcoal gray suit with a blinding white shirt offset by a paisley tie, cut to add flow to his tall, angular frame. The ensemble was stylish, brand-new, and smelling of money. War profiteering, to be exact. Sejanus's father was a District 2 manufacturer who had sided with the president. He had made such a fortune off munitions that he'd been able to buy his family's way into a life in the Capitol. The Plinths now enjoyed privileges that the oldest, most powerful families had earned over generations. It was unprecedented that Sejanus, a district-born boy, was a student at the Academy, but his father's lavish donation had allowed for much of the school's postwar reconstruction. A Capitol-born citizen would have expected a building to be renamed for them. Sejanus's father had only requested an education for his son.

For Coriolanus, the Plinths and their kind were a threat to all he held dear. The newly rich climbers in the Capitol were chipping away at the old order simply by virtue of their presence. It was particularly vexing because the bulk of the Snow family fortune had also been invested in munitions — but in District 13. Their sprawling complex, blocks and blocks of factories and research facilities, had been bombed to dust. District 13 had been nuked, and the entire area still emitted unlivable levels of radiation. The center of the Capitol's military manufacturing had shifted to District 2 and fallen right into the Plinths' laps. When news of District 13's demise had reached the Capitol, Coriolanus's grandmother had publicly brushed it off, saying it was fortunate that they had plenty of other assets. But they didn't.

Sejanus had arrived on the school playground ten years ago, a shy, sensitive boy cautiously surveying the other children with a pair of soulful brown eyes much too large for his strained face. When word had gotten out that he'd come from the districts, Coriolanus's first impulse had been to join his classmates' campaign to make the new kid's life a living hell. On further reflection, he'd ignored him. If the other Capitol children took this to mean that baiting the district brat was beneath him, Sejanus took it as decency. Neither take was quite accurate, but both reinforced the image of Coriolanus as a class act.

A woman of formidable stature, Professor Sickle cruised into Satyria's circle, scattering her inferiors to the four winds. "Good morning, Professor Click."

"Oh, Agrippina, good. You remembered your shield," said Satyria, accepting a firm handshake. "It worries me that the young people will forget the real meaning of the day. And, Sejanus. How smart you look."

Sejanus attempted a bow, sending a wayward lock of hair into his eyes. The cumbersome shield caught him in the chest.

"Too smart," said Professor Sickle. "I told him if I wanted a peacock, I'd call the pet store. They should all be in their uniforms." She eyed Coriolanus. "That's not terrible. Your father's old mess dress shirt?"

Was it? Coriolanus had no idea. A vague memory of his father in a dashing evening suit dripping in medals came to him. He decided to play out the hand. "Thank you for noticing, Professor. I had it redone so as not to suggest I'd seen combat myself. But I wanted him here with me today."

"Very fitting," said Professor Sickle. Then she directed her attention to Satyria and her views on the latest deployment of Peacekeepers, the nation's soldiers, to District 12, where the coal miners were failing to produce their quotas.

With their teachers engaged, Coriolanus nodded at the shield. "Getting a workout this morning?"

Sejanus gave a wry smile. "Always an honor to be of service."

"That's a fine polish job," Coriolanus replied. Sejanus tensed at the implication that he was, what, a suck-up? A lackey? Coriolanus let it build a moment before he diffused it. "I should know. I do all Satyria's wine goblets."

Sejanus relaxed at that. "Really?"

"No, not really. But only because she hasn't thought of it," said Coriolanus, seesawing between disdain and camaraderie.

"Professor Sickle thinks of everything. She doesn't hesitate to call me, day or night." Sejanus looked as if he might continue, then just sighed. "And, of course, now that I'm graduating, we're moving closer to the school. Perfect timing, as usual."

Coriolanus suddenly felt wary. "Whereabouts?"

"Somewhere on the Corso. A lot of those grand places will be going on the market soon. Owners not being able to afford the taxes, or some such, my father said." The shield scraped the floor, and Sejanus hefted it up.

"They don't tax properties in the Capitol. Only in the districts," said Coriolanus.

"It's a new law," Sejanus told him. "To get more money for rebuilding the city."

Coriolanus tried to tamp down the panic rising inside him. A new law. Instating a tax on his apartment. For how much? As it was, they barely eked out a living on Tigris's pittance, the tiny military pension his grandmother received for her husband's service to Panem, and his own dependent benefits as the child of a slain war hero, which would cease on graduation. If they couldn't pay the taxes, would they lose the apartment? It was all they had. Selling the place would be of no help; he knew his grandmother had borrowed every cent on it she could. If they sold, there would be next to nothing left. They would have to move to some obscure neighborhood and join the grimy ranks of everyday citizens, without status, without influence, without dignity. The disgrace would kill his grandmother. It would be kinder to toss her out the window of the penthouse. At least that would be quick.

"You all right?" Sejanus peered at him, puzzled. "You just went white as a sheet."

Coriolanus regained his composure. "I think it's the posca. Turns my stomach."

"Yeah," Sejanus agreed. "Ma was always forcing it down me during the war."

Ma? Was Coriolanus's place about to be usurped by someone who referred to his mother as "Ma"? The cabbage and posca threatened to make a reappearance. He took a deep breath and forced his stomach to hang on to it, resenting Sejanus more than he had since the well-fed district boy with the cloddish accent first wandered up to him, clutching a bag of gumdrops.

Coriolanus heard a bell ringing and saw his fellow students converging at the front of the dais.

"I guess it's time to assign us tributes," Sejanus said glumly.

Coriolanus followed him to where a special section of chairs, six rows by four, had been set up for the mentors. He tried to push the apartment crisis out of his head, to focus on the crucial task at hand. More than ever, it was essential that he excel, and to excel, he must be assigned a competitive tribute.

Dean Casca Highbottom, the man credited with the creation of the Hunger Games, was overseeing the mentor program personally. He presented himself to the students with all the verve of a sleepwalker, dreamy-eyed and, as usual, doped up on morphling. His once-fine physique was shrunken and draped with sagging skin. The close-clipped precision of a recent haircut and crisp suit only threw his deterioration into relief. Due to his fame as the Games' inventor, he still had a tenuous hold on his position, but there were rumors that the Academy Board was losing patience.

"Ho there," he slurred, waving a crumpled piece of paper over his head. "Reading the things off now." The students hushed, trying hard to hear him above the din of the hall. "Read you a name, then you who gets that one. Right? So, fine. District One, boy, goes to . . ." Dean Highbottom squinted at the paper, trying hard to focus. "Glasses," he mumbled. "Forgot them." Everyone stared at his glasses, already perched on his nose, and waited while his fingers found them. "Ah, here we go. Livia Cardew."

Livia's pointed little face broke into a grin and she punched the air in victory, shouting "Yes!" in her shrill voice. She had always been prone to gloating. As if the plum assignment was solely a reflection on her, and not on her mother running the largest bank in the Capitol.

Coriolanus felt increasing desperation as Dean Highbottom stumbled through the list, assigning each district's boy and girl a mentor. After ten years, a pattern had emerged. The better-fed, more Capitol-friendly districts of 1 and 2 produced more victors, with the fishing and farming tributes from 4 and 11 also being contenders. Coriolanus had hoped for either a 1 or a 2, but neither was assigned to him, which was made more insulting when Sejanus scored the District 2 boy. District 4 passed without mention of his name, and his last real chance for a victor — the District 11 boy — was assigned to Clemensia Dovecote, daughter of the energies secretary. Unlike Livia, Clemensia received news of her good fortune with tact, pushing her sheet of raven hair over her shoulder as she studiously made note of her tribute in her binder.

Something was amiss when a Snow, who also happened to be one of the Academy's high-honor students, had gone unrecognized. Coriolanus was beginning to think they had forgotten him — perhaps they were giving him some special position? — when, to his horror, he heard Dean Highbottom mumble, "And last but least, District Twelve girl . . . she belongs to Coriolanus Snow."

The District 12 girl? Could there be a bigger slap in the face? District 12, the smallest district, the joke district, with its stunted, joint-swollen kids that always died in the first five minutes, and not only that . . . but the girl? Not that a girl couldn't win, but in his mind the Hunger Games were largely about brute force, and the girls were naturally smaller than the boys and therefore at a disadvantage. Coriolanus had never been a particular favorite of Dean Highbottom, whom he jokingly called High-as-a-Kite-Bottom among his friends, but he had not expected such a public humiliation. Had the nickname gotten back to him? Or was this just an acknowledgment that, in the new world order, the Snows were fading into insignificance?

He could feel the blood burning his cheeks as he tried to remain composed. Most of the other students had risen and were chatting among themselves. He must join them, pretend this was of no consequence, but he seemed incapable of movement. The most he could manage was to turn his head to the right, where Sejanus still sat beside him. Coriolanus opened his mouth to congratulate him but stopped at the barely concealed misery on the other boy's face.

"What is it?" he asked. "Aren't you happy? District Two, the boy — that's the pick of the litter."

"You forget. I'm part of that litter," said Sejanus hoarsely.

Coriolanus let that sink in. So ten years in the Capitol and the privileged life it provided had been wasted on Sejanus. He still thought of himself as a district citizen. Sentimental nonsense.

Sejanus's forehead creased in consternation. "I'm sure my father requested it. He's always trying to get my mind right."

No doubt, thought Coriolanus. Old Strabo Plinth's deep pockets and influence were respected if his lineage was not. And while the mentorships were supposedly based on merit, strings clearly had been pulled.

The audience had settled into seats now. At the back of the dais, curtains parted to reveal a floor-to-ceiling screen. The reaping aired live from each district, moving from the east coast to the west, and was broadcast around the country. That meant District 12 would kick off the day. Everyone rose as the seal of Panem filled the screen, accompanied by the Capitol anthem.

Gem of Panem,
Mighty city,
Through the ages, you shine anew.

Some of the students fumbled for the words, but Coriolanus, who had heard his grandmother butcher it daily for years, sang all three verses in a forceful voice, garnering a few nods of approval. It was pathetic, but he needed every drop of approval he could get.

The seal dissolved to show President Ravinstill, his hair streaked with silver, dressed in his prewar military uniform as a reminder that he'd been controlling the districts long before the Dark Days of the rebellion. He recited a brief passage from the Treaty of Treason, which laid out the Hunger Games as a war reparation, young district lives taken for the young Capitol lives that had been lost. The price of the rebels' treachery.

The Gamemakers cut to the bleak square of District 12, where a temporary stage, now lined with Peacekeepers, had been erected before the Justice Building. Mayor Lipp, a squat, freckled man in a hopelessly outdated suit, stood between two burlap sacks. He dug his hand deeply in the bag on his left, pulled out a slip of paper, and barely glanced at it.

"The District Twelve girl tribute is Lucy Gray Baird," he said into a mic. The camera swept over the crowd of gray, hungry faces in gray, shapeless clothing, seeking the tribute. It zoomed in toward a disturbance, girls drawing back from the unfortunate chosen one.

The audience gave a surprised murmur at the sight of her.

Lucy Gray Baird stood upright in a dress made of a rainbow of ruffles, now raggedy but once fancy. Her dark, curly hair was pulled up and woven with limp wildflowers. Her colorful ensemble drew the eye, as to a tattered butterfly in a field of moths. She did not make straight for the stage but began to weave through the girls off to her right.

It happened quickly. The dip of her hand into the ruffles at her hip, the wriggle of bright green transported from her pocket and deposited down the collar of a smirking redhead's blouse, the rustle of her skirt as she moved on. Focus stayed on the victim, her smirk changing to an expression of horror, her shrieks as she fell to the ground, pawing at her clothes, the shouts of the mayor. And in the background, her assailant was still weaving, still gliding her way to the stage, not looking back even once.

Heavensbee Hall came to life as people elbowed their neighbors.

"Did you see that?"

"What did she drop down her dress?"

"A lizard?"

"I saw a snake!"

"Did she kill her?"

Coriolanus scanned the crowd and felt a spark of hope. His long shot of a tribute, his throwaway, his insult had captured the Capitol's attention. That was good, right? With his help, perhaps she could keep it, and he could turn disgrace into a respectable showing. One way or another, their fates were irrevocably linked.

Up on the screen, Mayor Lipp flew down the steps of the stage, pushing his way through the assembled girls to reach the fallen one on the ground. "Mayfair? Mayfair?" he cried. "My daughter needs help!" A circle had opened up around her, but the few half-hearted attempts to help her were blocked by her thrashing limbs. The mayor broke into the clearing just as a small, iridescent green snake shot out of the folds of her dress and into the crowd, bringing screams and scrambles to avoid it. The departure of the snake calmed Mayfair, but her distress was immediately replaced by embarrassment. She looked straight into the camera as she realized all the citizens of Panem were watching. One hand tried to straighten a bow that had gone askew in her hair, the other moved to right her garments, filthy with the coal dust that coated everything and torn from her clawing. As her father helped her to her feet, it was apparent she had wet herself. He removed his jacket to wrap around her and handed her over to a Peacekeeper to lead away. He turned back to the stage and trained a murderous look on District 12's newest tribute.

As Coriolanus watched Lucy Gray Baird take the stage, he felt a stab of uneasiness. Could she be mentally unstable? There was something vaguely familiar but disturbing about her. The rows of raspberry pink, royal blue, and daffodil yellow ruffles . . .

"She's like a circus performer," one of the girls remarked. The other mentors made sounds of agreement.

That was it. Coriolanus reached back into his memory to the circuses of his early childhood. Jugglers and acrobats, clowns and dancing girls in puffy dresses twirling around while his brain grew giddy with spun sugar. His tribute's choosing such festive attire for the darkest event of the year showed a strangeness beyond a simple lapse of judgment.

The allotted time for District 12's reaping had no doubt come and gone, but they still lacked a male tribute. Even so, when Mayor Lipp retook the stage, he ignored the bags of names, made a beeline for the girl tribute, and struck her in the face so powerfully that she was knocked to her knees. He had raised his hand to hit her again, when a couple of the Peacekeepers intervened, grabbing his arms and attempting to redirect him to the business at hand. When he resisted, they hauled him back into the Justice Building, bringing the whole proceeding to a standstill.

Attention shifted to the girl on the stage. As the camera zoomed in on her, Coriolanus was not reassured about Lucy Gray Baird's sanity. Where she'd gotten the makeup he had no idea, for it was only just becoming accessible again in the Capitol, but her eyes were shadowed blue and lined with black, her cheeks rouged, and her lips stained a somewhat greasy red. Here in the Capitol, it would have been bold. In District 12, it felt immoderate. She was impossible to look away from as she sat there running her hand over her skirt, compulsively smoothing the ruffles. Only when they were neatly arranged did she raise her hand to touch the mark on her cheek. Her lower lip trembled slightly and her eyes shone with tears that threatened to spill over.

"Don't cry," Coriolanus whispered. He caught himself and looked around nervously to find that the other students were riveted. Their faces showed concern. She had won their sympathy, despite her oddness. They had no idea who she was or why she had attacked Mayfair, but who couldn't see that the smirking thing was spiteful, and her father a brute who would flatten a girl he'd just sentenced to death?

"I bet they rigged it," Sejanus said quietly. "Her name wasn't on that slip."

Just as the girl was about to lose her battle with the tears, a strange thing happened. From somewhere in the crowd, a voice began to sing. A young voice, which might belong to either a boy or a girl, but of such a pitch that it carried across the silent square.

You can't take my past.
You can't take my history.

A puff of wind blew across the stage, and the girl slowly lifted her head. Somewhere else in the crowd, a deeper, distinctly male voice sang out.

You could take my pa,
But his name's a mystery.

The shadow of a smile played on Lucy Gray Baird's lips. She suddenly pushed herself to her feet, strode to the center of the stage, grabbed the mic, and let loose.

Nothing you can take from me was ever worth keeping.

Her free hand dug into the ruffles of her skirt, swishing it side to side, and all of it began to make sense — the costume, the makeup, her hair. Whoever she was, she had been dressed for a performance all along. She had a fine voice, bright and clear on the high notes, husky and rich on the low, and she moved with assurance.

You can't take my charm.
You can't take my humor.
You can't take my wealth,
'Cause it's just a rumor.
Nothing you can take from me was ever worth keeping.

Singing transformed her, and Coriolanus no longer found her so disconcerting. There was something exciting, even attractive, about her. The camera drank her in as she crossed to the front of the stage and leaned out over the audience, sweet and insolent.

Thinking you're so fine.
Thinking you can have mine.
Thinking you're in control.
Thinking you'll change me, maybe rearrange me.
Think again, if that's your goal,
'Cause . . .

And then she was off, sashaying around the stage, right past the Peacekeepers, some of whom were having trouble suppressing smiles. None of them moved to stop her.

You can't take my sass.
You can't take my talking.
You can kiss my ass
And then keep on walking.
Nothing you can take from me was ever worth keeping.

The doors to the Justice Building banged open and the Peacekeepers who had taken the mayor off burst back onto the stage. The girl was facing front, but you could see her register their arrival. She headed to the far end of the stage for her big finish.

No, sir,
Nothing you can take from me is worth dirt.
Take it, 'cause I'd give it free. It won't hurt.
Nothing you can take from me was ever worth keeping!

She managed to blow a kiss before they were on her. "My friends call me Lucy Gray — I hope you will, too!" she called out. One of the Peacekeepers wrested the mic from her hand as another picked her up and carried her back to the middle of the stage. She waved as if to raucous applause, not dead silence.

For a few moments, they were silent in Heavensbee Hall as well. Coriolanus wondered if, like him, they were hoping she'd keep singing. Then everybody broke out talking, first about the girl, then about who'd been lucky enough to get her. The other students were craning their heads around, some giving him a thumbs-up, some shooting resentful looks. He gave a bemused shake of his head, but inside he was glowing. Snow lands on top.

Peacekeepers brought the mayor back out and planted themselves on either side of him to avoid further conflict. Lucy Gray ignored his return, having seemingly regained her poise by performing. The mayor glowered at the camera as he slapped his hand into the second bag and pulled several slips out. A few fluttered down to the stage and he read the remaining paper. "The District Twelve boy tribute is Jessup Diggs."

The kids in the square stirred and made way for Jessup, a boy with a fringe of black hair plastered down on his prominent forehead. As District 12 tributes went, he was a fine specimen, bigger than average and strong-looking. His griminess suggested he was already employed in the mines. A halfhearted attempt at washing had revealed a relatively clean oval in the middle of his face, but it was ringed with black, and coal dust caked his nails. Awkwardly, he ascended the stairs to take his place. As he neared the mayor, Lucy Gray stepped forward and extended her hand. The boy hesitated, then reached out and shook. Lucy Gray crossed in front of him, switched her right hand for her left, and they were standing side by side, holding hands, when she made a deep curtsy, pulling the boy into a bow. A smattering of applause and a lone whoop came from the District 12 crowd before the Peacekeepers closed in and the reaping broadcast cut to District 8.

Coriolanus acted engrossed in the show as 8, 6, and 11 called their tributes, but his brain spun with the repercussions of landing Lucy Gray Baird. She was a gift, he knew it, and he must treat her as such. But how best to exploit her showstopping entrance? How to wrangle some success from a dress, a snake, a song? The tributes would be given precious little time with the audience before the Games began. How could he get the audience to invest in her and, by extension, him, in just an interview? He half registered the other tributes, mostly pitiful creatures, and took note of the stronger ones. Sejanus got a towering fellow from District 2, and Livia's District 1 boy looked like he could be a contender as well. Coriolanus's girl seemed fairly healthy, but her slight build was more suited to dancing than hand-to-hand combat. He bet she could run fast enough, though, and that was important.

As the reaping drew to a close, the smell of food from the buffet wafted over the audience. Fresh-baked bread. Onions. Meat. Coriolanus could not keep his stomach from growling, and risked another couple swallows of posca to quiet it. He felt wired, light-headed, and ravenous. After the screen went dark, he had to use all the discipline he could muster not to rush for the buffet.

The endless dance with hunger had defined his life. Not the very early years, before the war, but every day since had been a battle, a negotiation, a game. How was it best to stave off hunger? Eat all the food at one meal? Spread it through the day in dribs and drabs? Wolf it down or chew every morsel to liquid? It was all just a mind game to distract himself from the fact that it was never enough. No one would ever let him have enough.

During the war, the rebels had held the food-producing districts. Taking a page out of the Capitol's playbook, they'd tried to starve the Capitol into submission using food — or a lack thereof — as a weapon. Now the tables had turned again, with the Capitol controlling the supply and taking it one step further, twisting the knife into the districts' hearts with the Hunger Games. Amid the violence of the Games, there was a silent agony that everyone in Panem had experienced, the desperation for enough sustenance to bring you to the following sunrise.

That desperation had turned upstanding Capitol citizens into monsters. People who dropped dead from starvation in the streets became part of a gruesome food chain. One winter's night, Coriolanus and Tigris had slipped out of the apartment to scavenge some wooden crates they'd spotted earlier in an alley. On the way, they passed three bodies, recognizing one as that of a young maid who served tea so nicely at the Cranes' afternoon gatherings. A heavy, wet snow began falling and they thought the streets deserted, but on the way home, a bundled figure sent them scurrying behind a hedge. They watched as their neighbor Nero Price, a titan in the railroad industry, carved the leg from the maid, sawing back and forth with a terrifying knife until the limb came free. He wrapped it in the skirt he ripped from her waist and then bolted down the side street that led to the back of his town house. The cousins never spoke of it, even to each other, but it was burned into Coriolanus's memory. The savagery distorting Price's face, the white anklet and scuffed black shoe at the end of the severed limb, and the absolute horror of realizing that he, too, could now be viewed as edible.

Coriolanus credited both his literal and moral survival to the Grandma'am's foresight early in the war. His parents were dead, Tigris orphaned as well, and both children were living with their grandmother. The rebels had been making slow but steady progress to the Capitol, although arrogance kept that reality from being widely acknowledged in the city. Food shortages required even the richest to seek out certain supplies on the black market. That was how Coriolanus found himself at the back door of a once-trendy nightclub one late October afternoon, holding the handle of a small red wagon in one hand and the Grandma'am's gloved hand in the other. There was a bitter chill in the air that warned ominously of winter, and a blanket of gloomy, gray clouds overhead. They had come to see Pluribus Bell, an aging man with lemon-tinted spectacles and a white powdered wig that fell to his waist. He and his partner, Cyrus, a musician, owned the shuttered club and now made do by trafficking goods from its back alley. The Snows had come for a case of canned milk, the fresh stuff having disappeared weeks ago, but Pluribus said he was sold out. What had just arrived were crates of dried lima beans, stacked high on the mirrored stage behind him.

"They'll keep for years," Pluribus promised the Grandma'am. "I plan on setting aside twenty or so for personal use."

Coriolanus's grandmother had laughed. "How ghastly."

"No, my dear. Ghastly is what happens without them," Pluribus said.

He didn't elaborate, but the Grandma'am stopped laughing. She shot a look at Coriolanus, and her hand clenched his for a second. It seemed involuntary, almost a spasm. Then she looked at the crates and appeared to be figuring something in her head. "How many can you spare?" she asked the club owner. Coriolanus pulled one crate home in his wagon, and the other twenty-nine arrived in the dead of night, as hoarding was technically illegal. Cyrus and a friend hauled the crates up the stairs and piled them in the middle of the lavishly furnished living room. On the top of the pile, they placed a single can of milk, compliments of Pluribus, then bid them good night. Coriolanus and Tigris helped the Grandma'am hide them in closets, in fancy wardrobes, even in the old clock.

"Who's going to eat all these?" he asked. At this time, there was still bacon in his life, and chicken, and the occasional roast. Milk was spotty but cheese plentiful, and some sort of dessert could be counted on at dinner, even if it was just jam bread.

"We'll eat some. Perhaps some we can trade," said the Grandma'am. "They'll be our secret."

"I don't like lima beans." Coriolanus pouted. "At least, I don't think I do."

"Well, we'll have Cook find a good recipe," said the Grandma'am.

But the cook had been called to serve in the war, then died of the flu. The Grandma'am, it turned out, did not even know how to turn on the stove, let alone follow a recipe. It fell to eight-year-old Tigris to boil the beans to the thick stew, then the soup, then the watery broth, which was to sustain them throughout the war. Lima beans. Cabbage. The ration of bread. They lived on it, day in, day out, for years. Surely, it had impeded his growth. Surely, he would be taller, his shoulders broader, had he had more food. But his brain had developed properly; at least he hoped it had. Beans, cabbage, brown bread. Coriolanus grew to hate the stuff, but it kept them alive, without shame, and without cannibalizing the dead bodies in the streets.

Coriolanus swallowed the saliva flooding his mouth as he reached for the gilt-edged plate embossed with the Academy's seal. Even in the leanest days, the Capitol had not lacked fancy dishware, and he had eaten many a cabbage leaf from fine china at home. He collected a linen napkin, a fork, a knife. As he raised the lid on the first sterling silver chafing dish, the steam bathed his lips. Creamed onions. He took a modest spoonful and tried not to drool. Boiled potatoes. Summer squash. Baked ham. Hot rolls and a pat of butter. On second thought, two pats. A full plate, but not a greedy one. Not for a teenage boy.

He set his plate on the table next to Clemensia and went to retrieve his dessert from a cart, because last year they had run out and he'd missed the tapioca entirely. His heart skipped a beat when he saw the rows of apple pie wedges, each decorated with a paper flag sporting the seal of Panem. Pie! When had he last tasted that? He was reaching for a medium-sized piece when someone thrust a plate with an enormous slice under his nose. "Oh, take a big one. Growing boy like you can handle it."

Dean Highbottom's eyes were rheumy, but they had lost the glazed look of the morning. In fact, they were trained on Coriolanus with an unexpected sharpness.

He took the plate of pie with a grin he hoped was boyishly good-natured. "Thank you, sir. I can always find room for pie."

"Yes, pleasures are never hard to accommodate," said the dean. "No one would know better than I."

"I suppose not, sir." But that sounded wrong. He had meant to agree with the part about pleasures, but it sounded like a snide remark about the dean's character.

"You suppose not." Dean Highbottom's eyes narrowed as he continued to stare at Coriolanus. "So, what are your plans, Coriolanus, after the Games?"

"I hope to go on to university," he replied. What a strange question. Surely, his academic record made that evident.

"Yes, I saw your name among the prize contenders," said Dean Highbottom. "But if you shouldn't be awarded one?"

Coriolanus stammered. "Well, then we'd . . . we'd pay the tuition, of course."

"Would you?" Dean Highbottom laughed. "Look at you, in your makeshift shirt and your too-tight shoes, trying to hold it together. Strutting around the Capitol, when I doubt the Snows have a pot to piss in. Even with a prize, it would be a stretch, and you don't yet have one, do you? What then, I wonder, would happen to you? What then?"

Coriolanus could not help but glance around to see who else had heard the terrible words, but most people were engaged in mealtime chatter.

"Don't worry — nobody knows. Well, hardly anyone. Enjoy that pie, boy." Dean Highbottom walked away without bothering to take a piece himself.

Coriolanus wanted nothing so much as to drop his pie and run for the exit, but instead he carefully set the oversized slice back on the cart. The nickname. It could only be that the nickname had found its way back to Dean Highbottom, with Coriolanus given the credit. It had been stupid on his part. The dean was too powerful a person, even now, to be ridiculing in public. But was it really such a horrible thing? Every teacher had at least one nickname, many far less flattering. And it wasn't as if High-as-a-Kite-Bottom had made much effort to hide his habit. He seemed to invite derision. Could there be some other reason he hated Coriolanus so much?

Whatever it was, Coriolanus needed to set it right. He could not risk losing his prize over such a thing. After university he planned to embark on some lucrative profession. Without an education, what doors would be open to him? He tried to imagine his future in some low-level city position . . . doing what? Managing the coal distribution to the districts? Cleaning cages of genetic freaks in the muttations lab? Collecting taxes from Sejanus Plinth in his palatial apartment on the Corso while he lived in some rat hole fifty blocks out? That's if he were lucky! Capitol jobs were hard to come by, and he would be a penniless Academy graduate, no more. How was he to live? Borrow? Being in debt in the Capitol was historically a ticket to being a Peacekeeper, and that came with a twenty-year commitment to who knew where. They'd ship him off to some horrid backwater district where the people were hardly better than animals.

The day, which had held such promise, came crashing down around him. First the threat of losing his apartment, then the lowliest tribute assignment — who, on further reflection, was definitely crazy — and now the revelation that Dean Highbottom detested him enough to kill his prize chances and condemn him to a life in the districts!

Everyone knew what happened if you went to the districts. You were written off. Forgotten. In the eyes of the Capitol, you were basically dead.

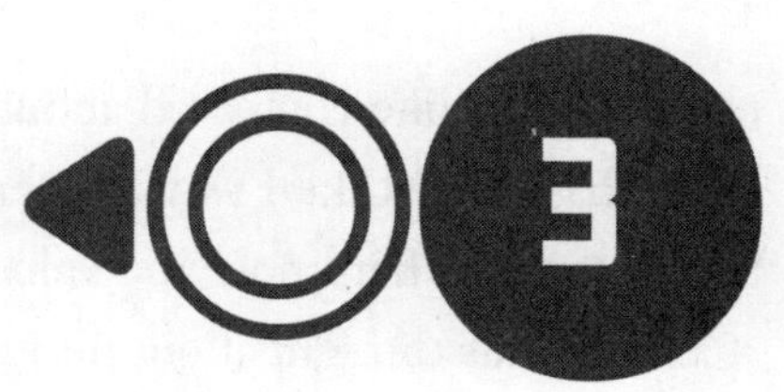

Coriolanus stood on the empty train platform, awaiting his tribute's arrival, a long-stemmed white rose balanced carefully between his thumb and index finger. It had been Tigris's idea to bring her a gift. She had arrived home very late on the night of the reaping, but he had waited up to consult with her, to tell her of his humiliations and fears. She refused to let the conversation spin into despair. He would get a prize; he would have to! And have a brilliant university career. As to the apartment, they must find out the specifics first. Perhaps the tax would not affect them, or even if it did, maybe not soon. Maybe they could scrape up enough for the taxes somehow. But he was to think of none of that. Only of the Hunger Games, and how he might make a success of it.

At Fabricia's reaping party, Tigris said, everyone was nuts about Lucy Gray Baird. His tribute had "star quality," her friends had declared as they drunkenly slurped their posca. The cousins agreed that he needed to make a good first impression on the girl so that she would be willing to work with him. He should treat her not as a condemned prisoner, but as a guest. Coriolanus had decided to greet her early at the train station. It would give him a jump on the assignment, as well as an opportunity to win her trust.

"Imagine how terrified she must be, Coryo," Tigris had said. "How alone she must feel. If it was me, anything you could do to make me feel like you cared about me would go a long way. No, more than that. Like I was of value. Take her something, even a token, that lets her know you value her."

Coriolanus thought about his grandmother's roses, which were still prized in the Capitol. The old woman nurtured them arduously in the roof garden that came with the penthouse, both out of doors and in a small solar greenhouse. She parceled out her flowers like diamonds, though, so it had taken a good bit of persuasion to get this beauty. "I need to make a connection with her. As you always say, your roses open any doors." It was a testament to how worried his grandmother was about their situation that she had allowed it.

Two days had passed since the reaping. The city had held on to the oppressive heat, and even though it was just past dawn, the train station was beginning to bake. Coriolanus felt conspicuous on the wide, deserted platform, but he couldn't risk missing her train. The only information he could get out of his downstairs neighbor, Gamemaker-in-Training Remus Dolittle, was that it was supposed to arrive Wednesday. Remus had recently graduated from the University, and his family had pulled in every favor they had to get him the position, which paid just enough and provided a stepping-stone to the future. Coriolanus could have inquired through the Academy, but he didn't know if greeting the train would be frowned upon. No rules had been laid out, per se, but he thought most of his classmates would wait to meet their tributes at a session overseen by the Academy the following day.

An hour passed, then two, and still no train of any kind appeared. The sun beat down through the glass panes of the station ceiling. Perspiration trickled down his back, and the rose, so majestic that morning, began to bend in resignation. He wondered if the whole idea was ill-conceived and if he would get no thanks for greeting her in this way. Another girl, a typical girl, would be impressed, but there was nothing typical about Lucy Gray Baird. In fact, there was something intimidating about a girl who could pull off such a brazen performance on the heels of the mayor's assault. And that, just after she had dropped a venomous snake down another girl's dress. Of course, he didn't know that it was venomous, but that was where the mind went, wasn't it? She was terrifying, really. And here he was in his uniform, clutching a rose like some lovestruck schoolboy, hoping she would — what? Like him? Trust him? Not kill him on sight?

Her cooperation was imperative. Yesterday, Satyria had led a mentor meeting in which their first assignment had been detailed. In the past, the tributes had gone directly into the arena the morning after they'd all arrived in the Capitol, but the time line had been extended now that the Academy students were involved. It had been decided that each mentor was to interview their tribute and would be given five minutes to present them to Panem on a live television program. If people had someone to root for, they might actually have an interest in watching the Hunger Games. If all went well, it would be prime-time viewing — the mentors might even be invited to comment on their tributes during the Games. Coriolanus promised himself that his five minutes would be the standout of the night.

Another hour crawled by and he was just about ready to give up, when a train whistle sounded deep in the tunnel. Those first few months of the war, the whistle had signaled his father's arrival from the battlefield. His father had felt that, as a munitions tycoon, military service enhanced his legitimacy in the family business. With an excellent head for strategy, nerves of steel, and a commanding presence, he'd quickly climbed the ranks. To publicly display their commitment to the Capitol cause, the Snow family would all travel to the station, Coriolanus in his velvet suit, to await the great man's return. Until the day the train brought only the news that a rebel bullet had found its mark. It was hard, in the Capitol, to find a spot that wasn't linked to a terrible memory, but this was particularly bad. He could not say he had felt great love for the remote, strict man, but he had certainly felt protected by him. His death was associated with a fear and a vulnerability that Coriolanus had never been able to shake off.

The whistle blew as the train sped into the station and screeched to a halt. It was a short train, only an engine and two cars. Coriolanus looked for a glimpse of his tribute in the windows before he realized the cars had none. They were designed not for passengers but for cargo. Heavy metal chains attached by old-fashioned padlocks secured the goods.

The wrong train, he thought. *Might as well go home.* But then a distinctly human cry came from one of the cargo cars and he remained in place.

He expected a rush of Peacekeepers, but the train sat ignored for twenty minutes before a few made their way to the rails. One of them exchanged words with an unseen engineer, and a set of keys was tossed out the window. The Peacekeeper took his time meandering down to the first car, flipping through the keys before he selected one, stuck it in the padlock, and gave it a twist. The lock and chains fell away, and he rolled back the heavy door. The car appeared empty. The Peacekeeper pulled out his baton and banged it against the doorframe. "All right, you lot, let's move!"

A tall boy with dark brown skin and patched burlap clothing appeared in the doorway. Coriolanus recognized him as Clemensia's tribute from District 11, rangy but muscular. A girl with similar coloring but a skeletal frame and a hacking cough joined him. Both of them were barefoot with their hands cuffed in front of their bodies. It was a five-foot drop to the ground, so they sat on the edge of the car before launching themselves awkwardly onto the platform. A small, pasty-faced girl in a striped dress and red scarf crawled to the door but seemed unable to figure out how to cover the distance to the ground. The Peacekeeper yanked her down and she landed hard, barely catching herself with her bound hands. Then he reached into the car and dragged out a boy who looked about ten years old but had to be at least twelve, and hauled him onto the platform as well.

By now the smell of the car, musty and heavy with manure, had reached Coriolanus. They were transporting the tributes in livestock cars, and not very clean ones at that. He wondered if they had been fed and let out for fresh air, or just locked in after their reapings. Accustomed as he was to viewing the tributes on-screen, he had not prepared himself properly for this encounter in the flesh, and a wave of pity and revulsion swept through him. They really were creatures out of another world. A hopeless, brutish world.

The Peacekeeper moved on to the second car and released the chains. The door slid open, revealing Jessup, the male District 12 tribute, squinting into the brightly lit station. Coriolanus felt a jolt run through him, and his body straightened in anticipation. Surely, she would be with him. Jessup hopped stiffly to the ground and turned back to the train.

Lucy Gray Baird stepped into the light, her cuffed hands half covering her eyes as they adjusted. Jessup reached up his arms, his wrists spread as wide as the chain on his restraints would allow, and she fell forward, letting him catch her by the waist and swing her to the ground in a surprisingly graceful move. She patted the boy's sleeve in thanks and tilted her head back to drink in the sunlight streaming into the station. Her fingers began combing through her curls, untangling the knots and picking out bits of straw.

Coriolanus's attention turned for a moment to the Peacekeepers, who were hollering threats into the train car. When he gazed back, Lucy Gray was staring directly at him. He started a bit but then remembered that he was the only one on the platform besides the Peacekeepers. The soldiers were cursing now as they hoisted one of their number into the train car to retrieve the reluctant tributes.

It was now or never.

He crossed to Lucy Gray, extended the rose, and gave a small nod. "Welcome to the Capitol," he said. His voice was slightly gravelly, as he had not spoken for hours, but he thought it gave him a nice maturity.

The girl sized him up, and for a minute he feared she was going to either walk away or, worse, laugh at him. Instead she reached out and delicately plucked a petal from the flower in his hand.

"When I was little, they used to bathe me in buttermilk and rose petals," she said in a manner that, despite the unlikeliness of her claim, seemed totally believable. She ran her thumb over the glossy, white surface and slipped the petal into her mouth, closing her eyes to savor the flavor. "Tastes like bedtime."

Coriolanus took the moment to examine her. She looked different than she had at the reaping. Except for flecks here and there, the makeup had been wiped away, and without it she appeared younger. Her lips were chapped, her hair loose, her rainbow dress dusty and rumpled. The mark from the mayor's blow had turned to a deep purple bruise. But there was something else, too. He again had the impression that he was witnessing a performance, but a private one this time.

When she opened her eyes, she trained all her attention on him. "You don't look like you should be here."

"I probably shouldn't be," he admitted. "But I'm your mentor. And I wanted to meet you on my own terms. Not the Gamemakers'."

"Ah, a rebel," she said.

That word was poison in the mouths of Capitol citizens, but she had said it approvingly, as a compliment. Or, was she mocking him? He remembered she carried snakes in her pocket and the usual rules didn't apply to her.

"And what does my mentor do for me, besides bring me roses?" she asked.

"I do my best to take care of you," he said.

She glanced over her shoulder, where the Peacekeepers were tossing two half-starved children onto the platform. The girl broke a front tooth on the platform, while the boy received several sharp kicks upon landing.

Lucy Gray smiled up at Coriolanus. "Well, good luck, Gorgeous," she said, and walked back to Jessup, leaving him and his rose behind.

As the Peacekeepers herded the tributes across the station to the main entrance, Coriolanus felt his chance slipping away. He had not secured her trust. He had not done anything except perhaps amuse her for a moment. Clearly, she thought he was useless, and maybe she was right, but with all that was at stake, he had to try. He ran across the station, catching up to the pack of tributes as they reached the door.

"Excuse me," he said to the Peacekeeper in charge. "I'm Coriolanus Snow from the Academy." He inclined his head toward Lucy Gray. "This tribute has been assigned to me for the Hunger Games. I wonder if I might accompany her to her quarters."

"That's why you been hanging around here all morning? To catch a ride to the show?" asked the Peacekeeper. He reeked of liquor and his eyes were rimmed with red. "Well, by all means, Mr. Snow. Join the party."

It was then that Coriolanus saw the truck that awaited the tributes. Less a truck than a cage on wheels. The bed was enclosed by metal bars and topped with a steel roof. He again flashed back to the circus of his childhood, where he had seen wild animals — big cats and bears — confined to such transport. Following orders, the tributes presented their cuffs for removal and climbed into the cage.

Coriolanus hung back but then saw Lucy Gray watching him and knew this was the moment of judgment. If he backed down now, it would all be over. She would think he was a coward and dismiss him entirely. He took a deep breath and hoisted himself up into the cage.

The door slammed shut behind him, and the truck lurched forward, knocking him off balance. He reflexively grabbed for the bars on his right and wound up with his forehead crammed between them as a couple of the tributes fell into him. He pushed back forcefully and twisted his body around to face his fellow passengers. Everyone had hold of at least one bar now except the girl with the broken tooth, who was clinging to the leg of the boy from her district. As the truck rumbled down a wide avenue, they began to settle in.

Coriolanus knew he had made a mistake. Even in the open air, the stench was overwhelming. The tributes had absorbed the odor of the cattle car and it mixed with an unwashed human smell that made him feel slightly nauseous. Up close, he could see how grubby they were, how bloodshot their eyes, how bruised their limbs. Lucy Gray was crammed into a corner at the front, dabbing a fresh scrape on her forehead with her ruffled hem. She seemed indifferent to his presence, but the rest of them stared at him like a pack of feral animals eyeing a pampered poodle.

At least I'm in better condition than they are, he thought, and he made a fist around the stem of the rose. *If they attack, I'll stand a chance.* But would he? Against so many?

The truck slowed to let one of the colorful street trolleys, packed with people, cross in front of it. Although he was in the back, Coriolanus hunched down to avoid being noticed.

The trolley passed, the truck began to roll, and he dared to straighten up. They were laughing at him, the tributes, or at least some of them were grinning at his obvious discomfort.

"What's the matter, pretty boy? You in the wrong cage?" said the boy from District 11, who was not laughing at all.

The undisguised hatred rattled Coriolanus, but he tried to look unimpressed. "No, this is exactly the cage I was waiting for."

The boy's hands came up fast, encircling Coriolanus's throat with his long, scarred fingers and slamming him back. His forearms pinned Coriolanus's body against the bars. Overpowered, Coriolanus resorted to the one move that had yet to fail him in schoolyard scuffles, driving his knee up hard into his opponent's crotch. The district boy gasped and doubled over, releasing him.

"He might kill you now." The girl from District 11 coughed in Coriolanus's face. "He killed a Peacekeeper back in Eleven. They never found out who did it."

"Shut it, Dill," the boy growled.

"Who cares now?" said Dill.

"Let's all kill him," the tiny boy said viciously. "Can't do nothing worse to us."

Several other tributes murmured in agreement and took a step in.

Coriolanus went rigid with fear. Kill him? Did they really mean to beat him to death, right here in broad daylight, in the middle of the Capitol? Suddenly, he knew they did. What, after all, did they have to lose? His heart pounded in his chest, and he crouched slightly, fists extended, in anticipation of the imminent attack.

From the corner, Lucy Gray's melodic voice broke the tension. "Not to us, maybe. You got family back home? Someone they could punish there?"

This seemed to take the wind out of the other tributes' sails. She wriggled through and placed herself between them and Coriolanus.

"Besides," she said, "he's my mentor. Supposed to help me. I might need him."

"How come you get a mender?" asked Dill.

"Mentor. You each get one," explained Coriolanus, trying to sound on top of the situation.

"Where are they, then?" Dill challenged. "Why didn't they come?"

"Just not inspired, I guess," said Lucy Gray. Turning from Dill, she gave Coriolanus a wink.

The truck veered onto a narrow side street and bumped down to what appeared to be a dead end. Coriolanus could not quite get his bearings. He tried to remember where the tributes had been held in previous years. Hadn't it been in the stables that housed the Peacekeepers' horses? Yes, he thought he had heard some mention of that. As soon as they arrived, he would find a Peacekeeper and explain things, perhaps ask for a bit of protection given the hostility. After Lucy Gray's wink, it might be worthwhile to stay.

They were backing in now to a dimly lit building, maybe a warehouse. Coriolanus inhaled a musky mix of rotten fish and old hay. Confused, he tried to get a better fix on his surroundings, and his eyes strained to make out two metal doors swinging open. A Peacekeeper opened the back door to the truck, and before anyone could climb out, the cage tipped and dumped them onto a slab of cold, damp cement. Not a slab, actually more like a chute, for it was tilted at such an extreme angle that Coriolanus began to slide immediately, along with the rest. He dropped the rose as his hands and feet scrabbled for purchase but found none. They all traveled a good twenty feet before they landed in a jumbled heap on a gritty floor. Sunlight glared down on Coriolanus as he scrambled to untangle his body from the pack. He staggered out a few yards, righted himself, and froze in horror. This was not the stables. While he had not visited in many years, he remembered it clearly now. The stretch of sand. The artificial rock formations twisting high in the air. The row of metal bars engraved to look like vines curved in a wide arc to protect the audience. Between the sets of bars, the faces of Capitol children gawked at him.

He was in the monkey house at the zoo.

He could not have felt more exposed had he been standing naked in the middle of the Corso. At least then he would've had the option to escape. Now he was trapped and on display, for the first time appreciating the animals' inability to hide. Children had begun to chatter excitedly and point at his school uniform, drawing the attention of the adults. Faces were filling all the available space between the bars. But the real horror was a pair of cameras positioned at either end of the visitors.

Capitol News. With their omnipresent coverage and their saucy slogan, *"If you didn't see it here, it didn't happen."*

Oh, it was happening. To him. Now.

He could feel his image going live all over the Capitol. Fortunately, shock rooted him to the spot, because the only thing worse than him standing among the district riffraff in the zoo would be him running around like a fool trying to escape. There was no easy way out. It was built for wild animals. Attempting to hide would be even more pathetic. Imagine how delicious that footage would be for Capitol News. They would play it ad nauseam. Add silly music and captions. *Snow's meltdown!* Make it part of the weather report. *Too hot for Snow!* They would rerun it as long as he lived. His disgrace would be complete.

What option did that leave him? Only to stand his ground, looking the cameras dead in the eye, until he was rescued.

He straightened up to his full height, subtly shifted back his shoulders, and attempted to look bored. The audience began to call out to him — first the high-pitched children's voices, then the adults joining in, asking what he was doing, why was he in the cage, did he need help? Someone recognized him, and his name spread like wildfire through the crowd, which was becoming deeper by the minute.

"It's the Snow boy!"

"Who's that again?"

"You know, the ones with the roses on their roof!"

Who were all these people hanging around on a weekday at the zoo? Didn't they have jobs? Shouldn't the children be in school? No wonder the country was such a mess.

The district tributes began to circle, taunting him. There was the pair from District 11, and the vicious little boy who had called for his death, and several new ones, too. He remembered the hatred in the truck and wondered what would happen if they attacked him as a pack. Perhaps the audience would only cheer them on.

Coriolanus tried not to panic, but he could feel sweat running down his sides. All the faces — of the nearby tributes, of the crowd at the bars — began to blur. Their features became indistinct, leaving only dark and light patches of skin broken by the pinkish red of their open mouths. His limbs felt numb, his lungs starved for air. He was beginning to consider making a break for the chute and attempting to climb it when a voice behind him softly said, "Own it."

Without turning he knew it was the girl, his girl, and he felt immense relief that he was not entirely alone. He thought of how cleverly she had played the audience after the mayor's assault, how she had won them all with her song. She was right, of course. He had to make this moment look intentional or it was all over.

He took a deep breath and turned to where she sat, casually

fixing the white rose behind her ear. She always seemed to be improving her appearance. Arranging her ruffles in District 12, grooming her hair at the train station, and now adorning herself with the rose. He extended his hand to her as if she was the grandest lady in the Capitol.

The edges of Lucy Gray's mouth curled up. As she took his hand, her touch sent a tiny electrical spark up his arm, and he felt as if a bit of her onstage charisma had been transferred to him. He made a small bow as she stood with exaggerated elegance.

She's onstage. You're onstage. This is the show, he thought. He lifted his head and asked, "Would you care to meet a few of my neighbors?"

"I would be delighted," she said as if they were at an afternoon tea. "My left side is better," she murmured, lightly brushing her cheek. He wasn't sure what to do with the information, so he started to guide her to the left. Lucy Gray gave the spectators a big smile, seemingly pleased to be there, but as he led her to the bars he could feel her fingers clenching his like a vise.

A shallow moat that ran between the rocky structures and the bars of the monkey house had once formed a watery barrier between the animals and the visitors, but it was bone-dry now. They descended three steps, crossed the moat, and climbed back up to a shelf that ran around the enclosure, putting them eye-to-eye with the patrons. Coriolanus chose a spot several yards from one of the cameras — let it come to him — where a gaggle of small children stood in a cluster. The bars were spaced about four inches apart — not enough room to slide a whole body between, but ample if you wanted to reach your hand through. The children fell silent as they approached, pressing back into their parents' legs.

Coriolanus thought the afternoon tea image was as good as any, so he continued to treat the situation with the same lightness.

"How do you do?" he said, leaning over to the children. "I brought along a friend of mine today. Would you like to meet her?"

The children shifted around, and there were a few giggles. Then one little boy shouted, "Yes!" He slapped the bars with his hands a few times, then shoved them in his pockets uncertainly. "We saw her on the television."

Coriolanus led Lucy Gray right up to the bars. "May I present Miss Lucy Gray Baird?"

The audience had fallen silent now, nervous at her proximity to the children but eager to hear what the strange tribute was going to say. Lucy Gray went down on one knee about a foot from the bars. "Hi there. I'm Lucy Gray. What's your name?"

"Pontius," the boy said, glancing up to his mother for reassurance. She looked warily at Lucy Gray, but the girl ignored her.

"How do you do, Pontius?" she said.

Like any well-bred Capitol lad, the boy thrust his hand out to shake. Lucy Gray raised her hand to meet his but refrained from sticking it through the bars, which might have appeared threatening. As a result, it was the boy who reached into the cage to make contact. She squeezed his little hand warmly.

"So nice to meet you. Is this your sister?" Lucy Gray nodded to the little girl next to him. She stood saucer-eyed as she sucked on a finger.

"That's Venus," he said. "She's only four."

"Well, I think four is a very smart age to be," said Lucy Gray. "Nice to meet you, Venus."

"I liked your song," whispered Venus.

"You did?" said Lucy Gray. "That's so sweet. Well, you keep watching, Precious, and I'll try to sing you another. Okay?"

Venus nodded and then buried her face in her mother's skirt, bringing laughter and a few *aws* from the crowd.

Lucy Gray began to sidestep her way along the fence, engaging the children as she went. Coriolanus hung back a bit to give her space.

"Did you bring your snake?" a girl clutching a dripping strawberry ice pop asked hopefully.

"I sure wish I could have. That snake was a particular friend of mine," Lucy Gray told her. "Do you have a pet?"

"I have a fish," said the girl. She leaned into the bars. "His name is Bub." She transferred her treat to her other hand and reached through the bars for Lucy Gray. "Can I touch your dress?" Streaks of ruby syrup ran from her fist to her elbow, but Lucy Gray just laughed and offered up a bit of her skirt. The girl ran a tentative finger over the ruffles. "It's pretty."

"I like yours, too." The girl's dress was a faded, printed thing, nothing to remark on. But Lucy Gray said, "Polka dots always make me feel happy," and the girl beamed.

Coriolanus could sense the audience beginning to warm up to his tribute, no longer bothering to keep their distance. People were easy to manipulate when it came to their children. So pleased to see them pleased.

Instinctively, Lucy Gray seemed to know this, ignoring the adults as she moved along. She had almost reached one of the cameras and its accompanying reporter. She must have sensed it, but when she rose and found it directly in her face, she gave a slight start, then laughed. "Oh, hi there. Are we on television?"

The Capitol reporter, a young man eager for a story, leaned in hungrily. "We certainly are."

"And who might you be?" she asked.

"I'm Lepidus Malmsey with Capitol News," he said, flashing a grin. "So, Lucy, you're the tribute from District Twelve?"

"It's Lucy Gray and I'm not really from Twelve," she said. "My people are Covey. Musicians by trade. We just took a wrong turn one day and were obliged to stay."

"Oh. So . . . what district are you from, then?" asked Lepidus.

"No district in particular. We move from place to place as the fancy takes us." Lucy Gray caught herself. "Well, we used to anyway. Before the Peacekeepers rounded us up a few years back."

"But now you're District Twelve citizens," he insisted.

"If you say so." Lucy Gray's eyes drifted back to the crowd as if she was in danger of being bored.

The reporter could feel her slipping away. "Your dress has been a big hit in the Capitol!"

"Has it? Well, the Covey love color, and me more than most. But this was my mama's, so it's extra special to me," she said.

"She in District Twelve?" Lepidus asked.

"Just her bones, darling. Just her pearly white bones." Lucy Gray stared directly at the reporter, who seemed to have trouble forming his next question. She watched him struggle for a moment, then gestured to Coriolanus. "So, do you know my mentor? Says his name is Coriolanus Snow. He's a Capitol boy and clearly I got the cake with the cream, 'cause nobody else's mentor even bothered to show up to welcome them."

"Well, he gave us all a surprise. Did your teachers tell you to be here, Coriolanus?" asked Lepidus.

Coriolanus stepped toward the camera and tried for likable with a hint of roguishness. "They didn't tell me not to." Laughter rippled through the crowd. "But I do remember them saying that I was to introduce Lucy Gray to the Capitol, and I take that job seriously."

"So you didn't have a second thought about diving into a cage of tributes?" prompted the reporter.

"A second, a third, and I imagine the fourth and fifth will be hitting me sometime soon," admitted Coriolanus. "But if she's brave enough to be here, shouldn't I be?"

"Oh, for the record, I didn't have a choice," said Lucy Gray.

"For the record, neither did I," said Coriolanus. "After I heard you sing, I couldn't keep away. I confess, I'm a fan." Lucy Gray gave her skirt a swish as a smattering of applause came from the crowd.

"Well, I hope for your sake the Academy agrees with you, Coriolanus," said Lepidus. "I think you're about to find out."

Coriolanus turned to see metal doors, their windows reinforced with grates, swinging open in the back of the monkey house. A quartet of Peacekeepers marched in and headed straight for him. He turned to the camera, intent on making a good exit.

"Thank you for joining us," he said. "Remember, it's Lucy Gray Baird, representing District Twelve. Drop by the zoo if you have a minute and say hello. I promise she's well worth the effort."

Lucy Gray extended her hand to him with the delicate droop of the wrist that invited a kiss. He obliged, and when his lips brushed her skin, he felt a pleasant tingle. After giving the audience one last wave, he stepped up calmly to meet the Peacekeepers. One nodded tersely, and without a word he followed them from the enclosure to a respectable applause.

When the doors closed behind him, his breath came out in a huff and he realized how afraid he'd been. He silently congratulated himself for maintaining grace under pressure, but the scowls of the Peacekeepers suggested they did not share his opinion.

"What are you playing at?" a Peacekeeper demanded. "You're not allowed in there."

"So I thought, until your cohorts unceremoniously dumped me down a chute," Coriolanus replied. He thought the combination of *cohorts* and *unceremoniously* had just the right note of superiority. "I only signed up for the ride to the zoo. I'd be happy to explain the whole thing to your presiding officer and identify the Peacekeepers who did this. But to you, I offer my thanks."

"Uh-huh," she said flatly. "We have orders to escort you to the Academy."

"Even better," said Coriolanus, sounding more confident than he felt. The quick reaction from the school unsettled him.

Although the television in the backseat of the Peacekeeper van was broken, he was able to catch glimpses of the story along the way on the huge public screens that dotted the Capitol. Nervous energy began to bubble up as he saw images of first Lucy Gray, then himself, beaming out over the city. He could never have planned anything this audacious, but since it had happened, he might as well enjoy it. And really, he thought, he had given a fine performance. Kept his head. Stood his ground. Featured the girl, and she was a natural. Handled it all with dignity and a little ironic humor.

By the time he reached the Academy, he had recovered his composure and ascended the steps with assurance. It helped that every head was turning his way, and had there been no Peacekeepers to hold them at bay, he felt sure his schoolmates would have swarmed him. He thought he'd be taken to the office, but the guard deposited him on the bench outside the door to, of all places, the high biology lab, which was restricted to the senior students most gifted in the science. Although it was not his favorite subject — the smell of formaldehyde triggered his gag reflex, and he loathed working with a partner — he did sufficiently well in genetic manipulation to have landed a spot in the class. Nothing like that whiz Io Jasper, who seemed to have been born with a microscope attached to her eye. He was always gracious to Io, though, and as a result, she adored him. With unpopular people, such a minor effort went such a long way.

But who was he to feel superior? Across from the bench, on the bulletin board for student notices, a memo had been posted. It read:

10th HUNGER GAMES
MENTOR ASSIGNMENTS

DISTRICT 1
Boy — *Livia Cardew*
Girl — *Palmyra Monty*
DISTRICT 2
Boy — *Sejanus Plinth*
Girl — *Florus Friend*
DISTRICT 3
Boy — *Io Jasper*
Girl — *Urban Canville*
DISTRICT 4
Boy — *Persephone Price*
Girl — *Festus Creed*
DISTRICT 5
Boy — *Dennis Fling*
Girl — *Iphigenia Moss*
DISTRICT 6
Boy — *Apollo Ring*
Girl — *Diana Ring*
DISTRICT 7
Boy — *Vipsania Sickle*
Girl — *Pliny Harrington*

DISTRICT 8

Boy *Juno Phipps*

Girl *Hilarius Heavensbee*

DISTRICT 9

Boy *Gaius Breen*

Girl *Androcles Anderson*

DISTRICT 10

Boy *Domitia Whimsiwick*

Girl *Arachne Crane*

DISTRICT 11

Boy *Clemensia Dovecote*

Girl *Felix Ravinstill*

DISTRICT 12

Boy *Lysistrata Vickers*

Girl *Coriolanus Snow*

Could there be a more stinging public reminder of his precarious position than to be dangling there at the end like an afterthought?

After Coriolanus spent a few minutes puzzling over why he'd been brought to the lab, the guard told him he could go in. At his tentative knock, a voice he recognized as Dean Highbottom's bid him enter. He had expected Satyria to be present but found only one other person in the lab — a small, stooped old woman with frizzy gray hair who was teasing a caged rabbit with a metal rod. She poked at it through the mesh until the creature, which had been modified to have the jaw strength of a pit bull, yanked the thing from her hand and snapped it in two. Then she straightened as well as she could, turned her attention to Coriolanus, and exclaimed, "Hippity, hoppity!"

Dr. Volumnia Gaul, the Head Gamemaker and mastermind behind the Capitol's experimental weapons division, had unnerved Coriolanus since childhood. On a school field trip, his class of nine-year-olds had watched as she'd melted the flesh off a lab rat with some sort of laser and then asked if anyone had any pets they were tired of. Coriolanus had no pets — how could they afford to feed one? But Pluribus Bell had a fluffy white cat named Boa Bell that would lie in her owner's lap and bat around the ends of his powdered wig. She had taken a fancy to Coriolanus and would start up a raspy, mechanical purr the moment he petted her head. On those dreary days when he'd slogged through the wintry slush to trade back a bag of lima beans for more cabbage, it was her silly, silky warmth that had consoled him. It upset him to think of Boa Bell ending up in the lab.

Coriolanus knew Dr. Gaul taught a class at the University, but he'd seldom seen her at the Academy. As Head Gamemaker, though, anything related to the Hunger Games fell under her purview. Could his trip to the zoo have brought her here? Was he about to lose his mentorship?

"Hippity, hoppity." Dr. Gaul grinned. "How was the zoo?" Then she was laughing. "It's like a children's rhyme. Hippity, hoppity, how was the zoo? You fell in a cage and your tribute did, too!"

Coriolanus's lips stretched into a weak smile as his eyes darted over to Dean Highbottom for some clue as to how to react. The man sat slumped at a lab table, rubbing his temple in a way that suggested he had a pounding headache. No help there.

"I did," Coriolanus said. "We did. We fell in a cage."

Dr. Gaul raised her eyebrows at him, as if expecting more. "And?"

"And . . . we . . . landed onstage?" he added.

"Ha! Exactly! That's exactly what you did!" Dr. Gaul gave him an approving look. "You're good at games. Maybe one day you'll be a Gamemaker."

The thought had never crossed his mind. No disrespect to Remus, but it didn't seem like much of a job. Or like it required any particular skill, tossing kids and weapons in an arena and letting them fight it out. He supposed they had to organize the reapings and film the Games, but he hoped for a more challenging career. "I've got a great deal to learn before I can even think of that," he said modestly.

"The instinct is there. That's what matters," said Dr. Gaul. "So, tell me, what made you go into the cage?"

It had been an accident. He was about to say so when he thought of Lucy Gray whispering the words *Own it.*

"Well . . . my tribute, she's on the small side. The kind who's gone in the first five minutes of the Hunger Games. But she's appealing in a scruffy sort of way, with the singing and all." Coriolanus paused for a moment, as if reviewing his plan. "I don't think she stands a chance of winning, but that isn't the point, is it? I was told we were trying to engage the audience. That's my assignment. To get people to watch. So I asked myself, how do I even reach the audience? I go where the cameras are."

Dr. Gaul nodded. "Yes. Yes, there's no Hunger Games without the audience." She turned to the dean. "You see, Casca, this one took the initiative. He understands the importance of keeping the Games alive."

Dean Highbottom squinted at him skeptically. "Does he? Or is he just showboating for a better grade? What do you think the purpose of the Hunger Games is, Coriolanus?"

"To punish the districts for the rebellion," Coriolanus said without hesitation.

"Yes, but punishment could take a myriad of forms," said the dean. "Why the Hunger Games?"

Coriolanus opened his mouth and then hesitated. Why the Hunger Games? Why not just drop bombs, or cancel food shipments, or stage executions on the steps of the district Justice Buildings?

His mind jumped to Lucy Gray kneeling at the bars of the cage, engaging the children, the thawing of the crowd. They were connected in some way that he couldn't quite articulate. "Because . . . It's because of the children. How they matter to people."

"How do they matter?" Dean Highbottom pressed.

"People love children," said Coriolanus. But even as the words came out of his mouth, he questioned them. During the war, he had been bombed and starved and abused in multiple ways, and not just by the rebels. A cabbage ripped from his hands. A Peacekeeper bruising his jaw when he mistakenly wandered too close to the president's mansion. He thought of the time he had collapsed and lain in the street with the swan flu and no one, no one would stop to help. Racked with chills, burning with fever, limbs spiked with pain. Even though she was sick herself, Tigris had found him that night and somehow gotten him home.

He faltered. "Sometimes they do," he added, but it lacked conviction. When he thought about it, people's love of children seemed a very fickle thing. "I don't know why," he admitted.

Dean Highbottom shot Dr. Gaul a look. "You see? It's a failed experiment."

"It is if no one watches!" she snapped back. She gave Coriolanus an indulgent smile. "He's a child himself. Give him time. I've got a good feeling about this one. Well, I'm off to visit my mutts." She patted Coriolanus on the arm as she shuffled toward the door.

"Very hush-hush, but there's something wonderful going on with the reptiles."

Coriolanus made as if to follow, but Dean Highbottom's voice stopped him. "So your whole performance was planned. That's odd. Because when you stood up in the cage, I thought you were thinking about running."

"It was a rather more physical entrance than I had envisioned. It took some time to get my bearings. Again, I have a great many things to learn," said Coriolanus.

"Boundaries being among them. You'll be receiving a demerit for engaging in reckless behavior that could have injured a student. You, namely. It will go on your permanent record," said the dean.

A demerit? What did that even mean? Coriolanus would have to review the Academy student guide so he could object to the punishment. He was distracted by the dean, who pulled a small bottle from his pocket, twisted it open, and applied three drops of clear liquid to his tongue.

Whatever was in the bottle, most likely morphling, worked quickly, because Dean Highbottom's whole body relaxed and a dreaminess settled in his eyes. He smiled unpleasantly. "Three such demerits, and you'll be expelled."

Coriolanus had never received an official reprimand of any kind, nothing that would stain his spotless record. "But —" he started to protest.

"Go, before you receive a second for insubordination," said Dean Highbottom. There was no give in the statement, no invitation to negotiate. Coriolanus did as he'd been directed.

Had Dean Highbottom actually used the word *expelled*?

Coriolanus left the Academy in a state of agitation, but once again the rush of attention quieted his distress. From his fellow students in the hallway, from Tigris and the Grandma'am as they ate a quick supper of fried eggs and cabbage soup, from complete strangers as he made his way back to the zoo that evening, eager to keep his hand in the Games.

The soft orange glow of the sunset suffused the city, and a cool breeze swept away the suffocating heat of the day. Officials had extended the zoo's hours until nine o'clock, allowing the citizens to see the tributes, but there had been no more live coverage since his earlier visit. Coriolanus had decided to make another appearance to check on Lucy Gray and suggest she sing another song. The audience would love that, and perhaps it would draw the cameras back again.

As he wound through the paths of the zoo, he was filled with nostalgia for the pleasant days he'd spent there as a child, but he felt saddened by the emptiness of the cages. They had once been full of fascinating creatures from the Capitol's genetic ark. Now, in one, a lone tortoise lay in the mud, wheezing. A bedraggled toucan squawked high in the branches, fluttering freely from one enclosure to the next. They were rare survivors of the war, as most animals had starved or been eaten. A pair of scrawny raccoons that had likely wandered in from the adjacent city park dug in an overturned trash can. The only beasts thriving were the rats that chased one another around the edges of fountains and scurried across the path mere feet away.

As Coriolanus neared the monkey house, the paths became more populated, and a crowd of about a hundred people curved from one side of the bars to the other. Someone jostled his arm as they sped by, and he recognized Lepidus Malmsey pushing ahead through the visitors with the cameraman. A sort of commotion was occurring down front, and he climbed up on a boulder to get a better view.

To his chagrin, he saw Sejanus standing at the edge of the cage with a large backpack beside him. He held what appeared to be a sandwich through the bars, offering it to the tributes within. For the moment, they were all hanging back. Coriolanus could not hear his words, but he seemed to be trying to coax Dill, the girl from District 11, to take it. What was Sejanus up to? Was he trying to outdo him and steal the day's thunder? To take his idea of coming to the zoo and then dress it up in a way Coriolanus could never compete with, because he could never afford to? Was that whole pack filled with sandwiches? That girl wasn't even his tribute.

When Sejanus caught sight of Coriolanus, his face brightened and he waved him over. Casually, Coriolanus made his way through the crowd, soaking up their attention. "Trouble?" he said as he surveyed the backpack. It was overflowing with not only sandwiches, but fresh plums as well.

"None of them trust me. And why should they?" asked Sejanus.

A self-important little girl marched up beside them and pointed to a sign on the pillar at the edge of the enclosure. "It says, 'Please don't feed the animals.'"

"They're not animals, though," said Sejanus. "They're kids, like you and me."

"They're not like me!" the little girl protested. "They're district. That's why they belong in a cage!"

"Once again, like me," said Sejanus drily. "Coriolanus, do you think you could get your tribute to come over? If she does, the others might. They have to be starving."

Coriolanus's mind worked quickly. He had already received one demerit today and did not wish to push his luck with Dean Highbottom. On the other hand, the demerit had been for endangerment of a student, and he was perfectly safe on this side of the bars. Dr. Gaul, who was arguably more influential than Dean Highbottom, had complimented his initiative. And in truth, he had no interest in ceding the stage to Sejanus. The zoo was his show, and he and Lucy Gray were the stars. Even now, he could hear Lepidus whispering his name to the cameraman, feel the viewers in the Capitol watching him.

He spotted Lucy Gray at the back of the enclosure, washing her hands and face at a faucet that jutted from the wall at knee height. She dried herself on the ruffled skirt, arranged her curls, and adjusted the rose behind her ear.

"I can't treat her like it's feeding time at the zoo," Coriolanus told Sejanus. It was not consistent with his treatment of her as a lady to be shoving food to her through the bars. "Not mine. But I could offer her dinner."

Sejanus nodded immediately. "Take whatever. Ma made extra. Please."

Coriolanus chose two sandwiches and two plums from the pack

and crossed to the edge of the monkey house, where a flat rock provided a likely seat. Never in his life, not even in the worst years, had he left home without a clean handkerchief in his pocket. The Grandma'am insisted on certain civilities that held chaos at bay. There were great drawers of them going back generations, plain to lacy to embroidered with flowers. He spread out the worn, slightly rumpled square of white linen and laid out the food. As he seated himself, Lucy Gray drifted up to the bars unbidden.

"Are those sandwiches for anybody?" she asked.

"Just for you," he answered.

She tucked her feet under her and accepted a sandwich. After examining its contents, she took a nibble from the corner. "Aren't you eating?"

He wasn't sure. The optics so far were good, singling her out again, presenting her as someone of value. But to eat with her? That might cross a line.

"I'd rather you have it," he said. "Keep up your strength."

"Why? So I can break Jessup's neck in the arena? We both know that's not my forte," she said.

His stomach growled at the smell of the sandwich. A thick slice of meat loaf on white bread. He'd missed his lunch at the Academy today, and breakfast and supper had been meager at home. A dollop of ketchup oozing out of Lucy Gray's sandwich tipped the scale. He lifted the second sandwich and sank his teeth in. A little shock of delight ran through his body, and he resisted the impulse to devour the sandwich in a couple of bites.

"Now it's like a picnic." Lucy Gray looked back at the other tributes, who had moved in closer but still seemed uncertain. "You all should get one. They're real good!" she called. "Go on, Jessup!"

Emboldened, her hulking district partner slowly approached Sejanus and took the sandwich from his hand. He waited until a plum followed and then walked off without a word. Suddenly, the other tributes rushed the fence, hands thrusting through the bars. Sejanus filled them as fast as he could, and within a minute the backpack was almost depleted. The tributes spread out around the cage, crouched protectively over their food, wolfing it down.

The only tribute who had not approached Sejanus was his own, the boy from District 2. He stood at the back of the cage, arms folded across his colossal frame, staring down his mentor.

Sejanus pulled one final sandwich from the backpack and held it out to him. "Marcus, this is for you. Take it. Please." But Marcus remained stone-faced and immobile. "Please, Marcus," Sejanus, pleaded. "You must be starving." Marcus looked Sejanus up and down, then pointedly turned his back on him.

Lucy Gray watched the standoff with interest. "What's going on there?"

"What do you mean?" Coriolanus asked.

"I don't know exactly," she said. "But it feels personal."

The tiny boy who'd wanted to murder Coriolanus in the truck sprinted up and snatched the unclaimed sandwich. Sejanus made no move to stop him. The news team tried to engage Sejanus, but he brushed them off and disappeared into the crowd, the limp pack over his shoulder. They shot a bit more of the tributes, then headed toward Lucy Gray and Coriolanus, who sat up straighter and ran his tongue over his teeth to clean off the meat loaf.

"We're here at the zoo with Coriolanus Snow and his tribute, Lucy Gray Baird. Another student just passed out sandwiches. Is he a mentor?" Lepidus thrust the mic at them for an answer.

Coriolanus didn't like sharing the spotlight, but Sejanus's presence could protect him. Would Dean Highbottom give a demerit to the son of the man who had rebuilt the Academy? A few days ago he would've thought the name Snow carried more weight than Plinth, but the reaping assignments had proven him wrong. If Dean Highbottom wanted to call him on the carpet, he'd prefer to have Sejanus by his side.

"He's my classmate, Sejanus Plinth," he informed Lepidus.

"What's he up to, bringing fancy sandwiches to the tributes? Surely, the Capitol feeds them," said the reporter.

"Oh, for the record, I last ate the night before the reaping," Lucy Gray announced. "So I guess it's been three days."

"Oh. Okay, well, you enjoy that sandwich!" said Lepidus. He signaled the camera to turn back to the other tributes.

Lucy Gray was on her feet in a flash, leaning into the bars and pulling back the focus. "You know, Mr. Reporter, what might be nice? If anybody has any food to spare, they might bring it on down to the zoo. No fun watching the Games if we're all too weak to fight, don't you think?"

"There's some truth to that," said the reporter, unsure.

"Me, I like sweet things, but I'm not picky." She smiled and bit into her plum.

"Okay. Okay, then," he said, easing away.

Coriolanus could tell the reporter was on shaky ground. Should he really be helping her solicit the citizens for food? Did it seem a condemnation of the Capitol?

As the news team moved to the other tributes, Lucy Gray settled back down across from him. "Too much?"

"Not for me. I'm sorry I didn't think to bring you food," he said.

"Well, I've been working my way through these rose petals when nobody's looking." She shrugged. "You didn't know."

They finished their food in silence, watching the reporter's failed attempts at getting the other tributes to talk. The sun had set now, and a rising moon had taken over the lighting. The zoo would be closing soon.

"I was thinking that it might be a good idea for you to sing again," said Coriolanus.

Lucy Gray sucked the last bit of flesh off the plum pit. "Mm-hmm, it might be, at that." She dabbed the corners of her mouth with a ruffle and then straightened her skirt. Her usual playful tone shifted to a sober one. "So, as my mentor, what do you get out of this? You're at school, right? So you get what? A better grade the more I shine?"

"Maybe." He felt embarrassed. Here, in the relative privacy of the corner, he realized for the first time that she would be dead in a few days. Well, of course, he'd always known that. But he had thought about her more as his contender. His filly in a race, his dog in a fight. The more he had treated her as something special, the more she'd become human. As Sejanus had told the little girl, Lucy Gray was not really an animal, even if she was not Capitol. And he was here doing what? Showboating, like Dean Highbottom had said?

"I don't even know what I get, really," he told her. "They've never had mentors before. You don't have to. Sing, I mean."

"I know," she said.

He still wanted her to, though. "But if people like you, they might bring you more food. We don't have much extra at home."

His cheeks burned in the dark. Why on earth had he admitted that to her?

"No? I always thought you had plenty to spare in the Capitol," she said.

Idiot, he said to himself. But then he met her gaze and realized that, for the first time, she looked genuinely interested in him. "Oh, no. Especially not during the war. One time I ate half a jar of paste just to stop the pains in my stomach."

"Yeah? How was it?" she asked.

That threw him, and he surprised himself by laughing. "Really sticky."

Lucy Gray grinned. "I'll bet. Still, sounds better than some of the stuff I made do with. Not to make this a competition."

"Of course not." He grinned back. "Look, I'm sorry. I'll find you some food. You shouldn't have to perform for it."

"Well, this wouldn't be the first time I sang for my supper. Not by a long shot," she said. "And I do so love to sing."

A voice came over the speaker to announce the zoo was closing in fifteen minutes.

"I ought to be going. But I'll see you tomorrow?" he asked.

"You know where to find me," she said.

Coriolanus rose and brushed off his pants. He shook out the handkerchief, folded it, and passed it through the bars to her. "It's clean," he assured her. At least she'd have something to dry her face with.

"Thanks. I left mine at home," she replied.

Lucy Gray's mention of home hung in the air between them. A reminder of a door she'd never reopen, loved ones she'd never see again. He couldn't stand the thought of being torn from his own home. The apartment was the one place he unquestioningly belonged, his safe harbor, his family's stronghold. Since he didn't know how else to respond, he simply nodded good night.

Coriolanus had not gone twenty paces when he was stopped by the sound of his tribute's voice, singing sweet and clear through the night air.

Down in the valley, valley so low,
Late in the evening, hear the train blow.

The train, love, hear the train blow.
Late in the evening, hear the train blow.

The audience, which had been trailing out, turned to listen to her.

Go build me a mansion, build it so high,
So I can see my true love go by.
See him go by, love, see him go by.
So I can see my true love go by.

Everyone had hushed now — the audience, the tributes. There was just Lucy Gray and the whir of the camera closing in on her. She still sat in their corner, her head leaning against the bars.

Go write me a letter, send it by mail.
Bake it and stamp it to the Capitol jail.
Capitol jail, love, to the Capitol jail.
Bake it and stamp it to the Capitol jail.

She sounded so sad, so lost. . . .

Roses are red, love; violets are blue.
Birds in the heavens know I love you.
Know I love you, oh, know I love you,
Birds in the heavens know I love you.

Coriolanus stood transfixed by the music and the rush of memories that accompanied it. His mother used to sing him a song at bedtime. Not this one, exactly, but it had used those same words, *roses are red* and *violets are blue*. It had mentioned loving him. He thought of the photo in the silver frame he kept on the nightstand by his bed. His beautiful mother, holding him when he was about two. They were looking at each other, laughing. Try as he might, he could never remember the moment the picture was taken, but this song caressed his brain, calling her from the depths. He could sense her presence, almost smell the delicate scent of the rose powder she wore, and feel the warm blanket of security that had enveloped him each night. Before she died. Before that awful stretch of days a few months into the war, when the first major rebel air raid had immobilized the city. When she went into labor, and they were unable to get her to the hospital, and something had gone wrong. Hemorrhage, maybe? A great deal of blood soaking the sheets and Cook and the Grandma'am trying to stop it and Tigris dragging him from the room. Then she was gone, and the baby — who would've been his sister — she was gone, too. The death of his father came right on the heels of his mother's, but that loss had not hollowed out the world in the same way. Coriolanus still kept his mother's compact in a drawer in his nightstand. In difficult times, when he had trouble falling asleep, he would click it open and inhale the rose scent of the silken cake of powder within. It never failed to calm him with the memory of how it had felt to be loved like that.

Bombs and blood. That was how the rebels had killed his mother. He wondered if they had killed Lucy Gray's, too. *"Just her pearly white bones."* She seemed to have no love for District 12, always separating herself from it, saying she was, what was it . . . Covey?

"Thanks for stepping up." Sejanus's voice startled him. He had been sitting a few feet back, concealed by one of the boulders, listening to the song.

Coriolanus cleared his throat. "It was nothing."

"I doubt any of our other classmates would've helped me," Sejanus pointed out.

"None of our other classmates have even made an appearance," Coriolanus replied. "That already sets us apart. What made you think of feeding the tributes?"

Sejanus looked down at the empty backpack by his feet. "Ever since the reaping, I keep imagining I'm one of them."

Coriolanus almost laughed before he realized Sejanus was serious. "That seems like an odd pastime."

"Can't help it." Sejanus's voice dropped so low, Coriolanus had to strain to hear it. "They read my name. I walk to the stage. Now they've cuffed me. Now they're hitting me for no reason. Now I'm on the train, in the dark, starving, alone except for kids I'm supposed to kill. Now I'm on display, with all these strangers bringing their children to stare at me through the bars. . . ."

The sound of rusty wheels turning drew their attention to the monkey house. A dozen or so bales of hay came bursting out of the chute and rolled into a heap on the cage floor.

"Look, that must be my bed," said Sejanus.

"It isn't going to happen to you, Sejanus," Coriolanus told him.

"It could've, though. Easily. If we weren't so rich now," he said. "I would be back in District Two, maybe still in school or maybe in the mines, but definitely in the reaping. You saw my tribute?"

"He's hard to miss," admitted Coriolanus. "I think there's a good chance he'll win."

"He was my classmate. You know, before I came here. Back home. His name's Marcus," Sejanus continued. "Not a friend exactly. But certainly not an enemy. One day I caught my finger in the door, smashed it good, and he scooped a cup of snow off the windowsill to bring down the swelling. Didn't even ask the teacher, just did it."

"Do you think he even remembers you?" said Coriolanus. "You were little. And a lot has happened since then."

"Oh, he remembers me. The Plinths are notorious back home." Sejanus looked pained. "Notorious and deeply despised."

"And now you're his mentor," said Coriolanus.

"And now I'm his mentor," Sejanus echoed.

The lights in the monkey house dimmed. A few of the tributes moved about, making nests of hay for the night. Coriolanus spotted Marcus drinking from the spigot, splashing water over his head. When he rose and crossed to the bales of hay, he dwarfed the others.

Sejanus gave the backpack a little kick. "He wouldn't take a sandwich from me. He'd rather go into the Games starving than take food from my hand."

"That's not your fault," said Coriolanus.

"I know. I know. I'm so blameless I'm choking on it," said Sejanus.

Coriolanus was trying to unravel that thought when a fight broke out in the cage. Two boys had claimed the same bale of hay and had come to blows over it. Marcus intervened and, grabbing each by the collar, tossed them apart like a pair of rag dolls. They flew in the air, traveling several yards before landing in awkward heaps. As they slunk into the shadows, Marcus took the bale for his own bed, unimpressed by the scuffle.

"He'll still win," said Coriolanus. If he'd had any doubts, Marcus's display of superior power had silenced them. He again felt the bitterness of a Plinth being granted the mightiest tribute. And he was tired of Sejanus's whining over his father's buying him the victor. "Any one of us would've been happy to get him."

Sejanus brightened a bit. "Really? Then take him. He's yours."

"You're not serious," said Coriolanus.

"A hundred percent." Sejanus sprang to his feet. "I want you to have him! And I'll take Lucy Gray. It will still be horrible, but at least I don't know her. I know the crowd likes her, but what good will that do her in the arena? There's no way she'll beat him. Trade tributes with me. Win the Games. Take the glory. Please, Coriolanus, I would never forget the favor."

For a moment, Coriolanus could taste it — the sweetness of the victory, the cheers of the crowd. If he could make Lucy Gray a favorite, imagine what he could do with a powerhouse like Marcus! And really, what chance did she have? His eyes traveled to Lucy Gray leaning against the bars like a trapped animal. In the shadowy light, her color, her specialness, had faded, making her just another drab, bruised creature. Not much of a match for the other girls, even less so for the boys. The idea of her defeating Marcus was laughable. Like pitting a songbird against a grizzly bear.

His mouth was forming the word *done*, when he stopped.

To win with Marcus was no win at all. It took no brains, or skill, or even particular luck. To win with Lucy Gray would be an incredible long shot but historic if he pulled it off. Besides, was winning even the point? Or was it to engage the audience? Thanks to him, Lucy Gray was the current star of the Games, the most memorable tribute no matter who won. He thought of their hands locked together in the zoo as they took on the world. They were a team. She trusted him. He couldn't imagine telling her he'd dumped her for Marcus. Or, even worse, telling the audience.

In addition, what guarantee did he have that Marcus would respond to him any more than he did to Sejanus? He seemed like just the kind to stonewall the lot of them. And then Coriolanus would look like a fool, begging for a crumb of attention from Marcus while Lucy Gray did pirouettes around Sejanus.

There was one more consideration. He had something Sejanus Plinth wanted, and wanted badly. Sejanus had already usurped his position, his inheritance, his clothes, his candy, his sandwiches, and the privilege due a Snow. Now he was coming for his apartment, his spot at the University, his very future, and had the gall to be resentful of his good fortune. To reject it. To consider it a punishment, even. If having Marcus as a tribute made Sejanus squirm, then good. Let him squirm. Lucy Gray was one thing belonging to Coriolanus that he would never, ever get.

"Sorry, my friend," he said mildly. "But I think I'll keep her."

Coriolanus relished the disappointment on Sejanus's face, but not for long, because that would've been petty. "Look, Sejanus, you may not think so, but this *is* me doing you a favor. Think about it. What would your father say if he found out you'd traded the tribute he'd lobbied for?"

"I don't care," said Sejanus, but it didn't sound convincing.

"All right, forget about your father. What about the Academy?" he asked. "I doubt trading tributes is allowed. I've already been slapped with one demerit just for meeting Lucy Gray early. What if I tried to trade her? Besides, the poor thing is already attached to me. Dumping her would be like kicking a kitten. I don't think I'd have the heart."

"I shouldn't have asked. I never even considered I might be making things difficult for you. I'm sorry. It's just . . ." Sejanus's words began to spill out. "It's just this whole Hunger Games thing is making me crazy! I mean, what are we doing? Putting kids in an arena to kill each other? It feels wrong on so many levels. Animals protect their young, right? And so do we. We try to protect children! It's built into us as human beings. Who really wants to do this? It's unnatural!"

"It's not pretty," Coriolanus agreed, glancing around.

"It's evil. It goes against everything I think is right in the world. I can't be a part of it. Especially not with Marcus. I have to get out of it somehow," Sejanus said, his eyes filling with tears.

His distress made Coriolanus uncomfortable, especially when he valued his own chance to participate so highly. "You could always ask another mentor. I don't think you'd have a problem finding a taker."

"No. I'm not handing Marcus over to anyone else. You're the only one I'd trust with him." Sejanus turned to the cage, where the tributes had settled down for the night. "Oh, what does it matter anyway? If it's not Marcus, it will be someone else. It might be easier, but it still won't be right." He collected his backpack. "I better get home. That's sure to be pleasant."

"I don't think you've broken any rules," said Coriolanus.

"I've publicly aligned myself with the districts. In my father's eyes, I've broken the only rule that matters." Sejanus gave him a small smile. "Thanks again, though, for helping me out."

"Thank you for the sandwich," said Coriolanus. "It was delicious."

"I'll tell Ma you said so," said Sejanus. "It'll make her night."

Coriolanus's own return home was somewhat marred by the Grandma'am's disapproval of his picnic with Lucy Gray.

"To feed her is one thing," she said. "To dine with her suggests that you consider her your equal. But she isn't. There's always been something barbaric about the districts. Your own father used to say those people only drank water because it didn't rain blood. You ignore that at your own peril, Coriolanus."

"She's just a girl, Grandma'am," Tigris said.

"She's district. And trust me, that one hasn't been a girl in a long time," the Grandma'am replied.

Coriolanus thought uneasily of the tributes on the truck debating whether or not to kill him. They'd certainly demonstrated a taste for his blood. Only Lucy Gray had objected.

"Lucy Gray is different," he argued. "She took my side in the truck when the others wanted to attack me. And she had my back in the monkey house, too."

The Grandma'am held her ground. "Would she have bothered if you weren't her mentor? Of course not. She's a wily little thing who began to manipulate you the minute you met. Tread carefully, my boy — that's all I'm saying."

Coriolanus didn't bother arguing, as the Grandma'am always took the worst view of anything she deemed district. He went straight to bed, dropping with fatigue, but couldn't quiet his mind. He took his mother's powder compact from the drawer of his nightstand and ran his fingers over the rose engraved on the heavy silver case.

Roses are red, love; violets are blue.
Birds in the heavens know I love you. . . .

When he clicked the latch, the lid opened and the floral scent wafted out. In the shadowy light from the Corso, his pale blue eyes reflected back from the round, slightly distorted mirror. "Just like your father's," the Grandma'am frequently reminded him. He wished he had his mother's eyes instead, but never said so. Maybe it was best to take after his father. His mother had not really been tough enough for this world. He finally drifted off, thinking of her, but it was Lucy Gray, spinning in her rainbow dress, who sang in his dreams.

In the morning, Coriolanus awoke to a delicious smell. He went to the kitchen and found that Tigris had been baking since before dawn.

He gave her shoulder a squeeze. "Tigris, you need to get more sleep."

"I couldn't sleep, thinking about what's going on at the zoo," she said. "Some of the kids look so young this year. Or maybe I'm just getting older."

"It's disturbing to see them locked up in that cage," Coriolanus admitted.

"It was disturbing to see you there as well!" she said, pulling on an oven mitt and taking a pan of bread pudding from the oven. "Fabricia told me to throw out the stale bread from the party, but I thought, why waste it?"

Hot from the oven, drizzled in corn syrup, bread pudding was one of his favorites. "It looks amazing," he told Tigris.

"And there's plenty, so you can take a piece to Lucy Gray. She said she liked sweet things — and I doubt there are many left in her future!" Tigris set the pan on the oven with a bang. "Sorry. Didn't mean to do that. I don't know what's gotten into me. I'm wound up tight as a spring."

Coriolanus touched her arm. "It's the Games. You know I have to do the mentorship, right? If I'm to stand a chance at getting a prize. I need to win that for all of us."

"Of course, Coryo. Of course. And we're so proud of you and how well you're doing." She cut a large slice of the bread pudding and slid it onto a plate. "Now eat up. You don't want to be late."

At the Academy, Coriolanus felt his apprehension melt away as he basked in the response to his recklessness the previous day. With the exception of Livia Cardew, who made it clear she thought he had cheated and should be dismissed as a mentor immediately, his classmates congratulated him. If his professors were not so openly supportive, he still received several smiles and subtle pats on the back.

Satyria took him aside after homeroom. "Well done. You've pleased Dr. Gaul, and that's won you some points with the faculty. She'll give a good report to President Ravinstill, and that will reflect well on all of us. Only, you need to be careful. You were lucky how it played out. What if those brats had attacked you in the cage? The Peacekeepers would have been bound to rescue you, and there could've been casualties on both sides. Things might've been quite different if you hadn't landed your little rainbow girl."

"Which is why I turned down Sejanus's offer to trade tributes," he said.

Satyria's mouth dropped open. "No! Imagine what Strabo Plinth would say if that went public."

"Imagine what he owes me if it doesn't!" The thought of blackmailing old Strabo Plinth had definite appeal.

She laughed. "Spoken like a Snow. Now get to class. We need the rest of your record spotless if you're going to go racking up demerits."

The twenty-four mentors spent the morning in a seminar led by Professor Crispus Demigloss, their excitable old history professor. The class brainstormed ideas — beyond the addition of mentors — to get people to watch the Hunger Games. "Show me I haven't been wasting my time with you for four years," he said with a titter. "If history teaches you anything, it's how to make the unwilling comply." Sejanus's hand went up directly. "Ah, Sejanus?"

"Before we talk about making people watch, shouldn't we begin with the question of whether or not watching is the right thing to do?" he said.

"Let's stay on topic, please." Professor Demigloss scanned the room for a more productive answer. "How do we get people to watch?"

Festus Creed raised his hand. Bigger and burlier than most his age, he'd been one of Coriolanus's inner circle since birth. His family was old Capitol money. Their fortune, largely in District 7 timber, had taken a hit during the war but had rebounded nicely during the reconstruction. His scoring the District 4 girl reflected his status quite accurately. High, but not stellar.

"Enlighten us, Festus," said Professor Demigloss.

"Simple. We go straight to the punitive," Festus answered. "Instead of suggesting people watch, make it the law."

"What happens if you don't watch?" asked Clemensia, not bothering to raise her hand or even look up from her notes. She was popular with both students and faculty, and her niceness excused a lot.

"In the districts, we execute you. In the Capitol, we make you move to the districts, and if you mess up again next year, then we execute you," Festus said cheerfully.

The class laughed, then began to give it serious thought. How could you enforce it? You couldn't send the Peacekeepers door-to-door. Perhaps some random sampling where you needed to be prepared to answer questions that proved you'd watched the Games. And if you hadn't, what would an appropriate punishment be? Not execution or banishment — those were too extreme. Maybe some loss of privilege in the Capitol, and a public whipping in the districts? That would make the punishment personal to all.

"The real problem is, it's sickening to watch," said Clemensia. "So people avoid it."

Sejanus jumped in. "Of course they do! Who wants to watch a group of children kill each other? Only a vicious, twisted person. Human beings may not be perfect, but we're better than that."

"How do you know?" said Livia snippishly. "And how does someone from the districts have any idea what we want to watch in the Capitol? You weren't even here during the war."

Sejanus fell silent, unable to deny it.

"Because most of us are basically decent people," said Lysistrata Vickers, folding her hands neatly on her notebook. Everything about her was neat. From her carefully braided hair to her evenly filed nails to the crisp, white cuffs of her uniform blouse setting off her smooth, brown skin. "Most of us don't want to watch other people suffer."

"We watched worse things during the war. And after," Coriolanus reminded her. There had been some bloody stuff broadcast over the airwaves during the Dark Days, and many a brutal execution after the Treaty of Treason had been signed.

"But we had a real stake in that, Coryo!" said Arachne Crane, giving him a sock on the arm from the seat to his right. Always so loud. Always socking people. The Cranes' apartment faced the Snows', and sometimes even from across the Corso, he could hear her bellowing at night. "We were watching our enemies die! I mean, rebel scum and whatnot. Who cares about these kids one way or another?"

"Possibly their families," said Sejanus.

"You mean a handful of nobodies in the districts. So what?" Arachne boomed. "Why should the rest of us care which one of them wins?"

Livia looked pointedly at Sejanus. "I know I don't."

"I get more excited over a dogfight," admitted Festus. "Especially if I'm betting on it."

"So you'd like it if we gave odds on the tributes?" Coriolanus joked. "That would make you tune in?"

"Well, it would certainly liven things up!" Festus exclaimed.

A few people chuckled, but then the class went quiet as they mulled over the idea.

"It's gruesome," said Clemensia, twisting her hair around her finger thoughtfully. "Did you mean it for real? You think we should have betting on who wins?"

"Not really," Coriolanus said, then cocked his head. "On the other hand, if it's a success, then absolutely, Clemmie. I want to go down in history as the one who brought gambling to the Games!"

Clemensia shook her head in exasperation. But as he walked to lunch, Coriolanus couldn't help thinking that the idea had some merit.

The dining hall cooks were still working with the reaping buffet leftovers, and the creamed ham on toast had to be the high point of the school lunch year. Coriolanus savored every bite, unlike at the original buffet, when he'd been so distraught over Dean Highbottom's threatening manner that he'd barely tasted a thing.

The mentors had been instructed to gather on the balcony of Heavensbee Hall after lunch, ahead of their first official meetings with their tributes. Each mentor had been given a brief questionnaire to complete with their assignee, partly as an icebreaker, and partly as a matter of record. Very little information had been archived on previous tributes, and this was an effort to correct that. Many of his classmates had difficulty hiding their nerves as they headed over, talking and joking a little too loudly, but Coriolanus had gotten a leg up by meeting Lucy Gray twice already. He felt completely at ease, even eager to see her again. To thank her for the song. To give her Tigris's bread pudding. To strategize over their interview.

The chatter died away as the mentors pushed through the swinging balcony doors and caught sight of what awaited them below. All signs of the reaping festivities had been stripped away, leaving the vast hall cold and imposing. Twenty-four small tables flanked with two folding chairs each were spread out in orderly rows. Each table bore a sign with a district number followed by a *B* or a *G* and next to it sat a concrete block with a metal ring on the top.

Before the students could discuss the layout, two Peacekeepers entered and stood guard by the main entrance and the tributes were brought in single file. The Peacekeepers outnumbered them two to one, but it was unlikely that any of the tributes could make a break for it, given the heavy shackles attached to their wrists and ankles. The tributes were led to the tables corresponding to their district and sex, directed to sit, and then chained to the concrete weights.

Some of the tributes drooped in their seats, chins almost on their chests, but the more defiant ones tilted their heads back and surveyed the hall. It was one of the most impressive chambers in the Capitol, and several mouths gaped open, awed by the grandeur of the marble columns, the arched windows, the vaulted ceiling. Coriolanus thought it must be a marvel to them, compared to the flat, ugly structures that were the signature style in many of the districts. As the tributes' eyes traveled around the room, they eventually made their way to the mentors' balcony, and the two groups found themselves locked in one another's gazes for a long, raw moment.

When Professor Sickle banged the door behind them, the mentors gave a collective jump. "Stop eyeballing your tributes and get down there," she ordered. "You only have fifteen minutes, so use them wisely. And remember, complete the paperwork for our records as best you can."

Coriolanus led the way down the steps that spiraled into the hall. When his eyes met Lucy Gray's, he could tell she'd been looking for him. Seeing her in chains disquieted him, but he gave her a reassuring smile, and some of the worry left her face.

Sliding into the seat across from her, he frowned at her shackled hands and gestured to the nearest Peacekeeper. "Excuse me, would it be possible to have these removed?"

The Peacekeeper did him the favor of checking with the officer at the door but then gave him a sharp shake of the head.

"Thanks for trying, just the same," said Lucy Gray. She'd braided back her hair in a pretty fashion, but her face looked sad and tired, and the bruise still marred her cheek. She noticed him looking and touched it. "Is it hideous?"

"It's just healing," he said.

"We don't have a mirror, so I can only imagine." She didn't bother to put on her sparkly camera personality for him, and in a way he was glad. Maybe she was beginning to trust him.

"How are you?" he asked.

"Sleepy. Scared. Hungry," said Lucy Gray. "Only a couple people came by the zoo this morning to feed us. I got an apple, which was more than most but not exactly filling."

"Well, I can help a bit with that." He pulled Tigris's packet from his book bag.

Lucy Gray brightened some and carefully unwrapped the waxed paper to reveal the big square of bread pudding. Suddenly, her eyes filled with tears.

"Oh, no. You don't like it?" he exclaimed. "I can try and bring something else. I can —"

Lucy Gray shook her head. "It's my favorite." She swallowed hard, broke off a bit, and slipped it between her lips.

"Mine, too. My cousin Tigris made it this morning, so it should be fresh," he said.

"It's perfect. It tastes just like my mama's did. Please tell Tigris I said thank you." She took another bite, but she was still fighting tears.

Coriolanus felt a twinge inside him. He wanted to reach out

and touch her face, to tell her that things were going to be all right. But, of course, they weren't. Not for her. He fumbled in his back pocket for a handkerchief and offered it to her.

"I still have the one from last night." She reached for her pocket.

"We've got drawers full," he said. "Take it."

Lucy Gray did, dabbing her eyes and wiping her nose. Then she took a deep breath and straightened up. "So, what's our plan today?"

"I'm supposed to fill out this questionnaire about your background. Do you mind?" He pulled out the single sheet of paper.

"Not a bit. I love talking about myself," she said.

The page began with basic stuff. Name, district address, date of birth, hair and eye colors, height and weight, and any disability. Things got more difficult with family makeup. Both Lucy Gray's parents and her two older siblings were dead.

"Is your whole family gone?" asked Coriolanus.

"I have a couple of cousins. And the rest of the Covey." She leaned in to check the paper. "Is there a space for them?"

There wasn't. But there should be, he thought, given how fractured families were by the war. There should be a place for anyone who cared for you at all. In fact, maybe that should be the question to start with: *Who cares about you?* Or even better, *Who can you count on?*

"Married?" He laughed, then remembered they married young in some of the districts. How did he know? Maybe she had a husband back in 12.

"Why? Are you asking?" said Lucy Gray seriously. He looked up in surprise. "Because I think this could work."

Coriolanus felt himself blush a little at her teasing. "I'm pretty sure you could do better."

"Haven't yet." A flicker of pain crossed her face, but she hid it with a smile. "I bet you've got sweethearts lined up around the block."

Her flirtation left Coriolanus tongue-tied. Where were they? He checked the paper. Oh, yes. Her family. "Who raised you? After you lost your parents, I mean."

"An old man took us in for a fee — the six Covey kids who were left. He didn't much raise us, but he didn't mess with us either, so it could've been worse," she said. "Really, I'm grateful. People weren't excited about taking in six of us. He died last year of the black lung, but some of us are old enough to manage things now."

They moved on to occupation. At sixteen, Lucy Gray wasn't old enough for the mines, but she didn't attend school either. "I make my living entertaining people."

"People pay you to . . . sing and dance?" asked Coriolanus. "I wouldn't think district people could afford that."

"Most can't," she said. "Sometimes they pool their money, and two or three couples get married the same day, and they hire us. Me and the rest of the Covey, that is. What's left of us. The Peacekeepers let us keep our instruments when they rounded us up. They're some of our best customers."

Coriolanus remembered how they'd tried not to smile at the reaping, how no one had interfered with her singing and dancing. He made a note of her employment, finishing the form, but he had plenty of questions of his own. "Tell me about the Covey. What side did you take in the war?"

"Neither. My people didn't take a side. We're just us." Something behind him captured her attention. "What's your friend's name again? The one with the sandwiches? I think he's having trouble."

"Sejanus?" He looked over his shoulder and back through the rows to where Sejanus sat across from Marcus. An untouched meal of roast beef sandwiches and cake languished between them. Sejanus was speaking entreatingly, but Marcus just stared fixedly ahead, his arms crossed, his whole being unresponsive.

Around the room the other tributes were in various stages of engagement. Several had covered their faces and were refusing to communicate. A few were crying. Some warily answered questions, but even they looked hostile.

"Five minutes," Professor Sickle announced.

That reminded Coriolanus of another five minutes they needed to address. "So, the night before the Games begin, we're going to get a five-minute interview on television in which we can do whatever we want. I thought you might sing again."

Lucy Gray considered it. "I'm not sure there's a point to it. I mean, when I sang that song at the reaping, that didn't have anything to do with you all here. I didn't plan it. It's just part of a long, sad tale that nobody but me gives a hoot about."

"It hit a nerve with people," Coriolanus observed.

"And the valley song was, like you told me, maybe a way to get food," she said.

"It was beautiful," he said. "It made me feel like when my mother . . . She died when I was five. It made me remember a song she used to sing to me."

"What about your daddy?" she asked.

"Lost him, too, actually. The same year," Coriolanus told her.

She nodded sympathetically. "So, you're an orphan, like me."

Coriolanus didn't like being called that. Livia had taunted him about his parentless state when he was small, making him feel alone and unwanted when he was neither. Still, there was that emptiness that most other kids didn't really understand. But Lucy

Gray did, being an orphan herself. "It could be worse. I have the Grandma'am. That's my grandmother. And Tigris."

"Do you miss your parents?" Lucy Gray asked.

"Oh, I wasn't that close with my father. My mother . . . sure." It was still hard to talk about her. "Do you?"

"A lot. Both of them. Wearing my mama's dress is the only thing keeping me together right now." She ran her fingers down the ruffles. "It's like she's wrapping her arms around me."

Coriolanus thought of his mother's compact. The scented powder. "My mother always smelled like roses," he said, and then felt awkward. He rarely mentioned his mother, even at home. How had the conversation gotten here? "Anyway, I think your song moved a lot of people."

"That's nice of you to say. Thank you. But it's not really a reason to sing in the interview," she said. "If it's the night before, we can rule food out. I've got no reason to win over anybody at that point."

Coriolanus tried hard to think of a reason, but this time her singing would only benefit him. "It's a shame, though. With your voice."

"I'll sing you a few bars backstage," she promised.

He would have to work to persuade her, but for the moment, he let it drop. Instead he let her interview him for a few minutes, answering more questions about his family and how they'd survived the war. He found her easy to tell things to, somehow. Was it because he knew that all he recounted would vanish in the arena in a few days?

Lucy Gray seemed in better spirits; there had been no more tears. As they'd shared their stories, a sense of familiarity had begun to grow between them. When the whistle blew to signal the end of the session, she tucked his handkerchief neatly back into the pocket of his book bag and gave his forearm a squeeze of thanks.

The mentors headed obediently to the main exit, where Professor Sickle instructed them, "You're to go to the high biology lab for a debriefing."

No one questioned her, but in the halls they wondered aloud about the reason. Coriolanus was hoping it meant Dr. Gaul would be there. His neatly completed questionnaire was in stark contrast to the spotty efforts of his classmates, and this could be another moment for him to stand out.

"Mine wouldn't speak. Not a word!" said Clemensia. "All I've got is what I had after the reaping. His name. Reaper Ash. Can you imagine naming your child Reaper and them ending up in the reaping?"

"There was no reaping when he was born," Lysistrata pointed out. "That's just a farming name."

"I guess that's true," said Clemensia.

"Mine spoke. I almost wish she hadn't!" Arachne practically yelled.

"Why? What did she say?" asked Clemensia.

"Oh, it seems she spends most of her time in District Ten butchering hogs." Arachne made a gagging motion. "Yech. What am I supposed to do with that? I wish I could make up something better." Suddenly, she stopped, causing Coriolanus and Festus to run into her. "Wait! That's it!"

"Watch it!" said Festus, pushing her forward.

She ignored him and chattered on, demanding everyone's attention. "I could make up something brilliant! I've visited District Ten, you know. It's practically my second home!" Before the war, her family had developed luxury hotels in vacation destinations, and Arachne had traveled extensively in Panem. She still bragged about it, even though she'd been as Capitol-bound as anyone else since the war. "Anyway, I could come up with something better than the ups and downs of a slaughterhouse!"

"You're lucky," said Pliny Harrington. Everybody called him Pup to differentiate him from his naval commander father, who watched over the waters off District 4. The commander had tried to mold him into his image, insisting Pup have a crew cut and shined shoes, but his son was a natural slob. He dug a piece of ham out of his braces with his thumbnail and flicked it to the floor. "At least she isn't afraid of blood."

"Why? Is yours?" asked Arachne.

"No idea. She cried for fifteen minutes straight." Pup grimaced. "I don't think District Seven prepared her for a hangnail, let alone the Games."

"You'd better button your jacket before class," Lysistrata reminded him.

"Oh, right," Pup sighed. He worked the top button, and it came off in his hand. "Stupid uniform."

As they filed into the lab, Coriolanus's pleasure at seeing Dr. Gaul again was dampened by the sight of Dean Highbottom stationed behind the professor's table, collecting the questionnaires. He ignored Coriolanus, but then, he wasn't particularly friendly to anyone else either. He left the talking to the Head Gamemaker.

Dr. Gaul poked at the muttation rabbit until the class had settled in, then greeted them with "Hippity, hoppity, how did you fare? Did they greet you like friends or just sit there and stare?" The students shot confused glances at one another as she retrieved the questionnaires. "For those of you who don't know, I'm Dr. Gaul, the Head Gamemaker, and I will be mentoring your mentorships. Let's see what I have to work with, shall we?" She flipped through the papers, frowned, then pulled one out and held it up before the class. "This is what you were asked to do. Thank you, Mr. Snow. Now, what happened to the rest of you?"

Inside he glowed, but he maintained a neutral expression. The best move now was to support his classmates. After a long pause, he spoke up. "I had good luck with my tribute. She's a talker. But most of the kids wouldn't communicate. And even my girl can't see the point of making an effort at the interview."

Sejanus turned to Coriolanus. "Why should they? What does it get them? No matter what they do, they'll be thrown into the arena and left to fend for themselves."

A murmur of assent came from the room.

Dr. Gaul peered at Sejanus. "You're the boy with the sandwiches. Why did you do it?"

Sejanus stiffened and avoided her gaze. "They were starving. We're going to kill them; do we have to torture them ahead of time as well?"

"Huh. A rebel sympathizer," said Dr. Gaul.

Keeping his eyes on his notebook, Sejanus persisted. "Hardly rebels. Some of them were two years old when the war ended. The oldest were eight. And now that the war's over, they're just citizens of Panem, aren't they? Same as us? Isn't that what the anthem says the Capitol does? 'You give us light. You reunite'? It's supposed to be everyone's government, right?"

"That's the general idea. Go on," Dr. Gaul encouraged him.

"Well, then it should protect everyone," said Sejanus. "That's its number-one job! And I don't see how making them fight to the death achieves that."

"Obviously, you don't approve of the Hunger Games," said Dr. Gaul. "That must be hard for a mentor. That must interfere with your assignment."

Sejanus paused for a moment. Then he sat up straight, seeming to steel himself, and looked her in the eye. “Perhaps you should replace me and assign someone more worthy.”

There was an audible gasp from the classroom.

“Not on your life, boy,” Dr. Gaul chuckled. “Compassion is the key to the Games. Empathy, the thing we lack. Right, Casca?” She glanced at Dean Highbottom, but he only fiddled with a pen.

Sejanus’s face fell, but he didn’t argue back. Coriolanus felt he’d ceded the battle but could not believe he’d given up on the war. He was tougher than he looked, Sejanus Plinth. Imagine throwing a mentorship back in Dr. Gaul’s face.

But the exchange only seemed to invigorate her. “Now, wouldn’t it be wonderful if everyone in the audience felt as passionately about the tributes as this young man here? That should be our goal.”

“No,” said Dean Highbottom.

“Yes! For them to really get involved!” continued Dr. Gaul. She struck her forehead. “You’ve given me a marvelous idea. A way to let people personally affect the outcome of the Games. Suppose we let the audience send the tributes food in the arena? Feed them, like your friend here did in the zoo. Would they feel more involved?”

Festus perked up. “I would if I could bet on the one I was feeding! Just this morning, Coriolanus said maybe we should give odds on the tributes.”

Dr. Gaul beamed at Coriolanus. “Of course, he did. All right, then, you all put your heads together and figure it out. Write me a proposal on how this could work, and my team will consider it.”

“Consider it?” asked Livia. “You mean you might actually use our ideas?”

“Why not? If they have merit.” Dr. Gaul tossed the stack of questionnaires onto the table. “What young brains lack in experience they sometimes make up for in idealism. Nothing seems impossible to them. Old Casca over there came up with the concept for the Hunger Games when he was my student at the University, just a few years older than you are now."

All eyes turned to Dean Highbottom, who addressed Dr. Gaul. "It was just theoretical."

"And so is this, unless it proves useful," said Dr. Gaul. "I'll expect it on my desk tomorrow morning."

Coriolanus sighed inwardly. Another group project. Another opportunity to compromise his ideas in the name of collaboration. Either have them cut entirely or, worse, watered down until they had lost their bite. The class voted on a committee of three mentors to draw the thing up. Of course, he was elected, and he could hardly decline. Dr. Gaul had to leave for a meeting and directed the class to discuss the proposal among themselves. He and Clemensia and Arachne were to convene that evening, but since they all wanted to visit their tributes first, they agreed to meet at eight o'clock at the zoo. Later, they'd go to the library to write up the proposal.

Since lunch had been substantial, he didn't feel deprived by a dinner of yesterday's cabbage soup and a plate of red beans. At least they weren't lima. And when Tigris had scooped the last cupful into an elegant china bowl and garnished it with a few fresh herbs from the roof garden, it didn't look too humble to offer to Lucy Gray. Presentation mattered to her. As for the beans, well, she was starving.

Optimism flowed through him as he walked to the zoo. Morning attendance may have been scanty, but now visitors were pouring in so quickly he wasn't sure he'd get a spot up front at the monkey house. His newfound status helped. As people recognized him, they allowed him to pass and even told others to clear a path. He was no common citizen — he was a mentor!

He made straight for his corner, only to find the twins, Pollo and Didi Ring, camped out on his rock. The pair embraced their twinship wholeheartedly, sporting identical outfits, hair buns, and sunny personalities. They cleared out without Coriolanus having to ask.

"You can take it, Coryo," Didi said as she pulled her brother up from the rock.

"Sure, we've already fed our tributes," added Pollo. "Hey, sorry you got stuck with the proposal."

"Yeah, we voted for Pup, but no one backed us up!" They laughed and ran off into the crowd.

Lucy Gray joined him immediately. Even though he wasn't dining with her, she devoured the beans after admiring how fancy they looked.

"Have you gotten any more food from the crowd?" he asked her.

"I got an old cheese rind from a lady, and a couple other kids fought over some bread a man threw in. I can see all kinds of people holding food, but I think they're afraid to get too close, even though they've got these Peacekeepers in here with us now." She pointed to the back wall of the cage, where a quartet of Peacekeepers stood guard. "Maybe they'll feel safer now that you're here."

Coriolanus noticed a boy of about ten hovering in the crowd, holding a boiled potato. He gave him a wink and a wave of the hand. The boy looked up at his father, who nodded approval. He moved up behind Coriolanus, still keeping his distance. "Did you bring that potato for Lucy Gray?" Coriolanus asked.

"Yes. I saved it from dinner. I wanted to eat it, but I wanted to feed her more," he said.

"Go on, then," Coriolanus encouraged him. "She doesn't bite. Mind you, use your manners."

The boy took a shy step in her direction. "Well, hey there," said Lucy Gray. "What's your name?"

"Horace," said the boy. "I saved you my potato."

"Aren't you sweet? Should I eat it now or save it?" she asked.

"Now." The boy gingerly held it out to her.

Lucy Gray took the potato as though it were a diamond. "My. That's about the nicest potato I've ever seen." The boy blushed with pride. "Okay, here I go." She took a bite, closed her eyes, and almost seemed to swoon. "Nicest tasting, too. Thank you, Horace."

The cameras closed in on them as Lucy Gray received a withered carrot from a little girl and a boiled soupbone from the girl's grandmother. Someone tapped on Coriolanus's shoulder, and he turned to see Pluribus Bell standing there with a small can of milk. "For old times' sake," he said with a smile as he punched a couple of holes in the lid and passed it to Lucy Gray. "I enjoyed your act at the reaping. Did you write that song yourself?"

Some of the more accommodating — or possibly the hungriest — tributes began to station themselves up by the bars. They sat on the ground, held out their hands, ducked their heads, and waited. Here and there someone, usually a child, would run up and place something in their hands and then jump back. The tributes began to compete for attention, drawing the cameras to the center of the cage. A limber little girl from District 9 did a back handspring after she received a bread roll. The boy from District 7 made a good show of juggling three walnuts. The audience rewarded those who would perform with applause and more food.

Lucy Gray and Coriolanus resumed their picnic seats and watched the show. "We're a regular circus troupe, we are," she said as she picked bits of meat off her bone.

"None of them can hold a candle to you," said Coriolanus.

Mentors who had been avoided before were now approached by their tributes if they offered food. When Sejanus arrived with bags of hard-boiled eggs and wedges of bread, all the tributes ran up to him except Marcus, who made a point of ignoring him entirely.

Coriolanus nodded at them. "You were right about Sejanus and Marcus. They used to be classmates in District Two."

"Well, that's complicated. At least we don't have to deal with that," she said.

"Yes, this is complicated enough." He meant it as a joke, but it fell flat. It *was* complicated enough, and it got more so by the minute.

She gave him a wistful smile. "Sure would've been nice to meet you under different circumstances."

"Like how?" It was a dangerous line of questioning, but he couldn't help himself.

"Oh, like you came to one of my shows and heard me sing," she said. "And afterward you came up to chat, and maybe we had a drink and a dance or two."

He could imagine it, her singing somewhere like Pluribus's nightclub, him catching her eye, connecting before they'd ever even met. "And I'd come back the next night."

"Like we had all the time in the world," she said.

Their musing was interrupted by a loud "Woo-hoo!" The tributes from District 6 began a funny dance, and the Ring twins got some of the audience to clap along in rhythm. After that, things became almost festive. The crowd ventured closer, and a few people began to converse with the captives.

On the whole, Coriolanus thought it a good development — it would take more than Lucy Gray to justify the prime-time slot for the interviews. He decided to let the other tributes have their moment and to ask her to sing at closing time. In the meantime, he filled her in on the mentors' discussions that day and stressed what her popularity could mean in the arena, now that there was a possibility that people could send gifts.

Secretly, he worried about his resources again. He'd need more affluent viewers, who could afford to buy her things. It would look bad if a Snow's tribute received nothing in the arena. Maybe he should make it a provision of the proposal that you couldn't send your own tribute gifts. Otherwise, how could he compete? Certainly not with Sejanus. And there, by the bars, Arachne had laid out a little picnic for her tribute. A fresh loaf of bread, a block of cheese, and were those grapes? How could she afford those? Maybe the travel industry was picking up.

He watched as Arachne sliced the cheese with a mother-of-pearl-handled knife. Her tribute, the talkative girl from District 10, squatted right in front of her, eagerly leaning into the bars. Arachne made a thick sandwich but didn't hand it right over. She seemed to be lecturing the girl about something. It was quite a speech. At one point, the girl reached through the bars, and Arachne withdrew the sandwich, drawing a laugh from the audience. She turned and flashed them a grin, shook her finger at her tribute, held out the sandwich again, and then pulled it away a second time, much to the crowd's amusement.

"She's playing with fire there," Lucy Gray observed.

Arachne waved to the crowd and then took a bite of the sandwich herself.

Coriolanus could see the tribute's face darkening, the muscles tightening in her neck. He could see something else, too. Her fingers sliding down the bar, darting out, circling the handle of the knife. He started to rise, opening his mouth to shout out a warning, but it was too late.

In one movement, the tribute yanked Arachne forward and slit her throat.

Shrieks came from the audience members nearest to the attack. Arachne's face drained of color as she dropped the sandwich and clawed at her neck. The blood poured down her fingers as the District 10 girl released her and gave her a small shove. Arachne stepped back, turning and reaching out a dripping hand, imploring the audience for help. People were either too stunned or too scared to respond. Many drew away as she fell to her knees and began to bleed out.

Coriolanus's initial reaction was to recoil like the others, to grab hold of the monkey house bars for support, but Lucy Gray hissed, "Help her!" He remembered the cameras streaming live to the Capitol audience. He had no idea what to do for Arachne, but he did not want to be seen cringing and clinging. His terror was a private thing, not meant for public display.

He forced his legs into motion and was the first to reach Arachne. She clutched his shirt as the life seeped out of her. "Medic!" he cried as he eased her to the ground. "Is there a doctor? Please, someone help!" He pressed his hand over the wound to stem the blood but removed it when she made a choking sound. "Come on!" he screamed at the crowd. A couple of Peacekeepers were shouldering their way toward him, but much, much too slowly.

Coriolanus glanced over in time to see the District 10 girl retrieve the cheese sandwich and take a furious bite before the bullets pierced her body, slamming her into the bars. She slipped into a heap as her blood commingled with Arachne's. Bits of half-chewed food fell from her mouth and floated in the red pool.

The crowd surged back as panicked people tried to flee the area. The fading light added a level of desperation. Coriolanus saw one small boy fall and watched his leg being trampled before a woman yanked him from the ground. Others weren't so lucky.

Arachne's lips made soundless words that he could not decipher. When her breathing stopped abruptly, he guessed it was pointless to try to resuscitate her. If he forced air into her mouth, wouldn't it only spill out the gaping wound in her neck? Festus was next to him now, and the two friends exchanged helpless looks.

Stepping back from Arachne, Coriolanus flinched at the red, shiny stuff coating his hands. He turned and found Lucy Gray huddled against the bars of the cage, her face hidden in her ruffled skirt, her body shaking, and realized he was shaking as well. That's how it was with him: The wash of blood, the whiz of bullets, the screams in the crowd all caused flashbacks to the worst moments of his childhood. Rebel boots pounding through the streets, he and the Grandma'am pinned down by gunfire, dying bodies twitching around them . . . his mother on the bloodstained bed . . . the stampedes during the food riots, the smashed faces, the moaning people . . .

He took immediate steps to mask his terror. Cramming his hands into fists at his sides. Trying to take slow, deep breaths. Lucy Gray began to vomit, and he turned away to keep his own stomach in check.

Medics appeared, lifting Arachne onto a stretcher. Others assessed those who had been wounded by stray bullets or tromped by the feet of the audience. A woman was in his face, asking was he hurt, was this his blood? Once they'd confirmed it wasn't, they gave him a towel to wipe himself with and moved on.

As he scrubbed at the blood, he spotted Sejanus kneeling near the dead tribute. He had reached through the bars, and he seemed to be sprinkling a handful of something white over her body while he mumbled some words. Coriolanus only caught a glimpse before a Peacekeeper came and pulled Sejanus back. The soldiers were swarming the place now, clearing out the last remnants of the audience and lining up the tributes along the back of the cage with their hands on top of their heads. Calmer, Coriolanus tried to catch Lucy Gray's attention, but her eyes were locked on the ground.

A Peacekeeper took him by the shoulders and gave him a respectful but firm push toward the exit. He found himself following Festus up to the main path. They stopped at a water fountain and worked a bit more on removing the blood. Neither knew what to say. Arachne hadn't been his favorite person, but she'd always been in his life. They'd played as babies, been at birthday parties, stood on ration lines, attended classes together. She'd been dressed head to toe in black lace at his mother's funeral, and he'd cheered her brother's graduation only last year. As part of the wealthy old guard of the Capitol, she was family. And you didn't have to like your family. The bond was a given.

"I couldn't save her," he said. "I couldn't stop the blood."

"I don't think anyone could have. At least you tried. That's what matters," Festus consoled him.

Clemensia found them, her whole body trembling in distress, and they made their way out of the zoo together.

"Come to my place," Festus said, but when they reached his apartment, he suddenly broke into tears. They saw him onto the elevator and said good night.

It was not until Coriolanus had walked Clemensia home that they remembered the assignment Dr. Gaul had given them. The proposal about sending tributes food in the arena and the option to bet on them. “Surely, she won’t still expect it,” said Clemensia. “I couldn’t do it tonight. I couldn’t possibly think about it. You know, without Arachne.”

Coriolanus agreed, but on the way home he thought about Dr. Gaul. She would be just the type to penalize them for missing such a deadline, regardless of the circumstances. Maybe he should write something up to be on the safe side.

When he’d climbed the twelve flights to the apartment, he found the Grandma’am in a state, railing at the districts and airing out her best black dress for Arachne’s funeral. She flew at him, patting his chest and arms, making sure he was uninjured. Tigris simply wept. “I can’t believe Arachne is dead. I just saw her this afternoon at the market, buying those grapes.”

He comforted them and did his best to reassure them of his safety. “It won’t happen again. It was like a freak accident. And now the security’s bound to be even tighter.”

When things had calmed down, Coriolanus went to his bedroom, stripped off his bloodstained uniform, and headed to his bathroom. In the near-scalding water of the shower, he scoured the remainder of Arachne’s blood from his body. For about a minute, a painful sobbing made his chest ache, but then it passed, and he wasn’t sure if it had to do with sorrow over her death or unhappiness over his own difficulties. Probably some of both. He pulled on a worn silk robe that had been his father’s and decided to take a shot at the proposal. It wasn’t as if he would be able to sleep, not with the burbling sound of Arachne’s throat still fresh in his ears. No amount of rose-scented powder could temper that. Losing himself in the assignment helped to calm him, and he preferred working in solitude, not having to parry the thoughts of his classmates diplomatically. Without interference, he created a simple but solid proposal.

Reflecting on the classroom discussion with Dr. Gaul and the electricity in the audience when they'd fed the starving tributes at the zoo, he focused on the food. For the first time, sponsors would be able to buy items — a piece of bread, a chunk of cheese — to be delivered by drone to a specific tribute. A panel would be established to review the nature and value of each item. A sponsor would have to be a Capitol citizen in good standing who was not directly related to the Games. This ruled out Gamemakers, mentors, Peacekeepers assigned to guard the tributes, and any of the aforementioned parties' immediate family members. When it came to his idea of betting, he suggested a second panel to create a venue that would allow Capitol citizens to officially wager on the victor, establish the odds, and oversee the payments to the winners. Proceeds from either program would be funneled toward the costs of the Games, making them essentially free for the government of Panem.

Coriolanus worked steadily until Friday morning dawned. As the first rays came through his window, he dressed in a clean uniform, tucked his proposal under his arm, and left the apartment as quietly as possible.

Dr. Gaul wore several hats between her research, military, and academic duties, so he had to venture a guess as to where her desk might be located. Since it was Hunger Games business, he walked to the imposing structure known as the Citadel, which housed the War Department. The Peacekeepers on duty had no intention of letting him into the high-security zone, but they assured him the pages of the proposal would be placed on her desk. It was the best he could do.

As he walked back to the Corso, the screen that had shown only the seal of Panem in the early hours came alive with the events of the previous night. Again and again they aired the tribute slitting Arachne's throat, him arriving to help her, and the gunning down of the murderer. He felt strangely detached from the action, as if all his emotional reserve had been depleted by his brief outburst in the shower. Since his initial reaction to Arachne's death had been somewhat lacking, he was relieved to see that the cameras had only recorded his attempt to save her, the moments when he appeared brave and responsible. You would only notice his shaking if you looked closely for it.

He was particularly pleased to catch a quick shot of Livia Cardew flailing her way through the crowd at the sound of the gunfire. In rhetoric class, she'd once attributed his inability to decipher the deeper meaning of a poem to the fact that he was too self-absorbed. The irony, coming from Livia, of all people! But actions spoke louder than words. Coriolanus to the rescue, Livia to the nearest exit.

By the time he reached home, Tigris and the Grandma'am had recovered somewhat from the shock of Arachne's death and were declaring him a national hero, which he waved off but secretly relished. He should have been exhausted, but he felt a nervous energy running through him, and the announcement that the Academy would still be holding classes gave him a boost. Being a hero at home had its limitations; he needed a larger audience.

After a breakfast of fried potatoes and cold buttermilk, he made his way to the Academy with the somberness the occasion demanded. Since he was known to be Arachne's friend, and had proven it by trying to save her, he seemed to have been designated chief mourner. In the hallways, condolences came in from every side, along with praise for his actions. Someone suggested that he cared for her like a sister, and although he'd done nothing of the sort, he allowed it. No need to disrespect the dead.

As dean of the Academy, it should've been Highbottom who led the schoolwide assembly, but he did not make an appearance.

Instead it was Satyria who spoke of Arachne in glowing terms: her audacity, her outspokenness, her sense of humor. All the things, Coriolanus thought as he dabbed his eyes, that were so annoying about her and had ultimately brought on her death. Professor Sickle took the mic and commended him, and to a lesser extent Festus, for their response to a fallen comrade in arms. Hippocrata Lunt, the school counselor, invited anyone with grief issues to visit her office, especially if they were having violent impulses toward themselves or others. Satyria came back and announced that Arachne's official funeral would be the following day, and the entire student body would attend to honor her memory. It would be aired live to all of Panem, so they were encouraged to look and behave as befitted the youth of the Capitol. Then they were allowed to mingle, to remember their friend, and to console one another for her loss. Classes would resume after lunch.

After a gloppy fish salad on toast, the mentors were scheduled to meet with Professor Demigloss again, although no one really felt like going. It didn't help that the first thing he did was pass out a mentor sheet, updated with the tributes' names, saying, "This should facilitate keeping track of your progress in the Games."

10th HUNGER GAMES
MENTOR ASSIGNMENTS

DISTRICT 1	
Boy (Facet)	*Livia Cardew*
Girl (Velvereen)	*Palmyra Monty*
DISTRICT 2	
Boy (Marcus)	*Sejanus Plinth*
Girl (Sabyn)	*Florus Friend*

DISTRICT 3	
Boy (Circ)	*Io Jasper*
Girl (Teslee)	*Urban Canville*
DISTRICT 4	
Boy (Mizzen)	*Persephone Price*
Girl (Coral)	*Festus Creed*
DISTRICT 5	
Boy (Hy)	*Dennis Fling*
Girl (Sol)	*Iphigenia Moss*
DISTRICT 6	
Boy (Otto)	*Apollo Ring*
Girl (Ginnee)	*Diana Ring*
DISTRICT 7	
Boy (Treech)	*Vipsania Sickle*
Girl (Lamina)	*Pliny Harrington*
DISTRICT 8	
Boy (Bobbin)	*Juno Phipps*
Girl (Wovey)	*Hilarius Heavensbee*
DISTRICT 9	
Boy (Panlo)	*Gaius Breen*
Girl (Sheaf)	*Androcles Anderson*
DISTRICT 10	
Boy (Tanner)	*Domitia Whimsiwick*
Girl (Brandy)	*Arachne Crane*
DISTRICT 11	
Boy (Reaper)	*Clemensia Dovecote*
Girl (Dill)	*Felix Ravinstill*
DISTRICT 12	
Boy (Jessup)	*Lysistrata Vickers*
Girl (Lucy Gray)	*Coriolanus Snow*

Coriolanus, along with several people around him, automatically crossed off the name of the girl from District 10. But then what? It would make sense to cross off Arachne's name as well, but that felt different. His pen hovered over her name and then left it alone for the moment. It seemed pretty cold to scratch her off the list like that.

About ten minutes into class, a note arrived from the office instructing him and Clemensia to leave class and report immediately to the Citadel. This could only be in response to his proposal, and Coriolanus felt a combination of excitement and nervousness. Did Dr. Gaul like it? Hate it? What did it mean?

Since he hadn't bothered to tell her about his proposal, Clemensia was put out. "I can't believe you wrote up some proposal while Arachne's body was still warm! I cried all night long." Her puffy eyes backed up the claim.

"Well, it's not like I could sleep either," Coriolanus objected. "After holding her while she died. Working kept me from freaking out."

"I know, I know. Everyone handles grief differently. I didn't mean that like it sounded." She sighed. "So, what's in this thing I supposedly cowrote?"

Coriolanus gave her a quick overview, but she still seemed annoyed. "I'm sorry, I meant to tell you. It's pretty basic stuff, and some of it we already discussed as a group. Look, I already got one demerit this week — I can't afford to let my grades take a hit, too."

"Did you at least put my name on it? I don't want it to seem like I was too feeble to pull my weight," she said.

"I didn't put anyone's name on it. It's more of a class project."

Coriolanus threw up his hands in exasperation. "Honestly, Clemmie, I thought I was doing you a favor!"

"Okay, okay," she said, relenting. "I guess I owe you. But I wish I'd at least had a chance to read it. Just cover for me if she starts grilling us about it."

"You know I will. She'll probably hate it anyway," he said. "I mean, I think it's pretty solid, but she's operating with a whole different rule book."

"That's true," Clemensia agreed. "Do you think there will even be a Hunger Games now?"

He hadn't thought of that. "I don't know. What with Arachne, and then the funeral . . . If they happen, they'll be delayed, I suppose. I know you don't like them anyway."

"Do you? Does anyone, really?" Clemensia asked.

"Maybe they'll just send the tributes home." The idea was not entirely unappealing when he thought of Lucy Gray. He wondered how the fallout from Arachne's death was affecting her. Were all the tributes being punished? Would they allow him to see her?

"Yes, or make them Avoxes, or something," said Clemensia. "It's awful, but not as bad as the arena. I mean, I'd rather be alive without a tongue than dead, wouldn't you?"

"I would, but I'm not sure my tribute would," said Coriolanus. "Can you still sing without a tongue?"

"I don't know. Hum, maybe." They had reached the gates of the Citadel. "This place scared me when I was little."

"It scares me still," said Coriolanus, which made her laugh.

At the Peacekeeper station, their retinas were scanned and checked against the Capitol files. Their book bags were taken and a guard escorted them down a long, gray corridor and onto an elevator that plunged down at least twenty-five floors. Coriolanus had never been so far underground and, surprisingly, found he liked it. Much as he loved the Snows' penthouse apartment, he'd felt so vulnerable when the bombs had fallen during the war. Here, it seemed nothing could reach him.

The elevator doors parted, and they stepped into a gigantic open laboratory. Rows of research tables, unfamiliar machines, and glass cases spread out into the distance. Coriolanus turned to the guard, but she closed the doors and left them without giving further instructions. "Shall we?" he asked Clemensia.

They began to make their way cautiously into the lab. "I have a terrible feeling I'm going to break something," she whispered.

They walked along a wall of glass cases fifteen feet high. Inside, a menagerie of creatures, some familiar, some altered to the point that no label could easily be attached, roamed and panted and flopped around in apparent unhappiness. Oversized fangs, claws, and flippers swiped the glass as they passed.

A young man in a lab coat intercepted them and led them to a section of reptile cases. Here they found Dr. Gaul, peering into a large terrarium filled with hundreds of snakes. They were artificially bright, their skins almost glowing in shades of neon pink, yellow, and blue. No longer than a ruler and not much thicker than a pencil, they twisted into a psychedelic carpet that covered the bottom of the case.

"Ah, here you are," Dr. Gaul said with a grin. "Say hello to my new babies."

"Hello there," said Coriolanus, putting his face close to the glass to see the writhing mess. They reminded him of something, but he couldn't think what.

"Is there a point to the color?" asked Clemensia.

"There is a point to everything or nothing at all, depending on your worldview," said Dr. Gaul. "Which brings me to your proposal. I liked it. Who wrote it? Just you two? Or did your brassy friend weigh in before her throat was cut?"

Clemensia pressed her lips together, upset, but then Coriolanus saw her face tighten. She was not going to be intimidated. "The whole class discussed it as a group."

"And Arachne was planning to help write it up last night, but then . . . as you said," he added.

"But you two forged ahead, is that it?" asked Dr. Gaul.

"That's right," said Clemensia. "We wrote it up at the library, and I printed it out at my apartment last night. Then I gave it to Coriolanus so he could drop it off this morning. As assigned."

Dr. Gaul addressed Coriolanus. "Is that how it happened?"

Coriolanus felt put on the spot. "I did drop it off this morning, yes. Well, just to the Peacekeepers on guard; I wasn't allowed in," he said evasively. Something was strange about this line of questioning. "Was that a problem?"

"I just wanted to make sure you'd both had your hands on it," said Dr. Gaul.

"I can show you the parts the group discussed and how they were developed in the proposal," he offered.

"Yes. Do that. Did you bring a copy?" she asked.

Clemensia looked at Coriolanus expectantly. "No, I didn't," he said. He wasn't thrilled with Clemensia laying it at his door, when she'd been too shaky to even help write the thing. Especially since she was one of his most formidable competitors for the Academy prizes. "Did you?"

"They took our book bags." Clemensia turned to Dr. Gaul. "Perhaps we could use the copy we gave you?"

"Well, we could. But my assistant lined this very case with it while I was having my lunch," she said with a laugh.

Coriolanus stared down into the mass of wriggling snakes, with their flicking tongues. Sure enough, he could catch phrases of his proposal between the coils.

"Suppose you two retrieve it?" Dr. Gaul suggested.

It felt like a test. A weird Dr. Gaul test, but still. And somehow planned, but he couldn't begin to guess to what end. He glanced at Clemensia and tried to remember if she was afraid of snakes, but he scarcely knew if he was himself. They didn't have snakes in the lab at school.

She gave Dr. Gaul a clenched smile. "Of course. Do we just reach in through the trapdoor on the top?"

Dr. Gaul removed the entire cover. "Oh, no, let's give you some room. Mr. Snow? Why don't you start?"

Coriolanus reached in slowly, feeling the warmth of the heated air.

"That's right. Move gently. Don't disrupt them," Dr. Gaul instructed.

He scooped his fingers under the edge of a sheet of his proposal and slowly slid it out from under the snakes. They slumped down into a heap but didn't seem to mind much. "I don't think they even noticed me," he said to Clemensia, who looked a little green.

"Here I go, then." She reached into the tank.

"They can't see too well, and they hear even less," said Dr. Gaul. "But they know you're there. Snakes can smell you using their tongues, these mutts here more than others."

Clemensia hooked a sheet with her fingernail and lifted it up. The snakes stirred.

"If you're familiar, if they have pleasant associations with your scent — a warm tank, for instance — they'll ignore you. A new scent, something foreign, that would be a threat," said Dr. Gaul. "You'd be on your own, little girl."

Coriolanus had just begun to put two and two together when he saw the look of alarm on Clemensia's face. She yanked her hand from the tank, but not before a half dozen neon snakes sank their fangs into her flesh.

Clemensia gave a bloodcurdling scream, shaking her hand madly to rid it of the vipers. The tiny puncture wounds left by their fangs oozed the neon colors of their skins. Pus dyed bright pink, yellow, and blue dripped down her fingers.

Lab assistants in white jackets materialized. Two pinned Clemensia to the floor while a third injected her with a scary-looking hypodermic needle filled with black fluid. Her lips turned purple and then bloodless before she passed out. The assistants dropped her onto a stretcher and whisked her away.

Coriolanus began to follow them, but Dr. Gaul stopped him with her voice. "Not you, Mr. Snow. You stay here."

"But I — She —" he stammered. "Will she die?"

"Anyone's guess," said Dr. Gaul. She had dipped a hand back into the tank and was lightly trailing her gnarled fingers over her pets. "Clearly, her scent was not on the paper. So, you wrote the proposal alone?"

"I did." There was no point in lying. Lying had probably killed Clemensia. Obviously, he was dealing with a lunatic who should be handled with extreme care.

"Good. The truth, finally. I've no use for liars. What are lies but attempts to conceal some sort of weakness? If I see that side of you again, I'll cut you off. If Dean Highbottom punishes you for it, I won't stand in his way. Are we clear?" She wrapped one of the pink snakes around her wrist like a bracelet and seemed to be admiring it.

"Very clear," said Coriolanus.

"It's good, your proposal," she said. "Well thought out and simple to execute. I'm going to recommend my team review it and implement a version of the first stage."

"All right," said Coriolanus, afraid to make more than the blandest of responses, surrounded as he was by lethal creatures that did her bidding.

Dr. Gaul laughed. "Oh, go home. Or go see your friend if she's still there to see. It's time for my crackers and milk."

Coriolanus hurried off, bumping into a lizard tank and sending its inhabitants into a frenzy. He made a wrong turn, then another, and found himself in a ghoulish section of the lab where the glass cases housed humans with animal parts grafted to their bodies. Tiny feathered ruffs around their necks; talons, or even tentacles, in place of fingers; and something — perhaps gills? — embedded in their chests. His appearance startled them, and when a few opened their mouths to plead with him, he realized they were Avoxes. Their cries reverberated and he caught a glimpse of small black birds perched above them. The name *jabberjay* popped into his mind. A brief chapter in his genetics class. The failed experiment, the bird that could repeat human speech, that had been a tool for espionage until the rebels had figured out its abilities and sent it back carrying false information. Now the useless creatures were creating an echo chamber filled with the Avoxes' pitiful wails.

Finally, a woman in a lab coat and oversized pink bifocals intercepted him, scolded him for disturbing the birds, and escorted him back to the elevator. As he waited, a security camera blinked down at him and he compulsively tried to smooth out the lone, crumpled page of his proposal he'd crushed in his hand. Peacekeepers met him above, returned both his and Clemensia's book bags, and marched him out of the Citadel.

Coriolanus made it down the street and around the corner before his legs gave way and he dropped onto the curb. The sun hurt his eyes, and he couldn't seem to catch his breath. He was exhausted, having not slept the night before, but hyper with adrenaline. What had just happened? Was Clemensia dead? He had not begun to come to terms with Arachne's violent end, and now this. It was like the Hunger Games. Only they weren't district kids. The Capitol was supposed to protect them. He thought of Sejanus telling Dr. Gaul it was the government's job to protect everybody, even the people in the districts, but he still wasn't sure how to square that with the fact that they'd been such recent enemies. But certainly the child of a Snow should be a top priority. He could be dead if Clemensia had written the proposal instead of him. He buried his head in his hands, confused, angry, and most of all afraid. Afraid of Dr. Gaul. Afraid of the Capitol. Afraid of everything. If the people who were supposed to protect you played so fast and loose with your life . . . then how did you survive? Not by trusting them, that was for sure. And if you couldn't trust them, who could you trust? All bets were off.

Coriolanus knotted up at the memory of the snake fangs sinking into flesh. Poor Clemmie, could she really be dead? And in that nightmarish way. If she was, was it his fault? For not calling her out for lying? It seemed such a minor infraction, but would Dr. Gaul place blame on him for covering for her? If she died, he could be in all kinds of trouble.

He guessed that in an emergency, a person would be taken to the nearby Capitol Hospital, so he found himself running in its direction. Once inside the cool entrance hall, he followed the signs to the emergency room. As soon as the automated door slid open, he could hear Clemensia screaming, just as she had when the snakes bit her. At least she was still alive. He babbled something to the nurse at the counter, and she made enough sense of it to have him take a seat just as a wave of dizziness hit him. He must have looked terrible, because she brought him two packets of nutritional crackers and a glass of sweet, fizzy lemon drink, which he tried to sip and ended up gulping down, longing for a refill. The sugar made him feel a bit better, although not enough to try the crackers, which he pocketed. By the time the attending doctor emerged from the back, he was almost in control of himself. The doctor reassured him. They'd treated the victims of mishaps at the lab before. Since the antidote had been swiftly administered, there was every reason to believe Clemensia would survive, although there might be some neurological damage. She'd be hospitalized until they were sure she was stable. If he checked back in a few days, she might be ready for visitors.

Coriolanus thanked the doctor, handed over her book bag, and agreed when he suggested that the best thing would be to return home. As he retraced his steps to the entrance, he spotted Clemensia's parents rushing in his direction and managed to conceal himself in a doorway. He didn't know what the Dovecotes had been told, but he had no interest in talking to them, especially before he'd worked out his story.

The lack of a plausible story, preferably one that absolved him of being an accessory to her condition, made his return to school or even home impossible.

Tigris would not be home until supper at the earliest, and the Grandma'am would be horrified by his situation. Strangely, he found the only person he wanted to talk to was Lucy Gray, who was both clever and unlikely to repeat his words.

His feet carried him to the zoo before he had really considered the difficulties he would encounter there. A pair of impressively armed Peacekeepers were on guard at the main entrance, with several more milling around behind them. At first they waved him away; instructions were to allow no visitors to the zoo. But Coriolanus played the mentor card, and at this point some of them recognized him as the boy who'd tried to save Arachne. His celebrity was enough to convince them to call in a request for an exception. The Peacekeeper spoke to Dr. Gaul directly, and Coriolanus could hear her distinctive cackle shooting out of the phone, even though he stood several yards away. He was allowed in with a Peacekeeper, but only for a short time.

Trash from the fleeing crowd was still strewn along the path to the monkey house. Dozens of rats darted about, gnawing on leftovers, from bits of rotting food to shoes lost in the panic. Although the sun was high, several raccoons foraged, scooping up tidbits in their clever little hands. One chewed on a dead rat, warning the others to give it a wide berth.

"Not the zoo I remember," said the Peacekeeper. "Nothing but kids in cages and vermin running loose."

At points along the path, Coriolanus could see small containers of white powder tucked under boulders or against walls. He remembered the poison used by the Capitol during the siege — a time with little food but plenty of rats. Humans, particularly dead ones, had become their daily fare. During the worst of it, of course, humans had eaten humans as well. There was no point in feeling superior to the rats.

"Is that rat poison?" he asked the Peacekeeper.

"Yeah, some new stuff they're trying out today. But the rats are so smart, they won't go near it." He shrugged. "It's what they gave us to work with."

Inside the cage, the tributes, shackled again, pressed against the back wall or positioned themselves behind the rock formations, as if trying to make themselves as inconspicuous as possible.

"You have to keep your distance," said the Peacekeeper. "Your girl isn't likely a threat, but who knows? Another might attack you. You have to stay back where they can't touch you."

Coriolanus nodded and went to his usual rock but remained standing behind it. He didn't feel threatened by the tributes — they were the least of his problems — but he didn't want to give Dean Highbottom any other excuse to punish him.

At first he couldn't locate Lucy Gray. Then he made eye contact with Jessup, who sat propped against the back wall, holding what appeared to be the Snows' handkerchief to his neck. Jessup gave something beside him a shake, and Lucy Gray sat straight up with a start.

For a moment she seemed disoriented. When she spotted Coriolanus, she wiped the sleep from her eyes and combed her loose hair back with her fingers. She lost her balance as she rose, and reached out to catch herself on Jessup's arm. Still unsteady, she began to make her way across the cage to him, dragging the chains with her. Was it the heat? The trauma of the killing? Hunger? Since the Capitol wasn't feeding the tributes, she'd had nothing since Arachne's murder, when she'd vomited up the precious food from the crowd, and probably his bread pudding and the apple from the morning as well. So she'd gone almost five days on a meat loaf sandwich and a plum. He was going to have to find a way to get her more to eat, even if it was cabbage soup.

When she'd crossed the waterless moat, he held up a cautionary hand. "I'm sorry, we can't get close."

Lucy Gray stopped a few feet from the bars. "Surprised you got in at all." Her throat, her skin, her hair — everything seemed parched in the hot afternoon sun. A bad bruise on her arm had not been there the previous night. Who had hit her? Another tribute, or a guard?

"I didn't mean to wake you," he said.

She shrugged. "It's nothing. Jessup and I take turns sleeping. Capitol rats have a taste for people."

"The rats are trying to eat you?" Coriolanus asked, revolted at the thought.

"Well, something bit Jessup's neck the first night we were here. Too dark to see what, but he mentioned fur. And last night, something crawled over my leg." She indicated a container of white powder by the bars. "That stuff doesn't do a lick of good."

Coriolanus had a terrible image of her lying dead under a swarm of rats. It wiped away the last few shreds of resistance he had, and despair engulfed him. For her. For himself. For the both of them. "Oh, Lucy Gray, I'm so sorry. I'm so sorry about all of this."

"It's not your fault," she said.

"You must hate me. You should. I would hate me," he said.

"I don't hate you. The Hunger Games weren't your idea," she replied.

"But I'm participating in them. I'm helping them happen!" His head dropped in shame. "I should be like Sejanus and at least try to quit."

"No, don't! Please don't. Don't leave me to go through this alone!" She took a step toward him and almost fainted. Her hands caught the bars, and she slid down to the ground.

Ignoring the guard's warning, he impulsively stepped over the rock and crouched down across the bars from her. "Are you all right?" She nodded, but she didn't look all right. He'd wanted to tell her about the scare with the snakes and Clemensia's brush with death. He'd hoped to ask her advice, but it all paled in comparison to her situation. He remembered the crackers the nurse had given him and fumbled for the crumpled packets in his pocket. "I brought you these. They're not big, but they're very nutritious."

That sounded stupid. How could their nutritional value matter to her? He realized he was just parroting what his teachers had said during the war, when one of the incentives for going to school had been the free snack provided by the government. The scratchy, tasteless things washed down with water were all some of the kids had to eat for the day. He remembered their little clawlike hands tearing into the wrapping and the desperate crunching that followed.

Lucy Gray immediately ripped open a packet and stuffed one of the two crackers into her mouth, chewing and swallowing the dry thing with difficulty. She pressed a hand against her stomach, sighed, and ate the second more slowly. The food seemed to focus her, and her voice sounded calmer.

"Thanks," she said. "That's better."

"Eat the others," he urged, nodding to the second packet.

She shook her head. "No. I'll save these for Jessup. He's my ally now."

"Your ally?" Coriolanus was perplexed. How could one have an ally in the Games?

"Uh-huh. The tributes from District Twelve are going down together," said Lucy Gray. "He's not the brightest star in the Dipper, but he's strong as an ox."

Two crackers seemed a small price to pay for Jessup's protection. "I'll get you more to eat as soon as I can. And it looks like people are going to be allowed to send food into the arena. It's official now."

"That'd be good. More food would be good." She leaned her head forward and rested it on the bars. "Then, like you said, it might make sense to sing. Make people want to help me."

"At the interview," he suggested. "You could sing the valley song again."

"Maybe." Her brow furrowed in thought. "They showing this in all Panem, or just the Capitol?"

"All Panem, I think," he answered. "But you won't get anything from the districts."

"Not expecting to. Not the point," she said. "Maybe I will sing, though. Be better with a guitar or something."

"I can try to find you one." Not that the Snows had any instruments. Except for the Grandma'am's daily anthem and his mother's long-ago bedtime songs, there'd been little music in his life until Lucy Gray appeared. He rarely listened to the Capitol radio broadcast, which mostly played marches and propaganda songs. Those all sounded the same to him.

"Hey!" The Peacekeeper waved at him from the path. "That's too close! Time's up anyway."

Coriolanus rose. "I better go if I want them to let me in again."

"Sure. Sure. And thanks. For the crackers and all," said Lucy Gray, grasping the bars to struggle to her feet.

He reached through the bars to help her up. "It's nothing."

"Not to you maybe," she said. "But it's meant the world having someone show up like I mattered."

"You do matter," he said.

"Well, there's a lot of evidence to the contrary." She rattled her chains and gave them a tug. And then, as if remembering something, she looked up at the sky.

"You matter to me," he insisted. The Capitol may not value her, but he did. Hadn't he just poured his heart out to her?

"Time to go, Mr. Snow!" the Peacekeeper called.

"You matter to me, Lucy Gray," he repeated. His words drew her eyes back to him, but she still seemed distant.

"Look, kid, don't make me report you," said the Peacekeeper.

"I've got to go." Coriolanus started to leave.

"Hey!" she said with a certain urgency. He turned back. "Hey, I want you to know I don't really believe you're here for grades or glory. You're a rare bird, Coriolanus."

"You, too," he said.

She dipped her head in agreement and headed back to Jessup, her chains leaving a trail in the dirty straw and rat droppings. When she reached her partner, she lay down and curled up in a ball, as if exhausted by the brief encounter.

Twice he tripped on his way out of the zoo, and he recognized that he was too tired to come up with any good solutions to anything. It was late enough now that his arrival at home wouldn't seem suspicious, so he headed back to the apartment. He had the misfortune to bump into his classmate Persephone Price, the daughter of the infamous Nero Price, who'd once cannibalized the maid. They ended up walking together, since they were neighbors. She'd been assigned to mentor Mizzen, a sturdy thirteen-year-old boy from District 4, and so had been present when he and Clemensia had been called from class. He dreaded any discussion of the proposal, but she was still too distraught over Arachne's death to talk about anything else. Usually, he avoided Persephone altogether, because he could never help wondering if she had known the ingredients of her wartime stew. For some time, he'd felt afraid of her, but now she only inspired disgust, no matter how many times he reminded himself of her innocence. With her dimples and hazel green eyes, she was prettier than any girl in his year, with the possible exception of Clemensia . . . well, pre-snakebite Clemensia. But the idea of kissing her repulsed him. Even now, as she gave him a tearful hug good-bye, all he could think of was that severed leg.

Coriolanus dragged himself up the stairs, his thoughts darker than ever at the memory of the poor maid collapsed from hunger in the street. How long could he expect Lucy Gray to last? She was fading fast. Weak and distracted. Injured and broken. But most of all, slowly starving to death. By tomorrow, she might not be able to stand. If he didn't find a way to feed her, she'd be dead before the Hunger Games even began.

When he reached the apartment, the Grandma'am took one look at him and suggested a nap before supper. He fell on his bed, feeling too stressed to ever sleep again. The next thing he knew, Tigris was gently shaking his shoulder. A tray on his night table gave off the comforting smell of noodle soup. Sometimes the butcher would give her chicken carcasses for free, and she'd boil them into something wonderful.

"Coryo," she said. "Satyria has called three times, and I can't think of any more excuses. Come on, eat some supper and call her back."

"Did she ask about Clemensia? Does everyone know?" he blurted out.

"Clemensia Dovecote? No. Why would she?" Tigris asked.

"It was so awful." He told her the story in all its gory detail.

As he spoke, the color left her face. "Dr. Gaul made the snakes bite her? Over a little white lie like that?"

"She did. And she didn't care at all whether Clemmie survived," he said. "Just shooed me out so she could get her afternoon snack."

"That's sadistic. Or completely demented," said Tigris. "Should you report her?"

"To who? She's the Head Gamemaker," he said. "She works directly with the president. She'll say it was our fault for lying."

Tigris thought it over. "All right. Don't report her. Or confront her. Just avoid her as much as possible."

"That's hard as a mentor. She keeps showing up at the Academy to play with this rabbit mutt and ask a lot of crazy questions. One word from her could make or break my prize." He rubbed his face with his hands. "And Arachne's dead, and Clemensia's all full of venom, and Lucy Gray . . . well, that's another really awful story. I doubt she'll make it to the Games, and maybe that's for the best."

Tigris tucked a spoon into his hand. "Eat your soup. We've gotten through worse than this. Snow lands on top?"

"Snow lands on top," he said with so little conviction they had to laugh. It made him feel a bit more normal. He took a few bites of soup to please her, then realized he was starving and made short work of it.

When Satyria called again, he almost launched into his confession, but it turned out that all she wanted to do was ask him to sing the anthem at Arachne's funeral in the morning. "Your heroics at the zoo, combined with the fact that you're the only one who knows all the words, made you the faculty's first choice."

"I'd be honored, of course," he replied.

"Good." Satyria slurped something, causing the ice to clink in her glass, then came up for air. "How are things with your tribute?"

Coriolanus hesitated. To complain might seem childish, like he couldn't handle his own problems. He almost never asked Satyria for help. But then he thought of Lucy Gray buckling under the weight of her chains and threw caution to the wind. "Not well. I saw Lucy Gray today. Just for a minute. She's very weak. The Capitol hasn't fed her at all."

"Since she left District Twelve? Why, that's been, what? Four days?" Satyria asked, surprised.

"Five. I don't think she's going to make it to the Hunger Games. I'm not even going to have a tribute to mentor," he said. "A lot of us won't."

"Well, that's not fair. It's like telling you to do an experiment with broken equipment," she responded. "And now the Games will be delayed at least another day or two." She paused, then added, "Let me see what I can do."

He hung up and turned to Tigris. "They want me to sing at the funeral. She didn't mention Clemensia. They must be keeping it a secret."

"Then that's what you do, too," said Tigris. "Maybe they'll pretend the whole thing didn't happen."

"Maybe they won't even tell Dean Highbottom," he said, brightening. Then another thought hit him. "Tigris? I just remembered, I can't really sing." And somehow, this was the funniest thing either of them had ever heard.

The Grandma'am, however, thought it was no laughing matter, and the following morning she had him up at dawn so she could coach him. At the end of every line she'd poke him in his ribs with a ruler and shout, "Breathe!" until he couldn't imagine making any other choice. For the third time that week, she sacrificed one of her darlings to his future, pinning a light blue rosebud to his carefully pressed uniform jacket and saying, "There. It matches your eyes." Looking sharp, with a belly full of oatmeal and a rib cage dotted with bruises reminding him to inhale, he set off for the Academy.

Although it was Saturday, the entire student body reported to homeroom before they assembled on the front steps of the Academy, divided neatly and alphabetically by class. By virtue of his assignment, Coriolanus found himself in the front row with faculty and distinguished guests, first and foremost President Ravinstill. Satyria gave him a quick overview of the program, but the only thing that stuck in his head was that his rendition of the anthem opened the ceremonies. He didn't mind public speaking but had never sung publicly — there was little occasion to in Panem. It was one reason that Lucy Gray's song had caught people's attention. He calmed his nerves by reminding himself that even if he howled like a dog, there wasn't much to compare him to.

Across the avenue, the temporary stands set up for the funeral procession quickly filled with mourners dressed in black, the one color everyone could be counted on to have, given the loss of loved ones during the war. He looked for the Cranes but couldn't spot them in the crowd. The Academy and the surrounding buildings were festooned with funereal banners and sported Capitol flags in every window. Numerous cameras were positioned to record the event, and multiple Capitol TV reporters streamed live commentary. Coriolanus thought it was quite a display for Arachne, disproportionate to both her life and death, the latter of which could have been avoided if she'd refrained from being such an exhibitionist. So many people had died heroically in the war, with so little recognition, that it grated on him. He was relieved that he was singing instead of having to praise her talents, which, if memory served, were limited to being loud enough to fill the school auditorium without a mic and the ability to balance a spoon on her nose. And Dean Highbottom had accused *him* of showboating? Still, he reminded himself, she was practically family.

The Academy clock struck nine, and the crowd fell silent. On cue, Coriolanus rose and walked to the podium. Satyria had promised accompaniment, but the silence stretched so long he actually drew breath to begin the anthem before a tinny version began to play over the sound system, giving him sixteen measures of introduction.

Gem of Panem,
Mighty city,
Through the ages, you shine anew.

His singing was more like sustained talking than a melodic tour de force, but the song was not particularly challenging. The high note the Grandma'am consistently missed was optional; most people sang it an octave lower. With the memory of her ruler prodding him, he sailed through it, never missing a note or running out of breath. He sat to generous applause and an approving nod from the president, who now took the podium.

"Two days ago, Arachne Crane's young and precious life was ended, and so we mourn another victim of the criminal rebellion that yet besieges us," the president intoned. "Her death was as valiant as any on the battlefield, her loss more profound as we claim to be at peace. But no peace will exist while this disease eats away at all that is good and noble in our country. Today we honor her sacrifice with a reminder that while evil exists, it does not prevail. And once again, we bear witness as our great Capitol brings justice to Panem."

The drums began a slow, deep boom, and the crowd turned as the funeral procession rounded a corner onto the street. Although not as wide as the Corso, Scholars Road easily held the honor guard of Peacekeepers, standing shoulder to shoulder, twenty wide and forty deep, that stepped in flawless uniformity to the rhythm of the drums.

Coriolanus had wondered about the strategy of telling the districts about a tribute killing a Capitol girl, but now he saw the point. Behind the Peacekeepers came a long flatbed truck with a crane affixed to it. High in the air, the bullet-ridden body of the District 10 girl, Brandy, dangled from its hook. Shackled to the truck bed, looking utterly filthy and defeated, were the remaining twenty-three tributes. The length of their restraints made it impossible to stand, so they either crouched or sat on the bare metal floor. This was just another chance to remind the districts that they were inferior and that there would be repercussions for their resistance.

He could see Lucy Gray trying to hold on to a shred of dignity, sitting as upright as the chains would allow and gazing straight ahead, ignoring the corpse swinging gently over her head. But it was no use. The dirt, the shackles, the public display — it was too much to overcome. He tried to imagine conducting himself under those circumstances, until he realized this was undoubtedly what Sejanus was doing, and snapped out of it.

Another battalion of Peacekeepers followed the tributes, paving the way for a quartet of horses. They were decked in garlands and pulled an ornate wagon with a pure white coffin draped in flowers. Behind the coffin came the Cranes, riding in a horse-drawn chariot. At least her family had the decency to look uncomfortable. The procession halted when the coffin drew up in front of the podium.

Dr. Gaul, who'd been sitting next to the president, approached the mic. Coriolanus thought it was a mistake to let her speak at such a moment, but she must have left the crazy lady and her pink snake bracelets at home, because she spoke with a stern and intelligent clarity. "Arachne Crane, we, your fellow citizens of Panem, vow that your death will not be in vain. When one of ours is hit, we hit back twice as hard. The Hunger Games will go forward, with more energy and commitment than ever before, as we add your name to the long list of the innocent who died defending a righteous and just land. Your friends, family, and fellow citizens salute you and dedicate the Tenth Hunger Games to your memory."

So now that loudmouth Arachne was a defender of a righteous and just land. *Yes, she laid down her life taunting her tribute with a sandwich*, thought Coriolanus. *Maybe her gravestone could read, "Casualty of cheap laughs."*

A row of Peacekeepers in red sashes lifted their guns and sent several volleys over the procession, which then rolled down a few blocks and disappeared around a corner.

As the crowd thinned, several people took the pained look on Coriolanus's face as sorrow at Arachne's death, when ironically he felt like killing her all over again. Still, he felt he'd handled himself well, until he turned to find Dean Highbottom looking down at him.

"My condolences on the loss of your friend," the dean said.

"And on your student. It's a difficult day for all of us. But the procession was very moving," Coriolanus replied.

"Did you think so? I found it excessive and in poor taste," said Dean Highbottom. Taken by surprise, Coriolanus let out a short laugh before he recovered and tried to look shocked. The dean dropped his gaze to Coriolanus's blue rosebud. "It's amazing, how little things change. After all the killing. After all the agonized promises to remember the cost. After all of that, I can't distinguish the bud from the blossom." He gave the rose a tap with his forefinger, adjusting the angle, and smiled. "Don't be late to lunch. I hear we're having pie."

The only good thing about the encounter was that it turned out there really was pie, peach this time, at the special buffet in the school dining hall. Unlike on the day of the reaping, Coriolanus loaded his plate with fried chicken and took the largest wedge of pie he could find. He slathered his biscuits with butter and had three refills of grape punch, filling the last glass so much it spilled over and he stained his linen napkin sopping it up. Let people talk. The chief mourner needed sustenance. But even as he ate, he recognized it as a sign that his usual gift for self-control was eroding. He blamed it on Dean Highbottom and his continual harassment. What was he babbling on about today anyway? Buds? Blossoms? He should be locked up somewhere or, even better, deported to a far-off outpost to leave decent Capitol people in peace. Just the thought of him sent Coriolanus back for more pie.

Sejanus, however, poked at his chicken and biscuits without taking even one bite. If Coriolanus had disliked the funeral parade, it had to have been misery for Sejanus.

"They'll report you if you throw out all that food," Coriolanus reminded him. He wasn't crazy about the guy, but he didn't particularly want to see him punished.

"Right," said Sejanus. But he still seemed unable to down more than a sip of punch.

As the luncheon was finishing up, Satyria gathered the twenty-two active mentors to inform them that not only were the Hunger Games still on, they were supposed to be the most visible yet. With this in mind, they were to escort their tributes on a tour of the arena that very afternoon. It was to be aired live to the entire country, somehow driving home the resolution Dr. Gaul had made at the funeral. The Head Gamemaker felt that separating the Capitol kids from the district ones suggested weakness, as if they were too afraid of their enemies to be in their presence. The tributes would be handcuffed but not fully shackled. The Peacekeepers' top sharpshooters would be among their guards, but the mentors were to be seen side by side with their charges.

Coriolanus could sense some reluctance among his classmates — several of their parents had lodged complaints about shoddy security after Arachne's death — but no one spoke up, none of them wanting to seem cowardly. The whole thing seemed dangerous and ill-advised to him — what would prevent other tributes from turning on their mentors? — but he'd never say so. A part of him wondered if Dr. Gaul wasn't hoping for another act of violence so she could punish another tribute, maybe a live one this time, in front of the cameras.

This further display of Dr. Gaul's callousness made him feel mutinous. He glanced over at Sejanus's plate. "All done?"

"I can't eat today," said Sejanus. "I don't know what to do with this."

Their section had emptied. Under the table, Coriolanus spread his stained linen napkin on his lap. He felt even more delinquent when he realized it was emblazoned with the Capitol seal. "Put it here," he said with a furtive glance.

Sejanus gave a look around and quickly transported the chicken and biscuits to the napkin. Coriolanus gathered it up and stuffed the whole thing in his book bag. They were not allowed to take food from the dining hall, and certainly not for a tribute, but where else would he get some before the tour? Lucy Gray couldn't eat the stuff in front of the cameras, but her dress had deep pockets. He resented that half of his takings would go to Jessup now, but maybe that investment would pay off when the Games began.

"Thanks. You're quite the rebel," said Sejanus as they carried their trays to the conveyor belt that ran to the kitchen.

"I'm bad news, all right," said Coriolanus.

The mentors piled into a few Academy vans and headed for the Capitol Arena, which had been built across the river to prevent crowds from swamping the downtown. In its day, the huge, state-of-the-art amphitheater had been the site of many an exciting sporting, entertainment, or military event. High-profile executions of the enemy were staged there during the war, making it a target for the rebel bombers. While the original structure stood, it was battered and unstable now, useful only as a venue for the Hunger Games. The lush field of meticulously tended grass had died from neglect. It was riddled with bomb craters, with weeds providing the only greenery on the expanse of dirt. Rubble from the explosions — chunks of metal and stone — lay everywhere, and the fifteen-foot wall that encircled the field was fissured and pockmarked from the shrapnel. Each year, the tributes would be locked in with nothing but an arsenal of knives, swords, maces, and the like to facilitate the bloodshed while the audience watched from home. At the end of the Games, the one who had managed to survive would be shipped back to their district, the bodies removed, the weapons collected, and the doors locked until the following year. No maintenance. No cleanup. Wind and rain might wash away the bloodstains, but Capitol hands would not.

Professor Sickle, their chaperone for the outing, ordered the mentors to leave their belongings in the vans when they arrived. Coriolanus stuffed the food-filled napkin in one of his front pants pockets and kept it covered with the hem of his jacket. As they stepped from the air-conditioning into the blazing sun, he saw the tributes standing in a line in handcuffs, heavily guarded by Peacekeepers. The mentors were directed to take their places beside their respective tributes, who'd been lined up numerically, so he was near the end with Lucy Gray. Only Jessup and his mentor, Lysistrata, who couldn't tip the scales at a hundred pounds, were behind him. In front of him, Clemensia's tribute, Reaper — the one who'd strangled him in the truck — stood glowering at the ground. If it came to a mentor-tribute showdown, the odds were not in Coriolanus's favor.

Despite her delicate appearance, Lysistrata had some grit. The daughter of the physicians who treated President Ravinstill, she'd been lucky to get a mentorship, and she'd apparently been working hard to connect with Jessup. "I brought you some cream for your neck," Coriolanus heard her whisper. "But you must keep it hidden." Jessup made a grunt of assent. "I'll put it in your pocket when I can."

The Peacekeepers removed the heavy bars from the entrance. The massive doors swung open, revealing a huge lobby lined with boarded-up booths and fly-specked posters advertising events from before the war. Holding their formation, the kids followed the soldiers deep within to the far side of the lobby. A bank of full-height turnstiles, each with three curved metal arms, stood covered in a thick layer of dust. They required a Capitol token for admittance, the same one still used for the price of a trolley fare.

This entrance was for the poor people, Coriolanus thought. Or perhaps not poor. The word *plebeian* came to mind. The Snow family had entered the arena at another entrance, demarcated by a velvet rope. Certainly, their box could not be accessed with a trolley token. Unlike much of the arena, it had a roof, a retractable glass window, and air-conditioning that had made the hottest day comfortable. An Avox had been assigned to them, bringing food and drink and toys for him and Tigris. If he grew bored, he'd nap on the plush, cushioned seats.

Peacekeepers posted at two turnstiles pumped tokens into the slots so each tribute and mentor could pass through simultaneously. At each rotation, a cheerful voice piped, "Enjoy the show!"

"Can't you override the ticket barrier?" asked Professor Sickle.

"We could if we had the key, but no one seems to know where it is," said a Peacekeeper.

"Enjoy the show!" the turnstile told Coriolanus as he passed through. He gave the arm at his waist a backward push and realized that no exit was possible. His eyes traveled to the tops of the turnstiles, where iron bars filled the space to the arched doorway. He guessed the patrons of the cheap seats left the building through passages elsewhere. While that was probably seen as a plus for crowd dispersal, it did nothing to calm a jittery mentor on a questionable field trip.

On the far side of the turnstiles, a squad of Peacekeepers marched into a passageway, guided only by the red glow of emergency lights on the floor. On either side, smaller arches leading to different seating levels were marked. The line of tributes and mentors fell into step, flanked by tight columns of Peacekeepers. As they moved into the gloom, Coriolanus took a page from Lysistrata's book and used the opportunity to slip the napkin of food into Lucy Gray's cuffed hands. It swiftly disappeared into her ruffled pocket. There. She was not going to starve to death on his watch. Her hand found his, intertwining their fingers and sending a buzz through his body at their closeness. At this small intimacy in the dark. He gave her hand a final squeeze and released it as they headed into the sunlight at the end of the passageway, where such a display would have been inexplicable.

He'd been to the arena several times as a small boy, to see the circus, mostly, but also to cheer military displays under his father's command. For the past nine years he'd watched at least part of the Games on television. But nothing prepared him for the sensation of walking out through the main gate, beneath the enormous scoreboard, and onto the field. Some of the mentors and tributes gasped at the sheer size of the place and the grandeur that defied even the decay. Staring up at the towering rows of seats made him feel diminished to the point of insignificance. A raindrop in a flood, a pebble in an avalanche.

The sight of the camera crews brought him back to himself, and he adjusted his face to say that nothing much really impressed a Snow. Lucy Gray, who seemed more alert and moved better without the weight of the chains, gave a wave to Lepidus Malmsey, but like all the reporters, he remained stony-faced and didn't engage. Their directive had been clear; gravity and retribution were the hallmarks of the day.

Satyria's use of the term *tour* had suggested a sightseeing excursion, and while he had not anticipated pleasure, he had not expected the palpable sadness of the place either. The Peacekeepers who'd been flanking them spread out as the kids dutifully followed the lead squad around the inside perimeter of the oval, forming a dusty, joyless parade. Coriolanus remembered the circus performers taking the same route, riding elephants and horses, bespangled and brimming with mirth. With the exception of Sejanus, probably all of his classmates would have been in the audience, too. Ironically, Arachne would have been in the box adjacent to his, dressed in a sequined costume and cheering at the top of her lungs.

Coriolanus surveyed the arena, looking for anything that might be an advantage for Lucy Gray. The high wall that enclosed the field, keeping the audience above the action, had some promise. The damaged surface provided hand- and footholds, offering access to the seats for a nimble climber. Several of the gates spaced symmetrically around the wall looked compromised as well, but as he was unsure what lay beyond in the tunnels, he thought those should be approached with caution. Too easy to get trapped. The stands would definitely be her best bet, if she could climb up. He made mental notes for later.

As the line began to stretch out, he initiated a whispered conversation with Lucy Gray. "It was awful this morning. Seeing you like that."

"Well, at least they fed us first," she said.

"Really?" Had his conversation with Satyria triggered that?

"A couple of kids blacked out when they tried to round us up last night. I think they decided that if they want to have anyone left for their show, they're going to have to feed us. Mostly bread and cheese. We got dinner, and breakfast, too. But don't worry, I've got plenty of room left for whatever's in my pocket." She sounded more like her old self. "Was that you I heard singing?"

"Oh. Yes," he admitted. "They asked me to sing because they thought Arachne and I were such great friends. We weren't. And I'm embarrassed you heard me."

"I like your voice. My daddy would've said it had real authority. Just didn't much care for the song," Lucy Gray replied.

"Thanks. That means a lot, coming from you," he said.

She nudged him with her elbow. "I wouldn't broadcast that. Most people here think I'm lower than a snake's belly."

Coriolanus shook his head and grinned.

"What?" she said.

"You just have funny expressions. Not funny, per se, more colorful," he told her.

"Well, I don't say 'per se' much, if that's what you mean," she quipped.

"No, I like it. It makes the way I talk seem so stiff. What was it you called me that day in the zoo? Something about cake?" he remembered.

"Oh, the cake with the cream? You don't say that?" she asked. "Well, it's a compliment. Where I come from, cake can be pretty dry. And cream's as scarce as hen's teeth."

For a moment he laughed, forgetting where they were, how depressing the backdrop. For a moment there was just her smile, the musical cadence of her voice, and the hint of flirtation.

Then the world exploded.

Coriolanus knew bombs, and they terrified him. Even as the impact threw him off his feet and tossed him farther into the arena, his arms lifted to cover his head. When he hit the ground, he automatically flattened onto his belly, cheek pressed into the dust, one arm bent up to guard his exposed eye and ear.

The first explosion, which seemed to have come from the main gate, initiated a chain of eruptions around the arena. Running was out of the question. It was all he could do to cling to the rumbling ground, hope for it to stop, and try to keep his panic in check. He entered what he and Tigris had nicknamed "bomb time," that surreal period when moments stretched and contracted in ways that seemed to defy science.

During the war, the Capitol had assigned every citizen a shelter near their residence. The Snows' magnificent building had a basement level so sturdy and spacious it accommodated not only its residents but half the block. Unfortunately, the Capitol's surveillance system depended heavily on electricity. With the power sketchy and the grid flickering on and off like a firefly due to rebel interference in District 5, the sirens were unreliable, and they were often caught unawares with no time to retreat to the basement. At these times, he, Tigris, and the Grandma'am — unless she was singing the anthem — would hide under the dining table, an impressive thing carved from a single block of marble, which sat in an interior room. Even with the absence of windows and the solid rock over his head, Coriolanus's muscles always went rigid with terror when he heard the whistling of the bombs, and it would be hours before he felt he could walk right. The streets weren't safe either, nor the Academy. You could be bombed anywhere, but usually he had a better place to shelter than this. Now, naked to the attack, lying in the open air, he waited for the interminable "bomb time" to end and wondered how much damage his internal organs were incurring.

No hovercraft. The realization bubbled up in his brain. There had been no hovercraft. These bombs had been planted, then? He could smell smoke, so some of them were probably incendiary. He pressed his daily handkerchief over his mouth and nose. Squinting through the black haze thickened with dirt from the arena, he could see Lucy Gray about fifteen feet away, curled up in a ball, forehead on the ground and fingertips lodged in her ears, which was the best she could do with the cuffs on. She coughed helplessly.

"Cover your face! Use the napkin!" he called out. She didn't look over but must have heard, because she rolled to her side and retrieved it from her pocket. The biscuits and chicken fell to the ground as she pressed the cloth to her face. He had a vague thought that this would not be conducive to her singing.

A lull fooled him into thinking the episode had ended, but just as he lifted his head, a final explosion in the stands above him demolished what had once been a snack stand — that pink spun sugar, those caramel-coated apples — and burning debris rained down on him. Something struck his head hard, and the heavy weight of a beam landed diagonally across his back, pinning him to the ground.

Stunned, Coriolanus lay almost senseless for a bit. The acrid smell of burning stung his nose, and he realized the beam was on fire. He tried to pull himself together and wriggle free, but the world swam and the peach pie turned sour in his stomach.

"Help!" he cried. Similar pleas came from around him, but he couldn't see the injured through the cloud. "Help!"

The fire singed his hair, and with renewed effort he tried to struggle from under the beam, to no avail. A searing pain began to eat into his neck and shoulder as the horrifying realization that he was burning to death overtook him. He screamed, again and again, but seemed alone in a bubble of dark smoke and flaming rubble. Then he could make out a figure rising from the inferno. Lucy Gray said his name, then snapped her head around, something out of his view catching her attention. Her feet took a few steps away from him, then she hesitated, apparently torn.

"Lucy Gray!" he pleaded in a ragged voice. "Please!"

She gave a last look at whatever had tempted her and ran to his side. The beam shifted off his back but then slammed down again. It rose a second time, leaving him just enough room to drag himself from beneath it. She helped him to his feet, and with his arm slung across her shoulders, they limped away from the flames until they collapsed somewhere in the middle of the arena.

At first, coughing and gagging required all his attention, but he slowly registered the pain in his head, the burns along his neck, back, and shoulders. Somehow his fingers were knotted in Lucy Gray's scorched skirt, as if it were his lifeline. Her cuffed hands, visibly burned, curled nearby.

The smoke settled enough that he could see the pattern the bombs had been planted in at intervals around the arena, with the mother lode of explosives placed at the entrance. So great was the damage there that he caught a glimpse of the street beyond and two forms fleeing the arena. Was that what had given Lucy Gray pause before she came to his aid? The possibility of escape? Other tributes had surely availed themselves of the opportunity. Yes, he heard the sirens now, the shouts from the street.

Medics picked their way over the rubble and ran for the wounded. "It's okay," he told Lucy Gray. "Help is here." Hands reached for him, settled him onto a stretcher. He released her ruffles, thinking there would be another stretcher for her, but as they carried him off, he could see a Peacekeeper force her to her stomach and jam the barrel of a gun into her neck, yelling a string of profanities at her. "Lucy Gray!" Coriolanus cried out. No one paid any attention to him.

The blow to his head made concentration hard, but he was aware of the ambulance ride, banging through the doors to the same waiting area where he'd drunk his fizzy lemon soda just a day before, and then being moved onto a table under a bright light while a team of doctors tried to assess the damage. He wanted to sleep, but they kept pushing their faces into his and demanding answers, their stale lunch breath making him queasy again. Into machines, out of machines, needles jabbing him, and finally, blissfully, being allowed to drift off. Periodically throughout the night, someone would wake him and shine lights in his eyes. As long as he could answer a few basic questions, they let him fall back into oblivion.

When he finally woke, really woke, on Sunday, the light through the window said afternoon, and the Grandma'am and Tigris were leaning over him with worried looks. He felt a warm reassurance. *I'm not alone*, he thought. *I'm not in the arena. I'm safe.*

"Hi, Coryo," said Tigris. "It's us."

"Hello." He attempted a smile. "You missed bomb time."

"Turns out it's worse than being there," said Tigris, "knowing you were going through it all alone."

“I wasn’t alone,” he said. The morphling and the concussion made it hard to recall things clearly. “Lucy Gray was there. She saved my life, I think.” He couldn’t quite get his mind around the idea. Sweet, but unsettling, too.

Tigris gave his hand a squeeze. “I’m not surprised. She’s obviously a good person. Right from the beginning, she tried to protect you from the other tributes.”

The Grandma’am needed more convincing. After he’d patched together a time line of the bombing for her, she came to this conclusion: “Well, like as not she decided the Peacekeepers would gun her down if she ran, but still, it shows some character. Perhaps, as she claims, she is not really district.”

High praise indeed, or as high as the Grandma’am was likely to muster.

As Tigris filled him in on the details he had missed, he realized how on edge this event had made the Capitol. What had happened — at least what the Capitol News claimed had happened — frightened citizens with both its immediate fallout and its ramifications for the future. They didn’t know who had set the bombs — rebels, yes, but from where? They could’ve been from any of the twelve districts, or a ragtag bunch that had escaped from District 13, or even, fate forbid, some long-dormant cell in the Capitol itself. The time line for the crime was baffling. Since the arena stood empty, locked, and ignored between Hunger Games, the bombs could’ve been placed six days or six months before. Security cameras covered the entrances around the oval, but the crumbling exterior made scaling the structure possible. They didn’t even know if the bombs had been triggered remotely or by a false step, but the unexpected losses shook the Capitol to its core. That the two tributes from District 6 had been killed by shrapnel caused little concern, but the same explosion had taken the lives of the Ring twins. Three mentors had been hospitalized — Coriolanus, and Androcles Anderson and Gaius Breen, who'd been assigned the District 9 tributes. His two classmates were in critical condition, Gaius having lost both his legs, and almost everyone else, whether mentor, tribute, or Peacekeeper, had needed medical care of some sort.

Coriolanus felt bewildered. He'd genuinely liked Pollo and Didi, how they'd doted on each other, how upbeat they'd been. Somewhere nearby, Androcles, who aspired to be a reporter at Capitol News like his mother, and Gaius, a Citadel brat with an endless supply of terrible jokes, were barely hanging on to life.

"What about Lysistrata? Is she all right?" She'd been behind him.

The Grandma'am looked uncomfortable. "Oh, her. She's fine. She's going around saying that big, ugly boy from District Twelve protected her by throwing his body over her, but who knows? The Vickers family loves the spotlight."

"Do they?" asked Coriolanus skeptically. He could not recall, not once, ever seeing a Vickers in the spotlight, except for a brief annual news conference in which they gave President Ravinstill a clean bill of health. Lysistrata was a self-contained, efficient person who never drew attention to herself. To even suggest she could be put in the same class as Arachne rubbed him the wrong way.

"She only made one quick statement to a reporter right after the bombing. I expect it was the truth, Grandma'am," said Tigris. "Perhaps the people of District Twelve are not quite so bad as you paint them. Both Jessup and Lucy Gray have behaved bravely."

"Have you seen Lucy Gray? On the television, I mean. Does she look all right?" he asked.

"I don't know, Coryo. They haven't shown any footage of the zoo. But she's not on the list of the dead tributes," said Tigris.

"Are there more? Than the ones from District Six?" Coriolanus didn't want to sound morbid, but they were Lucy Gray's competition.

"Yes, some others died after the bombing," Tigris told him.

Both pairs from Districts 1 and 2 had made for the hole blown open near the entrance. The District 1 kids had been shot dead, the girl from 2 had made it to the river and leaped over the wall only to die in the fall, and Marcus had disappeared completely, leaving a desperate, dangerous, powerful boy loose somewhere in the city. A displaced manhole cover suggested that he might have climbed underground to the Transfer, the network of tracks and roadways built under the Capitol, but no one knew for sure.

"I suppose they see the arena as a symbol," said the Grandma'am. "Just as they did during the war. The worst part is that it took almost twenty seconds before they cut the transmission to the districts, so no doubt it was a cause for celebration. Beasts that they are."

"But they say hardly anyone in the districts saw it, Grandma'am," Tigris countered. "The people there don't like to watch the Hunger Games coverage."

"It will only take a handful to get the word out," said the Grandma'am. "It's just the kind of story that catches fire."

The doctor who'd talked to Coriolanus after the snake attack entered, introducing himself as Dr. Wane. He sent Tigris and the Grandma'am home and gave Coriolanus a quick checkup, explaining the nature of the concussion (fairly mild) and the burns, which were responding well to treatment. It would take some time to heal completely, but if he behaved himself and continued to improve, he'd be released in a couple of days.

"Do you know how my tribute is doing? Her hands were burned rather badly," said Coriolanus. Each time he thought of her he felt a stab of uneasiness, but then the morphling would wrap around it like cotton wool.

"I wouldn't know," said the doctor. "But they've got a top-notch veterinarian over there. I expect she'll be fine by the time they've got the Games up and running. But that's not your concern, young man. Your concern is to get well, and for that, you need some sleep."

Coriolanus was happy to oblige. He slipped back into sleep and didn't fully come to until Monday morning. With his aching head and battered body, he felt in no rush to leave the hospital. The air-conditioning eased the burns on his skin, and generous portions of bland food appeared regularly. He caught up on the news on the large-screen television while he sipped as much fizzy lemon drink as he could hold. A double funeral was to be held for the Ring twins the following day. The manhunt for Marcus continued. Both the Capitol and the districts were under heightened security.

Three mentors dead, three hospitalized — really, four if you counted Clemensia. Six tributes dead, one escaped, several wounded. If Dr. Gaul wanted a makeover for the Hunger Games, she'd gotten it.

In the afternoon, the parade of visitors began with Festus, sporting a sling on his arm and a few stitches where a shard of metal had sliced his cheek. He said that the Academy had canceled classes, but the students were supposed to show up the next morning for the Rings' funeral. He choked up at the mention of the twins, and Coriolanus wondered if he would have a more emotional response himself once they removed the morphling drip, which muted both pain and joy. Satyria popped in with some bakery cookies, relayed the well-wishes of the faculty, and told him that while the incident was unfortunate, it could only improve his chances for a prize. After a bit, an uninjured Sejanus appeared with Coriolanus's book bag from the van and a stack of his mother's delicious meat loaf sandwiches. He had little to say on the subject of his runaway tribute. Finally, Tigris came without the Grandma'am, who'd remained home to rest but had sent a clean uniform for him to wear on discharge. If there were cameras, she wanted him to look his best. They split the sandwiches and then Tigris stroked his aching head until he dozed off, just as she had when headaches plagued him as a child.

When someone awakened him in the wee hours of Tuesday, he supposed a nurse had come to check his vital signs, then started at the sight of Clemensia's ravaged face above his. The snake venom, or the antidote perhaps, had left her golden brown skin peeling and the whites of her eyes the color of egg yolks. But much worse was the twitching that affected her entire body, causing her face to grimace, her tongue to jut periodically from her mouth, and her hands to jerk away even as they reached for his.

"Shh!" she hissed. "I shouldn't be here. Don't tell them I came. But what are they saying? Why has no one come to see me? Do my parents know what happened? Do they think I'm dead?"

Groggy from sleep and medication, Coriolanus couldn't quite wrap his mind around what she was saying. "Your parents? But they've been here. I saw them."

"No. No one has seen me!" she cried. "I have to get out of here, Coryo. I'm afraid she's going to kill me. It's not safe. We're not safe!"

"What? Who's going to kill you? You're not talking sense," he said.

"Dr. Gaul, of course!" She clutched his arm, awakening his burns. "You know, you were there!"

Coriolanus tried to free her fingers. "You need to go back to your room. You're sick, Clemmie. It's the snakebites. They're making you imagine things."

"Did I imagine this?" She ripped back the opening of her hospital gown to reveal a patch of skin that extended over her chest and down one shoulder. Mottled with bright blue, pink, and yellow scales, it had the reptilian quality of the snakes in the tank. When he gasped, she shrieked, "And it's spreading! It's spreading!"

Two of the hospital staff had her then, lifting her up and carrying her from the room. He lay awake the rest of the night, thinking of the snakes, and her skin, and the glass cases of Avoxes with their gruesome animal modifications in Dr. Gaul's lab. Is that where Clemensia was headed? If not, why hadn't her parents seen her? Why did no one except him seem to know what had happened? If Clemensia died, would he disappear as well, the only witness? Had he put Tigris at risk by telling her the story?

The pleasant cocoon of the hospital now seemed an insidious trap shrinking to suffocate him. No one checked on him as the hours crept by, which added to his distress. Finally, just as dawn was breaking, Dr. Wane appeared by his bedside. "I hear Clemensia visited you last night," he said cheerfully. "Did she give you a scare?"

"A bit." Coriolanus tried to appear nonchalant.

"She'll be all right. The venom causes a lot of unusual side effects as it works itself out of the system. That's why we haven't let her parents see her. They think she's quarantined with a highly contagious flu. She'll be presentable in a day or two," the doctor told him. "You can go visit her if you're up to it. Might cheer her up."

"All right," said Coriolanus, slightly reassured. But he could not unsee what he'd seen, not at the hospital, and not at the lab.

The removal of the morphling drip brought all the fuzzy edges into sharp relief. His suspicions tainted every comfort, from the large breakfast of hotcakes and bacon, to the basket of fresh fruit and sweets from the Academy, to the news that his performance of the anthem would be replayed for the Rings' funeral, as both a mark of its quality and a nod to his own sacrifices.

The pre-funeral coverage started at seven, and by nine the student body again filled the stairs in front of the Academy. Just over a week ago, he'd felt he was falling into insignificance with his District 12 girl assignment, and now he was being honored for his courage in front of the entire nation. He'd expected them to show a tape of him singing, but instead his holographic self appeared behind the podium, and while it was a little watery at first, it settled into a clean, crisp image. People were always saying he resembled his handsome father more every day, but for the first time he could really see it. Not just the eyes but the jawline, the hair, the proud carriage. And Lucy Gray was right; his voice did have real authority. Overall, the performance was quite impressive.

The Capitol doubled the efforts made for Arachne's funeral, which Coriolanus felt appropriate for the twins. More speeches, more Peacekeepers, more banners. He didn't mind seeing the twins praised, even extravagantly, and wished they somehow could've known his hologram had opened the event. The dead tribute count had escalated, with the two tributes from District 9 having died from their injuries. Apparently, the veterinarian had done her best, but her repeated requests to admit them to the hospital had been refused. Their scarred bodies, along with what remained of the District 6 tributes, were draped over the backs of horses and paraded down Scholars Road. The two tributes from District 1 and the girl from District 2, as befitting their cowardly escape attempt, were dragged behind them. Then came a pair of those caged trucks Coriolanus had ridden in on his way to the zoo, one for the boys and one for the girls. He strained to see Lucy Gray but couldn't locate her, which added to his worries. Was she lying inert on the floor, overcome by injuries and hunger?

As the twins' matching silver coffins came into focus, all he could think of was this silly game they'd made up on the playground during the war called Ring-around-the-Rings. The rest of the kids would chase down Didi and Pollo and then grab hands, forming a circle around them and trapping them. It always ended with the whole lot of them, Rings included, laughing their heads off in a heap on the ground. Oh, to be seven again, in a happy pile with his friends, with nutritional crackers waiting at his desk.

After lunch, Dr. Wane said he could be released if he promised to stay calm and get bed rest, and as the charms of the hospital had diminished, he changed into his clean uniform at once. Tigris collected him and accompanied him home on the trolley, but then had to return to work. Both he and the Grandma'am spent the afternoon napping, and he awoke to a nice casserole Sejanus's ma had sent over.

At Tigris's urging he went to bed with the sun, but sleep eluded him. Every time he closed his eyes, he'd see the flames all around, feel the trembling of the earth, smell the choking black smoke. Lucy Gray had been nibbling around the edges of his thoughts, but now he could think of no one else. How was she? Healing and fed, or suffering and starving in that awful monkey house? While he had been lying in the air-conditioned hospital with his morphling drip, had the veterinarian attended to her hands? Had the smoke damaged that remarkable voice? In helping him, had she ruined her chances for sponsors in the arena? He felt some embarrassment when he thought of his terror under the beam, but even more so when he remembered what had followed. On

Capitol TV, the coverage they'd shown of the bombing had been obscured by the smoke. But did it exist? Footage of her rescuing him and, much worse, of him clinging to her ruffled skirt as they waited for help to come?

His hand fumbled in the drawer of his nightstand and found his mother's compact. As he inhaled the rose-scented powder, his thoughts quieted a bit, but restlessness drove him from his bed. For the next few hours, he wandered the apartment, looking out at the night sky, down at the Corso, into the neighbors' windows across the way. At some point he found himself up on the roof amid the Grandma'am's roses and didn't remember having climbed the stairs to the garden. The fresh night air perfumed by the flowers helped, but soon brought on a bout of shivering that made everything hurt again.

Tigris found him sitting in the kitchen a few hours before dawn. She made tea and they ate the remainder of the casserole straight from the pan. The savory layers of meat, potato, and cheese consoled him, as did Tigris's gentle reminder that the situation with Lucy Gray was not of his making. They were both, after all, still children whose lives were dictated by powers above them.

Somewhat comforted, he managed to doze for a few hours before a phone call from Satyria woke him. She encouraged him to attend school that morning if he could manage. Another mentor-tribute meeting had been scheduled with the idea of working toward the interviews, which would now be on a completely voluntary basis.

Later at the Academy, as he looked down from the balcony into Heavensbee Hall, the empty chairs rattled him. He knew, in his head, that eight tributes had died, that one was missing, but he'd not envisioned how that would ripple through the pattern of the twenty-four little tables, leaving a jagged, disconcerting mess. No tributes at all from Districts 1, 2, 6, or 9, and only one from 10. Most of the kids who remained were injured, and all looked unwell. As the mentors joined their assignees, the losses became even more pronounced. Six mentors were either dead or hospitalized, and those partnered with the escapees of Districts 1 and 2 had no tributes at their tables and therefore no reason to show up. Livia Cardew had been vocal about this turn of events, demanding new tributes be brought from the districts, or at least that she be given Reaper, the boy assigned to Clemensia, who everyone thought had been hospitalized with the flu. Her wishes had not been accommodated, and Reaper sat alone at his table, a bandage stained with rusty dried blood wrapped around his head.

As Coriolanus took the seat opposite her, Lucy Gray didn't even attempt a smile. A ragged cough racked her chest, and soot from the fire still clung to her clothing. The veterinarian had exceeded Coriolanus's expectations, though, as the skin on her hands was healing nicely.

"Hi," he said, scooting a nut butter sandwich and two of Satyria's cookies across the table.

"Hey," she said hoarsely. Any attempt at flirtation or even camaraderie had been abandoned. She patted the sandwich but seemed too tired to eat it. "Thanks."

"No, thank *you* for saving my life." He said it lightly, but as he gazed into her eyes, the levity leached away.

"Is that what you're telling people?" she asked. "That I saved your life?"

He had said as much to Tigris and the Grandma'am and then, perhaps unsure what to do with the information, let it drift from his thoughts like a dream. Now, with the empty seats of the fallen around them, the memory of how she'd rescued him in the arena demanded his attention, and he could not ignore its significance. If Lucy Gray had not helped him, he would be utterly, irrevocably dead. Another shiny coffin dripping flowers. Another empty chair. When he spoke again, the words caught in his throat before he forced them out. "I told my family. Really. Thank you, Lucy Gray."

"Well, I had some time on my hands," she said, tracing the frosted flower on a cookie with a shaky forefinger. "Pretty cookies."

Then came confusion. If she had saved his life, he owed her, what? A sandwich and two cookies? That was how he was repaying her. For his life. Which apparently he held quite cheaply. The truth was, he owed her everything. He felt the blush burn over his cheeks. "You could have run. And if you had, I would have gone up in flames before they reached me."

"Run, huh? Seemed like a lot of effort to get shot," she said.

Coriolanus shook his head. "You can joke, but it won't change what you did for me. I hope I can repay you in some way."

"I hope so, too," she said.

In those few words he sensed a shift in their dynamic. As her mentor, he'd been the gracious giver of gifts, always to be met with gratitude. Now she'd upended things by giving him a gift beyond compare. On the surface, everything looked the same. Chained girl, boy offering food, Peacekeepers guarding that status quo. But deep down, things could never be the same between them. He would always be in her debt. She had the right to demand things.

"I don't know how," he admitted.

Lucy Gray glanced around the room, taking in her wounded competitors. Then she looked him in the eye, and impatience tinged her voice. "You could start by thinking I can actually win."

PART II

"THE PRIZE"

Lucy Gray's words stung but, on reflection, were well deserved. Coriolanus had never really considered her a victor in the Games. It had never been part of his strategy to make her one. He had only wished that her charm and appeal would rub off on him and make him a success. Even his encouragement to sing for sponsors was an attempt to prolong the attention she brought him. Only a moment ago, her healed hands were good news because she could use them to play the guitar on interview night, not to defend herself from an attack in the arena. The fact that she mattered to him, as he'd claimed in the zoo, only made things worse. He should've been trying to preserve her life, to help her become the victor, no matter the odds.

"I meant what I said about you being the cake with the cream," Lucy Gray said. "You're the only one who even bothered to show up. You and your friend Sejanus. You two acted like we were human beings. But the only way you can really repay me now is if you help me survive this thing."

"I agree." Stepping up made him feel a bit better. "From now on, we're in it to win."

Lucy Gray reached out. "Shake on that?"

Coriolanus gave her hand a careful shake. "You have my word." The challenge energized him. "Step one: I think of a strategy."

"*We* think of a strategy," she corrected. But she smiled and bit into the sandwich.

"*We* think of a strategy." He did the math again. "You've only got fourteen competitors left, unless they find Marcus."

"If you can keep me alive a few more days, I might just win by default," she said.

Coriolanus looked around the hall at her broken, sickly competitors, draped in chains, which encouraged him until he admitted that Lucy Gray's condition wasn't much better. Still, with Districts 1 and 2 out of play, Jessup watching over her, and the new sponsorship program, her odds were vastly improved from what they'd been when she'd arrived in the Capitol. Perhaps, if he could keep her fed, she could run and hide somewhere in the arena while the others fought it out or starved to death. "I have to ask one thing," he said. "If it came to it, would you kill someone?"

Lucy Gray chewed, weighing the question. "Maybe in self-defense."

"It's the Hunger Games. It's all self-defense," he said. "But maybe it's best if you run away from the other tributes, and we get you sponsors for food. Wait it out a bit."

"Yeah, that's a better strategy for me," she agreed. "Enduring horrible things is one of my talents." A dry bit of bread set her to coughing.

Coriolanus passed her a water bottle from his book bag. "They're still doing the interviews, but on a voluntary basis. Are you up for it?"

"Are you kidding? I've got a song that was made for this whiskey voice," she said. "You find me a guitar?"

"No. But I will today," he promised. "Someone must have one I can borrow. If we can get you some sponsors, it will go a long way toward you getting that victory."

She began to talk with a bit of animation about what she might sing. They'd only been allotted ten minutes, though, and the brief meeting ended with Professor Sickle ordering the mentors back to the high biology lab.

Following what had to be heightened security measures, Peacekeepers escorted them, and Dean Highbottom checked off their names as they filed to their places. The able-bodied mentors of the dead and missing tributes, including Livia and Sejanus, already sat at the lab tables, watching Dr. Gaul drop carrots into the rabbit's cage. Coriolanus's skin broke into a sweat at the sight of her, so close, and so crazy.

"Hippity, hoppity, carrot or stick? Everyone's dying and you're . . ." She turned to them expectantly, and everyone but Sejanus averted their gaze.

"Feeling sick," said Sejanus.

Dr. Gaul laughed. "It's the compassionate one. Where's your tribute, boy? Any clue?"

Capitol News had continued coverage of the manhunt for Marcus, but it was less frequent now. The official word was that he was trapped down in a remote level of the Transfer, where he'd be apprehended soon. The city had relaxed, the general consensus being that he'd either died or would be captured any moment. At any rate, he seemed more bent on escaping than rising out of the Transfer to murder innocents in the Capitol.

"Possibly on his way to freedom," said Sejanus in a strained voice. "Possibly captured and under wraps. Possibly injured and hiding. Possibly dead. I've no idea. Do you?"

Coriolanus couldn't help admiring his pluck. Of course, Sejanus didn't know how dangerous Dr. Gaul could be. He might end up in a cage with a pair of parakeet wings and an elephant's trunk if he wasn't careful.

"No, don't answer," Sejanus spat out. "He's either dead or about to be, when you catch him and drag him through the streets in chains."

"That's our right," Dr. Gaul countered.

"No, it isn't! I don't care what you say. You've no right to starve people, to punish them for no reason. No right to take away their life and freedom. Those are things everyone is born with, and they're not yours for the taking. Winning a war doesn't give you that right. Having more weapons doesn't give you that right. Being from the Capitol doesn't give you that right. Nothing does. Oh, I don't even know why I came here today." With that, Sejanus sprang up and bolted for the door. When he tried the handle, it wouldn't turn. He jiggled it and then confronted Dr. Gaul. "Locking us in now? It's like our own little monkey house."

"You have not been dismissed," said Dr. Gaul. "Sit down, boy."

"No." Sejanus said it quietly, but it still caused several people to jump.

After a pause, Dean Highbottom intervened. "It's locked from the outside. The Peacekeepers have orders to leave us undisturbed until notified. Sit down, please."

"Or should we have them chaperone you somewhere else?" suggested Dr. Gaul. "I think your father's offices are nearby." Clearly, despite her insistence on calling him boy, she'd known exactly who Sejanus was all along.

Sejanus burned with anger and humiliation, unwilling or unable to move. He just stood there, staring down Dr. Gaul, until the tension became unbearable.

"There's an empty seat by me." The words came unbidden from Coriolanus's mouth.

The offer distracted Sejanus, and then he seemed to deflate. He took a deep breath, walked back down the aisle, and slid onto the stool. One hand clenched the strap on his book bag, while the other formed a fist on the table.

Coriolanus wished he'd kept quiet. He noticed Dean

Highbottom giving him a quizzical look and busied himself by opening his notebook and uncapping his pen.

"Your emotions are running high," Dr. Gaul told the class. "I understand. I do. But you must learn to harness and contain them. Wars are won with heads, not hearts."

"I thought the war was over," said Livia. She seemed angry, too, but not in the same way as Sejanus. Coriolanus guessed she was just peeved about losing her strapping tribute.

"Did you? Even after your experience in the arena?" asked Dr. Gaul.

"I did," interjected Lysistrata. "And if the war is over, then technically the killing should be over, shouldn't it?"

"I'm beginning to think it will never be over," conceded Festus. "The districts will always hate us, and we'll always hate them."

"I think you might be onto something there," said Dr. Gaul. "Let's consider for a moment that the war is a constant. The conflict may ebb and flow, but it will never really cease. Then what should be our goal?"

"You're saying it can't be won?" asked Lysistrata.

"Let's say it can't," said Dr. Gaul. "What's our strategy then?"

Coriolanus pressed his lips together to keep from blurting out the answer. So obvious. Too obvious. But he knew Tigris was right about avoiding Dr. Gaul, even if it might bring praise. As the class chewed over the question, she paced up and down the aisle, finally coming to a stop at his table. "Mr. Snow? Any thoughts on what we should do with our endless war?"

He comforted himself with the thought that she was old and no one lived forever.

"Mr. Snow?" she persisted. He felt like he was the rabbit being prodded by her metal rod. "Want to take a wild guess?"

"We control it," he said quietly. "If the war's impossible to end, then we have to control it indefinitely. Just as we do now. With the Peacekeepers occupying the districts, with strict laws, and with reminders of who's in charge, like the Hunger Games. In any scenario, it's preferable to have the upper hand, to be the victor rather than the defeated."

"Though, in our case, decidedly less moral," Sejanus muttered.

"It's not immoral to defend ourselves," Livia shot back. "And who wouldn't rather be the victor than the defeated?"

"I don't know that I have much interest in being either," said Lysistrata.

"But that wasn't an option," Coriolanus reminded her, "given the question. Not if you think about it."

"Not if you think about it, eh, Casca?" said Dr. Gaul as she headed back up the aisle. "A little thought can save a lot of lives."

Dean Highbottom doodled on the list. *Maybe Highbottom's just as much a rabbit as I am*, Coriolanus thought, and wondered if he was wasting his time worrying about him.

"But take heart," Dr. Gaul continued cheerfully. "Like most of life's circumstances, war has its ups and downs. And that's your next assignment. Write me an essay on everything attractive about war. Everything you loved about it."

Many of his classmates looked up in surprise, but not Coriolanus. The woman had set snakes on Clemensia for fun. Clearly, she relished witnessing pain and probably assumed they all did.

Lysistrata frowned. "Loved about it?"

"That shouldn't take long," said Festus.

"Is it a group project?" asked Livia.

"No, individual. The problem with group assignments is that one person usually does all the work," said Dr. Gaul, giving

Coriolanus a wink that made his skin crawl. "But feel free to pick your families' brains. You might be surprised. Be as honest as you dare. Bring them to Sunday's mentor meeting." She pulled some more carrots out of her pocket, turned back to the rabbit, and seemed to forget about them.

When they were released, Sejanus followed Coriolanus down the hall. "You have to stop rescuing me."

Coriolanus shook his head. "I can't seem to control it. It's like a tic."

"I don't know what I'd do if you weren't here." Sejanus's voice dropped. "That woman is evil. She should be stopped."

Coriolanus felt any attempt to dethrone Dr. Gaul would be futile, but he adopted a sympathetic manner. "You tried."

"I failed. I wish my family could just go home. Back to District Two, where we belong. Not that they'd want us," said Sejanus. "Being Capitol is going to kill me."

"It's a bad time, Sejanus. With the Games and the bombing. No one is at their best. Don't do anything rash like running off." As Coriolanus clapped him on the shoulder, he thought, *I might need a favor.*

"Running off where? How? With what?" said Sejanus. "But I really do appreciate your support. I wish I could think of some way to thank you."

There was actually something Coriolanus needed. "You don't happen to have a guitar I could borrow, do you?"

The Plinths did not, so he devoted the rest of Wednesday afternoon to fulfilling his promise to Lucy Gray. He asked around in school, but the closest thing he got was a maybe from Vipsania Sickle, mentor of the District 7 boy, Treech, who'd juggled the walnuts in the zoo.

"Oh, I think we used to have one during the war," she told

him. "Let me check and get back to you. I'd love to hear your girl sing again!" He didn't know whether or not to believe her; the Sickles did not impress him as a musical crowd. Vipsania had inherited her aunt Agrippina's love of competition, and for all he knew, she was trying to spoil Lucy Gray's performance. But two could play at that game, so he told her she was a lifesaver and then continued his search.

After coming up empty-handed at the Academy, he thought of Pluribus Bell. Possibly, he still had instruments lying around from his nightclub days.

The minute the door in the back alley opened, Boa Bell wove between Coriolanus's legs, purring like an engine. At seventeen, she was getting long in the tooth, and he used care as he lifted her into his arms.

"Ah, she's always happy to see an old friend," Pluribus said, and invited Coriolanus in.

The defeat of the districts had made little difference to Pluribus's trade, as he still secured a living dealing in black market goods, even if they now had a more luxurious bent. Decent liquor, makeup, and tobacco were still hard to get hold of. District 1 had slowly turned its attention to supplying the Capitol with pleasures, but not everyone had access to them, and they came at a high price. The Snows were no longer regular customers, but Tigris made occasional visits to sell him the ration coupons that would allow them to buy meat or coffee, which they usually couldn't afford. People were happy to pay for the privilege of buying an extra leg of lamb.

Known for his discretion, Pluribus remained one of the few people Coriolanus didn't need to pretend to be wealthy around. He knew the Snows' situation but never blabbed about it or made the family feel inferior. Today he poured Coriolanus a glass of cold tea, filled a plate with cakes, and offered him a chair. They chatted about the bombing and how it brought up bad memories of the war, but soon their talk turned to Lucy Gray, who'd made a very favorable impression on Pluribus.

"If I had a few like her, I might think of opening the club back up," Pluribus mused. "Oh, I'd still sell my pretties, but I could stage shows on the weekends. The truth is, we were all so busy killing each other that we forgot how to have fun. She knows, though. Your girl."

Coriolanus told him the plan for the interview and asked if there might be a guitar they could borrow. "We'd take good care of it, I promise. I'd keep it at home except when she's playing, and return it right after the show."

Pluribus needed no coaxing. "You know, I packed everything away after the bombs got Cyrus. Silly, really. As if I could forget the love of my life so easily." He got to his feet and moved a stack of perfume crates, revealing an old closet door. Inside, lovingly arranged on shelves, was a variety of musical instruments. Pluribus pulled out a surprisingly dust-free leather case and lifted the lid. A pleasant smell of old wood and polish hit Coriolanus's nose as he looked at the gleaming, golden thing inside. The body shaped like a woman's, the six strings running up the long neck to the tuning pegs. He strummed it lightly with his finger. Even though it was badly out of tune, the richness of the sound went right through him.

Coriolanus shook his head. "This one's too nice. I wouldn't want to risk damaging it."

"I trust you. And I trust your girl. Kind of like to hear what she does with it." Pluribus closed the case and held it out. "You take it and tell her I've got my fingers crossed for her. It's good to have a friend in the audience."

Coriolanus took the guitar gratefully. "Thank you, Pluribus. I hope you do reopen the club. I'll be a steady customer."

"Just like your father," said Pluribus with a chuckle. "When he was about your age, he used to close down this place every night with that rascal Casca Highbottom."

Every part of that sounded nonsensical. His stern father, so humorless and strict, living it up at a nightclub? And with, of all people, Dean Highbottom? He'd never heard them mentioned together, although they were about the same age. "You're kidding, right?"

"Oh, no. They were a pair of wild things," said Pluribus. But before he could elaborate, he was interrupted by a customer.

With great care, Coriolanus carried his prize home and laid it on his dresser. Tigris and the Grandma'am *ooh*ed and *aah*ed over it, but he couldn't wait to see Lucy Gray's reaction. Whatever instrument she'd had back in District 12 could never compare with Pluribus's.

His head ached enough to go to bed at sundown, but it took a while to fall asleep, so preoccupied was he with the relationship between his father and "that rascal Casca Highbottom." If they had been friends, as Pluribus had suggested, none of the goodwill remained. He couldn't help thinking that, however close they'd been during their clubbing days, things hadn't ended well. As soon as he could, he'd press Pluribus for more details.

The next few days gave him no such opportunity, though, as they were devoted to readying Lucy Gray for the interview, which had been set for Saturday night. Each mentor-tribute pair had been assigned a classroom to work in. Two Peacekeepers were on guard, but Lucy Gray had been freed of both chains and cuffs. Tigris had provided an old dress of hers, saying that if Lucy Gray was willing to trust her, she could wash and iron her rainbow ruffles for the broadcast. Lucy Gray hesitated, but when he gave her Tigris's other gift, a small cake of soap shaped like a flower and smelling of lavender, she had him turn his back while she changed.

The loving way she handled the guitar, as if it were a sentient being, gave him a hint of a past so unlike his own he had trouble imagining it. She took her time tuning the instrument and then played song after song, seemingly as starved for the music as for the meals he brought. He pumped her with all the food they could spare, along with bottles of tea sweetened with corn syrup to soothe her throat. Her vocal cords were much improved by the time the big night arrived.

The Hunger Games: A Night of Interviews kicked off in front of a live audience in the Academy auditorium while broadcasting throughout Panem. Hosted by the clownish Capitol TV weatherman, Lucretius "Lucky" Flickerman, it seemed both glaringly inappropriate and surprisingly welcome on the heels of all the killing. Lucky was dressed in a high-collared blue suit with rhinestone accents, his gelled hair was dusted in coppery powder, and his mood could only be described as merry. The back curtain of the stage, resurrected from some prewar production, depicted a starry sky and twinkled accordingly.

After a jaunty rendition of the anthem played, Lucky welcomed the audience to a brand-new Hunger Games for a brand-new decade, one in which every Capitol citizen could participate by sponsoring the tribute of their choice. In the chaos of the past few days, the best Dr. Gaul's team had been able to do was offer a half dozen basic food items the sponsors could send to the tributes.

"You're wondering, what's in it for you?" chirped Lucky. Then he explained the gambling, a simple system with win, place, and show options familiar to those who'd played the ponies before the war. Anyone who wanted to either send a monetary gift to feed a tribute, or place a bet on one, needed only to visit their local post office, where the staff would be happy to help. Starting tomorrow, they would be open from eight in the morning until eight at night, giving people time to place their bets before the Hunger Games kicked off on Monday. After he'd introduced the new wrinkle in the Games, Lucky had little to do but read the cue cards with the material that wrapped around the interviews, but he managed to work in a few magic tricks, like pouring different-colored wine from the same bottle to toast the Capitol and having a pigeon fly out of his bell-sleeved jacket.

Of the mentor-tribute pairs who were capable of participating, only half had something to present. Coriolanus asked to go last, knowing nothing could compete with Lucy Gray but wanting to be the closer for effect. The other mentors offered up background information about their tributes while trying to throw in something memorable and urging the public to sponsor them. To demonstrate his strength, Lysistrata sat primly in her chair while Jessup lifted her over his head easily. Io Jasper's District 3 boy, Circ, said he could start a fire with his glasses, and she, with her scientific know-how, suggested various angles and times of day that would facilitate the task. Snooty Juno Phipps admitted she'd been disappointed to get tiny Bobbin. Didn't a Phipps, a member of a founding family of the Capitol, deserve better than District 8? But he'd won her over when he told her five different ways he could kill someone with a sewing needle. Coral, Festus's District 4 girl, made a case for her ability to handle a trident, a weapon that was typically available in the arena. She demonstrated with an old broomstick, wielding it in a sinuous fashion that left little doubt of her expertise. The dairy heiress Domitia Whimsiwick's familiarity with cows turned out to be an asset. Bubbly by nature, she got her muscular District 10 tribute, Tanner, so engaged in talking about slaughterhouse techniques that Lucky had to cut them off when they ran over. Arachne had been wrong about the appeal of that topic, because Tanner garnered the most applause of the evening so far.

Coriolanus listened with one ear as he prepared to take the stage with Lucy Gray. Felix Ravinstill, the president's grandnephew, was trying to make an impression with the District 11 girl, Dill, but Coriolanus couldn't figure out his angle, because she'd become so sickly even her coughs were barely audible.

Tigris had worked another one of her miracles on Lucy Gray's dress. The filth and soot had vanished, leaving fresh, starchy rows of rainbow ruffles. She'd also sent a pot of blush Fabricia had discarded with just a smidgeon left in the bottom. Scrubbed clean, with rouged cheeks and lips, her hair piled up on her head as it had been for the reaping, Lucy Gray looked, as Pluribus had said, like someone who still knew how to have fun.

"I think your odds get better by the minute," said Coriolanus, adjusting a hot pink rosebud in her hair. It matched the one on his lapel, just in case anyone needed a reminder of who Lucy Gray belonged to.

"Well, you know what they say. The show's not over until the mockingjay sings," she said.

"The mockingjay?" He laughed. "Really, I think you're just making these things up."

"Not that one. A mockingjay's a bona fide bird," she assured him.

"And it sings in your show?" he asked.

"Not my show, sweetheart. Yours. The Capitol's anyway," said Lucy Gray. "I think we're up."

With her clean dress and his neatly pressed uniform, their very appearance brought a spontaneous round of applause from the audience. He didn't waste time asking her a lot of questions no one cared about. Instead he introduced himself and stepped back, leaving her alone in the spotlight.

"Good evening," she said. "I'm Lucy Gray Baird, of the Covey Bairds. I started writing this song back in District Twelve, before I knew what the ending would be. It's my words set to an old tune. Where I'm from, we call it a ballad. That's a song that tells a story. And I guess this is mine. 'The Ballad of Lucy Gray Baird.' I hope you like it."

Coriolanus had heard her sing dozens of songs over the past few days, full of everything from the beauty of springtime to the heart-wrenching despair of losing her mama. Lullabies and toe tappers, laments and ditties. She'd solicited his opinion, weighing his responses to each song. He'd thought they'd settled on a charming thing about the wonder of falling in love, but a few bars into this ballad, he knew this was nothing she'd rehearsed. The haunting melody set the tone, and her words did the rest as she began to sing in a voice husky from smoke and sadness.

When I was a babe I fell down in the holler.
When I was a girl I fell into your arms.
We fell on hard times and we lost our bright color.
You went to the dogs and I lived by my charms.

I danced for my dinner, spread kisses like honey.
You stole and you gambled and I said you should.
We sang for our suppers, we drank up our money.
Then one day you left, saying I was no good.

Well, all right, I'm bad, but then, you're no prize either.
All right, I'm bad, but then, that's nothing new.

You say you won't love me, I won't love you neither.
Just let me remind you who I am to you.

'Cause I am the one who looks out when you're leaping.
I am the one who knows how you were brave.
And I am the one who heard what you said sleeping.
I'll take that and more when I go to my grave.

It's sooner than later that I'm six feet under.
It's sooner than later that you'll be alone.
So who will you turn to tomorrow, I wonder?
For when the bell rings, lover, you're on your own.

And I am the one who you let see you weeping.
I know the soul that you struggle to save.
Too bad I'm the bet that you lost in the reaping.
Now what will you do when I go to my grave?

You could hear a pin drop in the auditorium when she finished. Then there were a few sniffles, some coughing, and finally Pluribus's voice shouting out "Bravo" from the back of the auditorium and the thunderous applause that followed.

Coriolanus knew it had hit home, this dark, moving, far too personal account of her life. He knew the gifts would pour into the arena for her. That her success, even now, reflected back on him, making it his success. Snow lands on top and all that. He knew he should be elated at this turn of events and jumping up and down inside while presenting a modest, pleased front.

But what he really felt was jealous.

"And last but least, District Twelve girl . . . she belongs to Coriolanus Snow."

"Things might've been quite different if you hadn't landed your little rainbow girl."

"The truth is, we were all so busy killing each other that we forgot how to have fun. She knows, though. Your girl."

His girl. His. Here in the Capitol, it was a given that Lucy Gray belonged to him, as if she'd had no life before her name was called out at the reaping. Even that sanctimonious Sejanus believed she was something he could trade for. If that wasn't ownership, what was? With her song, Lucy Gray had repudiated all that by featuring a life that had nothing to do with him, and a great deal to do with someone else. Someone she referred to as "lover," no less. And while he had no claim on her heart — he barely knew the girl! — he didn't like the idea of anyone else having it either. Although the song had been a clear success, he felt somehow betrayed by it. Even humiliated.

Lucy Gray rose and took a bow, then extended her hand to him. After a moment's hesitation, he joined her at the front of the stage while the applause built to a standing ovation. Pluribus led the cries for an encore, but their time had expired, as Lucky Flickerman reminded them, so they took a final bow and exited the stage, hand in hand.

As they reached the wings she started to release him, but he tightened his grip. "Well, you're a hit. Congratulations. New song?"

"I've been working on it awhile, but I only found that last stanza a few hours ago," she said. "Why? Didn't you like it?"

"It surprised me. You had so many others," he said.

"I did." Lucy Gray freed her hand and ran her fingers across the guitar strings, picking out one last bit of melody before she gently settled the instrument back in its case. "Here's the thing, Coriolanus. I'm going to fight like all-fire to win these Games, but I'm going to be in there with the likes of Reaper and Tanner and a few others who are no strangers to killing. There's no guarantee of anything."

"And the song?" he prodded.

"The song?" she repeated, and took a moment to consider her answer. "I left some loose ends back in District Twelve. Me being tribute . . . Well, there's bad luck and then there's bad business. That was bad business. And someone who owed me plenty had a hand in it. The song, it was payback of a kind. Most people won't know that, but the Covey will get the message, loud and clear. And they're all I really care about."

"Just on one hearing?" asked Coriolanus. "It went by pretty fast."

"One hearing's all my cousin Maude Ivory needs. That child never forgets anything with a tune," said Lucy Gray. "Looks like I'm being rounded up again."

The two male Peacekeepers who appeared at her side treated her with a certain friendliness now, asking if she was ready to go and trying to keep their smiles contained. Just like those Peacekeepers back in 12. Coriolanus couldn't help wondering just how friendly she could be. He gave them a disapproving look that had zero effect and heard them complimenting her performance as they took her away.

He swallowed his peevishness and accepted the congratulations that were pouring in from all sides. They helped to remind him that he was the real star of the evening. Even if Lucy Gray was confused on the issue, in the eyes of the Capitol, she belonged to him. What point would there be in crediting a district tribute? This held true until he ran into Pluribus, who gushed, "What a talent, what a natural she is! If she manages to survive, I'm determined to headline her in my club."

"That sounds a bit tricky. Won't they send her home?" said Coriolanus.

"I have one or two favors I could call in," he said. "Oh, Coriolanus, wasn't she stellar? I'm so glad you got her, my boy. The Snows were due a piece of good luck."

Silly old man with his ridiculous powdered wig and his decrepit cat. What did he know about anything? Coriolanus was about to set the record straight, when Satyria appeared and whispered in his ear, "I think that prize is in the bag," and he let it go.

Sejanus appeared, in another brand-new suit, with a rumpled little woman in an expensive flowered dress on his arm. It didn't matter. You could put a turnip in a ball gown and it would still beg to be mashed. Coriolanus had no doubt this could only be Ma.

As Sejanus introduced them, he extended his hand and gave her a warm smile. "Mrs. Plinth, what an honor. Please forgive me for my negligence. I've been meaning to write you a note for days, but every time I sit down to do it, my head throbs so from my concussion that I can't think straight. Thank you for the delicious casserole."

Mrs. Plinth crinkled with pleasure and gave an embarrassed laugh. "It's for us to thank you, Coriolanus. We're so glad that

Sejanus has such a good friend. If there's ever anything you need, I hope you'll know you can count on us."

"Well, that cuts both ways, madam. I am at your service," he said, laying it on so thick she was sure to be suspicious. But not Ma. Her eyes filled with tears and she made a gurgling sound, having been rendered speechless by his magnanimousness. She dug in her handbag, a ghastly thing the size of a small suitcase, pulled out a lace-trimmed handkerchief, and began blowing her nose. Fortunately, Tigris, who was genuinely sweet to everyone, came backstage to find him and took over chatting with the Plinths.

Things finally wound down, and as the cousins walked home together, they analyzed the evening, from Lucy Gray's restrained use of the blush to the unfortunate fit of Ma's dress. "But really, Coryo, I can't imagine things going any better for you," said Tigris.

"I'm certainly pleased," he said. "I think we'll be able to get her some sponsors. I just hope some people aren't put off by the song."

"I was very moved by it. I think most people were. Didn't you like it?" she asked.

"Of course I liked it, but I'm more open-minded than most," he said. "I mean, what do you think she was suggesting happened?"

"It sounded to me like she had a bad time of it. Someone she loved broke her heart," Tigris answered.

"That was only the half of it," he continued, because he couldn't let even Tigris think he'd felt envious of some no-account in the districts. "There was the part about her living by her charms."

"Well, that could be anything. She's a performer, after all," she said.

He considered it. "I suppose."

"You said she lost her parents. She's probably been fending for herself for years. I don't think anyone who survived the war and the years after can blame her for that." Tigris dropped her gaze. "We all did things we're not proud of."

"You didn't," he said.

"Didn't I?" Tigris spoke with an uncharacteristic bitterness. "We all did. Maybe you were too little to remember. Maybe you didn't know how bad it really was."

"How can you say that? That's all I remember," he shot back.

"Then be kind, Coryo," she snapped. "And try not to look down on people who had to choose between death and disgrace."

Tigris's rebuke shocked him, but less than her alluding to behavior that might be considered a disgrace. What had she done? Because if she'd done it, she'd done it to protect him. He thought about the morning of the reaping, when he'd casually wondered what she had to trade in the black market, but he'd never really taken that seriously. Or hadn't he? Would he have just preferred not to know what sacrifices she might be willing to make for him? Her comment was vague enough, and so many things were beneath a Snow, that he could say, as she had of Lucy Gray's song, "Well, that could be anything." Did he want to know the details? No. The truth was he did not.

As he pulled open the glass door to the apartment building, she gave a cry of disbelief. "Oh, no, it can't be! The elevator's working!"

He felt doubtful, as the thing hadn't worked since early in the war. But the door stood open and the lights reflected off the mirrored walls of the car. Glad for the distraction, he made a low bow, inviting her to enter. "After you."

Tigris giggled and paraded into the car like the grand lady she was born to be. "You're too kind."

Coriolanus swept in after her, and for a moment they both stared at the buttons designating the floors. "The last time I remember this working, we'd just been to my father's funeral. We got home, and we've been climbing ever since."

"The Grandma'am will be thrilled," said Tigris. "Her knees can't take those stairs anymore."

"*I'm* thrilled. Maybe she'll get out of the apartment once in a while," Coriolanus said. Tigris smacked him on the arm, but she was laughing. "Really. It would be nice to have the place to ourselves for five minutes. Maybe skip the anthem one morning, or not wear a tie to dinner. Then again, there's the danger of her talking to people. 'When Coriolanus is president, it will rain champagne every Tuesday!'"

"Perhaps people will just put it down to age," said Tigris.

"One can hope. Will you do the honors?" he asked.

Tigris reached out and gave the penthouse button a nice long push. After a pause the doors slid shut with nary a squeak, and they began to ascend. "I'm surprised the apartment board decided to fix it now. It must've been costly."

Coriolanus frowned. "You don't suppose they're spiffing up the building hoping to sell their places? You know, with the new taxes."

The playfulness drained out of Tigris. "That's very possible. I know the Dolittles would consider selling for the right price. They say the apartment is too big for them, but you know it's not that."

"Is that what we'll say? That our ancestral home has gotten too large?" Coriolanus said as the doors opened to reveal their front door. "Come on, I've still got homework."

The Grandma'am had waited up to sing his praises and said

they'd been replaying highlights from the interviews nonstop. "She's a sad, trashy little thing, your girl, but oddly appealing in her way. Perhaps it's her voice. It gets inside a person somehow."

If Lucy Gray had won over the Grandma'am, Coriolanus felt the rest of the nation could only fall in step. If no one else seemed to be bothered by her questionable past, why should he be?

He got a glass of buttermilk, changed into his father's silk robe, and settled down to write about everything he loved about the war. He began with *As they say, war is misery, but it's not without its charms.* It seemed a clever intro to him, but it led nowhere, and half an hour later he'd made no headway. It was, as Festus had suggested, destined to be a very short assignment. But he knew that would not satisfy Dr. Gaul, and a halfhearted effort would only bring him unwanted attention.

When Tigris came in to say good night, he bounced the topic off her. "Can you remember anything at all we liked?"

She sat on the end of his bed and thought it over. "I liked some of the uniforms. Not the ones they wear now. Do you remember the red jackets with the gold piping?"

"In the parades?" He felt a bit of a rush as he remembered hanging from the window with the soldiers and bands marching by. "Did I like the parades?"

"You loved them. You'd be so excited that we couldn't get you to eat your breakfast," said Tigris. "We always had a gathering on parade days."

"Front-row seats." Coriolanus jotted the words *uniforms* and *parades* on a scrap of paper, then added *fireworks*. "Any sort of spectacle appealed to me when I was little, I suppose."

"Remember the turkey?" Tigris said suddenly.

It had been the last year of the war, when the siege had reduced the Capitol to cannibalism and despair. Even the lima beans were running low, and it had been months since anything resembling meat had made its way to their table. In an attempt to raise morale, the Capitol had proclaimed December 15th National Heroes Day. They put together a television special and honored a dozen or so citizens who'd lost their lives in defense of the Capitol, with Coriolanus's father, General Crassus Snow, among them. The electricity came on in time for the broadcast, but it had been off — and with it the heat — for a solid day before. They'd been huddled together on the Grandma'am's boat of a bed, and so they remained to watch their heroes honored. Even then, Coriolanus's memory of his father had faded, and while he knew his face from photos, he was startled by the man's deep voice and uncompromising words against the districts. After the anthem played, a knock on the front door roused them from the bed, and they found a trio of young soldiers in dress uniforms delivering a commemorative plaque and a basket with a twenty-pound frozen turkey, compliments of the state. In an apparent attempt at the Capitol's former luxury, the basket also included a dusty jar of mint jelly, a can of salmon, three cracked sticks of pineapple candy, a loofah sponge, and a flowery-scented candle. The soldiers set the basket on a table in the foyer, read a statement of thanks, and bid them good night. Tigris burst into tears, and the Grandma'am had to sit down, but the first thing Coriolanus did was run and make sure the door was locked to protect their newfound riches.

They'd eaten salmon on toast and it was decided Tigris would stay home from school the next day to figure out how to cook the bird. Coriolanus delivered a dinner invitation on the Snows' engraved stationery to Pluribus, and he came bearing posca and a dented can of apricots. With the help of one of Cook's old recipe books, Tigris had outdone herself, and they'd feasted on jelly-glazed turkey with bread and cabbage stuffing. Nothing had ever, before or since, tasted so good.

"Still one of the best days of my life." He wasn't sure how to phrase it but finally added *relief from deprivation* to the list. "You were a wonder, the way you cooked that turkey. At the time you seemed so old to me, but you were really just a little girl," said Coriolanus.

Tigris smiled. "And you. With your victory garden on the roof."

"If you liked parsley, I was your man!" He laughed. But he'd taken pride in his parsley. It had livened up the soup, and sometimes he could trade it for other things. *Resourcefulness*, he put on the list.

So he wrote his assignment, recounting these childish delights, but in the end he did not feel satisfied. He thought about the last couple of weeks, with the bombing in the arena, losing his classmates, Marcus's escape, and how it all had revived the terror he'd felt when the Capitol had been under siege. What had mattered then, what mattered still, was living without that fear. So he added a paragraph about his deep relief on winning the war, and the grim satisfaction of seeing the Capitol's enemies, who'd treated him so cruelly, who'd cost his family so much, brought to their knees. Hobbled. Impotent. Unable to hurt him anymore. He'd loved the unfamiliar sense of safety that their defeat had brought. The security that could only come with power. The ability to control things. Yes, that was what he'd loved best of all.

The next morning, as the remaining mentors straggled in for the Sunday meeting, Coriolanus tried to imagine who they would've been had no war occurred. Barely more than toddlers when it started, they'd all been about eight when it ended. Although the hardships had eased, he and his classmates were still far removed from the opulent life they'd been born into, and the rebuilding of their world had been slow and disheartening. If he could erase the rationing and the bombings, the hunger and the fear, and replace it with the rosy lives promised to them at birth, would he even recognize his friends?

Coriolanus felt a twinge of guilt when his thoughts landed on Clemensia. He hadn't been to see her yet, between recovering and homework and readying Lucy Gray for the Games. It wasn't just a time issue, though. He had no desire to return to the hospital and see what state she was in. What if the doctor had been lying, and the scales were spreading to cover her entire body? What if she'd transformed into a snake entirely? That was silliness, but Dr. Gaul's lab had been so sinister that his mind went to extremes. A paranoid thought nibbled at him. What if Dr. Gaul's people were only waiting for him to visit so they could imprison him as well? It didn't make sense. If they'd wanted to hold him, his hospitalization would've been the time. The whole thing was ridiculous, he concluded. He'd go to see her at the first opportunity.

Dr. Gaul, clearly a morning person, and Dean Highbottom, clearly not, reviewed the previous night's performances. Coriolanus and Lucy Gray had obliterated the field, although points were given to those who'd at least managed to get their tributes to the interview stage. On Capitol TV, Lucky Flickerman was providing updates on the betting scene from the main post office, and while people were favoring Tanner and Jessup to win, Lucy Gray had racked up three times as many gifts as her nearest competitor.

"Look at all these people," said Dr. Gaul. "Sending bread to a slip of a girl with a broken heart, even though they don't believe she can win. What's the lesson there?"

"At the dogfights, I've seen people back mutts that can barely stand," Festus told her. "People love a long shot."

"People love a good love song, more like," said Persephone, showing her dimples.

"People are fools," sneered Livia. "She doesn't stand a chance."

"But there are a lot of romantics." Pup batted his eyes at her and made sloppy kissing sounds.

"Yes, romantic notions, idealistic notions, can be very attractive. Which seems like a good segue into your essays." Dr. Gaul settled herself on a lab stool. "Let's see what you've got."

Rather than collect their essays, Dr. Gaul had them read bits and pieces of them aloud. Coriolanus's classmates had touched on many points that hadn't crossed his mind. Some had been drawn to the courage of the soldiers, the chance to maybe one day be heroic themselves. Others mentioned the bond that formed between soldiers who fought together, or the nobility of defending the Capitol.

"It felt like we were all part of something bigger," said Domitia. She nodded solemnly, causing the ponytail on the top of her head to bob. "Something important. We all made sacrifices, but it was to save our country."

Coriolanus felt disconnected from their "romantic notions," as he didn't share a romanticized view of the war. Courage in battle was often necessary because of someone else's poor planning. He had no idea if he would take a bullet for Festus and had no interest in finding out. As to the noble ideas of the Capitol, did they really believe that? What he desired had little to do with nobility and everything to do with being in control. Not that he didn't have a strong moral code; certainly he did. But almost everything in war, between its declaration and the victory parades, seemed a waste of resources. He kept one eye on the clock while pretending to be engaged in the conversation, willing time to pass so he wouldn't have to read anything. The parades seemed shallow, the appeal of power still true but heartless compared to the ramblings of his classmates. And he wished he hadn't even written the bit about growing the parsley; it just sounded puerile now.

The best he could do, when his time came, was to read the story about the turkey. Domitia told him it was touching, Livia rolled her eyes, and Dr. Gaul raised her eyebrows and asked did he have more to share? He did not.

"Mr. Plinth?" said Dr. Gaul.

Sejanus had been silent and subdued through the entire class. He flipped a sheet of paper over and read, "'The only thing I loved about the war was the fact that I still lived at home.' If you're asking me if it had any value beyond that, I would say that it was an opportunity to right some wrongs."

"And did it?" asked Dr. Gaul.

"Not at all. Things in the districts are worse than ever," said Sejanus.

Objections came from around the room.

"Whoa!"

"He did not just say that."

"Go back to Two, then! Who'd miss you?"

He's really pushing it now, thought Coriolanus. But he was angry, too. It took two parties to make a war. A war that, by the way, the rebels had started. A war that had left him an orphan.

But Sejanus ignored his classmates, staying focused on the Head Gamemaker. "May I ask, what did you love about the war, Dr. Gaul?"

She looked at him for a long moment, then smiled. "I loved how it proved me right."

Dean Highbottom announced the lunch break before anyone ventured to ask how, and they all filed out, leaving their essays behind.

They were given a half hour to eat, but Coriolanus had forgotten to bring any food, and none was provided because it was Sunday. He spent the time stretched out in a shaded area of the front steps, resting his head while Festus and Hilarius Heavensbee, who was mentoring the District 8 girl, discussed strategies for female tributes. He vaguely remembered Hilarius's tribute from the train station, wearing a striped dress and red scarf, but mostly because she'd been with Bobbin.

"The trouble with girls is, they're not used to fighting the same way boys are," said Hilarius. The Heavensbees were ultrarich, the way the Snows had been before the war. But no matter his advantages, Hilarius always seemed to feel oppressed.

"Oh, I don't know," said Festus. "I think my Coral could give any of those guys a run for their money."

"Mine's a runt." Hilarius picked at his steak sandwich with his manicured nails. "Wovey, she calls herself. Well, I tried to train old Wovey for the interview, but zero personality. No one's backed her, so I can't feed her, even if she can avoid the others."

"If she stays alive, she'll get backers," said Festus.

"Are you even listening to me? She can't fight, and I've no money to work with since my family can't bet," Hilarius whined. "I'm just hoping she lasts until the final twelve so I can face my parents. They're embarrassed that a Heavensbee's making such a poor showing."

After lunch, Satyria took the mentors over to the Capitol News station so they could become acquainted with the behind-the-scenes machinery of the Hunger Games. The Gamemakers worked out of a handful of shabby offices, and while the control room assigned to them was sufficient, it seemed a little small for the annual event. Coriolanus found the whole thing a bit disappointing — he'd imagined something flashier — but the

Gamemakers were excited about the new elements of this year's Games and chattered on about mentor commentary and sponsor participation. The booth was abuzz as they checked the remote-operated cameras that had been fixtures back in the sports arena days. Half a dozen Gamemakers were busy testing the toy drones designated to deliver the sponsors' gifts. The drones found their recipients by facial recognition and could carry just one item at a time.

Lucky Flickerman, fresh off his interview success, had been tapped to host, backed up by a handful of Capitol News reporters. Coriolanus got a thrill when he saw himself slotted in at 8:15 the following morning, until Lucky said, "We wanted to make sure to get you in early. You know, before your girl buys it."

He felt as though someone had punched him in the gut. Livia was bitter and Dr. Gaul insane, so he'd been able to ignore their certainty that Lucy Gray wasn't a contender. But somehow goofy Lucky Flickerman's words hit home in a way theirs could not. As he walked back to the apartment to prepare for his final meeting with Lucy Gray, he ruminated over the likelihood that she'd be dead by the same time tomorrow. The previous night's jealousy over her loser of a boyfriend and the way her star quality sometimes outshone his own evaporated. He felt remarkably close to her, this girl who'd dropped into his life so unexpectedly and with such style. And it wasn't just about the accolades she'd brought him. He was genuinely fond of her, far more than he was of most of the girls he knew in the Capitol. If she could survive — oh, sweet only if — how could they help but have a lifelong connection? But for all his positive talk, he knew the odds were not in her favor, and a heavy melancholy descended upon him.

At home, he lay on his bed, dreading having to say good-bye. He wished he could give Lucy Gray something beautiful that would really show his thanks for what she'd given him. A renewed sense of his worth. An opportunity to shine. A prize in the bag. And, of course, his life. It would have to be something very special. Precious. Something of his own, not like the roses, which were really the Grandma'am's. Something that, if things went badly in the arena, she could wrap her fingers around as a reminder that he was with her, and find comfort in the fact that she was not dying alone. There was a silk scarf dyed a luscious deep orange that she could probably use in her hair. A gold pin he'd won for academic excellence, engraved with his name. Maybe a lock of his hair tied in a ribbon? What could be more personal than that?

Suddenly, he felt a surge of anger. What good were any of these unless she could use them to defend herself? What was he doing but dressing her up to be a pretty corpse? Perhaps she could strangle someone with the scarf, or stab them with the pin? But there was no shortage of weaponry in the arena, if that were the issue.

He was still trying to figure out a gift when Tigris called him to the table. She had bought a pound of chopped beef and fried up four patties. Hers was considerably smaller, which he would've objected to if he didn't know she always nibbled on the uncooked meat while she prepared the meal. Tigris craved it and would have eaten her whole portion raw if the Grandma'am hadn't forbidden it. One of the patties was reserved for Lucy Gray, layered with toppings and nestled in a large bun. Tigris also made fried potatoes and creamed cabbage slaw, and Coriolanus selected the finest fruits and sweets from the gift basket from the hospital. Tigris laid a linen napkin in a small cardboard box decorated with brightly plumed birds and arranged the feast, topping the snowy white fabric with one final rosebud from the Grandma'am. Coriolanus had chosen a rich shade of peach tinged with crimson, because the Covey loved color, and Lucy Gray more than most.

"Tell her," said Tigris, "that I am rooting for her."

"Tell her," the Grandma'am added, "that we are all so sorry she has to die."

After the soft, sun-warmed evening air, the chill of Heavensbee Hall reminded Coriolanus of the Snow family mausoleum, where his parents had been laid to rest. Empty of students and their bustle, everything from footsteps to sighs echoed loudly, giving an otherworldly feeling to an already gloomy meeting. No lights had been turned on, the late rays that slipped through the windows being thought sufficient, but that contrasted sharply with the brightness of their earlier meetings. As the remaining mentors gathered on the balcony and surveyed their counterparts down below, a hush fell over them.

"The thing is," Lysistrata whispered to Coriolanus, "I've become rather attached to Jessup." She paused a moment, arranging the wrapping on a chunk of baked noodles and cheese. "He did save my life." Coriolanus wondered what Lysistrata, who had been closer to him than anyone else in the arena, had seen when the bombs went off. Had she seen Lucy Gray save him? Was she hinting at that?

As they wove their way to their respective tables, Coriolanus forced himself to think positively. There was no profit in spending their last ten minutes together weeping when they could devote it to a winning strategy. It helped quite a bit that Lucy Gray looked better than in previous meetings in the hall. Clean and groomed, her dress still fresh in the shadowy light, you'd think she'd readied herself for a party and not a slaughter. Her eyes lit on the box.

Coriolanus presented it with a small bow. "I come bearing gifts."

Lucy Gray lifted the rose daintily and inhaled its fragrance. She plucked a petal and slipped it between her lips. "It tastes like bedtime," she said with a sad smile. "What a pretty box."

"Tigris was saving it for something special," he said. "Go ahead and eat if you're hungry. It's still warm."

"I think I will. Eat one last meal like a civilized person." She pulled open the napkin and admired the contents of the box. "Oh, this looks prime."

"There's a lot, so you can share it with Jessup," Coriolanus told her. "Although I think Lysistrata brought him something."

"I would, but he stopped eating." Lucy Gray shot Jessup a worried look. "Might just be nerves. He's acting kind of funny, too. Of course, all kinds of crazy's coming out of our mouths now."

"Like what?" asked Coriolanus.

"Like last night Reaper apologized to each of us personally for having to kill us," she explained. "He says he'll make it up to us when he wins. He's going to take revenge on the Capitol, although that part wasn't as clear as the killing us part."

Coriolanus's glance flitted over to Reaper, who was not only powerful but apparently good at mind games. "What was the response to that?"

"Most people just stared at him. Jessup spit in his eye. I told him it wasn't over until the mockingjay sang, but that only confused him. It's his way of making sense of all this, I guess. We're all reeling. It's not easy . . . saying good-bye to your life." Her lower lip began to tremble, and she pushed her sandwich aside without taking so much as a bite.

Feeling the conversation taking a fatalistic turn, Coriolanus steered it in another direction. "Lucky you don't have to. Lucky you have triple the gifts of anybody else."

Lucy Gray's eyebrows shot up. "Triple?"

"Triple. You're going to win this thing, Lucy Gray," he said. "I've thought it through. The moment they hit that gong, you run. Run as fast as you can. Get up in those stands and put as much distance as you can between you and the others. Find a good hiding space. I'll get you food. Then you move to another space. Just keep moving and stay alive until the others all kill each other or starve to death. You can do it."

"Can I? I know I'm the one who pushed you to believe in me, but last night I got to thinking about being in that arena. Trapped. All those weapons. Reaper coming after me. I feel more hopeful in the daytime, but when it gets dark, I get so afraid I —" Suddenly, tears began streaming down her face. It was the first time she hadn't been able to contain them. On the stage after the mayor had hit her, or the time Coriolanus had given her bread pudding, she'd been on the verge of crying but managed to keep her tears in check. Now, as if a dam had broken, they flooded out.

Coriolanus felt something inside him unravel as he saw her helplessness and felt his own. He reached for her. "Oh, Lucy Gray . . ."

"I don't want to die," she whispered.

His fingers brushed the tears from her cheeks. "Of course you don't. And I won't let you." She sobbed on. "I won't let you, Lucy Gray!"

"You should let me. I've never been anything but trouble to you," she choked out. "Putting you in danger and eating your food. And I could tell you hated my ballad. You'll be well rid of me tomorrow."

"I'll be a wreck tomorrow! When I told you that you mattered to me, I didn't mean as my tribute. I meant as you. You, Lucy Gray Baird, as a person. As my friend. As my —" What was the word for it? Sweetheart? Girlfriend? He could not claim more than a crush, and that might be one-sided. But what could he possibly have to lose by admitting she'd gotten to him? "I felt jealous after your ballad, because I wanted you to be thinking about me, not someone from your past. It's stupid, I know. But you're the most incredible girl I've ever met. Really. Extraordinary in every way. And I . . ." Tears welled in his own eyes, but he blinked them away. He had to stay strong for them both. "And I don't want to lose you. I refuse to lose you. Please, don't cry."

"I'm sorry. I'm sorry. I'll stop. It's just . . . I feel so alone," she said.

"You're not alone." He took her hand. "And you won't be alone in the arena; we'll be together. I'll be there every moment. I won't take my eyes off of you. We'll win this thing together, Lucy Gray. I promise."

She clung to him. "Sounds almost possible, the way you say it."

"It's more than possible," he asserted. "It's probable. It's inevitable, if you just follow the plan."

"You really believe that?" she said, watching his face. "Because if I thought you did, it could go a long way to making me believe it, too."

The moment required a grand gesture. Fortunately, he had one. He had been on the fence, weighing the risk, but he couldn't leave her like this, with nothing to hold on to. It was a matter of honor. She was his girl, she had saved his life, and he had to do everything he could to save hers.

"Listen. Are you listening?" She was still crying, but her sobs had quieted to small, intermittent gasps. "My mother left me something when she died. It's my most precious possession. I want you to have it in the arena, for good luck. It's a loan, mind you. I fully expect you to return it to me. Otherwise, I could never part with it." Coriolanus reached into his pocket, extended his hand, and fanned out his fingers. On his palm, gleaming in the last rays of the sun, sat his mother's silver compact.

Lucy Gray's mouth dropped open at the sight of it, and

she wasn't easy to impress. She reached out and caressed the exquisitely engraved rose, the antique silver, before drawing back regretfully. "Oh, I couldn't take it. It's too fine. It's enough you offered it, Coriolanus."

"Are you sure?" he asked, teasing her a bit. He smoothly clicked the latch and held it up so she could see her reflection in the mirror.

Lucy Gray drew in a quick breath and laughed. "Well, now you're playing on my weakness." And it was true. She was always so careful with her appearance. Not vain, really. Just conscious. She noticed the empty well where the cake of powder had sat an hour earlier. "Did there used to be powder here?"

"There did, but —" began Coriolanus. He paused. If he said it, there was no going back. On the other hand, if he didn't, he might be losing her for good. His voice dropped to a whisper. "I thought you might want to use your own."

Lucy Gray understood instantly. Her eyes darted to the Peacekeepers, none of whom were paying attention, and she leaned in and took a sniff of the compact. “Mm, you can still smell it, though. Lovely.”

“Like roses,” he said.

“Like you,” she said. “It really would be like having you with me, wouldn’t it?”

“Go on,” he urged her. “Take me with you. Take it.”

Lucy Gray wiped away her tears with the back of her hand. “Okay, but it’s a loaner.” She took the compact, slipped it into her pocket, and gave it a pat. “It helps to clarify my thinking. Somehow, winning the Games is just too large a thing to conceive of. But if I say, ‘I need to get this back to Coriolanus,’ I can wrap my mind around that.”

They talked a bit more, mostly about the layout of the arena and where the best hiding places might be, and he got half of the sandwich and all of a peach into her by the time Professor Sickle blew her whistle. Coriolanus wasn’t sure how it happened, but they must have both risen, both moved forward, because he found her in his arms, her hands clutching his shirtfront, as he locked her in an embrace.

“You’re all I’m going to think about in that arena,” she whispered.

“Not that guy back in Twelve?” he said only half-jokingly.

"No, he made sure he killed anything I felt for him," she said. "The only boy my heart has a sweet spot for now is you."

Then she gave him a kiss. Not a peck. A real kiss on the lips, with hints of peaches and powder. The feel of her mouth, soft and warm against his own, sent sensations surging through his body. Rather than pulling back, he held her even tighter as the taste and touch of her made his head spin. So this was what people were talking about! This was what made them so crazy! When they finally broke apart, he drew a deep breath, as if surfacing from the depths. Lucy Gray's lashes fluttered open, and the look in her eyes matched his own. They simultaneously leaned in for another kiss when the Peacekeepers laid hands on her and led her away.

Festus nudged him on the way out of the hall. "That was some good-bye."

Coriolanus just shrugged. "What can I say? I'm irresistible."

"I guess," Festus answered. "I tried to give Coral a reassuring pat on the shoulder and she about broke my wrist."

The kiss left him giddy. Beyond a doubt he'd crossed a line, but he didn't regret it. . . . It had been amazing. He walked home alone, savoring the bittersweet parting, electrified by his daring. Maybe he'd broken a rule or two by giving her the compact and suggesting she fill it with rat poison, who knew? There was no real rule book for the Hunger Games. Okay, he probably had. But even so, it was worth it. For her. Still, he wasn't telling anyone, not even Tigris.

It wasn't a game changer necessarily. It would take cleverness and luck to poison another tribute. But Lucy Gray was clever, and no more unlucky than the others. They would have to ingest the poison, so his job would be to get her the food to use as bait. He felt more in control, having something to do besides watch.

After the Grandma'am had gone to bed, he confided in Tigris. "I think she's fallen in love with me."

"Of course she has. What do you feel for her?" she asked.

"I don't know," he answered. "I kissed her good-bye."

Tigris raised her eyebrows. "On the cheek?"

"No. On the lips." He thought about how to explain it, but all he could muster was "She's something else." Which was undeniable, on so many levels. The truth was, he didn't have much experience when it came to girls, and even less when it came to love. Keeping the Snows' situation a secret had always been the top priority. The cousins rarely had anyone to the apartment, even when Tigris had fallen hard in her final year of the Academy. Her reluctance to bring her sweetheart home had been taken as lack of commitment and had been a deciding factor in the breakup. Coriolanus took the incident as a warning not to become too deeply entangled with anyone himself. Plenty of his classmates had been interested in him, but he'd skillfully kept them at arm's length. The excuse of that broken elevator had come in handy, and the Grandma'am had had several fictional ailments that required absolute quiet. There had been that one thing, last year, in the alley behind the train station, but that wasn't really a romance so much as a dare Festus had put him up to. Between the posca and the darkness, the memory was sketchy at best. On reflection, he had never even learned her name, but it had earned him the reputation of being rather a player.

But Lucy Gray was his tribute, headed into the arena. And even if the circumstances were different, she'd still be a girl from the districts, or at least not Capitol. A second-class citizen. Human, but bestial. Smart, perhaps, but not evolved. Part of a shapeless mass of unfortunate, barbaric creatures that hovered on the periphery of his consciousness. Surely, if there had ever been an exception to the rule, it was Lucy Gray Baird. A person who defied easy definition. A rare bird, just like him. Why else had the pressure of her lips on his turned his knees to water?

Coriolanus fell asleep that night replaying the kiss in his head. . . .

The morning of the Hunger Games dawned bright and clear. He readied himself, ate the eggs Tigris prepared for him, and made the long, hot walk to Capitol News. He declined the thick makeup that Lucky had spackled on his own face, but allowed a light dusting of powder, not wanting to be too sweaty for the cameras. Calm and unruffled: Those were the qualities a Snow should project. The powder smelled sweet but lacked the refinement of his mother's cake, which was tucked in his sock drawer back home.

"Good morning, Mr. Snow." Dr. Gaul's voice snapped him to attention. Of course, she was here at the television studio. Where else would she be on the opening morning of the Games?

Why Dean Highbottom had found it necessary to make an appearance, he didn't know, but his bleary eyes peered down at Coriolanus. "We hear there was quite a touching scene when you parted from your tribute last night."

Ugh. Would it be possible to find two people less capable of love? How did they even know about the kiss? Professor Sickle didn't seem like a gossip, so who was spreading it around? Probably most of the mentors had seen it. . . .

Never mind. These two would not get a rise out of him. "As Dr. Gaul pointed out, emotions are running high."

"Yes, it's too bad she's not likely to last the day," said Dr. Gaul.

How he hated the pair of them. Gloating. Baiting him. Still, all he could allow himself was an indifferent twitch of the shoulders. "Well, as they say, it's not over until the mockingjay sings." He felt satisfaction at the puzzlement on their faces. They did not have a chance to question him, because Remus

Dolittle appeared to inform them that the boy tribute from District 5 had passed away in the night due to complications from asthma or some such — anyway, the veterinarian couldn't save him — and they had to go off and address his loss.

Try as he might, Coriolanus couldn't remember the boy, or even which of his classmates had been assigned to mentor him. In preparation for the opening of the Games, he'd updated the mentor list he'd received from Professor Demigloss. He'd decided, for simplicity's sake, to cross the teams off in pairs, regardless of what had happened to them. He didn't mean to be ruthless, but there was no other way to keep it straight. He pulled the list out of his book bag now to record this latest casualty.

10th HUNGER GAMES
MENTOR ASSIGNMENTS

DISTRICT 1
~~*Boy (Facet) — Livia Cardew*~~
~~*Girl (Velvereen) — Palmyra Monty*~~
DISTRICT 2
~~*Boy (Marcus) — Sejanus Plinth*~~
~~*Girl (Sabyn) — Florus Friend*~~
DISTRICT 3
Boy (Circ) Io Jasper
Girl (Teslee) Urban Canville
DISTRICT 4
Boy (Mizzen) Persephone Price
Girl (Coral) Festus Creed
DISTRICT 5
~~*Boy (Hy) — Dennis Fling*~~
Girl (Sol) Iphigenia Moss

DISTRICT 6
~~*Boy (Otto)* *Apollo Ring*~~
~~*Girl (Ginnee)* *Diana Ring*~~
DISTRICT 7
Boy (Treech) *Vipsania Sickle*
Girl (Lamina) *Pliny Harrington*
DISTRICT 8
Boy (Bobbin) *Juno Phipps*
Girl (Wovey) *Hilarius Heavensbee*
DISTRICT 9
~~*Boy (Panlo)* *Gaius Breen*~~
~~*Girl (Sheaf)* *Androcles Anderson*~~
DISTRICT 10
Boy (Tanner) *Domitia Whimsiwick*
~~*Girl (Brandy)* *Arachne Crane*~~
DISTRICT 11
Boy (Reaper) *Clemensia Dovecote*
Girl (Dill) *Felix Ravinstill*
DISTRICT 12
Boy (Jessup) *Lysistrata Vickers*
Girl (Lucy Gray) *Coriolanus Snow*

The number of Lucy Gray's competitors had now dropped to thirteen. Another gone, and a boy, too. This could only be good news for her.

His mentor sheet had begun to get a bit crumpled, so he folded it in crisp quarters and decided to put it in the outside pocket of his book bag for easy access. When he opened it, he discovered a handkerchief. He puzzled a moment, since his were always on his person, then remembered that this was the one Lucy Gray had returned after drying her eyes the day he'd brought her the bread pudding. It felt good to have something so personal, a talisman of sorts, and he slid the list in carefully beside it.

The only mentors invited to appear on the pre-show were the seven who'd participated on interview night. They had, by default, become the Capitol faces of the Games, even though several of their tributes seemed like long shots. A corner of the studio had been outfitted with a few upholstered living room chairs, a coffee table, and a slightly crooked chandelier. Most of the mentors rehashed their tributes' backgrounds, playing up any dangerous elements they could.

Since Coriolanus had devoted his entire interview to Lucy Gray's song, he was the only one with fresh material. Pleased to have something new, Lucky Flickerman let him run over his allotted time. After filling in the usual details, Coriolanus spent most of the time talking about the Covey and emphasizing that Lucy Gray was not really district, no, not really at all. The Covey had a long history as musical performers, were artists of a kind rarely seen, and were no more like district residents than people from the Capitol were. In fact, if you thought about it, they almost *were* Capitol, and only by a series of misfortunes had somehow landed, or quite possibly been mistakenly detained, in District 12. Surely people could see how at home Lucy Gray seemed in the Capitol? And Lucky had to agree that yes, yes, there was something special about the girl.

Lysistrata shot him a look of annoyance as she took his seat, which he understood when he realized she was trying to tie Jessup to Lucy Gray in her interview and win sympathy for the two as a pair. While it was true that Jessup was District 12 coal miner stock through and through, hadn't the two of them shown a natural partnership from the first bow? And who hadn't noticed the unusual closeness between them, so often absent in tributes from the same district? In fact, Lysistrata was convinced that they were devoted to each other. With Jessup's strength and Lucy Gray's ability to charm the audience, she felt sure this year's victor would come from District 12.

The reason for Dean Highbottom's presence became clear when he followed on Lysistrata's heels. He managed to discuss the mentor-tribute program as if he hadn't been drugged the entire time. Actually, Coriolanus found it a little unsettling how lucid some of his observations were. He noted that the Capitol students had begun with certain prejudices against their district counterparts, but in the two weeks since the reaping, many had formed a new appreciation and respect for them. "It's essential, as they say, to know your enemy. So what better way to get to know each other than to join forces in the Hunger Games? The Capitol won the war only after a long, hard fight, and recently our arena was bombed. To imagine that on either side we lack intelligence, strength, or courage would be a mistake."

"But surely, you're not comparing our children to theirs?" asked Lucky. "One look tells you ours are a superior breed."

"One look tells you ours have had more food, nicer clothing, and better dental care," said Dean Highbottom. "Assuming anything more, a physical, mental, or especially a moral superiority, would be a mistake. That sort of hubris almost finished us off in the war."

"Fascinating," said Lucky, seemingly for lack of a better response. "Your views are absolutely fascinating."

"Thank you, Mr. Flickerman. I can think of no one whose opinion I value more," deadpanned the dean.

Coriolanus thought the dean's eye roll was implied, but Lucky blushed in response. "That's very kind, Mr. Highbottom. As we all know, I am only a humble weatherman."

"And a budding magician," Dean Highbottom reminded him.

"Well, perhaps I'll plead guilty to that!" said Lucky with a chortle. "Hold on, what's this?" He reached behind Dean Highbottom's ear and pulled out a small, flat candy with bright stripes. "I believe this is yours." He presented it to Dean Highbottom, the colors smearing his damp palm.

Dean Highbottom made no move to take it. "My goodness. Where did that come from, Lucky?"

"Secrets of the trade," said Lucky with a knowing grin. "Secrets of the trade."

Cars were waiting to carry them back to the Academy, and Coriolanus found himself with Felix and Dean Highbottom. The two seemed to know each other socially, and they largely ignored Coriolanus while they caught up on gossip. It gave him time to reflect on what Dean Highbottom had said about the people in the districts. That they were essentially the equals of those in the Capitol, only worse off materially. It was a somewhat radical idea for the dean to be putting out there. Certainly, the Grandma'am and many others would reject it, and it diminished Coriolanus's own effort, which had been to present Lucy Gray as someone completely other than district. He wondered how much of that had had to do with a winning strategy, and how much of it reflected his confusion about his feelings for her.

It was not until they were headed into the hall, and Felix was distracted by a camera crew, that Coriolanus felt a hand on his arm. "You know that friend of yours from Two? The emotional one?" Dean Highbottom asked him.

"Sejanus Plinth," said Coriolanus. Not that they were actually friends, but that wasn't any of Dean Highbottom's business.

"You might want to find him a seat near the door." The dean

slipped his bottle from his pocket, ducked behind a nearby pillar, and dosed himself with morphling drops.

Before he could consider this, Lysistrata appeared in a temper. "Honestly, Coriolanus, you could work with me a little! Jessup keeps calling Lucy Gray his ally!"

"I had no idea that was your pitch. Really, I didn't mean to trip you up. If we get another chance, I'll work in the team angle," he promised.

"That's a big if," said Lysistrata with an exasperated huff.

Satyria made her way through the crowd and didn't help the situation when she crowed, "What a clever interview, my dear. I half believe your girl was Capitol-born myself! Now come on. You, too, Lysistrata! You need your badges and communicuffs!"

She led them through the hall, which, unlike in previous years, was buzzing with excitement. People were shouting good luck to him, congratulating him on the interview. Coriolanus enjoyed the attention, but there was something undeniably disturbing about it as well. In the past, these had been subdued occasions, in which people avoided eye contact and spoke only when necessary. Now an eagerness filled the hall, as if a much-loved entertainment awaited them.

At a table, a Gamemaker oversaw the distribution of mentor supplies. While all were given a bright yellow badge with the word *Mentor* emblazoned on it to wear around their necks, only the ones with tributes still in the Games were issued communicuffs, making them the objects of envy. So much personal technology had disappeared during the war and its aftermath, as manufacturing had focused on other priorities. These days, even simple devices were a big deal. The cuffs buckled onto the wrist and featured a small screen, where the tally of sponsor gifts blinked in red. All the mentors had to do was scroll down the list of food items, select one from the menu, and double-click on it for a Gamemaker to set its delivery by drone in motion. Some of the tributes had no gifts at all coming to them. Despite not appearing at the interviews, Reaper had picked up a few sponsors from his time in the zoo, but Clemensia was nowhere to be seen, and her communicuff sat unclaimed at the table, drawing covetous looks from Livia.

Coriolanus drew Lysistrata aside and showed her his screen. "Look, I've got a small fortune to work with. If they're together, I'll send in food for both."

"Thank you. I'll do the same. I didn't mean to snap like that. It's not your fault. I should've brought it up before." Her voice dropped to a hush. "It's just . . . I couldn't sleep last night, thinking about sitting through this. I know it's to punish the districts, but haven't we punished them enough? How long do we have to keep dragging the war out?"

"I think Dr. Gaul believes forever," he said. "Like she told us in class."

"It's not just her. Look at everybody." She indicated the party-like atmosphere of the room. "It's revolting."

Coriolanus tried to calm her. "My cousin said to remember this isn't of our making. That we're still children, too."

"That doesn't help, somehow. Being used like this," said Lysistrata sadly. "Especially when three of us are dead."

Used? Coriolanus had not thought of being a mentor as anything but an honor. A way to serve the Capitol and perhaps gain a little glory. But she had a point. If the cause wasn't honorable, how could it be an honor to participate in it? He felt confused, then manipulated, then undefended. As if he were more a tribute than a mentor.

"Tell me it will be over quickly," Lysistrata said.

"It will be over quickly," Coriolanus reassured her. "Want to sit together? We can coordinate our gifts."

"Please," she said.

The whole school had assembled by this time. They made their way over to the section of twenty-four mentor seats, which were set in the same place they'd been for the reaping. Everyone able was required to attend, whether they had a viable tribute or not. "Let's not sit in the front," said Lysistrata. "I don't want that camera right in my face when he's killed." She was right, of course. The camera would go to the mentor, and if Lucy Gray died, *especially* if Lucy Gray died, he was assured a good, long close-up.

Coriolanus obliged her by heading toward the back row. As they settled themselves in, he turned his attention to the giant screen on which Lucky Flickerman acted as tour guide to the districts, giving background about their industries, spiced with weather facts and the occasional magic trick. The Hunger Games had been a big break for Lucky, and he was not above accompanying his District 5 spiel on energy with some gadget that made his hair stand on end. "It's electrifying!" he panted.

"You're an idiot," muttered Lysistrata, and then something caught her attention. "That must've been an awful flu."

Coriolanus followed her gaze to the table, where Clemensia had just collected her communicuff. She was scanning the room for someone. . . . Oh, it was him! The moment their eyes met, she made a beeline for the back row, and she didn't look happy. She looked terrible, really. The bright yellow of her eyes had faded to a pale pollen shade, and a long-sleeved, high-collared, white blouse concealed the scaly area, but even with those improvements, she radiated sickliness. She picked distractedly at the dry patches on her face, and her tongue, while not protruding from her mouth, seemed bent on exploring the inside of her cheek. She made her way to the seat directly in front of him and stood there, flicking bits of skin randomly into the air as she examined him.

"Thanks for visiting, Coryo," Clemensia said.

"I meant to, Clemmie, I was pretty beat-up —" he started to explain.

She cut him off. "Thanks for contacting my parents. Thanks for letting them know where I was."

Lysistrata looked puzzled. "We knew where you were, Clem. They said you couldn't have visitors because you were contagious. I tried to call once, but they said you were sleeping."

Coriolanus ran with that. "I tried, too, Clemmie. Repeatedly. They always gave me the runaround. And as to your parents, the doctors promised they were on the way." None of that was true, but what could he say? Obviously, the venom had unbalanced her, or she wouldn't even be bringing the whole incident up in such a public setting. "If I was wrong, I'm sorry. As I said, I've been recovering myself."

"Really?" she said. "You looked top-notch at the interview. You and your tribute."

"Easy, Clem. It's not his fault you got sick," said Festus, who'd arrived in time to hear enough of the conversation.

"Oh, shut up, Festus. You have no idea what you're talking about!" Clemensia spat out, and stomped off to take a seat near the front.

Festus settled down next to Lysistrata. "What's her problem? Other than she looks like she's molting."

"Oh, who knows? We're all a mess," said Lysistrata.

"Still, that isn't like her. I wonder what —" Festus began.

"Sejanus!" Coriolanus called out, happy for an interruption. "Over here!" There was an empty seat next to him, and he needed to shift the conversation.

"Thanks," said Sejanus, dropping into the seat on the end. He looked unwell, exhausted, with a feverish sheen on his skin.

Lysistrata reached across Coriolanus and pressed one of his hands. "The sooner it starts, the sooner it can be over."

"Until next year," he reminded her. But he gave her hand a grateful pat back.

The students had barely been instructed to take their seats when the seal of the Capitol overtook the screens and the anthem drew everyone to their feet. Coriolanus's voice rang out over those of the other mentors, who mumbled their way through. Honestly, by this point, couldn't they make a little effort?

When Lucky Flickerman returned and extended his hands in a welcoming gesture, Coriolanus could see the bright candy smear from the magic trick on his palm. "Ladies and gentlemen," he said, "let the Tenth Hunger Games begin!"

A wide shot of the arena's interior replaced Lucky. The fourteen tributes who remained on his list were positioned in a large circle, awaiting the opening gong. No one paid any attention to them, or to the new wreckage from the bombing that littered the field, or to the weapons strewn on the dusty ground, or to the flag of Panem strung from the stands, adding an unprecedented decorative touch to the arena.

All eyes moved with the camera, riveted as it slowly zoomed in to the pair of steel poles not far from the main entrance of the arena. They were twenty feet high, joined by a crossbeam of similar length. At the center of the structure, Marcus hung from manacled wrists, so battered and bloody that at first Coriolanus thought they were displaying his corpse. Then Marcus's swollen lips began to move, showing his broken teeth and leaving little doubt he was still alive.

Coriolanus felt ill but incapable of looking away. It would have been horrifying to see any creature displayed this way — a dog, a monkey, a rat, even — but a boy? And a boy whose only real crime had been to run for his life? Had Marcus gone on a killing spree throughout the Capitol, it would have been one thing, but no such reports had followed in the wake of his escape. Coriolanus flashed back to the funeral parades. The grisliest exhibits — Brandy dangling from a hook and the tributes being dragged through the streets — had been reserved for the dead. The Hunger Games themselves had the twisted brilliance of pitting district child against district child, so the Capitol kept its hands clean of actual violence. There was no precedent for Marcus's torture. Under Dr. Gaul's guidance, the Capitol had reached a new level of retaliation.

The image drained the party atmosphere from Heavensbee Hall. The interior of the arena had no microphones, except for a few around the oval wall, so none were close enough to hear if Marcus was trying to speak. Coriolanus desperately wished for the gong to sound, to release the tributes into action and distraction, but the opening stasis stretched on.

He could feel Sejanus shaking with rage, and he had just turned to put a quieting hand on him, when the boy sprang from his seat and ran forward. The mentor section had five empty chairs in the front reserved for their missing classmates. Sejanus grabbed the one on the corner and hurled it toward the screen, smashing it into the image of Marcus's ravaged face. "Monsters!" he screamed. "You're all monsters here!" Then he dashed back down the aisle and out the main entrance to the hall. No one moved a muscle to stop him.

The gong sounded at that moment, and the tributes scattered. Most fled to the gates that led to the tunnels, several of which had been blown open by the latest bombing. Coriolanus could see Lucy Gray's bright dress heading for the far side of the arena, and his fingers gripped the edge of his seat, willing her forward. *Run*, he thought. *Run! Get out of there!* A handful of the strongest sprinted for the weapons, but after grabbing a few, Tanner, Coral, and Jessup dispersed. Only Reaper, armed with a pitchfork and a long knife, seemed ready to engage. But by the time he was on the offensive, no one remained to fight. He turned to watch the receding backs of his opponents, threw back his head in frustration, and climbed into a nearby stand to begin his hunt.

The Gamemakers took this opportunity to cut back to Lucky. "Wish you'd placed a bet but couldn't make it to the post office? Finally decided on a tribute to back?" A phone number flashed at the bottom of the screen. "You can do it all by phone now! Just call the number below, give your citizen digits, the name of the tribute, and the dollar amount you'd like to bet or gift, and you'll be part of the action! Or if you'd rather make a transaction in person, the post office will be open daily from eight to eight. Come on, don't miss out on this historic moment. It's your chance to support the Capitol and make a tidy profit, too. Be a part of the Hunger Games and be a winner! Now back to the arena!"

Within a few minutes, the arena had cleared of every tribute except Reaper, and after roaming around the stands for a bit, he ducked out of sight, too. Marcus and his agony became the focus of the Games again.

"Should you go after Sejanus?" Lysistrata whispered to Coriolanus.

"I think he'd rather be alone," he whispered back. Which was probably true but secondary to the fact that he didn't want to miss anything, trigger a response from Dr. Gaul, or publicly link himself to Sejanus. This growing perception that they were great friends, that he was the confidant of the loose cannon from the districts, was beginning to worry him. Passing out sandwiches was one thing, throwing the chair quite another. There were sure to be repercussions, and he had enough troubles without adding Sejanus to the list.

A very long half hour passed before a distraction drew the audience's attention. The bombs near the entrance had blown open the main gate, but a barricade had been built under the scoreboard. With its multiple layers of concrete slabs, wooden planks, and barbed wire, it was both an eyesore and a reminder of the rebel attack, which was probably why the Gamemakers hadn't given it much screen time. However, with little else going on, they relented to show the audience a skinny, long-limbed girl creeping out from the fortification.

"That's Lamina!" Pup told Livia, who was seated next to him a couple of rows ahead of Coriolanus.

Coriolanus had no recollection of Pup's tribute except that she'd been unable to stop weeping at the first mentor-tribute meeting. Pup had failed to prepare her for the interview and had thus forfeited his chance to promote her. He couldn't recall her district . . . 5 maybe?

A rather jarring voice-over set him straight. "Now we see fifteen-year-old Lamina from District Seven," Lucky said. "Mentored by our own Pliny Harrington. District Seven has the honor of providing the Capitol with the lumber used to repair our beloved arena."

Lamina surveyed Marcus, taking in his plight. The summer breeze ruffled her blonde halo of hair, and she squinted against the brightness of the sun. She wore a dress that looked to be fashioned from a flour sack and belted with a piece of rope, and insect bites dotted her bare feet and legs. Her eyes, puffy and exhausted, were reddened but tearless. In fact, she seemed strangely calm for her circumstances. Without haste, without nervousness, she crossed to the weapons and took her time choosing first a knife, then a small ax, testing each blade for sharpness with the tip of her thumb. She stuck the knife in her belt and swung the ax loosely back and forth, feeling its weight. Then she made her way to one of the poles. Her hand ran down the steel, which was rusty and paint-splattered from some previous job. Coriolanus thought she might try to chop it down, being from the lumber district and all, but instead she secured the ax handle between her teeth and began to climb it, using her knees and calloused feet to grip the metal. It looked natural, like a caterpillar making its way up a stem, but as someone who'd put in extra hours to scale the rope in gym class, he knew the strength it took.

When she reached the top of the post, Lamina regained her feet and slid the ax into her belt. Although the crossbeam couldn't have measured more than six inches in width, she easily walked along it until she stood above Marcus. Straddling the beam, she locked her ankles for support and leaned over toward his battered head. She said something that the microphones couldn't pick up, but he must have heard, because his lips moved in response. Lamina sat upright and considered the situation. Then she braced herself again, swung down, and drove the ax blade into the curved side of Marcus's neck. Once. Twice. And on the third time, in a spray of blood, she succeeded in killing him. Regaining her seat, she wiped her hands clean on her skirt and stared off into the arena.

"That's my girl!" Pup cried out. Suddenly, he appeared on the screen as the Heavensbee Hall camera streamed his reaction. Coriolanus caught a glimpse of himself a couple of rows behind Pup and sat up straighter. Pup grinned, revealing bits of his morning eggs in his braces, and gave a fist pump. "First kill of the day! That's my tribute, Lamina, from District Seven," he said to the camera. He held up his wrist. "And my communicuff is open for business. Never too late to show your support and send a gift!"

The phone number flashed on the screen again, and Coriolanus could hear a few faint pings coming from Pup's communicuff as Lamina received some sponsor gifts. The Hunger Games felt more fluid, more changeful than he had prepared for. *Wake up!* he told himself. *You're not a spectator, you're a mentor!*

"Thank you!" Pup waved at the camera. "Well, I think she deserves a little something, don't you?" He fiddled with the communicuff and looked up at the screen expectantly as the camera jumped back to Lamina. The audience watched with anticipation, as this would be the first attempt to deliver a gift to a tribute. A minute passed, then five. Coriolanus had begun to wonder if the technology had failed the Gamemakers, when a small drone clutching a pint-sized bottle of water in its claws appeared over the top of the arena by the entrance and made its way shakily to Lamina. It looped and dipped and even reversed course before crashing into the crossbeam a good ten feet from her and falling to the ground like a swatted insect. The bottle had cracked, so the water soaked into the dirt and vanished.

Lamina stared down at her gift, expressionless, as if she'd expected nothing more, but Pup burst out angrily, "Wait a minute! That's not fair. Someone paid good money for that!" The crowd murmured in agreement. No immediate remedy followed, but a replacement bottle flew in ten minutes later, and this time,

Lamina managed to snatch it from the drone, which followed its predecessor to a dusty death.

Lamina took an occasional sip of her water, but other than that, little movement occurred except the gathering of flies around Marcus's body. Coriolanus could hear the occasional ping from Pup's communicuff signifying additional gifts to Lamina, who seemed content to remain on the crossbeam. It wasn't a bad strategy, really. Safer than the ground, for sure. She had a plan. She could kill. In less than an hour, Lamina had redefined herself as a contender in the Games. She seemed a lot tougher than Lucy Gray anyway. Wherever she was.

Time passed. With the exception of Reaper, who could occasionally be seen prowling the stands, none of the tributes presented themselves as hunters, not even the armed ones. Had it not been for Marcus's presentation and Lamina's finishing him off, it would have been an exceptionally slow opening. Usually, some sort of bloodbath could be counted on to kick off the Games, but with so many of the competitive tributes dead, the field consisted largely of prey.

The arena shrank to a small window at the corner of the screen as Lucky appeared, giving more district background and dropping in a weather report for good measure. Having a full-time host for the Games was new territory, and he struggled to create the role. When Tanner climbed up and strolled along the top row of the arena, he quickly threw the broadcast back, but the tribute only sat awhile in the sun before vanishing into the passages beneath the stands.

A rustling in the back of Heavensbee Hall turned heads, and Coriolanus spotted Lepidus Malmsey making his way up the aisle with his camera crew. He invited Pup to join him, and their interview went live. Pup, a previously untapped source, rattled off every detail he could think of about Lamina and then added several more that Coriolanus felt were fabricated, but even that only took a few minutes. This set the pattern for the morning. Brief informational interviews with mentors. Long expanses of inactivity in the arena. Everyone welcomed the lunch break.

"You lied about it being over quickly," Lysistrata muttered as they lined up for the bacon sandwiches stacked on a table in the hall.

"Things will pick up," Coriolanus said. "They have to."

But it seemed they didn't. The long, hot afternoon brought only a few more tribute sightings and a quartet of carrion birds that circled lazily above Marcus. Lamina managed to hack away at his restraints enough to send him tumbling to the ground. For her efforts, Pup sent her a slice of bread, which she broke up, rolled into small balls, and ate one at a time. Then she stretched out on her stomach, secured her spindly frame by tying her rope belt around the beam, and dozed off.

Capitol News found short-lived relief by streaming the plaza in front of the arena, where concession stands had been set up to sell drinks and sweets to citizens who'd come down to watch the Games on two large screens flanking the entrance. With so little happening in the arena, most of the attention ended up on a pair of dogs whose owner had dressed them up like Lucy Gray and Jessup. Coriolanus felt conflicted about it — he didn't really like seeing that silly poodle in her rainbow ruffles — until a couple of pings registered on his communicuff and he decided there was no bad publicity. But the dogs tired and were taken home, and still nothing happened.

Five o'clock was nearing when Lucky introduced Dr. Gaul to the audience. He'd become visibly frazzled under the strain of keeping the coverage going. Throwing his hands up in bewilderment, he said, "What gives, Head Gamemaker?"

Dr. Gaul basically ignored him, speaking directly to the camera. "Some of you may be wondering about the slow start to the Games, but let me remind you what a wild ride it's been just getting here. Over a third of the tributes never made it into the arena, and those who did, for the most part, weren't exactly the powerhouses. In terms of fatalities, we're running neck and neck with last year."

"Yes, that's true," said Lucky. "But I think I speak for a lot of people when I say, where are the tributes this year? Usually, they're easier to spot."

"Perhaps you've forgotten about the recent bombing," said Dr. Gaul. "In previous years, the areas open to the tributes were largely restricted to the field and the stands, but last week's attack opened up any number of cracks and crevices, providing easy access to the labyrinth of tunnels inside the walls of the arena. It's a whole new Games, first finding another tribute, and then ferreting them out of some very dark corners."

"Oh." Lucky looked disappointed. "So we might have seen the last of some tributes?"

"Don't worry. When they get hungry, they'll start poking their heads out," Dr. Gaul replied. "That's another game changer. With the audience providing food, the Games could last indefinitely."

"Indefinitely?" Lucky said.

"I hope you've got a lot more magic tricks up your sleeve!" cackled Dr. Gaul. "You know, I've got a rabbit mutt I'd love to see you pull out of a hat. It's part pit bull."

Lucky blanched a bit and attempted a laugh. "No, thanks. I've got my own pets, Dr. Gaul."

"I almost feel sorry for him," Coriolanus whispered to Lysistrata.

"I don't," she answered. "They deserve each other."

At five o'clock, Dean Highbottom dismissed the student body, but the fourteen mentors with tributes stayed on, largely because their communicuffs only worked through transmitters at the Academy or the Capitol News station itself.

Around seven o'clock, a real dinner appeared for the "talent," which made Coriolanus feel important and right at the center of things. The pork chops and potatoes were certainly better fare than what they had at home — another reason for wanting Lucy Gray to stay alive. Sopping up the gravy on his plate, he wondered if she was hungry. As they collected their blueberry tarts and cream, he pulled Lysistrata aside to discuss the situation. Their tributes should have a nice little stash of food from the good-bye meeting, especially if Jessup had lost his appetite, but what about water? Was there a source inside the arena? And even if they wanted to, how would they go about sending in supplies without revealing their tributes' hiding spot? Dr. Gaul was likely right about the tributes poking their heads out if they wanted something. Until then, they reasoned, the best strategy would be to sit tight.

As they finished dessert, some activity in the arena drew the mentors back to their seats. Io Jasper's District 3 boy, Circ, crawled out of the barricade near the entrance and looked around before waving someone in. A small, scruffy girl with dark, frizzy hair scrambled out after him. Lamina, still napping on the beam, opened one eye to determine their threat level.

"No worries, my sweet Lamina," said Pup to the screen. "Those two couldn't climb a stepladder." Apparently, Lamina agreed, because all she did was adjust her body to a more comfortable position.

Lucky Flickerman came up in the corner of the screen, a napkin tucked into his collar and a smudge of blueberry on his chin, and reminded the audience that the children were the tributes from District 3, the technology district. Circ was the boy who'd claimed he could ignite things with his glasses. "And the girl's name is . . ." Lucky glanced off-screen for a cue card. "Teslee! Teslee from Three! And she's being mentored by our own . . ." Lucky looked off again, but this time seemed lost. "That would be our own . . ."

"Oh, make an effort," Urban Canville grumbled from the first row. Like Io, his parents were some kind of scientists, physicists maybe? Urban was so ill-tempered everyone felt fine resenting the perfect scores he brought in on calculus tests. Coriolanus thought he could hardly blame Lucky for laziness after ditching the interview. Teslee looked small but not hopeless.

"Our own Turban Canville!" said Lucky.

"Urban, not Turban!" said Urban. "Honestly, could they get a professional?"

"Unfortunately, we did not see Turban and Teslee at the interview," said Lucky.

"Because she refused to speak to me!" Urban snapped.

"Somehow immune to his charms," said Festus, causing the back row to laugh.

"I'm going to send Circ something right now. No telling when I'll see him again," announced Io, working her communicuff. Coriolanus could see Urban following suit.

Circ and Teslee quickly skirted around Marcus's body and crouched down to examine the broken drones. Their hands moved delicately over the equipment, assessing the damage, probing into compartments that would have gone unnoticed otherwise. Circ removed a rectangular object that Coriolanus took for a battery and gave Teslee a thumbs-up. Teslee reattached some wires on hers, and the drone lights blinked. They grinned at each other.

"Oh, my!" exclaimed Lucky. "Something exciting happening here!"

"It would be more exciting if they had the controllers," said Urban, but he seemed a little less angry.

The pair was still examining the drones when two more flew in and dropped some bread and water in their general vicinity. As they gathered up their gifts, a figure appeared deep in the arena. They consulted, then each picked up a drone and hastily beat a path back to the barricade. The figure turned out to be Reaper, who ducked into one of the tunnels and emerged carrying someone in his arms. As the cameras trained on them, Coriolanus saw it was Dill, who seemed to have shrunk, her body curled up in the fetal position. She stared dully into the evening sun that dappled her ashen skin. A cough brought a strand of bloody spittle out of the side of her mouth.

"I'm surprised she lasted the day," Felix commented to no one in particular.

Reaper stepped around the debris from the bombing until he reached a sunny spot and laid Dill down on a charred piece of wood. She shivered despite the heat. He pointed up at the sun and said something, but she didn't react.

"Isn't he the one who promised to kill all the others?" asked Pup.

"Doesn't look so tough to me," said Urban.

"She's his district partner," said Lysistrata. "And she's almost dead now. Tuberculosis, probably."

That quieted people down, as a bad strain of the stuff still cropped up around the Capitol, where it was barely managed as a chronic condition, let alone cured. In the districts, of course, it was a death sentence.

Reaper paced restlessly for a minute, either eager to get back to the hunt or unable to handle Dill's suffering. Then he gave her one last pat and loped toward the barricade.

"Shouldn't you send him something?" Domitia said to Clemensia.

"What for? He didn't kill her; he just carried her. I'm not going to reward him for that," Clemensia retorted.

Coriolanus, who'd been avoiding her all day, decided he'd made the right decision. Clemensia wasn't herself. Maybe the snake venom had altered her brain.

"Well, I might as well use what little I have. It's hers," Felix said, and punched something into his communicuff.

Two bottles of water flew in by drone. Dill seemed oblivious to them. After a few minutes, the boy who Coriolanus remembered juggling sprinted out of a tunnel, his black hair flowing behind him. Without missing a step, he reached down and grabbed the water, then disappeared through a large crack in the wall. A voice-over from Lucky reminded the audience that the boy was Treech, from District 7, mentored by Vipsania Sickle.

"Well, that's harsh," said Felix. "Might've given her one last drink."

"That's good thinking," said Vipsania. "Saves me money, and I don't have much to work with."

The sun sank toward the horizon, and the carrion birds wheeled slowly over the arena. At last, Dill's body convulsed with a final, violent bout of coughing, and a gush of blood soaked her filthy dress. Coriolanus felt unwell. The blood pouring from her mouth both horrified and disgusted him.

Lucky Flickerman came on and announced that Dill, the girl tribute from District 11, had died of natural causes. Sadly, that meant they wouldn't be seeing much more of Felix Ravinstill. "Lepidus, can we have a few last words with him from Heavensbee Hall?"

Lepidus pulled Felix out and asked him how he felt about having to leave the Games.

"Well, it isn't a shock, really. The girl was on her last legs when she got here," said Felix.

"I think it's enormously to your credit that you got her through the interview," said Lepidus sympathetically. "Many mentors didn't manage even that."

Coriolanus wondered if Lepidus's high praise had more to do with Felix's being the grandnephew of the president than anything else, but he didn't begrudge it. It set a precedent for a level of success that he'd already surpassed, so even if Lucy Gray didn't last the night, he could still be viewed as a standout. But she *must* last the night, and then another, and then another until she won. He had promised to help her, but so far he'd done absolutely nothing except promote her to the audience.

Back in the studio, Lucky heaped a few more compliments on Felix and signed off. "As night falls on the arena, most of our tributes have bedded down, and so should you. We'll keep an eye on things here, but we don't really expect much action until morning. Pleasant dreams."

The Gamemakers cut to a wide shot of the arena, where the silhouette of Lamina on her beam was about all Coriolanus could make out. After dark, the arena had no lighting except what the moon provided, and that usually didn't make for good viewing. Dean Highbottom said they might as well go home, although bringing a toothbrush and a change of clothes for the future would be a good idea. They all shook hands with Felix and congratulated him on a job well done, and most of them meant it, as the day had cemented the mentor bond in a brand-new way. They were members of a special club that would dwindle down to one but always define them all.

As he walked home, Coriolanus did the math. Two more tributes were dead, but he'd stopped counting Marcus as a contender awhile back. Still, only thirteen left, and only twelve competitors that Lucy Gray needed to survive. And, as Dill and the asthmatic boy from District 5 had proven, a lot of it could come down to a matter of her simply outliving the others. He thought back to yesterday: wiping away her tears, the promise to keep her alive, the kiss. Was she thinking of him now? Was she missing him the way he was missing her? He hoped she would make an appearance tomorrow and he could get her some food and water. Remind the audience of her existence. He'd only had a few new gifts in the afternoon, and that might've been due to her alliance with Jessup. Lucy Gray's charming songbird persona was becoming less impressive with each grim moment in the Hunger Games. No one knew about the rat poison but him, so that didn't help her standing.

Hot and tired from the stressful day, he wanted nothing more than to shower and sink into bed, but the moment he stepped into the apartment, the fragrance of the jasmine tea reserved for company wafted over him. Who would be visiting at this hour? And on opening day, at that? It was far too late for the Grandma'am's friends, far too late for neighbors to be dropping in, and they weren't the dropping-in kind anyway. Something must be wrong.

The Snows rarely used the television in the formal living room, but, of course, they had one. Its screen showed the darkened arena, just as he'd left it at Heavensbee Hall. The Grandma'am, who'd pulled a decent robe over her nightdress, perched stiffly on a straight-backed chair at the tea table while Tigris poured out a steaming cup of pale liquid for their guest.

For there sat Mrs. Plinth, frumpier than ever, her hair disheveled and her dress awry, crying into a handkerchief. "You're such nice people," she sputtered. "I'm so sorry to have dropped in on you like this."

"Any friend of Coriolanus is a friend of us all," said the Grandma'am. "Plinch, did you say?"

Coriolanus knew she knew exactly who Ma was, but to be forced to entertain anyone, let alone a Plinth, at this hour challenged everything she stood for.

"Plinth," said the woman. "Plinth."

"You know, Grandma'am, she sent the lovely casserole when Coriolanus was injured," Tigris reminded her.

"I'm sorry. It's too late," said Mrs. Plinth.

"Please don't apologize. You did exactly the right thing," said Tigris, patting her shoulder. She spotted Coriolanus and looked relieved. "Oh, here's my cousin now! Perhaps he knows something."

"Mrs. Plinth, what an unexpected pleasure. Is everything all right?" Coriolanus asked, as if she wasn't dripping with bad news.

"Oh, Coriolanus. It isn't. Not at all. Sejanus hasn't come home. We heard he left the Academy this morning, and I haven't seen him since. I'm so worried," she said. "Where can he be? I know Marcus being like that hit him hard. Do you know? Do you know where he could be? Was he upset when he left?"

Coriolanus remembered that Sejanus's outburst, the throwing of the chair, the shouting of insults, had been confined to the audience in Heavensbee Hall. "He was upset, ma'am. But I don't know that it's any cause for worry. He probably just needed to blow off some steam. Took a long walk or something. I'd do the same thing myself."

"But it's so late. It isn't like him to up and disappear, not without letting his ma know," she fretted.

"Is there anywhere you can think of he might go? Or somebody he might visit?" asked Tigris.

Mrs. Plinth shook her head. "No. No. Your cousin's his only friend."

How sad, thought Coriolanus. *To have no friends.* But he only said, "You know, if he'd wanted company, I think he'd have come to me first. You can see how he might have needed some time alone to . . . to make sense of all this. I'm sure he's all right. Otherwise you'd have heard of it."

"Did you check with the Peacekeepers?" asked Tigris.

Mrs. Plinth nodded. "No sign of him."

"You see?" said Coriolanus. "There's been no trouble. Maybe he's even home by now."

"Perhaps you should go and check," suggested the Grandma'am, a little too obviously.

Tigris shot her a look. "Or you could just call."

But Mrs. Plinth had calmed down enough to take the hint. "No. Your grandma's right. Home is the place I should be. And I should let you all get to bed."

"Coriolanus will walk you," said Tigris firmly.

As she'd left him no choice, he nodded. "Of course."

"My car's waiting down the block." Mrs. Plinth rose and patted her hair down. "Thank you. You've all been so kind. Thank you." She'd gathered up her voluminous handbag and was starting to turn when something on the screen caught her eye. She froze.

Coriolanus followed her gaze and saw a shadowy shape slip out of the barricade and cross toward Lamina. The figure was tall, male, and carrying something in his hands. *Reaper or Tanner*, he thought. The boy stopped when he reached Marcus's corpse and looked up at the sleeping girl. *I guess one of the tributes finally decided to make a move on her.* He knew he should watch, as a mentor, but he really wanted to get rid of Mrs. Plinth first.

"Shall I walk you to your car?" he asked. "I bet you'll find Sejanus in bed."

"No, Coriolanus," said Mrs. Plinth in a hushed voice. "No." She nodded at the screen. "My boy's right there."

The moment Ma said it, Coriolanus knew she was right. Perhaps only a mother would make the connection in that gloom, but with her prompting he recognized Sejanus. Something about the posture, the slight stoop, the line of the forehead. The white Academy uniform shirt glowed faintly in the dark, and he could almost make out the bright yellow mentor badge, still hanging by the lanyard on his chest. How Sejanus had gotten into the arena, he had no idea. A Capitol boy, a mentor no less, might not have drawn too much attention at the entrance, where you could buy fried dough and pink lemonade, where you could join the crowd watching the Games on the screen. Had he merely blended in, or even used his minor celebrity to set suspicions at bay? *My tribute's finished, so I may as well enjoy myself!* Posed for pictures? Chatted up the Peacekeepers and slipped in somehow while their backs were turned? Who would think he'd want to enter the arena, and why on earth had he?

On-screen, a shadowy Sejanus knelt, set down a parcel, and rolled Marcus onto his back. He did his best to straighten the legs, to fold the arms on the chest, but the limbs had grown stiff and defied arrangement. Coriolanus couldn't tell what was happening next, something with the parcel, but then Sejanus rose to his feet and held his hand over the body.

That's what he did at the zoo, thought Coriolanus. He remembered when, after Arachne's death, he'd caught a glimpse of Sejanus sprinkling something over the dead tribute's body.

"That's your son in there? What's he doing?" asked the Grandma'am, aghast.

"He's putting bread crumbs on the body," said Ma. "So Marcus has food on his journey."

"His journey where?" asked the Grandma'am. "He's dead!"

"Back to wherever he came from," said Ma. "It's what we do, back home. When someone dies."

Coriolanus couldn't help feeling embarrassed for her. If you ever needed proof of the districts' backwardness, there you had it. Primitive people with their primitive customs. How much bread had they wasted with this nonsense? *Oh, no, he starved to death! Somebody get the bread!* He had a sinking feeling that his supposed friendship was going to come back to haunt him. As if on cue, the phone rang.

"Is the whole city up?" wondered the Grandma'am.

"Excuse me." Coriolanus crossed to the phone in the foyer. "Hello?" he said into the receiver, hoping it was a wrong number.

"Mr. Snow, it's Dr. Gaul." Coriolanus felt his insides contract. "Are you near a screen?"

"Just got home, actually," he answered, trying to buy time. "Oh, yes, there it is. My family's watching."

"What's going on with your friend?" she asked.

Coriolanus turned his head away from the gathering and lowered his voice. "He's not really . . . that."

"Nonsense. You've been thick as thieves," she said. "'Help me give away my sandwiches, Coriolanus!' 'Empty seat next to me, Sejanus!' When I asked Casca what classmates he was close to, yours was the only name he could think of."

His civility to Sejanus had obviously been misread. Really, they were hardly more than acquaintances. "Dr. Gaul, if you'd let me explain —"

"I don't have time for explanations. Right now the Plinth brat's loose in the arena with a pack of wolves. If they see him, they'll kill him on the spot." She turned to speak to someone else. "No, don't cut away abruptly, that will only draw attention. Just make it as dark as you can. Make it look natural. A slow blackout, as if a cloud has drifted over the moon." She was back in the next breath. "You're a smart boy. What message will that send to the audience? The damage will be considerable. We must remedy the situation at once."

"You could send in some Peacekeepers," Coriolanus said.

"And have him bolt like a rabbit?" she scoffed. "Imagine that for a moment, the Peacekeepers trying to chase him down in the dark. No, we'll have to lure him out, as uneventfully as possible, so we'll need people he cares about. He can't stand his father, no siblings, no other friends. That leaves you and his mother. We're trying to locate her now."

Coriolanus felt his heart sink. "She's right here," he admitted. So much for his "acquaintances" defense.

"Well, done and done. I want you both here at the arena in twenty minutes. More, and it will be me serving you with a demerit, not Highbottom, and you can kiss any chance of a prize good-bye." With that, she hung up.

On his television, Coriolanus could see that the image had darkened. He could barely make out Sejanus's figure at all now. "Mrs. Plinth, that was the Head Gamemaker. She'd like you to meet her at the arena to collect Sejanus, and I'm to accompany you." He could hardly admit to more without giving the Grandma'am a heart attack.

"Is he in trouble?" she asked, wide-eyed. "With the Capitol?"

Coriolanus found it strange that she'd be more worried about the Capitol than an arena full of armed tributes at this point, but maybe she had reason after what had happened to Marcus.

"Oh, no. They're just concerned with his well-being. Shouldn't be long, but don't wait up," he told Tigris and the Grandma'am.

As fast as he could, short of carrying her, he moved Mrs. Plinth out the door, down the elevator, and through the lobby. Her car rolled up soundlessly, and the driver, most likely an Avox, only nodded at his request to be taken to the arena.

"We're rather in a hurry," Coriolanus told the driver, and the car sped up immediately, gliding through the empty streets. If it was possible to cover the distance in twenty minutes, they would.

Mrs. Plinth clutched her handbag and stared out the window at the deserted city. "First time I saw the Capitol, it was night, like this."

"Oh, yes?" said Coriolanus, only to be polite. Honestly, who cared? His entire future was on the line because of her wayward son. And one had to question the parenting of a boy who thought breaking into the arena would solve anything.

"Sejanus sat right where you are, saying, 'It'll be all right, Ma. It'll be okay.' Trying to calm me down. When we both knew it was a disaster," said Mrs. Plinth. "But he was so brave. So good. Only thinking of his ma."

"Hm. Must have been a big change." What was it with the Plinths anyway? To be constantly turning advantage to tragedy? You needed only to take a cursory glance at the interior of this car, the tooled leather, the upholstered seats, the bar with its crystal bottles of gem-colored liquids, to know they were among the most fortunate people in Panem.

"Family and friends cut us off," Mrs. Plinth went on. "No new ones to be made here. Strabo — his pa, that is — still thinks it was the right thing to do. No kind of future in Two. His way of protecting us. His way of keeping Sejanus from the Games."

"Ironic, really. Given the circumstances." Coriolanus tried to redirect her. "Now, I don't know what Dr. Gaul has in mind, but I imagine she wants your help getting him out of there."

"I don't know if I can," she said. "Him so upset and all. I can try, but he'll have to think it's the right thing to do."

The right thing to do. Coriolanus realized that this was what had always defined Sejanus's actions, his determination to do the right thing. That insistence, the way, for instance, he would defy Dr. Gaul when the rest of them were just trying to get by, was another reason he alienated people. Frankly, he could be insufferable with those superior little comments of his. But playing on that might be the way to manipulate him.

As the car pulled up to the entrance of the arena, Coriolanus saw an effort had been made to conceal the crisis. Only a dozen or so Peacekeepers were present, and a handful of Gamemakers. The refreshment booths had shut down, the day's crowd had dispersed earlier, so there was little to draw curious spectators. Stepping out, he noticed how quickly the temperature had dropped since his walk home.

In the back of a van, a Capitol News monitor displayed a split screen with the actual feed of the arena next to the darkened version going out to the public. Dr. Gaul, Dean Highbottom, and a few Peacekeepers were gathered around it. As Coriolanus walked up with Mrs. Plinth, he made out Sejanus kneeling next to Marcus's body, still as a statue.

"At least you're punctual," said Dr. Gaul. "Mrs. Plinth, I presume?"

"Yes, yes," said Mrs. Plinth, a quaver in her voice. "I'm sorry if Sejanus has caused any inconvenience. He's a good boy, really. It's just he takes things so to heart."

"No one could accuse him of being indifferent," Dr. Gaul agreed. She turned to Coriolanus. "Any idea how we might rescue your best friend, Mr. Snow?"

Coriolanus ignored the barb and examined the screen. "What's he doing?"

"Just kneeling there, looks like," said Dean Highbottom. "Possibly in some kind of shock."

"He appears calm. Perhaps you could send the Peacekeepers in now without startling him?" suggested Coriolanus.

"Too risky," said Dr. Gaul.

"What about putting his mother on a speaker, or a bullhorn?" Coriolanus continued. "If you can darken the screen, surely you can manipulate the audio as well."

"On the broadcast. But in the arena, we'd alert every tribute to the fact that there's an unarmed Capitol boy in their midst," said Dean Highbottom.

Coriolanus began to get a bad feeling. "What do you propose?"

"We think someone he knows needs to slip in as unobtrusively as possible and coax him out," said Dr. Gaul. "Namely, you."

"Oh, no!" burst out Mrs. Plinth with surprising sharpness. "It can't be Coriolanus. The last thing we need is to put another child in danger. I'll do it."

Coriolanus appreciated the offer but knew the chances of this were slim. With her red, swollen eyes and wobbly high heels, she did not inspire confidence as a covert operator.

"What we need is someone who can make a run for it, if necessary. Mr. Snow is the man for the job." Dr. Gaul gestured to some Peacekeepers, and Coriolanus found himself being suited up in body armor for the arena. "This vest should protect your vital organs. Here's your pepper spray and a flash unit that will temporarily blind your enemies, should you make any."

He looked at the small bottle of pepper spray and the flash unit. "What about a gun? Or at least a knife?"

"Since you're not trained, this seems safer. Remember, you're not in there to do damage; you're in there to bring your friend out as quickly and quietly as possible," instructed Dr. Gaul.

Another student, or even the Coriolanus of a couple of weeks ago, would have protested this situation. Insisted on calling a parent or guardian. Pleaded. But after the snake attack on Clemensia, the aftermath of the bombing, and Marcus's torture, he knew it would be pointless. If Dr. Gaul decided he was to go into the Capitol Arena, that's where he would go, even if his prize was not at stake. He was just like the subjects of her other experiments, students or tributes, of no more consequence than the Avoxes in the cages. Powerless to object.

"You can't do this. He's just a boy. Let me call my husband," begged Mrs. Plinth.

Dean Highbottom gave Coriolanus a little smile. "He'll be all right. It takes a lot to kill a Snow."

Had this whole idea been the dean's? Had he seen a neat shortcut to his ultimate goal of destroying Coriolanus's future? At any rate, he seemed deaf to Ma's entreaties.

With Peacekeepers at either elbow — for his safety, or to prevent him from bolting? — he crossed to the arena. He had little recollection of being carried out after the bombing — perhaps they'd gone out another exit? — but now he could see the significant damage to the main entrance. One of the two great doors had been entirely blown away, leaving a wide hole framed with twisted metal. Besides the guard, little had been done to secure this area other than placing a few rows of waist-high concrete barriers across the opening. Sejanus wouldn't have had much trouble getting past those if there'd been a decent distraction, and there'd been the bustle of a carnival most of the day. If the Peacekeepers had been concerned about rebel activity, they would have been focused on someone targeting the crowd. Still, it seemed a little too relaxed. What if the tributes tried to make a break for it again?

Coriolanus and his escort wove their way through the barriers and into the lobby, which had taken multiple hits. The few unbroken electric bulbs around the admission and concession booths showed a layer of plaster dust coating chunks of ceiling and floor, toppled pillars and fallen beams. To reach the turnstiles required navigating the debris, and again he could see how Sejanus might have crossed it undetected, with a little patience and a bit of luck. The turnstiles on the far right side had been targeted, leaving gnarled, melted metal shards and open access. Here, the Peacekeepers had built the first real fortification, installing a temporary set of bars encased in barbed wire, and a half dozen armed guards. The undamaged turnstiles were still an effective blockade, as they did not allow reentry.

"So he had a token?" asked Coriolanus.

"He had a token," confirmed an old Peacekeeper who seemed to be in command. "Caught us off guard. We're not really looking for people breaking into the arena during the Games, only out." He produced a token from his pocket. "This one's for you."

Coriolanus turned the disk in his fingers but made no move to the turnstiles. "How did he think he'd get out?"

"I don't think he did," said the Peacekeeper.

"And how will I get out?" asked Coriolanus. This plan seemed dicey at best.

"There." The Peacekeeper pointed to the bars. "We can pull back the barbed wire and tilt the bars forward, creating an opening big enough for you to crawl under."

"You can do that quickly?" he said doubtfully.

"We've got you on camera. We'll start moving the bars when you're successfully bringing him out," the Peacekeeper assured him.

"And if I can't convince him to come?" Coriolanus asked.

"We have no instructions on that." The Peacekeeper shrugged. "I guess you stay until the mission is accomplished."

A cold sweat bathed Coriolanus's body as the words registered. He would not be allowed back out without Sejanus. He looked through the turnstile to the end of the passage, where the barricade had been erected under the scoreboard. The one he'd seen Lamina, Circ, and Teslee scampering in and out of earlier in the Games. "What about that?"

"That's for show, really. It blocks the view of the lobby, of the street. Can't put that on camera," the Peacekeeper explained. "But you won't have trouble getting through it."

Then neither would the tributes, Coriolanus thought. He ran his thumb over the slick surface of the token.

"We've got you covered up to the barricade," the Peacekeeper said.

"So you'll kill any tributes who attack me," Coriolanus clarified.

"Scare them off anyway," said the Peacekeeper. "Don't worry, we've got your back."

"Excellent," said Coriolanus, not at all convinced. He steeled himself and jammed the token in the slot, then he pushed the metal arms. "Enjoy the show!" the turnstile reminded him, sounding ten times louder in the stillness of the night. One of the Peacekeepers chuckled.

Coriolanus made for the wall on the right and walked forward as swiftly and silently as he could. The red emergency lights, his only illumination, suffused the passageway with a soft, bloody glow. He pressed his lips tightly together, controlling his breathing through his nose. Right, left, right, left. Nothing, no one stirred. Perhaps, as Lucky had suggested, the tributes had all bedded down for the night?

He paused for a moment at the barricade. Just as the Peacekeeper had said, it was a sham. Flimsy layers of barbed wire mounted on frames, rickety wooden structures and concrete slabs arranged to block the view, not imprison the tributes. Probably hadn't been enough time for a real one, or perhaps it had been deemed unnecessary with the bars and Peacekeepers behind him. As it was, he had only to wind his way through the backdrop to find himself at the edge of the field. He hesitated behind a final stretch of barbed wire, surveying the scene.

The moon had risen high in the sky, and in the pale, silvery light he could make out the figure of Sejanus, back toward him, still kneeling over Marcus's body. Lamina hadn't stirred. Other than that, the immediate area seemed deserted. Was it, though? The wreckage from the bombings provided ample hiding places. The other tributes could be concealed a few yards away and he'd never know it. In the chilly air, his sweat-soaked shirt felt clammy against his skin, and he wished for his jacket. He thought of Lucy Gray in her sleeveless dress. Had she curled up against Jessup for warmth? The image didn't sit well with him, so he pushed it away. He could not think of her now, only of the present danger, and Sejanus, and how to get him to the other side of that turnstile.

Coriolanus took a deep breath and stepped out onto the field. He padded across the dirt, channeling the circus wildcats he had seen here as a boy. Fearless, and powerful, and silent. He knew he must not spook Sejanus, but he needed to get close enough to converse.

When he was ten feet behind him, he stopped and spoke in a hushed voice. "Sejanus? It's me."

Sejanus stiffened, then his shoulders began to shake. At first, Coriolanus took it for sobbing, but it was quite the opposite. "You really can't stop rescuing me, can you?"

Coriolanus joined in the laughter under his breath. "Can't do it."

"They sent you in to fish me out? What madness." Sejanus's laughter trailed off, and he rose to his feet. "Did you ever see a dead body?"

"A lot. During the war." He took it as an invitation to join Sejanus and closed in. There. He could grab his arm now, but what then? It was unlikely he could drag him from the arena. He shoved his hands into his pockets instead.

"I haven't so much. Not this close. At funerals, I guess. And at the zoo the other night, only those girls hadn't been dead long enough to stiffen up," Sejanus said. "I don't know if I'd rather be burned or buried. Not that it matters, really."

"Well, you don't have to decide now." Coriolanus's eyes swept the field. Was that a person in the shadows behind the broken wall?

"Oh, it won't be up to me," said Sejanus. "I don't know what's taking the tributes so long to find me. I must have been in here awhile." He looked at Coriolanus for the first time, and his brow wrinkled in concern. "You should go, you know."

"I'd like to," Coriolanus said carefully. "I really would. Only there's the matter of your ma. She's waiting out front. Pretty upset. I promised I'd bring you to her."

Sejanus's expression turned indescribably sad. "Poor Ma. Poor old Ma. She never wanted any of this, you know. Not the money, not the move, not the fancy clothes or the driver. She just wanted to stay in Two. But my father . . . Bet he isn't here, is he? No, he'll keep his distance until this is settled. Then let the buying begin!"

"Buying what?" The breeze ruffled Coriolanus's hair and made hollow, echoing sounds in the arena. This was taking too long, and Sejanus was making no effort to speak softly.

"Buying everything! He bought our way here, bought my schooling, bought my mentorship, and he goes nuts because he can't buy me," said Sejanus. "He'll buy you if you let him. Or at least compensate you for trying to help me."

Buy away, thought Coriolanus, thinking of next year's tuition. He only said, "You're my friend. He doesn't need to pay me to help you."

Sejanus laid a hand on his shoulder. "You're the only reason I've lasted this long, Coriolanus. I need to stop causing you trouble."

"I didn't realize how bad this was for you. I should have traded tributes when you asked," he answered.

Sejanus sighed. "It doesn't matter anymore. Nothing does, really."

"Of course it matters," Coriolanus insisted. They were coming now, he could feel it. The sense of a pack closing in on him. "Come out with me."

"No. There's no point," said Sejanus. "There's nothing left to do but die."

Coriolanus pressed him. "That's it? That's your only choice?"

"It's the only way I might possibly make a statement. Let the world see me die in protest," Sejanus concluded. "Even if I'm not truly Capitol, I'm not district either. Like Lucy Gray, but without the talent."

"Do you really think they'll show this? They'll quietly remove your body and say you died of the flu." Coriolanus stopped, wondering if he'd said too much, if it pointed too directly at Clemensia's fate. But it wasn't as if Dr. Gaul and Dean Highbottom could hear him. "They've all but blacked out the screen now."

Sejanus's face clouded over. "They won't show it?"

"Not in a million years. You'll be dead for nothing, and you'll have wasted your chance to make things better." A cough, small and muffled, but definitely a cough. Coming from the stands to his right. Coriolanus had not imagined it.

"What chance?" asked Sejanus.

"You have money. Maybe not now, but one day you'll have a fortune. Money has a lot of uses. Look how it changed your world. Maybe you could make changes, too. Good ones. Maybe if you don't, a lot more people will suffer." Coriolanus's right hand tightened around his pepper spray, then flitted to his flash unit. Which would actually help if he was attacked?

"What makes you think I could do that?" said Sejanus.

"You're the only one who had the guts to stand up to Dr. Gaul," said Coriolanus. He hated giving that to him, but it was true. He was the sole member of the class who'd defied her.

"Thank you." Sejanus sounded tired but a bit saner. "Thank you for that."

Coriolanus put his free hand on Sejanus's arm, as if comforting him, but really to grip his shirt if he decided to run. "We're being surrounded. I'm going. Come with me." He could see Sejanus starting to cave. "Please. What do you want to do, fight the tributes or fight *for* them? Don't give Dr. Gaul the satisfaction of beating you. Don't give up."

Sejanus stared down at Marcus for a long moment, weighing his options. "You're right," he said finally. "If I believe what I say, it's my responsibility to take her down. To end this whole atrocity somehow." He lifted his head, as if suddenly realizing their situation. His eyes turned to the stands, where Coriolanus had heard the cough. "But I won't leave Marcus."

Coriolanus made a snap judgment. "I'll get his feet." The legs were stiff and heavy, reeking of blood and filth, but he crooked the knees in his arms as best he could and hoisted Marcus's lower half. Sejanus encircled his chest with his arms, and they began to move, half carrying, half dragging the body toward the barricade. Ten yards, five yards, not far now. Once they'd cleared it, the Peacekeepers should provide some cover.

He tripped on a rock and went down, driving his knee into something sharp and piercing, but sprang back up, heaving Marcus's body with him. Almost there. Almost —

The footsteps came from behind him. Quick and light. Speeding from the barricade, where the tribute had lain in wait. Coriolanus reflexively dropped Marcus and spun around just in time to see Bobbin bring down his knife.

The blade glanced off his body armor and sliced his left upper arm. As Coriolanus leaped backward, he swung at Bobbin but only encountered air. He landed in a pile of debris, old boards, and plaster as his hand searched for some kind of defense. Bobbin sprang at him again, aiming the knife at his face. Coriolanus's fingers closed around a two-by-four, and he brought it up, catching Bobbin in the temple hard, sending him to his knees. And then he was on his feet, using the board like a club, bringing it down again and again without being sure where it made contact.

"We have to go!" Sejanus shouted.

Coriolanus could hear catcalls now, and feet pounding down the bleachers. Confused, he made a move toward Marcus's body, but Sejanus yanked him away. "No! Leave him! Run!"

Needing no persuasion, Coriolanus sprinted for the barricade. Pain shot from his elbow to his shoulder, but he ignored it, pumping his arms as hard as he could, the way Professor Sickle had taught them. When he reached the barricade, barbed wire bit into his shirt, and as he turned to pull it free, he saw them. The two tributes from District 4, Coral and Mizzen, and Tanner — the slaughterhouse kid — making straight for him, armed to the teeth. Mizzen drew his arm back to throw a trident. The fabric on Coriolanus's sleeve ripped wide as he yanked it from the barbed wire and dove out of the line of fire, with Sejanus right behind him.

Only a few weak rays of moonlight penetrated the layers of the barricade, and Coriolanus found himself crashing into wood and fencing like a wild bird in a cage, surely alerting any tribute who'd somehow missed his presence. He ran facefirst into a concrete slab, and Sejanus plowed into him from behind, smacking his forehead into the unrelenting surface a second time. When he pushed back, it was as if the concussion had never left. His head throbbed, and a cloud of confusion descended.

The tributes started up a whooping sound, rattling their weapons against the barricade as they tracked the mentors through the labyrinth. Which direction to go? The tributes seemed to be all around them. Sejanus grabbed his arm and began to pull him, and he stumbled blindly along behind, wounded and terrified. Was this it, then? Was this how he died? The fury at the injustice of it all, the mockery it made of his existence, sent a surge of energy through him, and he crashed past Sejanus, finding himself on his hands and knees in a cloud of soft, red light. The passageway! Up ahead he could make out the turnstiles, where the Peacekeepers were clustered at the temporary bars. He ran for his life.

The passageway wasn't long, but it seemed interminable. His legs rose and fell as if he were waist-high in glue, and black specks dotted his vision. Sejanus stayed steady at his elbow, but he could hear the tributes gaining. Something heavy and unyielding — a brick? — clipped the side of his neck. Another object punctured his vest and stuck, bobbing behind him until it fell with a clank. Where was the cover? The protective gunfire from the Peacekeepers? There was nothing, nothing at all, and the bars still stood flush with the floor. He wanted to scream for them to kill the tributes, shoot them dead in their tracks, but his breath was in too short supply.

Someone heavy-footed shrank his lead to a few yards, but once again remembering Professor Sickle's training, he didn't dare waste a second looking back to see who it was. Before him, the Peacekeepers finally managed to tilt the unit of bars inward, achieving a gap of about twelve inches at the ground. Coriolanus dove, sanding several layers of skin off his chin on the rough floor and just getting his hands beneath the bars, where the Peacekeepers latched on to him and gave a great yank. Lacking time to turn his head, the rest of his face scraped against the filthy surface until he reached safety.

The guards dumped him immediately to retrieve Sejanus, who gave a sharp cry as Tanner's knife cut open the back of his calf before he slid out of range. The bars were slammed into place, and bolts locked down the unit, but the tributes were undeterred. Tanner, Mizzen, and Coral jabbed their weapons through the bars at Coriolanus and Sejanus, spewing hate-filled taunts while the Peacekeepers banged on the turnstiles with their batons. Not a shot was fired. Not even a shot of pepper spray. Coriolanus realized that they must have been under orders to leave the tributes untouched.

As the Peacekeepers helped him to his feet, he spat out in rage, "Thanks for having our backs!"

"Just following orders. Don't blame us if Gaul thinks you're expendable, boy," said the old Peacekeeper who'd promised him cover.

Someone tried to steady him but he shoved them off. "I can walk! I can walk, no thanks to you!" Then he listed sideways, almost hitting the floor before they hoisted him up again and made their way back through the lobby. Coriolanus babbled a long string of profanities, which made no impression, and hung in their grip like deadweight until they dropped him, unceremoniously, just outside the arena. After a minute they deposited

Sejanus beside him. They both lay panting on the tiles that graced the front of the arena.

"I'm so sorry, Coryo," said Sejanus. "I'm so sorry."

Coryo was a nickname for old friends. For family. For people Coriolanus loved. And this was the moment Sejanus decided to try it out? If he'd had the energy, Coriolanus would have reached over and strangled him.

No one paid them any attention. Ma had vanished. Dr. Gaul and Dean Highbottom debated audio levels as they watched the feeds in the van. The Peacekeepers stood in loose clumps, waiting for instructions. Five minutes passed before an ambulance drove up and popped open its back doors. The boys were loaded in without so much as a glance from the authorities.

The medic gave Coriolanus a pad to hold against his arm wound while she dealt with the more pressing issue of Sejanus's calf, which was producing quite a bit of blood. Coriolanus dreaded returning to the hospital and that untrustworthy Dr. Wane, until he saw through the small pane of glass that they'd arrived at the Citadel, which seemed twice as scary. Unloaded onto gurneys, they were swiftly transported deep down to the lab where Clemensia had been attacked, leaving Coriolanus to wonder just what modifications they had in store for him.

Accidents must've been frequent in the lab, as a small medical clinic awaited them. It had lacked the sophistication for Clemensia's resurrection yet seemed adequate to patch up the boys. A white curtain divided their two hospital beds, but Coriolanus could hear Sejanus giving one-word answers to the doctors' inquiries. He gave little more himself as they stitched his arm and cleaned his raw face. His head ached, but he didn't dare tell them about the rebound of his concussion for fear he'd end up being admitted to the hospital for an indefinite stay. All he wanted was to get away from these people. Despite his protests, they stuck an IV in his arm to rehydrate him and deliver some cocktail of drugs, and he lay rigid on the bed, willing himself not to flee. Although he'd done Dr. Gaul's bidding, although he'd succeeded, he felt more vulnerable than ever. And here he lay, wounded and trapped, hidden away in her lair.

The pain eased in his arm, but he did not feel the velvet curtain of morphling draw around him. Some alternative drug must have been administered, because, if anything, his mind felt a heightened sharpness, and he noticed everything, from the weave of the bedsheet, to the tug of the tape on his raw skin, to the bitter taste the metal cup of water left on his tongue. Peacekeeper boots approached and withdrew, taking a limping Sejanus with them. Deep in the lab, a round of squeals heralded some creature's feeding time, and the faint scent of fish reached him. After that, a relative hush fell over the place for a long time. He considered trying to slip away but knew in his heart he was expected to wait. To wait for the soft slipper tread that inevitably made its way to his cubicle.

When Dr. Gaul pulled back the curtain, the twilight of the nocturnal lab gave Coriolanus the strange impression that she stood on the edge of a cliff, that if he were to give her even the smallest shove, she would topple backward into some great chasm, never to be heard from again. *If only*, he thought. *If only.* Instead she moved forward and placed two fingers on his wrist, checking his pulse. He flinched at the feel of her cool, papery fingers.

"I started out as a medical doctor, you know," she said. "Obstetrics."

How awful, Coriolanus thought. *To have you be the first person in the world a baby sees.*

"Wasn't really for me," said Dr. Gaul. "Parents always want reassurances you can't give. About the futures their children face.

How could I possibly know what they'd encounter? Like you, tonight. Who would've imagined Crassus Snow's darling baby boy fighting for his life in the Capitol Arena? Not him, for one."

Coriolanus didn't know how to respond. He could barely remember his father, let alone divine his imaginings.

"What was it like? In the arena?" asked Dr. Gaul.

"Terrifying," said Coriolanus flatly.

"It's designed to be." She checked his pupils, shining a light into each of his eyes. "What about the tributes?"

The light hurt his head. "What about them?"

Dr. Gaul moved on to his stitches. "What did you think of them, now that their chains have been removed? Now that they've tried to kill you? Because it was of no benefit to them, your death. You're not the competition."

It was true. They'd been close enough to recognize him. But they'd hunted down him and Sejanus — Sejanus, who'd treated the tributes so well, fed them, defended them, given them last rites! — even though they could have used that opportunity to kill one another.

"I think I underestimated how much they hate us," said Coriolanus.

"And when you realized that, what was your response?" she asked.

He thought back to Bobbin, to the escape, to the tributes' bloodlust even after he'd cleared the bars. "I wanted them dead. I wanted every one of them dead."

Dr. Gaul nodded. "Well, mission accomplished with that little one from Eight. You beat him to a pulp. Have to make up some story for that buffoon Flickerman to tell in the morning. But what a wonderful opportunity for you. Transformative."

 "Was it?" Coriolanus remembered the sickening thuds of his

board against Bobbin. So he had what? Murdered the boy? No, not that. It was an open-and-shut case of self-defense. But what, then? He had killed him, certainly. There would never be any erasing that. No regaining that innocence. He had taken human life.

"Wasn't it? More than I could've hoped. I needed you to get Sejanus out of the arena, of course, but I wanted you to taste that as well," she said.

"Even if it killed me?" asked Coriolanus.

"Without the threat of death, it wouldn't have been much of a lesson," said Dr. Gaul. "What happened in the arena? That's humanity undressed. The tributes. And you, too. How quickly civilization disappears. All your fine manners, education, family background, everything you pride yourself on, stripped away in the blink of an eye, revealing everything you actually are. A boy with a club who beats another boy to death. That's mankind in its natural state."

The idea, laid out as such, shocked him, but he attempted a laugh. "Are we really as bad as all that?"

"I would say yes, absolutely. But it's a matter of personal opinion." Dr. Gaul pulled a roll of gauze from the pocket of her lab coat. "What do you think?"

"I think I wouldn't have beaten anyone to death if you hadn't stuck me in that arena!" he retorted.

"You can blame it on the circumstances, the environment, but you made the choices you made, no one else. It's a lot to take in all at once, but it's essential that you make an effort to answer that question. Who are human beings? Because who we are determines the type of governing we need. Later on, I hope you can reflect and be honest with yourself about what you learned tonight." Dr. Gaul began to wrap his wound in gauze. "And a few stitches in your arm is a cheap price to pay for it."

Coriolanus felt nauseous at her words but even more enraged that she had forced him to kill for the sake of her lesson. Something that significant should have been his decision, not hers. No one's but his. "So, if I'm a vicious animal, then who are you? You're the teacher who sent her student to beat another boy to death!"

"Oh, yes. That role has fallen to me." She neatly finished the bandage off. "You know, Dean Highbottom and I read your essay through. What you liked about the war. A lot of fluff. Drivel, really. Until that bit in the end. The part about control. For your next assignment, I'd like you to elaborate on that. The value of control. On what happens without it. Take your time with it. But it might be a nice addition to your prize application."

Coriolanus knew what happened without control. He'd seen it recently, at the zoo when Arachne died, in the arena when the bombs went off, and then again tonight. "Chaos happens. What else is there to say?"

"Oh, a good deal, I think. Start with that. Chaos. No control, no law, no government at all. Like being in the arena. Where do we go from there? What sort of agreement is necessary if we're to live in peace? What sort of social contract is required for survival?" She removed the drip from his arm. "We'll need you back in a couple of days to check those stitches. Until then, I would keep the night's events to yourself. Better get home and catch a few hours of sleep. Remarkably, your tribute still needs you."

After she left, Coriolanus slowly pulled on his sliced, torn, bloody shirt and fastened the buttons. He wandered until he found the elevator to street level, and the disinterested guards waved him out. The trolleys ended at midnight, and the Capitol clock showed two, so he pointed his filthy shoes toward home.

The Plinths' luxurious car slid up beside him, and the window lowered to reveal the Avox, who stepped out and opened the back door for him. Coriolanus guessed he'd already taken Sejanus home, and Ma had sent him back. Since the car was empty of Plinths, he got in. One last ride, then he wanted nothing to do with that family ever again. When the driver let him out at his apartment, Coriolanus was presented with a large paper bag. Before he could object, the car pulled away.

Upstairs, he peeked in to see Tigris waiting by the tea table, wrapped in a ratty fur coat that had been her mother's. It was her security blanket, much as the rose powder compact had been his before he revamped it as a weapon. He grabbed a school jacket from the coatrack and pulled it over his damaged shirt before he went in to see her.

Coriolanus tried to make light of the dreadful night. "Surely, it's not so bad you need the coat?"

Her fingers dug into the fur. "You tell me."

"I will. Every bit of it. But in the morning, okay?" he said.

"Okay." When she reached up to hug him good night, her hand felt the bulge of the bandage on his arm. Before he could stop her, she pulled back the jacket and saw the blood. She bit her lip. "Oh, Coryo. They made you go into the arena, didn't they?"

He hugged her. "Not that bad, really. I'm here. Got Sejanus out, too."

"Not that bad? It's horrific to think of you in there. To think of anyone in there!" she cried. "Poor Lucy Gray."

Lucy Gray. Now that he'd been in the arena himself, her circumstances seemed even more dire than before. The thought of her huddled somewhere in the cold blackness of the arena, too petrified to close her eyes, made him ache. For the first time, he felt glad he'd killed Bobbin. At least he'd saved her from that animal. "It's going to be okay, Tigris. But you have to let me get some rest. You need to sleep, too."

She nodded, but he knew she'd be lucky to snatch an hour or two. He handed her the bag. "Courtesy of Ma Plinth. Breakfast, by the smell of it. See you then?"

Not bothering to bathe, he collapsed into a comatose sleep until the sound of the Grandma'am singing the anthem woke him. Time to be getting up anyway. Aching head to toe, he teetered to the shower, removed the gauze from his arm, and let the hot water scream over his scraped flesh. He had a tube of ointment from his time in the hospital and, although unsure of its use, dabbed it on his raw face and chin. The stitches on his arm snagged on his clean shirt, but no new bleeding appeared. He'd wear his jacket today just in case. Throwing a toothbrush and fresh uniform in his book bag, he took one last look in the mirror and sighed. *Bicycle accident*, he thought. *That's the story. Not that I've had a working bicycle in years.* Well, now he had an excuse for its broken condition.

Once he was presentable, the first thing he did was check the television to make sure no harm had come to Lucy Gray. But the camera hadn't shifted, and the only tribute visible in the early morning light was Lamina on her beam. Avoiding the Grandma'am, he came into the kitchen, where Tigris was warming up the leftover jasmine tea.

"Running late," he said. "I better get going."

"Take this for breakfast." She put a packet in his hands and placed a pair of tokens in his pocket. "And take the trolley today."

Needing to conserve energy, he did as he was told, riding the trolley and eating two loaded egg-and-sausage rolls Mrs. Plinth had sent over. His only regret about ditching the Plinths would be the loss of her cooking.

The main student body had been told to report at a quarter to eight, so the early birds consisted of the active mentors and a few Avoxes tidying the hall. Coriolanus couldn't help throwing a guilty look at Juno Phipps, who sat discussing her strategy with Domitia when she could have slept in. He didn't much like her — she was always throwing her family lineage in his face, as if his wasn't as good — but last night hadn't been fair to her either. He wondered how they would reveal Bobbin's death and how he would feel when they did. Besides queasy.

The only thing being served at Heavensbee Hall was tea, which brought grumblings from Festus. "If we have to be here early, you'd think they could at least feed us. What happened to your face?"

"Bike accident," Coriolanus said, loud enough for everyone to hear. He tossed the bag with the last roll to Festus, happy to be able to offer food for a change. He owed the Creeds more meals than he cared to remember.

"Thanks. This looks great," said Festus, digging in immediately.

Lysistrata recommended a cream to prevent infection, and they went ahead and took their seats as their schoolmates began to arrive.

Although the sun had been up for a few hours, nothing much appeared changed on the screen except the disappearance of Marcus's body. "I guess they removed it," said Pup. But Coriolanus thought it might still be by the barricade where he and Sejanus had abandoned it last night, just out of range of the shot.

At the stroke of eight, they all rose for the anthem, which his classmates finally seemed to be getting a handle on, and then Lucky Flickerman appeared, welcoming them to day two of the Hunger Games. "While you were sleeping, something pretty important happened. Let's take a look, shall we?" They cut back to the wide shot of the arena, and then slowly panned the camera round to the barricade, zooming in. As Coriolanus had suspected, Marcus's body lay where he and Sejanus had dropped it. A few feet away, Bobbin's battered form slumped against a chunk of concrete. It looked much, much worse than he'd imagined. The bloody limbs, the dislodged eye, the face so swollen it was unrecognizable. Had he really done that to another boy? And such a young boy, too, for in death Bobbin looked tinier than ever. Lost in that dark web of terror, it seemed he had. Perspiration beaded Coriolanus's forehead, and he wanted to leave the hall, the building, the entire event behind. But, of course, that wasn't an option. Who was he — Sejanus?

After a good long look at the bodies, the show cut back to Lucky as he pondered who might have done the deed. Then his mood changed abruptly. "One thing we do know is that we've got something to celebrate!" Confetti fell from the ceiling, and Lucky blew madly away on a plastic horn. "Because we've just hit the halfway mark! That's right, twelve tributes down, and only twelve to go!" A string of brightly colored handkerchiefs shot out of his hand. He swung it around his head, dancing and cheering, "Whoowee!" When he finally wound down, he adopted a sad expression. "But that also means we've got to say our farewells to Miss Juno Phipps. Lepidus?"

Lepidus had already positioned himself at the end of the unsuspecting Juno's aisle, and she had no choice but to join him and work through her disappointment on camera. Given a little notice, Coriolanus imagined she'd have comported herself more graciously, but as it was, she came off as sour and suspicious, questioning the recent developments as she flashed a leather binder inlaid with the Phipps family crest. "Something seems fishy to me," she told Lepidus. "I mean, what's he doing over there with Marcus's body? Who moved it? And how did Bobbin end up dead? I can't even imagine a likely scenario. I feel like there might have been foul play!"

The reporter sounded genuinely puzzled. "What would qualify as foul play, exactly? I mean, in the arena?"

"Well, I don't know *exactly*," steamed Juno, "but I, for one, would really like to see a replay of last night's events!"

Good luck with that, Juno, thought Coriolanus. Then he realized it did exist. In the back of the van, Dr. Gaul and Dean Highbottom had been watching both versions, the real feed and the one they'd darkened to obscure his mission. Even the regular one would be hard to make out. Still, he didn't like it, the idea that somewhere there was a record, however shadowy, of him killing Bobbin. If it were ever to get out . . . well, he didn't know what. But it made him uneasy.

Lepidus didn't dally with Juno, a sore loser who lacked Felix's grace in defeat, and she was directed back to her seat with a consoling pat on the back.

Still sparkly with confetti, Lucky seemed oblivious to her pain. He leaned in toward the camera with barely contained glee. "And now, what do you suppose? We've got an extra-big surprise — especially if you're one of the twelve remaining mentors!"

Coriolanus only had a moment to exchange questioning looks with his friends before Lucky bounded across the studio to reveal Sejanus sitting side by side with his father, Strabo Plinth, whose stern expression seemed carved from the very granite of his home district. Lucky took the host chair and patted Sejanus on the leg. "Sejanus, I'm sorry we didn't get a moment with you yesterday to let you comment on the demise of your tribute, Marcus." Sejanus just stared at Lucky uncomprehendingly. Lucky seemed to notice the abrasions on his face for the first time. "What's going on here? You look like you've been mixing it up yourself."

"I fell off my bike," Sejanus rasped, and Coriolanus winced slightly. Two biking mishaps in the same twelve-hour period seemed more than coincidental.

"Ouch. Well, I guess you have some pretty big news to share with us!" Lucky said with an encouraging nod.

Sejanus lowered his eyes for a moment, and while neither father nor son acknowledged each other, a battle seemed to be occurring.

"Yes," Sejanus finally began. "We, the Plinth family, would like to announce that we will be giving a prize for a full ride to the University to the mentor whose tribute wins the Hunger Games."

Pup let out a whoop, and the other mentors grinned at one another. Coriolanus knew most of them didn't need the money as badly as he did, if at all, but it would be a feather in anyone's cap.

"Sensational!" said Lucky. "What a thrill those twelve remaining mentors must be experiencing right now. Was this your idea, Strabo? To create the Plinth Prize?"

"My son's, actually," said Strabo, curving the edges of his lips up in what Coriolanus thought might be an attempt at a smile.

"Well, what a generous and appropriate gesture, especially given Sejanus's defeat. You may not have won the Games, but you've certainly taken home the prize for good sportsmanship. I think I speak for the Capitol when I say many thanks!" Lucky beamed at the pair, but as nothing else was forthcoming, he made a sweeping gesture with his arm. "All right, then, back to the arena!"

Coriolanus's mind reeled with the new development. Sejanus had been right about his father's hasty attempt to bury his son's outrageous behavior in cash. Not that it didn't merit damage control. He hadn't heard much reaction from the others in Heavensbee

Hall about the outburst with the chair, but he expected stories were going around. A prize for the victor's mentor seemed a small price to pay, really. What would Plinth offer to prevent word of Sejanus's trip into the arena from going public? Could he be planning to buy Coriolanus's silence?

Never mind, never mind that, Coriolanus told himself. The bigger news was the possibility of winning the Plinth Prize. It was independent of the Academy, so Dean Highbottom wouldn't have a say in it. Even Dr. Gaul would not. A full ride that would free him from their power and lift this awful anxiety about the future from his shoulders! Already high, the stakes of these Games shot into the stratosphere. *Focus,* he told himself, drawing slow, deep breaths. *Focus on helping Lucy Gray.*

What was there to do, though, until she showed her face? As the morning passed, it seemed few of the tributes were tempted to do so. Coral and Mizzen roamed around together for a bit, collecting food and water from Festus and Persephone, their mentors. They'd been spending time together, trying to come up with a joint strategy for their tributes, and Coriolanus could see that Festus was falling for her. Did you tell your best friend his crush was a cannibal? Never a rule book when you needed one.

When they returned to the dais after lunch they found the mentor seats had been reduced to twelve, leaving only enough space for those with tributes still in the Games.

"The Gamemakers requested it," Satyria told the final dozen. "It makes it easier for the audience to keep track of who's still a contender. We're to keep removing seats as your tributes are killed."

"Like musical chairs," said Domitia with a pleased look.

"But with people dying," said Lysistrata.

The decision to bump the losers from the dais made Livia even more bitter, if that was possible, and Coriolanus was glad to see her relegated to the regular audience section, where he wouldn't have to hear her snarky comments. On the other hand, it made it harder to put distance between himself and Clemensia, who seemed to spend all her free time glaring at him. He positioned himself in the last row, bolstered by Festus and Lysistrata, and tried to look engaged.

As the afternoon unrolled, his head got heavier and heavier, until Lysistrata had to nudge him twice to keep him awake. Perhaps it was fortunate the day required so little of him, given that the night had almost killed him. There were few tribute sightings, and Lucy Gray stayed completely hidden.

Not until the late afternoon did the Hunger Games finally present the kind of action that people expected. The girl tribute from District 5, a rickety little thing who had been one of the unwashed herd to Coriolanus, made her way out onto the bleachers at the far end of the arena. Failing to find her name, Lucky just managed to connect her with her equally forgettable mentor, Iphigenia Moss, whose father oversaw the Agriculture Department, and thus the flow of food around Panem. Contrary to expectations, Iphigenia always seemed on the verge of malnutrition, often giving her school lunch to her classmates and even blacking out on occasion. Clemensia had once told Coriolanus it was the only revenge she could take on her father, but refused to give any more details.

True to form, Iphigenia began to unload every bit of food she could on her tribute, but even as the drones made the long trek across the arena, Mizzen, Coral, and Tanner, who appeared to have formed some sort of pack after the previous night's adventure, materialized from the tunnels and began their hunt. After a brief chase along the bleachers, the trio surrounded the girl, and Coral killed her with a trident to the throat.

"Well, that's that," said Lucky, still unable to locate the tribute's name. "What can her mentor tell us, Lepidus?"

Iphigenia had already sought out Lepidus. "Her name was Sol, or maybe Sal. She had a funny accent. Not much more to tell."

Lepidus seemed inclined to agree. "Nice job getting her to the second half, Albina!"

"Iphigenia," said Iphigenia over her shoulder as she walked off the dais.

"That's right!" said Lepidus. "And this means there's only eleven tributes left!"

Which means ten between me and that prize, thought Coriolanus as he watched an Avox remove Iphigenia's chair. He wished he could get food and water to Lucy Gray. What would happen if he sent it in without knowing her location? On-screen, the pack collected Sol's, or Sal's, food and moved back toward the tunnels, probably to get some rest before the night came. Should he risk it now?

He discussed it in whispers with Lysistrata, who felt that it might be worth a try if they sent in drones together. "We don't want them getting too weak and dehydrated. I don't think Jessup's gotten anything down in days. Let's wait and see if they try and contact us. Let's give them until the supper break."

But Lucy Gray made an entrance just as the student body was being released to go home. She darted out of a tunnel, running at full pitch, her hair loosening from her braids and flying free behind her.

"Where's Jessup?" said Lysistrata with a frown. "Why aren't they together?"

Before Coriolanus could venture a guess, Jessup staggered out of the same tunnel Lucy Gray had fled from. At first, Coriolanus thought he had been wounded, possibly while defending Lucy

Gray. But then, what accounted for her flight? Were other tributes in pursuit? As the camera moved in on Jessup, it became apparent that he was ill, not hurt. Stiff-limbed and feverish with excitement, he swiped at the sun a few times before crouching down and springing almost immediately back to his feet for his first close-up.

Coriolanus wondered if Lucy Gray had found a way to poison him, but that didn't make sense. Jessup was too valuable as a protector, especially with the pack that had formed last night running around. What, then, ailed him?

Any number of things could've sickened him, any range of maladies been suspected, if it hadn't been for the telltale foam that began to bubble over his lips.

"He's rabid," Lysistrata said softly.

Rabies had made a comeback in the Capitol during the war. With doctors needed in the field, and facilities and supply lines compromised by the bombings, medical treatment had become sketchy for humans, like Coriolanus's mother, and almost nonexistent for the pampered Capitol pets. Vaccinating your cat wasn't on the list of priorities when you couldn't scrape up enough money for bread. How it began remained a matter of debate — an infected coyote from the mountains? A nocturnal encounter with a bat? — but the dogs spread it. Most of them were starving, abandoned casualties of the war themselves. From dog to dog, and then to people. The virulent strain developed with unprecedented speed, killing over a dozen Capitol citizens before a vaccination program brought it under control.

Coriolanus remembered the posters alerting people to the warning signs in animals and humans alike, adding just one more potential threat to his world. He thought of Jessup with his handkerchief pressed against his neck. "The rat bite?"

"Not a rat," said Lysistrata, shock and sadness on her face. "Rats almost never spread rabies. Probably one of those mangy raccoons."

"Lucy Gray said he mentioned fur, so I'd assumed . . ." He trailed off. Not that it mattered what had bitten Jessup; it was a death sentence any way you sliced it. He must have been infected about two weeks ago. "It was fast, wasn't it?"

"Very fast. Because he was bit in the neck. The quicker it gets to the brain, the quicker you die," Lysistrata explained. "And, of course, he's half-starved and weak."

If she said so, it was probably true. This was just the sort of thing he imagined the Vickers family discussing over dinner, in their calm, clinical manner.

"Poor Jessup," said Lysistrata. "Even his death has to be horrible."

The recognition of Jessup's illness put the audience on edge, setting off a wave of comments thick with fear and revulsion.

"Rabies! How did he get that?"

"Brought it from the districts, I'll bet."

"Great, now he'll infect the whole city!"

All the students dropped back into their seats, not wanting to miss anything, dredging up childhood memories of the disease.

Coriolanus stayed silent in solidarity with Lysistrata, but his concern grew as Jessup zigzagged across the arena in Lucy Gray's direction. No telling what was going on in his mind. Under normal circumstances, Coriolanus was certain he'd protect her, but he'd clearly lost his reason if she'd run for her life.

The cameras tracked Lucy Gray as she sprinted across the arena and began to scramble up the broken wall into the stands holding the main press box. Positioned midway in the arena, it occupied several rows and had somehow been spared in the bombing. She stopped a moment, panting, while she considered Jessup's erratic pursuit, then she made for the debris of a nearby concession stand. The skeleton of the frame remained, but the center had been blasted into bits and the roof had been flung thirty feet away. Strewn with bricks and boards, the area presented a sort of obstacle course that she traversed until she planted herself at the top of the mess.

The Gamemakers took advantage of her stillness and zoomed in for a close-up. Coriolanus took one look at her cracked lips and reached for his communicuff. She appeared to have had no access to water since she'd been left in the arena, and that had been a day and a half ago. He punched in the order for a bottle of water. The promptness of the drone delivery was improving with each request. Even if she had to keep running, they would be able to get the water to her if she stayed in the open. If she could escape Jessup, Coriolanus would load her up with both food and drink, for her own use and to lace with the rat poison. But that seemed like a long-term plan at the moment.

Jessup had made his way across the arena and seemed confused by Lucy Gray's rejection. He began to climb after her into the stands, but he had trouble keeping his balance. As he entered the field of debris, his coordination diminished further, and twice he fell with great force, opening gashes on his knee and temple. After the second wound, which generated a fair amount of blood, he sat, somewhat stunned, on a step, reaching out to her. His mouth moved while the foam began dripping from his chin.

Lucy Gray remained motionless, watching Jessup with a pained expression. They created a strange tableau: rabid boy, trapped girl, bombed-out building. It suggested a tale that could only end in tragedy. Star-crossed lovers meeting their fate. A revenge story turned in on itself. A war saga that took no prisoners.

Please die, Coriolanus thought. What eventually killed you when you had rabies? You couldn't breathe, or maybe your heart stopped? Whatever it was, the sooner it happened to Jessup, the better it was for everyone involved.

A drone carrying a bottle of water flew into the arena, and Lucy Gray lifted her face to track its wobbly progress. Her tongue flicked across her lips as if in anticipation. However, as it passed over Jessup's head, something registered and a shudder racked his body. He swung at it with a board, and the drone crashed into the stands. The water pooling out of the cracked bottle sent him into a state of heightened agitation. He backed away, tripping over the seats, and then made straight for Lucy Gray. She, in turn, began to climb even higher.

Coriolanus panicked. While the strategy of putting the wreckage between herself and Jessup had some merit, she was in danger of being cut off from the field. The virus may have compromised Jessup's movement, but it also loaned a manic speed to his powerful body, and nothing distracted him from Lucy Gray. *Except that moment with the water*, he thought. The water. A word surfaced in his brain. A word from the poster that had papered the Capitol for a time. *Hydrophobia.* A fear of water. The inability to swallow made rabies victims go wild at the sight of it.

His fingers began to work his communicuff, to order bottles of water. Perhaps enough of them would frighten Jessup away. He would drain his bank if he had to.

Lysistrata placed her hand on his, stopping him. "No, let me. He's my tribute, after all." She began to order bottle after bottle. Sending in the water to drive Jessup over the brink. Her face registered little emotion, but a single tear slid down her cheek, just kissing the edge of her mouth before she brushed it away.

"Lyssie . . ." He hadn't called her that since they were tiny. "You don't have to."

"If Jessup can't win, I want Lucy Gray to. That's what he'd want. And she can't win if he kills her," she said. "Which might happen anyway."

On-screen, Coriolanus could see that Lucy Gray had indeed worked herself into a tough spot. To her left stood the high back wall of the arena, to her right the thick glass side of the press box. As Jessup continued his pursuit, she made several attempts to escape him, but he kept correcting his course to block her. When he came within twenty feet, she began to talk to him, putting her hand out in a soothing manner. It stopped him, but only momentarily, and he made for her again.

Far across the arena, the first bottle of Lysistrata's water, or perhaps the replacement for the one that had crashed, began its flight toward the tributes. This machine seemed steadier and truer in course, as did the small fleet that followed it. The moment Lucy Gray spied the drones she stopped her retreat. Coriolanus saw her hand pat the ruffles of her skirt over the pocket with the silver compact, and he took it as a sign that she had grasped the significance of the water. She pointed over at the drones, beginning to shout, and succeeded in getting Jessup to turn his head.

Jessup froze, and his eyes bulged with fear. As the drones closed in on him, he pawed at them but failed to connect. When they started releasing the bottles of water, he lost all control. Explosive devices could not have elicited a stronger response, and the impact of the bottles smacking into the seats whipped him into a frenzy. The contents of one splattered his hand, and he recoiled as if it were acid. He gained the aisle and bounded down toward the field, but another dozen drones arrived and bombarded him. Since they were directed to deliver right to the tribute, there was no escaping them. As he flew down toward the front-row seats his foot caught, and he tripped forward, hurtling over the arena wall and onto the field.

The sound of snapping bones that accompanied his landing surprised the audience, as Jessup had landed in a rare pocket of the arena with good audio. He lay on his back, motionless except for the heaving in his chest. The remaining bottles rained down on him while his lips curled back and his eyes stared unblinkingly at the bright sun glinting off the water.

Lucy Gray darted down the steps and hung over the railing. "Jessup!" The most he could do was shift his gaze to her face.

Coriolanus could barely hear Lysistrata whisper, "Oh, don't let him die alone."

Weighing the danger, Lucy Gray took a moment to assess the empty arena before she picked her way down the broken wall to his side. Coriolanus wanted to groan — she needed to get out of there — but he couldn't do it with Lysistrata beside him. "She won't," he reassured Lysistrata, thinking of how Lucy Gray had dragged the burning beam from his body. "It's not her style."

"I've got some money left," said Lysistrata, wiping her eyes. "I'll send some food."

Jessup followed Lucy Gray with his eyes as she jumped the last yard to the field, but he seemed unable to move. Was he paralyzed by the fall? She approached him with caution and knelt just out of reach of his long arms. Trying to smile, she said, "You go to sleep now, you hear, Jessup? You go on, it's my turn to stand guard." Something seemed to register, her voice or perhaps the repetition of words she'd spoken to him over the past two weeks. The rigidity eased in his face, and his eyelids fluttered. "That's right. Let yourself go. How are you going to dream if you don't go to sleep?" Lucy Gray scooted forward and laid a hand on his head. "It's okay. I'll watch over you. I'm right here. I'm staying right here." Jessup stared at her fixedly as the life slowly ebbed out of his body and his chest became still.

Lucy Gray smoothed his bangs and sat back on her heels. She heaved a deep sigh, and Coriolanus could feel her exhaustion.

She shook her head as if to wake herself, then grabbed the nearest bottle of water, twisting off the top and draining it in a few gulps. A second followed, then a third, before she wiped her mouth with the back of her hand. She stood up and examined Jessup, then opened another bottle and poured it over his face, washing away the foam and spittle. From her pocket she took the white linen napkin that had lined the picnic box Coriolanus brought her the final night. She leaned down and used the edge to gently shut his eyelids, then shook out the cloth and covered his face to hide it from the audience.

The food parcels from Lysistrata thumping down around her seemed to bring Lucy Gray back to the moment, and she quickly scooped up the pieces of bread and cheese and stuffed them in her pockets. She gathered the bottles of water in her skirt, but pulled up short as Reaper appeared at the far end of the arena. Lucy Gray lost no time in vanishing into the nearest tunnel with her gifts. Reaper let her go but walked over to collect the last few water bottles in the fading light, taking note of Jessup but leaving his body alone.

Coriolanus thought it might bode well for later. If the tributes kept making a habit of scavenging the gifts of the fallen, they'd play right into the poisoning plan. He didn't have much time to dwell on it, though, as Lepidus arrived to claim Lysistrata.

"Whoa!" Lepidus said. "That was unexpected! Did you know about the rabies?"

"Of course not. I would've alerted the authorities so they could test the raccoons in the zoo," she said.

"What? You mean he didn't bring it from the districts?" said Lepidus.

Lysistrata was firm. "No, he was bitten here in the Capitol."

"At the zoo?" Lepidus looked worried. "A lot of us have been spending time at the zoo. A raccoon was over by my equipment, you know, scratching around with those weird little hands and —"

"You don't have rabies," Lysistrata said flatly.

Lepidus made a clawing motion with his fingers. "It was touching my things."

"Did you have any questions about Jessup?" she asked.

"Jessup? No, I never got near him. Oh, um, you meant . . . Did *you* have any thoughts?" he asked.

"I do." She took a deep breath. "What I'd like people to know about Jessup is that he was a good person. He threw his body over mine to protect me when the bombs started going off in the arena. It wasn't even conscious. He did it reflexively. That's who he was at heart. A protector. I don't think he would've ever won the Games, because he'd have died trying to protect Lucy Gray."

"Oh, like a dog or something." Lepidus nodded. "A really good one."

"No, not like a dog. Like a human being," said Lysistrata.

Lepidus eyed her, trying to decipher whether she was joking. "Huh. Lucky, any thoughts from headquarters?"

The camera caught Lucky gnawing on a stubborn hangnail. "Oh, what? Hey! Nothing upstairs at present. Let's peek back at that arena, shall we?"

With the cameras averted, Lysistrata began to collect her things.

"Don't go yet. Stay for dinner with us," Coriolanus said.

"Oh, no. I just want to go home. But thanks for being there, Coryo. You're a good ally," she said.

He hugged her. "*You* are. I know that wasn't easy."

She sighed. "Well, at least I'm out of it."

The other mentors gathered around her, saying good job and whatever, before she left the hall without waiting for the rest of the student body to head out. That was soon to follow, and within a few minutes the ten remaining mentors were all that was left behind. They examined one another with new eyes now that the Plinth Prize was in play, each hoping not just to *have* a victor but to *be* a victor in the Games.

The same thought must have occurred to the Gamemakers, because Lucky reclaimed the screen to do a rundown of the remaining tributes and their mentors. A split screen showed photos of the pairings side by side, accompanied by his voice-over. Some of the mentors groaned when they realized their unflattering student ID photos had been downloaded, but Coriolanus felt relieved that they weren't highlighting his current scabby face. The tributes, who had no official photographs, showed up in random shots taken since the reaping.

The list went chronologically by district, starting with District 3's Urban-Teslee and Io-Circ pairings. "Our tech district tributes have us all wondering, what did they do with those drones?" said Lucky. Festus and Coral appeared next, followed by Persephone and Mizzen. "The District Four tributes are sailing high as we enter the final ten!" Lamina on her beam and Pup's photo brought a cheer from Pup until it was replaced by Treech juggling at the zoo and Vipsania. "And crowd favorites Lamina and Pliny Harrington are joined by the District Seven boy, Treech, and his mentor, Vipsania Sickle! So, Districts Three, Four, and Seven all have both their teams intact! Now to the solo tributes." A blurry picture of Wovey crouched down at the zoo, coupled with Hilarius with a bad acne outbreak. "Wovey from Eight with Hilarius Heavensbee as a guide!" Since they used his interview shot, Tanner looked better as he came up side by side with Domitia. "The boy from Ten can't wait to put his slaughterhouse techniques to good use!" Then Reaper, standing strong in the arena, matched with a flawless-looking Clemensia. "Here's a tribute you might want to rethink! Reaper from Eleven!" Finally, Coriolanus saw his own photo — not great, not bad — with a dazzling photo of Lucy Gray singing at the interview. "And the award for most popular goes to Coriolanus Snow and Lucy Gray from Twelve!"

Most popular? It was flattering, Coriolanus supposed, but not especially intimidating. Never mind, though. Popular had gotten Lucy Gray a pile of money. She was alive, watered, fed, and well stocked. Hopefully, she could hole up while the others thinned their ranks. Losing Jessup as her protector was a blow, but it would be easier for her to hide by herself. Coriolanus had promised her she would never really be alone in the arena, that he would be with her all the way. Was she holding on to that compact now? Thinking of him as he was of her?

Coriolanus updated his mentor sheet, taking no pleasure in crossing out Jessup and Lysistrata.

10th HUNGER GAMES
MENTOR ASSIGNMENTS

DISTRICT 1

~~*Boy (Facet)*~~	~~*Livia Cardew*~~
~~*Girl (Velvereen)*~~	~~*Palmyra Monty*~~

DISTRICT 2

~~*Boy (Marcus)*~~	~~*Sejanus Plinth*~~
~~*Girl (Sabyn)*~~	~~*Florus Friend*~~

DISTRICT 3

Boy (Circ)	*Io Jasper*
Girl (Teslee)	*Urban Canville*

DISTRICT 4	
Boy (Mizzen)	*Persephone Price*
Girl (Coral)	*Festus Creed*
DISTRICT 5	
~~*Boy (Hy)*~~	~~*Dennis Fling*~~
~~*Girl (Sol)*~~	~~*Iphigenia Moss*~~
DISTRICT 6	
~~*Boy (Otto)*~~	~~*Apollo Ring*~~
~~*Girl (Ginnee)*~~	~~*Diana Ring*~~
DISTRICT 7	
Boy (Treech)	*Vipsania Sickle*
Girl (Lamina)	*Pliny Harrington*
DISTRICT 8	
~~*Boy (Bobbin)*~~	~~*Juno Phipps*~~
Girl (Wovey)	*Hilarius Heavensbee*
DISTRICT 9	
~~*Boy (Panlo)*~~	~~*Gaius Breen*~~
~~*Girl (Sheaf)*~~	~~*Androcles Anderson*~~
DISTRICT 10	
Boy (Tanner)	*Domitia Whimsiwick*
~~*Girl (Brandy)*~~	~~*Arachne Crane*~~
DISTRICT 11	
Boy (Reaper)	*Clemensia Dovecote*
~~*Girl (Dill)*~~	~~*Felix Ravinstill*~~
DISTRICT 12	
~~*Boy (Jessup)*~~	~~*Lysistrata Vickers*~~
Girl (Lucy Gray)	*Coriolanus Snow*

The field had narrowed considerably, but several of the surviving tributes would be tough to beat. Reaper, Tanner, both of those District 4 tributes . . . and who knew what that brainy little pair from District 3 was up to?

As the ten mentors gathered for a delicious lamb stew with dried plums, Coriolanus missed Lysistrata. She had been his only real ally, just as Jessup had been Lucy Gray's.

After supper, he sat between Festus and Hilarius, doing his best to keep from nodding off. At around nine, with nothing eventful having happened since Jessup's death, they were sent home with orders to be there all the earlier the following morning. The walk home loomed, but he remembered the second token from Tigris and gratefully mounted the trolley, which dropped him a block from his apartment.

The Grandma'am had gone to bed, but Tigris waited for him in his bedroom, again enveloped in her mother's fur coat. He collapsed on the chaise longue at her feet, knowing he owed her an explanation of his time in the arena. It wasn't only fatigue that made him hesitate.

"I know you want to hear about last night," he told her, "but I'm afraid to tell you. I'm afraid you could get in trouble for knowing it."

"It's okay, Coryo. Your shirt's told me most of it." From the floor she retrieved the shirt he'd worn in the arena. "Clothes speak to me, you know." She smoothed it out on her lap and began to reconstruct the terrors of his night, first lifting the bloodstained slit in the material on the sleeve. "Right here. This is where the knife cut you." Her fingers tracked the damage down the fabric. "All these little rips, and the way the dirt's ground in, tell me you slid — or maybe even were dragged — which matches up with the scrape on your chin and the blood on your collar." Tigris touched the neckline, then moved on. "This other sleeve, the way it's torn, I'd say you caught it on barbed wire. Probably at the barricade. But this blood here, the stuff splattered on the cuff . . . I don't think it's yours. I think you had to do something really awful in there."

Coriolanus stared down at the blood and felt the impact of the beam on Bobbin's head. "Tigris . . ."

She rubbed her temple. "And I keep wondering how it came to this. That my baby cousin, who wouldn't hurt a fly, has to fight for his life in the arena."

This was the last conversation in the world he wanted to have right now. "I don't know. I didn't have any choice."

"I know that. Of course I know that." Tigris put her arms around him. "I just hate what they're doing to you."

"I'm okay," he said. "It won't last much longer. And even if I don't win, I'm a shoo-in for some sort of prize. Really, I think things are about to take a turn for the better."

"Right. Yes. I'm sure they are. Snow lands on top," she agreed. But the look on her face spoke otherwise.

"What is it?" he asked. She shook her head. "Come on, what?"

"I wasn't going to tell you until after the Hunger Games . . ." She fell silent.

"But now you have to," he said. "Or, I'll imagine the worst things possible. Please, just tell me."

"We'll figure something out." She started to rise.

"Tigris." He pulled her back down. "What?"

Tigris reluctantly reached into her coat pocket, pulled out a letter marked with the Capitol stamp, and handed it to him. "The tax bill came today."

She didn't have to elaborate. Her expression told him everything. With no money for the taxes, and no way to borrow more, the Snows were about to lose their home.

Coriolanus had been in a state of denial about the taxes, but now the reality of his family's displacement hit him like a truck. How could he say good-bye to the only home he'd ever known? To his mother, to his childhood, to those sweet memories of his life before the war? These four walls not only kept his family safe from the world, they protected the legend of the Snows' wealth. He would be losing his residence, his history, and his identity in one fell swoop.

They had six weeks to come up with the money. To scrape together the equivalent of Tigris's income for the whole year. The cousins tried to assess what they might still have to sell, but even if they sold every stick of furniture and every keepsake, it would only cover a few months, at the most. And the tax bills would keep showing up, every month, like clockwork. They would need the proceeds from selling their possessions, however paltry, to rent a new place. Eviction due to tax troubles had to be avoided at all cost; the public shame would be too great, too lasting. So move they must.

"What are we going to do?" Coriolanus asked.

"Nothing until the Hunger Games are finished. You have to focus on them so you can get that Plinth Prize, or at least another one. I'll handle this end," she said firmly. She made him a cup of hot milk laced with corn syrup and stroked his throbbing head until he fell asleep. He dreamed violent, unsettling things, replaying the events of the arena, and awoke to the usual.

Gem of Panem,
Mighty city,
Through the ages, you shine anew.

Would the Grandma'am still be singing it in their rental in a month or two? Or would she be too humiliated to raise her voice again? For all his derision of the morning recital, the thought saddened him.

As he dressed, the stitches on his arm pulled, and he remembered he was supposed to drop by the Citadel to get them checked. Dark red scabs had settled on his scraped face, but the swelling had abated. He dabbed some of his mother's powder on, and while it didn't really cover the scabs, the scent soothed him a bit.

Their hopeless financial situation made him accept the tokens Tigris offered without hesitation. Why bother pinching pennies when the dollars had fled long ago? On the trolley, he choked down his nut butter on soda crackers and tried not to compare it with Ma Plinth's breakfast rolls. It crossed his mind that, given his rescue of Sejanus, the Plinths might provide a loan, or even a payout for his silence, but the Grandma'am would never allow that, and the idea of a Snow groveling before a Plinth was unthinkable. The Plinth Prize, though, was fair game, and Tigris was right. These next few days would determine his future.

At the Academy, the ten mentors drank their tea and readied themselves for the cameras. Every day brought them more scrutiny. The Gamemakers had sent over a makeup person, who managed to tone down Coriolanus's scabs and give his eyebrows a little shape while she was at it. No one seemed in the mood to talk about the Games directly, except Hilarius Heavensbee, who could talk of nothing else.

"It's different for me," said Hilarius. "I checked my list last night. Every single one of the tributes left has had food, or at least water, since they've been in the arena. Except old no-show Wovey. Where is she anyway? I mean, how would I know if she just curled up and died somewhere in those tunnels? Maybe she's already dead, and I'm just sitting here like a jackass, playing with my communicuff!"

Coriolanus wanted to tell him to shut up because other people had real problems, but instead he maneuvered himself into a seat on the end, next to Festus, who was deep in discussion with Persephone.

Lucky Flickerman opened by recapping the remaining tributes and inviting Lepidus to take comments from the mentor pool. Coriolanus was called upon first thing to respond to the Jessup scare. He made a point of complimenting Lysistrata's brilliant handling of the rabies situation and thanking her for her generosity in the last minutes of Jessup's life. He turned to the section where the fallen mentors sat, asked her to stand, and invited the audience to give her a round of applause. Not only did they oblige, but at least half stood up, and while Lysistrata looked embarrassed, he thought she didn't really mind. Then he added that he hoped to properly thank her by fulfilling her prediction that the victor would be a tribute from District 12, namely, Lucy Gray. The audience could see for themselves how clever his tribute had been. And they shouldn't forget how she'd stood by Jessup until the bitter end. Again, that was behavior you might expect of a Capitol girl, but of one from the districts? It was something to think about, how much they rewarded character in the Hunger Games victor, how much she reflected their values. Something must've hit home with the audience, because at least a dozen pings sounded from his communicuff right off. He held up the cuff for the camera and thanked the generous sponsors.

As if unable to stand that much attention being showered on Coriolanus, Pup sat forward and loudly announced that he'd "Better get Lamina her breakfast!" and ordered up a storm of food and drink. No one else could compete, as she was the only tribute to be seen in the arena, so it was just one more way in which Pup was annoying. It gratified Coriolanus that no new pinging came from his rival's cuff.

Knowing he wouldn't be called upon again until the others had been interviewed, Coriolanus adopted an interested demeanor but barely listened to their pitches. The idea of approaching old Strabo Plinth for money — not blackmailing him, of course, but giving him the opportunity to make a financial gift of thanks — kept nagging at him. What if Coriolanus dropped by the Plinths' to check on Sejanus's health? That had been a bad cut on his leg. Yes, what if he just dropped by and then saw what happened?

Lucky interrupted Io's thoughts on what Circ might do with the drone — "Well, if the light-emitting diodes on the drone aren't broken, he might be able to fashion a flashlight of some sort, which would give him a great advantage at night" — to direct the audience's attention to Reaper's emergence from the barricade.

Lamina, who'd been collecting water, bread, and cheese from a half dozen drones, neatly lined up her provisions along the beam. She barely acknowledged Reaper's entrance, but he walked over to her with purpose. He pointed up at the sun and then to her face. For the first time, Coriolanus noticed the toll the long days outdoors were taking on Lamina's skin. She'd been badly sunburned, and her nose was peeling in response. On close inspection, the tops of her bare feet were red as well. Reaper indicated her food. Lamina rubbed her foot and seemed to consider whatever his offer might be. They went back and forth for a bit, then both nodded in agreement. Reaper jogged across the arena and climbed up to the flag of Panem. He pulled out his long knife and stabbed through the heavy fabric.

Loud objections came from the audience in the hall. This disregard for the sanctity of the national flag shook them. As Reaper began to saw his way through the flag, carving off a piece the size of a small blanket, the unease grew. Surely, this should not go unchecked. Surely, he should be punished in some way. But given that being in the Hunger Games was the ultimate punishment, no one knew what form it should take.

Lepidus hurried over to Clemensia to ask what she made of her tribute's behavior. "Well, it's a stupid move, isn't it? Who's going to sponsor him now?"

"Not that it matters, since you never feed him," Pup commented.

"I'll feed him when he does something that merits feeding," said Clemensia. "Anyway, I think you've got that covered today."

Pup frowned. "I do?"

Clemensia nodded to the screen as Reaper jogged back to the beam. Further negotiation occurred between him and Lamina. Then, on what appeared to be the count of three, Reaper tossed up the wadded piece of flag as Lamina dropped down a piece of bread. The flag didn't quite make it high enough for her to catch hold of. More negotiation ensued. When Reaper finally delivered it after several attempts, she rewarded him with a chunk of cheese.

It wasn't an official alliance, but the exchange seemed to bond the two a bit. While Lamina shook out the flag and draped it over her head, Reaper sat against one of the posts and ate his bread and cheese. They didn't speak to each other again, but a relative calm came over them, and when the pack appeared at the far end of the arena, Lamina pointed them out. Reaper gave her a nod of thanks before withdrawing behind the barricade.

Coral, Mizzen, and Tanner sat in the stands and made eating motions. Festus, Persephone, and Domitia all obliged them, and the three tributes shared the bread, cheese, and apples dropped by the drones.

Back in the studio, Lucky had brought his pet parrot, Jubilee, to the set, and he spent several minutes trying to coax it to say "Hi, Handsome!" to Dean Highbottom. The bird, a depressed creature in the midst of battling mange, perched wordlessly on Lucky's wrist as the dean folded his hands and waited. "Oh, say it! Come on! 'Hi, Handsome! Hi, Handsome!'"

"I don't think it wants to, Lucky," said Dean Highbottom finally. "Perhaps it doesn't find me handsome at all."

"What? Ha! Nooo. He's just shy in front of strangers." He held out the bird. "Would you like to hold him?"

The dean leaned back. "No."

Lucky pulled Jubliee back to his chest and stroked his feathers with a fingertip. "So, Dean Highbottom, what do you make of it all?"

"All . . . what?" Dean Highbottom asked.

"All this stuff. All this different stuff happening in the Hunger Games." Lucky waved his hand in the air. "All of it!"

"Well, what I'm noticing is the new interactivity of the Games," said Dean Highbottom.

Lucky nodded. "Interactivity. Go on."

"Right from the beginning. Even before, actually. When the bombing occurred in the arena, it not only took out participants, it changed the landscape," the dean continued.

"Changed the landscape," Lucky repeated.

"Yes. Now we have the barricade. The beam. Access to the tunnels. It's a brand-new arena, and it's made the tributes behave in a brand-new way," the dean explained.

"And we have drones!" said Lucky.

"Exactly right. Now the audience is an active player in the Games." Dean Highbottom inclined his head toward Lucky. "And you know what that means."

"What?" said Lucky.

The dean spoke the next words slowly, as if to a small child. "It means we're all in the arena together, Lucky."

Lucky furrowed his brow. "Huh. I don't quite get that."

Dean Highbottom tapped his temple with his forefinger. "Think it over."

"Hi, Handsome," squawked Jubilee despondently.

"Oh, there we go! I told you, didn't I?" crowed Lucky.

"You did," admitted the dean. "And yet it was still unexpected."

Nothing much else happened before lunch. Lucky did the weather report district by district, with the added fillip of Jubilee's company, but the bird refused to talk again, so Lucky began speaking for it in a high-pitched voice. "How's the weather look in District Twelve, Jubilee?" *"They've got snow, Lucky."* "Snow in July, Jubilee?" *"Coriolanus Snow!"*

Coriolanus gave the camera a thumbs-up when they cut for his reaction. He could not believe this was his life.

Lunch disappointed, as the menu consisted of nut butter sandwiches, and he'd had nut butter for breakfast. He ate it, because he ate anything free, and it was important to keep his strength up. A ripple went through the hall indicating something was happening on the screen, and he hurried to resume his seat. Maybe Lucy Gray had surfaced?

She had not, but the pack's morning laziness had given way to direction. The three strode across the arena until they were directly under Lamina's beam. She took no notice at first, but Tanner smacking a sword blade against one of the poles brought her to attention. Lamina sat up and surveyed the pack, and she must have sensed a change in the air, because she pulled out her ax and her knife and polished them on the flag.

After a brief huddle, in which the District 4 tributes relinquished their tridents to Tanner, the pack split up. Coral and Mizzen each went to one of the metal posts that supported the beam, and Tanner stood directly under Lamina, holding the pair of tridents. Knives in teeth, Coral and Mizzen gave each other a nod and then began to climb their respective posts.

Festus shifted in his seat. "Here we go."

"They'll never make it," said Pup in agitation.

"They're trained to work on ships. They climb ropes as part of it," Persephone pointed out.

"Rigging," said Festus.

"Yes, I get it. My father's a commander, after all," said Pup. "Rope climbing is different. The posts are more like trees."

But Pup had been getting on everyone's nerves, and even the mentors without a tribute in the confrontation seemed eager to comment.

"What about masts?" asked Vipsania.

"Or flagpoles?" Urban chimed in.

"They won't make it," said Pup.

While the District 4 pair lacked Lamina's smooth style, they were indeed making it, slowly pulling their way higher and higher. Tanner directed them, calling on Coral to wait a moment when Mizzen fell behind.

"Look, they're timing it so they reach the top together," said Io.

"They're making her choose who to fight, then the other one will reach the beam."

"So she'll kill one of them and climb down," said Pup.

"Where Tanner will be waiting," Coriolanus reminded him.

"Well, I know that!" said Pup. "What do you expect me to do? It's not like they have rabies and there's a simple fix like sending in water!"

"Never would have crossed your mind," said Festus.

"Of course, it would've," snapped Pup. "Shut up! All of you!"

A silence fell, but largely because Coral and Mizzen were nearing the top. Lamina's head went back and forth as she decided who to confront. Then she headed for Coral.

"No, not the girl, the boy!" exclaimed Pup, jumping to his feet. "Now she'll have to fight the boy on the beam."

"I'd do the same thing. I wouldn't want to fight that girl up there," said Domitia, and murmurs of agreement came from a few of the mentors.

"No?" Pup reconsidered. "Maybe you're right."

Lamina reached the end of the beam and swung the ax down at Coral without hesitation, just missing her scalp but shaving off a tuft of hair. Coral retreated, lowering herself about a yard, but Lamina struck at her a few more times, as if to drive the point home. As expected, this gave Mizzen time to mount the beam, but when Tanner threw the trident up to him, it peaked about two-thirds of the way up and fell back to the ground. Lamina took one last swipe at Coral and then moved swiftly for Mizzen. He was no match for her sure-footedness on the beam and only managed a few hesitant steps as she bore down on him. Tanner did better with his second throw, but the trident bounced off the underside of the beam and landed in the dirt. Occupied by crouching to try and catch it, Mizzen straightened up just as Lamina came in, bringing the flat side of the ax against the outer part of his knee. The force of the blow threw them both off balance. But while she recovered by straddling the beam, Mizzen fell, losing his knife and just barely catching himself with one arm.

Even the sound system in the arena picked up Coral's war cry as she gained the top. Tanner ran down to her end and managed to hurl the trident within range. The easy way Coral snatched the weapon from the air drew a few exclamations of admiration from the Capitol audience. Lamina gave Mizzen a glance, but his helpless condition posed no immediate threat, so she turned and braced herself for Coral's attack. Lamina had better balance, but Coral's weapon had more range. After Lamina managed to block the first few jabs with her ax, Coral wove the trident in a twisting move that distracted the eye before it plunged into her opponent's abdomen. Coral released the weapon and stepped back, using her knife as a backup, but none was needed. Lamina fell off the beam and died on impact.

"No!" cried Pup, and the word echoed around Heavensbee Hall. He stood stock-still for a long moment, then picked up his seat and left the mentor section, ignoring Lepidus's outstretched mic. He slammed his chair down next to Livia's and strode out of the hall. Coriolanus thought he was trying not to cry.

Coral crossed to Mizzen and stood over him for a disconcerting beat, in which Coriolanus wondered if she was planning to kick his arm free and send him after Lamina. Instead she sat down on the beam, locking her legs for support, and helped him to safety. The ax had damaged his knee, although it was difficult to gauge to what extent. He half slid, half lowered himself down the pole, closely followed by Coral, who picked up the unused trident from the ground where Tanner had abandoned it. Mizzen leaned back against the pole, testing his knee.

After performing some kind of dance over Lamina's body, Tanner bounded over to them. Mizzen grinned and raised his hands for a victory slap. Tanner had just made contact when Coral drove the second trident into his back. He fell forward into Mizzen, who, braced by the pole, shoved him away. Tanner turned in a circle, one hand swatting uselessly behind him as if to dislodge the trident, but the barbed tines were buried deep. He fell to his knees, his expression more wounded than shocked, and collapsed facedown in the dirt. Mizzen finished him with a knife to the neck. He then went back and sat against his pole while Coral tore a strip of fabric from Lamina's flag cloth and began to bind his knee.

At the studio, Lucky's face stretched into a comedic mask of shock. "Did you just see what I saw?"

Domitia had quietly gathered her things, her lips pressed together in disappointment. But when Lepidus pushed the mic at her, she spoke in a calm, detached voice. "It's a surprise. I thought Tanner might win this thing. And he probably would have if his allies hadn't betrayed him. I guess that's the takeaway. Be careful who you trust."

"In and out of the arena," said Lepidus, nodding sagely.

"Everywhere," Domitia agreed. "You know, Tanner was a very good-natured sort of person. And District Four took advantage of that." She looked sadly at Festus and Persephone, suggesting this reflected badly on them, and Lepidus gave a disapproving click of his tongue. "It's one of the many things I've learned from being a mentor in the Hunger Games. I'll always cherish my experience here, and I wish all the remaining mentors the best of luck."

"Well said, Domitia. I think you've just showed your fellow mentors how to be a good loser," said Lepidus. "Lucky?"

The cut revealed Lucky trying to lure Jubilee off the chandelier with a cracker. "What? Aren't you going to talk to the other one? What's his name? The commander's kid?"

"He declined to comment," said Lepidus.

"Well, let's get back to the show!" called Lucky.

The show was over for the moment, though. Coral finished bandaging Mizzen's knee and collected their tridents, yanking them from her victims' bodies. Mizzen limped as the pair walked unhurriedly across the arena to their preferred tunnel.

Satyria came over and had the mentors rearrange their chairs into two neat rows of four. Io, Urban, Clemensia, and Vipsania in the front. Coriolanus, Festus, Persephone, and Hilarius in the back. The musical chairs continued.

Perhaps the indignities of being Lucky's dummy had become too great, because Jubilee refused to come down from the chandelier. Lucky leaned heavily on his stringers in Heavensbee Hall and in front of the arena, where the crowd had set up cheering sections for the various tributes. Team Lucy Gray was well represented by young and old, male and female, and even a handful of Avoxes — but they didn't really count, having been brought along to hold signs.

Coriolanus wished Lucy Gray could see how many people loved her. He wished she knew how he advocated for her. He'd become more active, pulling Lepidus over during quiet stretches and praising Lucy Gray to the skies. As a result, her sponsor gifts had reached a new high, and he felt confident he could feed her for a week. There was really nothing left to do but watch and wait.

Treech came out long enough to snag Lamina's ax and for Vipsania to feed him. Teslee retrieved another fallen drone and collected some food from Urban. Little else occurred until late afternoon, when Reaper wandered out of the barricade, rubbing sleep from his eyes. He seemed unable to make sense of the scene before him, the stabbed bodies of Tanner and particularly Lamina. After walking around them for a time, he lifted Lamina up, carried her over to where Bobbin and Marcus lay, and arranged the three in a row on the ground. For a while, he paced around the beam, then he dragged Tanner over beside Lamina. Over the next hour, he collected first Dill and then Sol, adding them to his makeshift morgue.

Jessup remained the only one left out. Reaper was probably afraid of contracting rabies. Once he'd neatly lined up the others, he swatted at the flies that had gathered. After pausing a moment in thought, he went back and cut off a second piece of the flag, draping it over their bodies and causing another wave of outrage in the hall. Reaper shook out Lamina's flag remnant and tied it like a cape around his shoulders. The cape seemed to inspire him, and he began to spin slowly, looking back over his shoulder to watch it fly out behind him. He ran then, spreading his arms out as the flag streamed in the sunlight. Exhausted by the day's activities, he finally climbed into the stands and waited.

"Oh, for heaven's sake, feed him, Clemmie!" said Festus.

"Mind your own business," said Clemensia.

"You're heartless," Festus told her.

"I'm a good manager. It could be a long Hunger Games." She gave Coriolanus an unpleasant smile. "And it's not like I've abandoned him."

Coriolanus thought about inviting her to the Citadel for his follow-up appointment. He could use some company, and she could visit her snakes.

Five o'clock rolled around with the dismissal of the student body, and the eight remaining mentors gathered for beef stew and cake. He couldn't say he missed Domitia, and certainly not Pup, but he missed the buffer they had provided between him and the likes of Clemensia, Vipsania, and Urban. Even Hilarius, with his woeful tales of being a Heavensbee, had become a strain. When Satyria released them at around eight o'clock, he headed straight for the door, hoping it wasn't too late to have his arm checked.

The Citadel guards recognized him, and after they searched his book bag, he was allowed to keep it and go down to the lab unescorted. He wandered a bit before finding his destination, then sat in the clinic for half an hour before a doctor appeared. She checked his vitals, examined the stitches, which were doing their job, and told him to wait.

An unusual energy filled the lab. Quick footsteps, raised voices, impatient commands. Coriolanus listened hard but he couldn't make out the cause of the activity. He did hear the words *arena* and *Games* more than once, and wondered about the connection. When Dr. Gaul finally appeared, she made only a cursory check of his stitches.

"Another few days," she confirmed. "Tell me, Mr. Snow, did you know Gaius Breen?"

"Did I?" asked Coriolanus, picking up on the past tense immediately. "I do. I mean, we're classmates. I know he lost his legs in the arena. Is he —"

"He's dead. Complications from the bombing," said Dr. Gaul.

"Oh, no." Coriolanus couldn't process it. Gaius, dead? Gaius Breen? He remembered a joke Gaius had recently told him about how many rebels it took to tie a shoe. "I never even visited him in the hospital. When is the funeral?"

"That's being worked out. You must keep it to yourself until we make an official announcement," she warned him. "I'm only telling you now so that at least one of you will have something intelligent to say to Lepidus. I trust you can manage that."

"Yes, of course. That will be strange, announcing it during the Games. Like a victory for the rebels," said Coriolanus.

"Exactly. But rest assured, there will be repercussions. In fact, it was your girl who gave me the idea. If she wins, we should compare notes. And I haven't forgotten you owe me a paper." She left, pulling the curtain closed behind her.

Free to go, Coriolanus buttoned his shirt up and collected his book bag. What was he supposed to write about, again? Something about chaos? Control? Contracts? He felt fairly sure it began with a *C.* When he approached the elevator, he found a pair of lab assistants ahead of him, trying to maneuver a cart into the car. On the cart sat the large tank filled with the snakes that had attacked Clemensia.

"Did she say to bring the cooler?" asked one of the assistants.

"Not that I remember," said the other. "I thought they'd been fed. We better check. If we're wrong, she'll go ballistic." She noticed Coriolanus. "Sorry, need to back out."

"No problem," he said, and stepped aside so they could wheel the tank out. The elevator doors closed, and he could hear the whir of it ascending.

"Oh, sorry, it will be back in a minute," the second assistant said.

"No problem," Coriolanus repeated. But he was beginning to suspect a very great problem. He thought of the activity in the lab, and the Games being mentioned, and Dr. Gaul promising repercussions. "Where are you taking the snakes?" he asked as innocently as possible.

"Oh, just to another lab," said one, but the assistants exchanged a look. "Come on, the cooler takes two." The pair receded into the lab, leaving him alone with the tank. *"In fact, it was your girl who gave me the idea."* His girl. Lucy Gray. Who'd made an entrance into the Hunger Games by dropping a snake down the mayor's daughter's back. *"If she wins, we should compare notes."* Notes about what? How to use snakes as weapons? He stared into the undulating reptiles, imagining them being let loose in the arena. What would they do? Hide? Hunt? Attack? Even if he knew how snakes behaved, which he didn't, he doubted these would conform to any norms, as they were genetically designed by Dr. Gaul.

With a sharp pang, Coriolanus had a vision of Lucy Gray in their final meeting, clutching his hand as he promised her they could win. But there was no way he could protect her from the creatures in this tank, any more than he could protect her from tridents and swords. At least she could hide from those. He didn't know for sure, but he was guessing the snakes would head straight for the tunnels. The dark would not impair their sense of smell. They would not recognize Lucy Gray's scent, just the way they had not recognized Clemensia's. Lucy Gray would scream and fall to the ground, her lips turning purple, then bloodless, while bright pink and blue and yellow pus oozed onto her ruffled dress — That was it! The thing the snakes had reminded him of the first time he'd seen them. They matched her dress. As if they had always been her destiny . . .

Without knowing quite how, Coriolanus found the handkerchief in his hand, neatly balled up like a prop in one of Lucky's magic tricks. He moved to the snake tank, his back to the security camera, and leaned over, resting his hands on the cover as if fascinated by the snakes. From that vantage point, he watched the handkerchief fall through the trapdoor and disappear beneath the rainbow of bodies.

What had he done? What on earth had he done? His heart raced as he blindly turned down one street and then another, trying to make sense of his actions. He couldn't think clearly but had the dreadful feeling that he'd crossed some line that could not be uncrossed.

The avenue felt full of eyes. There were few pedestrians or drivers out, but even their notice felt glaring. Coriolanus ducked into a park and hid in the shadows, on a bench surrounded by bushes. He forced himself to control his breathing, counting four in and four out until his blood stopped pounding in his ears. Then he tried to think rationally.

All right, so he'd dropped the handkerchief with Lucy Gray's scent — the one from the outside pocket of his book bag — into the snake tank. He'd done it so they would not bite her as they had Clemensia. So they would not kill her. Because he cared about her. Because he cared about her? Or because he wanted her to win the Hunger Games so that he could secure the Plinth Prize? If it was the latter, he had cheated to win, and that was that.

Hold on. You didn't know if those snakes were going to the arena, he thought. The assistants had, in fact, told him otherwise. There was no history of such a thing ever occurring. Perhaps it had just been a temporary flight of madness. And even if the snakes did end up in the arena, Lucy Gray might never encounter them. It was a huge place, and he didn't think snakes just went around attacking people right and left. You had to step on them or something. And even if she did run into a snake, and it didn't bite her, how would anyone trace that back to him? It required too much high-security knowledge and access that no one would presume he had. And a handkerchief with her scent. And why would he have that? It was okay. He was going to be okay.

Except that line. Whether anyone pieced together his actions or not, he knew he had crossed it. In fact, he knew he'd been dancing on top of it for some time. Like when he'd taken Sejanus's food from the dining hall to feed Lucy Gray. It had been a small infraction, motivated by his desire to keep her alive and his anger at the Gamemakers' negligence. An argument could be made for basic decency there. But it was not a lone incident. He could see it all now, the slippery slope of the last few weeks that had started with Sejanus's leftovers and ended with him here, shivering in the dark on a deserted park bench. What awaited him farther down that slope if he was unable to stop his descent? What else might he be capable of? Well, that was it. It stopped now. If he didn't have honor, he had nothing. No more deception. No more shady strategies. No more rationalization. From now on he'd live honestly, and if he ended up as a beggar, at least he would be a decent one.

His feet had carried him far from home, but he realized the Plinth apartment was just a few minutes away. Why not pop in?

An Avox in a maid's outfit opened the door and gestured to ask if she should take his book bag. He declined and inquired if Sejanus was free. She led him to a drawing room and indicated that he should sit. While he waited, he took in the furnishings with a knowing eye. Fine furniture, thick carpets, embroidered tapestries, a bronze bust of someone. While the exterior of the apartment had not impressed, no expense had been spared on the interior. All the Plinths needed was an address on the Corso to solidify their status.

Mrs. Plinth bustled in, full of apologies and flour. Sejanus, it seemed, had gone to bed early, and he'd caught her in the kitchen. Would he come downstairs for a moment and have a cup of tea? Or perhaps she should serve tea in here, like the Snows had. No, no, he assured her, the kitchen would be fine. As if anyone served a guest in the kitchen but a Plinth. But he had not come to pass judgment. He had come to be thanked, and if that involved baked goods, all the better.

"Would you like pie? I've got blackberry. Or peach if you can wait for it." She nodded to a pair of newly assembled pies on the counter awaiting the oven. "Or maybe cake? I made custards this afternoon. The Avoxes like those best, because, you know, they're easy to swallow. Coffee or tea or milk?" The lines between Ma's eyebrows deepened in anxiety, as if nothing she could offer would be good enough.

Although he'd eaten dinner, the events at the Citadel and the walk had left him drained. "Oh, milk, please. And the blackberry pie would be a real treat. No one can compete with your cooking."

Ma filled a large glass to the brim. She carved out a full quarter of the pie and plunked it onto a plate. "Do you like ice cream?" she asked. Several scoops of vanilla followed. She pulled a chair up to the surprisingly simple wooden table. It sat under a framed needlepoint of a mountain scene overlaid with a single word: HOME. "My sister sent me that. She's the only one I really stay in touch with now. Or who stays in touch with me, I guess. Doesn't really fit with the rest of the house, but I have my corner down here. Please, sit. Eat."

Her corner boasted the table with three mismatched chairs, the needlepoint, and a shelf filled with little oddities. A pair of rooster salt and pepper shakers, a marble egg, and a soft doll with patched clothing. The sum total of the possessions, Coriolanus suspected, that she'd brought from home. Her shrine to District 2. It was pitiful, the way she clung to that backward mountain region. Poor little displaced person without a hope of ever fitting in, spending her days making custards for Avoxes who would never taste them, and pining for the past. He watched her slide the pies into the oven and took a bite of his slice. His taste buds tingled in pleasure.

"How is it?" she asked anxiously.

"Superb," he said. "Like everything you cook, Mrs. Plinth." It wasn't an exaggeration. Ma might be pathetic, but she was something of an artist in the kitchen.

She allowed herself a small smile and joined him at the table. "Well, if you ever want seconds, our door is always open. I don't even know how to begin to thank you, Coriolanus, for what you've done for us. Sejanus is my life. I'm sorry he can't visit with you. He's taken a lot of that sedative. Can't seem to sleep otherwise. So angry, so lost. Well, I don't have to tell you how unhappy he is."

"The Capitol isn't really the best fit for him," said Coriolanus.

"For any of us Plinths, really. Strabo says that while it's hard for us now, it will be better for Sejanus and his children, but I don't know." She glanced up at her shelf. "Your family and friends, that's your real life, Coriolanus, and we left all ours back in Two. But you know that already. I can see it. I'm glad you've got your grandma and that sweet cousin."

Coriolanus found himself trying to cheer her up, saying that things would be better once Sejanus graduated from the Academy. The University had more people, and more kinds of people from all over the Capitol, and he was sure to make new friends.

Mrs. Plinth nodded but didn't seem convinced. The Avox maid caught her attention and communicated in a kind of sign language. "All right, he'll come up after he finishes his pie," Mrs.

Plinth told her. "My husband would like to see you, if you don't mind. I think he wants to thank you."

When Coriolanus swallowed his last bite of pie, he bid Ma good night and followed the maid up the stairs to the main floor. The thick carpeting silenced their footsteps, so they arrived at the open library door without warning, and he was able to get a look at Strabo Plinth with his guard down. The man stood at a fancy stone fireplace, his tall frame propped up by an elbow on the mantel, staring down into where the flame would be in another season. Now the hearth was cold and empty, and Coriolanus had to wonder what he saw there that would provoke the profoundly sad expression on his face. One hand gripped the velvet lapel of his expensive smoking jacket, which seemed all wrong, like Mrs. Plinth's designer dress or Sejanus's suit. The Plinths' wardrobe always suggested they were trying too hard to be Capitol. The unquestionable quality of the clothes clashed with their district personae instead of disguising them, just as the Grandma'am in a flour-sack dress would still scream Corso.

Mr. Plinth met his gaze, and Coriolanus felt a sensation he remembered from encounters with his own father, a mix of anxiety and awkwardness, as if, at that moment, he'd been caught doing something foolish. This man, however, was a Plinth, not a Snow.

Coriolanus produced his best society smile. "Good evening, Mr. Plinth. I'm not disturbing you?"

"Not at all. Come in. Sit." Mr. Plinth gestured to the leather chairs before the fireplace rather than the ones before his imposing oak desk. This was to be personal, then, not business. "You've eaten? Of course, you couldn't get out of the kitchen without my wife stuffing you like a turkey. Do you want a drink? A whiskey maybe?"

Adults had never offered him any beverage stronger than

posca, which went quickly enough to his head. He couldn't risk that for this exchange. "I don't know where I'd put it," he said with a laugh, patting his stomach as he settled himself into a chair. "But please, you go ahead."

"Oh, I don't drink." Mr. Plinth folded himself into the facing chair and looked Coriolanus over. "You look like your father."

"I hear that a lot," said Coriolanus. "Did you know him?"

"Our business overlapped at times." He drummed his long fingers on the arm of the chair. "It's striking, the resemblance. But you're nothing like him, really."

No, thought Coriolanus. *I'm poor and powerless.* Although maybe the perceived difference was good for tonight's purposes. His district-hating father would have loathed seeing Strabo Plinth admitted to the Capitol and becoming a titan of the munitions industry. That was not why he'd given his life in the war.

"Nothing at all. Or you'd never have gone into that arena after my son," continued Mr. Plinth. "Impossible to imagine Crassus Snow risking his life for me. I keep asking myself why you did it."

Not much choice, really, thought Coriolanus. "He's my friend," he said.

"No matter how many times I hear that, it's difficult to believe. But even from the beginning, Sejanus singled you out. Maybe you take after your mother, huh? She was always gracious to me when I came here on business before the war. Despite my background. The very definition of a lady. Never forgot it." He gave Coriolanus a hard stare. "Are you like your mother?"

The conversation wasn't going the way Coriolanus had imagined. Where was the talk of reward money? He couldn't be persuaded to take it if it was never offered. "I'd like to think I am, in some respects."

"In what respects?" asked Mr. Plinth.

The line of questioning felt weird. In what way was he anything like that loving, adoring creature who'd sung him to sleep each night? "Well, we shared a fondness for music." Did they? She liked music, and he didn't hate it, he guessed.

"Music, huh?" said Mr. Plinth, as if Coriolanus had said something as frivolous as puffy clouds.

"And I do think we both believed that good fortune was . . . something to be repaid . . . on a daily basis. Not taken for granted," he added. He had no idea what that meant, but it seemed to register with Mr. Plinth.

He thought it over. "I'd agree with that."

"Oh, good. Yes, well, so . . . Sejanus," Coriolanus reminded him.

Mr. Plinth's face grew weary. "Sejanus. Thank you, by the way, for saving his life."

"No thanks necessary. As I said, he's my friend." Now was the time. The time for the money, the refusal, the persuasion, the acceptance.

"Good. Well, I guess you should get home. Your tribute's still in the Games, right?" asked Mr. Plinth.

Thrown by the dismissal, Coriolanus rose from his chair. "Oh. Yes. You're right. Just wanted to check on Sejanus. Will he be back to school soon?"

"No telling," said Mr. Plinth. "But thanks for stopping by."

"Of course. Tell him he's missed," said Coriolanus. "Good night."

"Night." Mr. Plinth gave him a nod. No money. Not even a handshake.

Coriolanus left off balance and disappointed. The heavy bag of food and the chauffeur assigned to drive him home made a decent consolation prize, but in the end his visit had been a waste of time, especially when Dr. Gaul's paper still awaited him. The *"nice addition to your prize application."* Why did everything have to be an uphill battle for him?

Coriolanus told Tigris he'd checked on Sejanus, and she didn't press him for further explanation of his lateness. She made him a cup of the special jasmine tea — an indulgence like splurging on the tokens, but who cared now? He settled down to work, writing the three *C*-words on a scrap of paper. Chaos, control, and what was the third? Oh, yes. Contract. What happened if no one was in control of humanity? That was the topic he was supposed to address. And he had said there was chaos. And Dr. Gaul had said to start there.

Chaos. Extreme disorder and confusion. *"Like being in the arena,"* Dr. Gaul had said. That *"wonderful opportunity,"* she had called it. *"Transformative."* Coriolanus thought about what it had felt like to be in the arena, where there were no rules, no laws, no consequences to one's actions. The needle of his moral compass had swung madly without direction. Fueled by the terror of being prey, how quickly he himself had become a predator, with no reservations about smashing Bobbin to death. He'd transformed, all right, but not into anything he was proud of — and being a Snow, he had more self-control than most. He tried to imagine what it would be like if the whole world played by those same rules. No consequences. People taking what they wanted, when they wanted, and killing for it if it came to that. Survival driving everything. There had been days during the war when they'd all been too scared to leave the apartment. Days when the lawlessness had made even the Capitol an arena.

Yes, the lack of law, that was at the heart of it. So people needed to agree on laws to follow. Was that what Dr. Gaul had meant by *"social contract"*? The agreement not to rob, abuse, or kill one another? It had to be. And the law required enforcement, and that was where control came in. Without the control to enforce the contract, chaos reigned. The power that controlled needed to be greater than the people — otherwise, they would challenge it. The only entity capable of this was the Capitol.

It took him until about two in the morning to sort that out, and then it barely filled a page. Dr. Gaul would want more, but that was all he could manage tonight. He crawled into bed, where he dreamed of Lucy Gray being hunted by the rainbow snakes. He awoke with a start, trembling, to the strains of the anthem. *You have got to hold yourself together*, he told himself. *The Games can't last much longer.*

The breakfast delights provided by Mrs. Plinth gave him a boost into day four of the Hunger Games. On the trolley, he gorged himself on a slice of blackberry pie, a sausage roll, and a cheese tart. Between the Games and the Plinths, his waistband was becoming snug. He would make an effort to walk home.

Velvet ropes cordoned off the section of the dais with the eight remaining mentors, and now a sign with the occupant's name hung on the back of each chair. Assigned seating — that was new, but probably an attempt to mitigate some of the snarkiness that had sprung up in the last few days. Coriolanus remained in the back row, between Io and Urban. Poor Festus was sandwiched between Vipsania and Clemensia.

Lucky welcomed the audience with the long-suffering Jubilee, who'd been confined in a cage more suited to a rabbit than a bird. Nothing stirred in the arena, and the tributes seemed to be sleeping in. The only new development was that someone, likely Reaper, had dragged Jessup's body to the line of the dead near the barricade.

Coriolanus nervously awaited the announcement of Gaius Breen's death, but no word was forthcoming. The Gamemakers spent time with the crowd in front of the arena, which continued to expand. The different fan clubs now sported shirts with tribute and mentor faces, and Coriolanus felt both pleased and embarrassed to see his image staring back at him from the giant screen.

Not until midmorning did the first tribute make an appearance, and it took the audience a moment to place her.

"It's Wovey!" Hilarius shouted in relief. "She's alive!"

Coriolanus remembered the child as scrawny, but now she looked skeletal, her arms and legs like sticks, her cheeks sunken. She crouched at the mouth of a tunnel in her filthy striped dress, squinting into the sunlight and clutching an empty water bottle.

"Hold on, Wovey! Food's on the way!" said Hilarius, hammering away at his cuff. She couldn't have much in the way of sponsors, but there was always someone willing to place a bet on a long shot.

Lepidus swooped in, and Hilarius spoke at length about Wovey's merits. He presented her absence as stealth, claiming it had been their strategy all along for her to hide and let the field clear. "And look at her! Here she is in the final eight!" As a half dozen drones sped across the arena toward her, Hilarius became even more excited. "There's her food and water now! All she has to do is grab it and get back in hiding!"

As the supplies showered her, Wovey lifted her hands but seemed in a daze. She pawed at the ground, located a bottle of water, and struggled to unscrew the cap. After a few gulps, she sank back against the wall and gave a small belch. A thin stream of silverish liquid trickled out of the side of her mouth and then she went still.

The audience watched uncomprehendingly for a minute.

"She's dead," announced Urban.

"No! No, she's not dead. She's just resting!" said Hilarius.

But the longer Wovey stared unblinkingly into the bright sunlight, the harder that was to believe. Coriolanus examined her spittle — neither clear nor bloody, but slightly off — and wondered if Lucy Gray had finally managed to put the rat poison to use. It would've been easy to poison the last swallow of water in a bottle and discard it in one of the tunnels. Desperate Wovey would not have thought twice about downing it. But no one else, not even Hilarius, seemed to find anything amiss.

"I don't know," said Lepidus to Hilarius. "I think your friend might be right."

They waited another ten long minutes without a flicker of life from Wovey before Hilarius gave in and lifted his chair. Lepidus heaped on the praise, and Hilarius, while disappointed, reckoned things could have gone a lot worse. "She managed to hang in there a long time, given her condition. I wish she'd have come out sooner so I could've fed her, but I feel like I can hold my head up. The final eight is nothing to sneeze at!"

Coriolanus mentally checked his list. Both tributes from 3, both from 4, and Treech and Reaper. That was all that stood between Lucy Gray and victory. Six tributes and a fair amount of luck.

Wovey's death went unnoticed for a while in the arena. It was almost lunchtime when Reaper came out from the barricade, still wearing his flag cape. He approached Wovey warily, but she had posed no threat alive, and she certainly didn't dead. Reaper crouched beside her and picked up an apple, then frowned as he examined her face more closely.

He knows, thought Coriolanus. *He at least suspects that it wasn't a natural death.*

Reaper dropped the apple, lifted Wovey into his arms, and headed to the dead tributes, abandoning the food and water on the ground.

"You see?" Clemensia asked no one in particular. "You see what I'm dealing with? My tribute's mentally unbalanced."

"I guess you're right," said Festus. "Sorry about earlier."

And that was it. Wovey's death caused no suspicion outside the arena, and inside it only Reaper questioned the cause. Lucy Gray was not prone to carelessness. Perhaps she'd even chosen frail Wovey as a target because the child's already-grave condition would mask the poisoning. He felt frustrated by his inability to communicate with her and update their strategy together. With so few left, was hiding still the best approach, or would it be better for her to act more aggressively? Of course, he didn't know. She could be planting poisoned food and water at this very moment. In which case, she'd need more, which he couldn't provide if she didn't make an appearance. Although he didn't believe in it, he tried to channel her telepathically. *Let me help, Lucy Gray. Or at least let me see that you're all right*, he thought. Then added, *I miss you.*

Reaper had returned to the tunnels by the time District 4 scavenged Wovey's food. Their absolute lack of concern with its origin reassured Coriolanus that the possibility of poisoning had flown under the radar. They sat right down where Wovey died and gobbled up every bite, then they strolled back to their tunnel. Mizzen walked with a limp, but he would still outmatch most of the remaining tributes if it came to a fight. Coriolanus wondered if, in the end, it would all come down to

Coral and Mizzen deciding which District 4 tribute took home the crown.

In all his years, Coriolanus had never left a school lunch unfinished, but the cardboard bowls of lima beans on noodles turned his stomach. Still full from the Plinths' breakfast, he just couldn't bring himself to swallow even a spoonful, and it required a quick exchange of his untouched bowl with Festus's empty one to avoid a reprimand. "Here. Lima beans still taste like the war to me."

"That's me and oatmeal. One whiff and I want to hide in a bunker," said Festus, who made quick work of the stuff. "Thanks. I overslept and missed breakfast."

Coriolanus hoped the lima beans hadn't been a bad omen. Then he admonished himself. This was no time to start embracing superstitions. He needed to keep his wits sharp, stay personable for the cameras, and get through the day. Lucy Gray must be getting hungry by now. He planned his next food delivery while he sipped his water.

With Hilarius gone, the three remaining mentor chairs in the back row had been centered, and Coriolanus resumed his seat in the middle. It was, as Domitia had called it, like a game of musical chairs, and these were the very people he'd played with during childhood. If he ever had children, and he planned to one day, would they still be among the elite Capitol social club? Or would they be relegated to lesser circles? It would help if they had a wider family network to draw on, but he and Tigris were the only Snows of their generation. Without her, he'd be headed into the future all alone.

Little occurred in the arena that afternoon. Coriolanus watched for Lucy Gray, hoping for a chance to feed her, but she remained elusive. The audience outside the arena provided most of the excitement when Coral fans mixed it up with Treech fans over who was worthiest to be crowned victor. A few punches were thrown before the Peacekeepers separated the two groups, sending them to opposite sides of the crowd. Coriolanus felt glad his own fans had a little more class.

In late afternoon, when Lucky resumed his coverage, Dr. Gaul sat across from him holding Jubilee in his cage. The bird rocked back and forth like a small child trying to comfort itself. Lucky eyed his pet with worry, perhaps anticipating its loss to the labs. "We have a special guest with us today: Head Gamemaker Dr. Gaul, who's been making friends with Jubilee. I hear you have some sad news for us, Dr. Gaul."

Dr. Gaul moved Jubilee's cage to the table. "Yes. Due to injuries sustained in the rebel bombing of the arena, another of our Academy students, Gaius Breen, has died."

As his classmates cried out, Coriolanus tried to center himself. Any minute he might be called upon to respond to Gaius's death, but that wasn't the source of his anxiety. Gaius would be easy enough to eulogize; he hadn't an enemy in the world.

"I think I speak for everyone when I say we extend our sympathies to the family," said Lucky.

Dr. Gaul's face hardened. "We do. But actions speak louder than words, and our rebel enemies seem somewhat hard of hearing. In response, we've planned something special for their children in the arena."

"Shall we tune in?" said Lucky.

In the center of the arena, Teslee and Circ squatted over a pile of rubble, poking around for who knew what. Apparently, they held no interest for Reaper, who sat high in the stands, his back to the arena wall, wrapped in his cape. Suddenly, Treech burst out of a tunnel and bore down on the District 3 tributes, who fled for the barricade.

Murmurs of confusion came from the audience. Where was the *"something special"* promised by Dr. Gaul? They were answered by the sight of an oversized drone flying into the arena, transporting the rainbow snake tank.

Coriolanus had all but convinced himself that the snake attack had been a product of an overheated imagination, but the entry of the tank ended that. His brain had assembled the puzzle pieces in exactly the right order. What he didn't know was how the snakes would respond to being unleashed, but he'd been in the lab. Dr. Gaul did not breed lapdogs; she designed weapons.

The unusual package caught Treech's attention. Perhaps he thought some extra-special gift had been earmarked for him, because he halted as the drone reached the middle of the arena. Teslee and Circ paused as well, and even Reaper rose to observe the delivery. The drone released the uncovered tank about ten yards above the ground. Rather than shattering, the container bounced on impact. Then, like a flower opening its petals, its walls fell to the ground.

Snakes shot out in all directions, creating a multicolored sunburst in the dust.

In the front row, Clemensia jumped to her feet and let out a bloodcurdling scream, almost causing Festus to fall out of his chair. As most people were only just registering the new development on the screen, her reaction seemed extreme. Afraid that Clemensia would spill the whole story in her panic, Coriolanus leaped up and wrapped his arms around her from behind, not sure if the move was meant to be comforting or confining. Clemensia went rigid but silent.

"They're not here. They're in the arena," Coriolanus said in her ear. "You're safe." But he continued to hold on to her as the action unfolded.

Maybe Treech's lumber district background had given him some familiarity with snakes. The second they erupted from the tank, he'd turned on his heel and sprinted for the stands. He bounced up the debris hill like a goat and kept moving, hurdling over seats as he ascended.

The few moments of confusion that Teslee and Circ experienced came at a great cost. Teslee made it to one of the poles and managed to shinny up a few yards to safety, but Circ stumbled over a rusty, old spear, and the snakes overtook him. A dozen pairs of fangs pierced his body and then, as if satisfied, the snakes moved on. Pink, yellow, and blue streaked his body as the wounds pumped out bright pus. Smaller than Clemensia, with double the venom in his system, Circ struggled to breathe for about ten seconds before he died.

Teslee stared at his fallen body and sobbed in terror as she clung to the pole. Below her, the delicate snakes bunched, rearing up and dancing around the base.

Lucky's voice-over boomed above the scene. "What's happening?"

"These are muttations we've developed in our labs in the Capitol," Dr. Gaul informed the audience. "They're only snakelets, but full-grown they'll easily outrun a human, and that post will be no problem for them to climb. They're designed to hunt humans and reproduce rapidly so any casualties can be swiftly replaced."

By this time, Treech had climbed out onto the narrow shelf over the scoreboard, and Reaper had found refuge on the roof of the press box. The few snakes that had managed to scale the rubble into the stands gathered below them.

The mics picked up the muted sounds of a girl's scream.

They got Lucy Gray, Coriolanus thought in despair. *The handkerchief didn't work.*

But just then, Mizzen exploded from the tunnel nearest the barricade, followed by a shrieking Coral. A single snake dangled from her arm. She tore it free, but dozens charged for her the moment it hit the ground, targeting her lower legs. Mizzen flung away his trident and made a flying leap to gain the pole across from Teslee. Despite his bad knee, he halved his previous time climbing to the top. From there he witnessed Coral's frantic, but blissfully short, end.

With the targets on the ground disposed of, most of the snakes regrouped under Teslee. Her grip on the pole began to fail, and she cried out to Mizzen for help, but he only shook his head, more stunned than malicious.

People in the audience began shushing each other then, although Coriolanus did not know why. As the hall quieted, he picked up on what sharper ears had detected. Somewhere, ever so faintly, someone was singing in the arena.

His girl.

Lucy Gray emerged from her tunnel moving in slow motion, and backward. She lifted each foot with care as she stepped behind herself, swaying gently to the rhythm of her music.

La, la, la, la,
La, la, la, la, la, la,
La, la, la, la, la, la . . .

That was the extent of the lyrics at the moment, but it was compelling nonetheless. Following her, as if mesmerized by the melody, came half a dozen snakes.

Coriolanus released Clemensia, who had calmed down, giving her a gentle push in Festus's direction. He stepped toward the screen, holding his breath as Lucy Gray continued to back in and then curve around toward where Jessup's body had lain. Her voice became louder as she, knowingly or not, worked her way back to the mic. Perhaps for one last song, one last performance.

None of the snakes were inclined to attack her, though. In fact, she seemed to be drawing them from around the arena. The bunch under Teslee's pole thinned, a few dropped from the stands, and dozens slithered out of the tunnels to join in a general migration to Lucy Gray. They surrounded her, flocking in from all sides, making it impossible for her to continue retreating. The bright bodies undulated over her bare feet, curling around her ankles as she lowered herself gently onto a chunk of marble.

With the tips of her fingers, she spread her ruffles out in the dust, as if by way of invitation. As the snakes swarmed her, the faded fabric vanished, leaving her with a brilliant skirt of weaving reptiles.

Coriolanus squeezed his hands into fists, unsure of the vipers' intentions. The snakes in the tank, having been exposed to his scent on the proposal, had entirely ignored him. But these seemed magnetically drawn to his tribute. Could it be that the environment made the difference? Violently released from the warm, close quarters of their tank into the vast, unsheltered arena, were they seeking her out as the only familiar scent they could find? Had they gravitated to her to harbor in the safety of her skirt?

Lucy Gray knew nothing of this, because that day in the zoo when he'd meant to tell her about Clemensia and the snakes, her circumstances had been so much worse than his own that he'd kept silent on the subject. Even if he had told her, it would be a real leap of faith in his abilities to imagine he'd found a way to tamper with the snakes in the Games. What did she think was keeping them in check? It had to be her singing. Had she sung to the snakes at home? *"That snake was a particular friend of mine,"* she'd told the little girl in the zoo. Perhaps she'd befriended several snakes back in District 12. Perhaps she thought if she stopped singing, they would indeed kill her now. Perhaps this was her swan song. She would never want to go out without a finale. She would want to die with her boots on, in the brightest spotlight she could find.

When Lucy Gray began the lyrics, her voice was soft but clear as a bell.

You're headed for heaven,
The sweet old hereafter,
And I've got one foot in the door.
But before I can fly up,
I've loose ends to tie up,
Right here in
The old therebefore.

An old song, Coriolanus thought. With talk of the hereafter, which reminded him of Sejanus and his bread crumbs, but also that funny line about the therebefore. That must mean the present. Here. Now. While she was still alive.

I'll be along
When I've finished my song,
When I've shut down the band,
When I've played out my hand,
When I've paid all my debts,
When I have no regrets,
Right here in
The old therebefore,
When nothing
Is left anymore.

The Gamemakers cut to a longer shot, which made Coriolanus want to shout an objection until he realized why. Every snake in the arena appeared to have fallen subject to her siren's song and flocked to her. Even those in the nest under Teslee, who was ready prey, had abandoned their target and made for Lucy Gray. Still shuddering from the trauma, Teslee slid shakily to the ground and hobbled over to a chain-link fence on one section of the barricade. She climbed her way to a safe height while the song continued.

I'll catch you up
When I've emptied my cup,
When I've worn out my friends,
When I've burned out both ends,
When I've cried all my tears,
When I've conquered my fears,
Right here in
The old therebefore,
When nothing
Is left anymore.

The camera made its way back to a tight shot of Lucy Gray. Coriolanus had the feeling that she usually catered to an audience well plied with liquor. In the days before her interview, he'd listened to many a number that conjured up a drunken group waving tin cups of gin from side to side in some dive bar. Although the liquor didn't seem essential, because when he took a quick look over his shoulder, he saw that several people in Heavensbee Hall had begun to sway to her rhythm. Her voice rose in volume, echoing around the arena . . .

I'll bring the news
When I've danced off my shoes,
When my body's closed down,
When my boat's run aground,
When I've tallied the score,
And I'm flat on the floor,
Right here in

The old therebefore,
When nothing
Is left anymore

. . . and then reaching a crescendo as she brought it home.

When I'm pure like a dove,
When I've learned how to love,
Right here in
The old therebefore,
When nothing
Is left anymore.

The last note hung in the air while the audience held its collective breath. The snakes waited for it to fade, and then — or was it his imagination? — began to stir. Lucy Gray responded by softly humming, as if to a restless baby. The viewers quietly relaxed as the snakes relaxed around her.

Lucky looked as spellbound as the snakes when the cameras cut back to him, eyes a bit glazed, mouth slackly open. He snapped back when he saw his own image on the feed, and turned his attention to a stone-faced Dr. Gaul. "Well, Head Gamemaker, take . . . a . . . bow!"

Heavensbee Hall erupted into a standing ovation, but Coriolanus could not peel his eyes off Dr. Gaul. What was going on behind that inscrutable expression? Did she attribute the snakes' behavior to Lucy Gray's singing, or did she suspect foul play? Even if Dr. Gaul knew about the handkerchief, perhaps she would forgive him, as the result had been so dramatic.

Dr. Gaul allowed herself a small nod of acknowledgment. "Thank you. But the focus today should be not on me, but on

Gaius Breen. Perhaps his classmates might share some remembrances with us."

Lepidus leaped into action in Heavensbee Hall, collecting stories from Gaius's classmates. It was well that Dr. Gaul had given him a heads-up, because while everybody had a joke or a funny story to share, only Coriolanus managed to tie in the heroic loss, the snakes, and the retribution they had witnessed in the arena. "We could never let the death of such a stellar youth of the Capitol go without repercussions. When hit, we hit back twice as hard, just as Dr. Gaul has mentioned in the past."

Lepidus tried to turn the conversation to Lucy Gray's extraordinary performance with the snakes, but Coriolanus only said, "She's remarkable. But Dr. Gaul is right. This moment belongs to Gaius. Let's save Lucy Gray for tomorrow."

After a full half hour of remembrance, Lepidus bid the show's adieus to Festus and Io, as Coral and Circ had succumbed to venom. Coriolanus gave Festus a bear hug, surprisingly emotional at seeing his reliable friend leave the dais. He felt the loss of Io as well, since she veered more toward clinical than combative, which was more than he could say for the others remaining. Except perhaps Persephone, who he decided to share his supper hour with. Cannibals over cutthroats.

The student body went home, leaving the handful of active mentors to their steak dinners. Coriolanus glanced around at his competitors. Being in the final five, he should have been flying high. But if one of the others won, Dean Highbottom could still give him a prize that was insufficient to pay for university, perhaps citing the demerit as his reason. Only the Plinth Prize would truly protect him.

He shifted his focus to the screen, where Lucy Gray continued to hum to her pets, Teslee disappeared behind the barricade, and

Mizzen, Treech, and Reaper held their lofty positions. Clouds rolled in, portending a storm and creating a dazzling sunset. The bad weather brought a quick nightfall, and he had not yet finished his pudding when Lucy Gray faded from view, and a deep rumble of thunder shook the arena. He hoped for lightning to provide some illumination, but the heavy downpour that followed made the night impenetrable.

Coriolanus decided to sleep in Heavensbee Hall, as did the other four remaining mentors. No one except Vipsania had thought to bring bedding, so the rest arranged themselves in the padded chairs, propping up their feet and using book bags as makeshift pillows. As the rainy night cooled the hall, Coriolanus dozed in his chair, one eye half-open for any activity on the screen. The storm obscured all, and eventually he drifted off. Near dawn, he woke with a start and looked around. Vipsania, Urban, and Persephone slept soundly. From a few yards away, Clemensia's large dark eyes shone in the dim light.

He did not want to be her enemy. If the Snow fortress was about to fall, he would need friends. Until the snake incident, he'd counted Clemensia among his best. And she'd always gotten on well with Tigris, too. But how to make amends?

Clemensia had one hand tucked inside her shirt, where she fingered the collarbone she'd presented in the hospital. The one covered in scales.

"Did they go away?" he whispered.

Clemensia tensed. "They're fading. Finally. They said it may take as long as a year."

"Are they painful?" It was the first time the idea had occurred to him.

"Not painful. They pull. On my skin." She rubbed the scales. "It's hard to explain."

Heartened by the confidence, he took the plunge. "I'm sorry, Clemmie. Really. About all of it."

"You didn't know what she had planned," said Clemensia.

"No, I didn't. But after, in the hospital, I should've been there for you. I should've broken down the doors to make sure you were okay," he insisted.

"Yes!" she said emphatically, but she seemed to relent a little. "But I know you were hurt, too. In the arena."

"Oh, don't make excuses for me." He threw up his hands. "I'm worthless and we both know it!"

A hint of a smile. "Almost. I guess I should thank you for keeping me from making a complete fool of myself today."

"Did I?" He squinted as if trying to recall. "All I remember is clinging to you. Not necessarily hiding behind you. But there was definitely clinging."

She laughed a little but then became serious. "I shouldn't have blamed so much on you. I'm sorry. I was terrified."

"With good reason. I wish you hadn't had to watch that today," he said.

"Maybe it was cathartic. I feel better somehow," she confessed. "Am I terrible?"

"No," he said. "The only thing you are is brave."

And so their friendship was shakily renewed. They let the others sleep while they shared the last cheese tart in Coriolanus's stash, talking of this and that and even rolling around the idea of trying to set up an alliance between Lucy Gray and Reaper in the arena. Since it seemed out of their control, they abandoned it. The two would pair up together or they would not.

"At least we're allies again," he said.

"Well, not enemies anyway," Clemensia allowed. But when they went to wash their faces for the cameras, she loaned him her soap so he wouldn't have to use the abrasive liquid goop in the bathrooms, and somehow the small but intimate gesture let him know he was forgiven.

No breakfast was provided, but Festus came in early to pass out egg sandwiches and apples in the spirit of camaraderie. Persephone beamed at him over her teacup. Now that Clemensia had lightened up, Coriolanus didn't feel as threatened by the mentor pool. They all wanted to win, but that was largely in their tributes' hands. He assessed Lucy Gray's competitors. Teslee, small and brainy. Mizzen, deadly but injured. Treech, athletic but still something of an unknown. Reaper, too strange for words.

The last of the clouds rolled out with the sunrise. Dead snakes littered the arena, draped over rubble, floating in puddles. Drowned, perhaps, or unable to survive the cold, wet night. Some genetically engineered creatures didn't do well outside the lab. Lucy Gray and Teslee were nowhere to be seen, but the three boys in soggy clothes hadn't ventured down from the heights. Mizzen was sleeping, his body belted to the beam. As the other students filed into Heavensbee Hall, Vipsania and Clemensia, who seemed almost normal, sent food to their tributes.

When the drones arrived, Treech ate hungrily, but Reaper again brushed off his food, climbing down into the arena to scoop water from a puddle. Indifferent to Treech and Mizzen, who finally awoke, he went about collecting Coral and Circ and adding them to his row. The other boys watched him warily, but neither engaged him, put off either by his eccentric behavior or the possibility of stray snakes. They were probably hoping that someone else would finish him off, but his work remained uninterrupted, and he returned to the press box when he'd tidied his morgue. Treech sat on the edge of the scoreboard, swinging his feet, while Mizzen mimed eating. Persephone responded immediately, ordering him a large breakfast.

After a minute, Teslee showed up. Her face pinched in concentration, she hauled out a drone that, while much like the original delivery craft, appeared slightly altered. She positioned herself directly under Mizzen.

"Does she think that will fly?" asked Vipsania dubiously. "Even if it does, how can she control it?"

Urban, who'd been scowling at the screen, sat forward suddenly in his seat. "She wouldn't have to. She wouldn't need to if— But how did she . . ." He trailed off, trying to puzzle something out.

Teslee flipped a switch, raised her arms, and launched the drone into the air. It ascended, revealing a cable that connected the base of the drone to a loop on her wrist. Thus tethered, the drone began to fly in a circle about halfway between her and Mizzen. He looked down, clearly perplexed, but got distracted by the arrival of his first drone from Persephone. It dropped a chunk of bread down to him and made as if to return home as usual. Then, a few yards out, it swerved and came back at him. Mizzen leaned back, surprised. He reflexively swatted at it, but it only passed over him, opening its claws to deliver a nonexistent gift, and came in again.

"What's wrong with that drone?" asked Persephone.

No one knew, but at that moment, a second drone came in with water, and a third with cheese. They, too, deposited their packets, only to hang around, attempting repeated deliveries. But the drones, which had been timed for a smooth airdrop, began to bump into one another, and sometimes into Mizzen. The tail of one caught him in the eye, and he cried out, lashing at it.

“Is there any way for me to contact the Gamemakers? I mean, I sent three more!” said Persephone.

“There’s nothing they can do,” said Urban in amusement. “She found a way to hack them. She’s blocked their homing direction, so his face is their only destination.”

Sure enough, as the other three drones arrived, one at a time, they malfunctioned in a similar fashion. Mizzen was their sole target, and what had seemed at first funny turned deadly. He got to his feet and attempted to flee down the beam, but they swarmed around him like bees to a honeypot. Having left his trident on the ground, he pulled his knife and attempted to fight them, but the most he achieved was momentarily knocking them off course. They weren’t programmed to make contact with him, but as they ricocheted off one another and his blade, more and more collided into him, until they gave the appearance of an attack. Mizzen began to grope his way to a pole — the very one on which he’d left Teslee to her fate — but his knee would not cooperate. Frantic now, he took a wild swing at the drones, throwing his weight onto his injured leg, which wobbled and then gave way. He lost his balance and plummeted toward the ground, snapping his neck sideways on contact.

“Oh!” Persephone exclaimed as he hit the ground. “Oh, she killed him!”

Vipsania frowned at the screen. “She’s smarter than she looks.”

Teslee gave a satisfied smile and reeled in her drone, switching it off and giving it a loving hug.

“Do not judge a book by its cover.” Urban chuckled as he tapped some gifts into his communicuff. “Especially if it belongs to me.”

His glee was short-lived. While featuring the drone incident, the Gamemakers had neglected to show the wider picture, in which Treech had climbed down from the scoreboard and through the stands, dropping into the arena. He seemed to appear out of thin air, making a gigantic leap into the frame and bringing his ax down on Teslee in one fell swoop. She had barely taken a step when the blade connected with her skull, splitting it open and killing her instantly. Treech leaned his hands on his knees, puffing with exertion, and then sat right on the ground next to her, watching the blood ooze into the sand. The drones arriving with a shower of food for her set him in motion again. He collected a dozen parcels and withdrew behind the barricade.

Urban covered his moment of disbelief with disgust and rose to go. He could not escape Lepidus's ever-present mic, though, and barely managed not to snarl when he said, "That's it for me. Laugh a minute, wasn't it?" Then he walked off, leaving Persephone to expand on her regrets and her gratitude for the opportunity to be a mentor.

"You made the top five!" Lepidus beamed at her. "No one can ever take that away from you."

"No," she said somewhat dubiously. "No, that's the kind of thing that sticks."

Coriolanus looked from Clemensia to Vipsania. "Just us, I guess." The three arranged their chairs in a row, with Coriolanus in the middle, while others cleared away the seats of the defeated.

Lucy Gray. Treech. Reaper. Final three. Final girl. Final day? Maybe that, too.

Lucky made his entrance in a hat stuck with five sparklers. "Hello, Panem! Had this hat done especially for the final five, but they've been sending off their own sparks!" He pulled two sparklers out of the hat and hurled them over his shoulder blindly. "Final three, anybody?"

One of the sparklers fizzled out on the floor, but the second set a curtain to smoking, eliciting a high-pitched yipping sound and panicked footwork from Lucky. A crew member ran on-screen with a fire extinguisher to handle the crisis, allowing Lucky to regain his composure. As his three remaining hat sparklers died, the number for sponsors and gamblers began flashing at the bottom of the screen. "Whoowee! The betting's getting hot and heavy! Do not miss out on the fun!"

Coriolanus's communicuff pinged healthily, but so did Vipsania's and Clemensia's. "A lot of good it will do me," Clemensia murmured to Coriolanus. "He doesn't trust me enough to eat anything I send."

Lucy Gray had to be hungry, but he assumed she was resting in the tunnels. He wanted to send her food and water, both for sustenance and as a conduit for the poison. Since her last two opponents could easily overpower her, he had to do something to put the odds in her favor. For now, he could think of nothing but to keep the crowd on her side. When Lepidus approached him for his promised thoughts on Lucy Gray's performance, he laid it on thick. Coriolanus didn't know what it would take to prove to people she was not district if she hadn't convinced them by now. "I feel a great injustice may have occurred by her being not just in the reaping, but in District Twelve at all. People will need to judge for themselves. If you agree with me, or even suspect I might be right, you know what to do." While the new barrage of donations hitting his communicuff was affirming, he didn't know how it would help. He could probably feed her for weeks on what he already had.

But the only tribute moving around the arena was Reaper, who had descended from the press box, cutting off another large swath of flag on his way. Gaunt and unsteady, he teetered over to add Teslee and Mizzen to his collection, using the new piece of flag to cover them. With effort, he climbed up to the back row of the arena, where he dozed in the sunlight, rocking gently back and forth, his cape spread out to dry. Coriolanus wondered if he would soon perish of natural causes. If starving to death was a natural cause. He wasn't entirely sure. Was it natural if hunger had been used as a weapon?

To his relief, Lucy Gray materialized just before noon in the shadows of a tunnel. She surveyed the arena and, judging it safe, stepped into the sunlight. The mud on the hem of her ruffled skirt had begun to cake, but the damp dress still clung to her. While Coriolanus ordered her a feast on his communicuff, Lucy Gray crossed to Reaper's puddle and knelt. She scooped up water, slaking her thirst and washing her face. After combing out her hair with her fingers, she twisted it into a loose knot, finishing just as a dozen drones entered the arena.

She appeared not to notice them as she took a bottle from her pocket and dipped the neck into the puddle, collecting an inch or so of water. After swishing it around, Lucy Gray poured the water back into the puddle and was making to refill the bottle when the incoming drones caught her attention. As the food and water began to drop around her, she tossed away the old bottle and gathered her gifts into her skirt.

Lucy Gray started for the nearest tunnel but then glanced up at Reaper lolling in the stands. She changed course, hurried to his morgue, and lifted the flag material. Her lips moved as she counted the fallen.

"She's trying to figure out who's left in the Games," Coriolanus said into the mic that Lepidus had pushed in his face.

"Maybe we should put it up on the scoreboard," joked Lepidus.

"I'm sure the tributes would find that helpful," said Coriolanus. "Seriously, that's a good idea."

Suddenly, Lucy Gray's head shot up, and the provisions in her skirt fell to the dirt as she turned on her heel and ran. She had heard what the audience could not. Treech swung out from behind the barricade, wielding his ax, and caught her wrist as she passed under the beam. Lucy Gray twisted around, dropping to her knees, fighting wildly as he raised the ax.

"No!" Coriolanus jumped to his feet, pushing Lepidus aside. "Lucy Gray!"

Then two things happened simultaneously. As the ax began to fall, she flung herself into Treech's arms and clung to him, avoiding the blade. Bizarrely, they seemed to embrace each other for a long moment, until Treech's eyes widened in horror. He shoved her away, dropping the ax, and tore something from the back of his neck. His hand shot into the air, fingers gripped tightly around the bright pink snake. Then he collapsed to his knees and smashed it into the ground, again and again, until he fell dead in the dirt, the lifeless snake still clutched in his fist.

Her chest rising and falling, Lucy Gray whipped around to locate Reaper, but he still sat rocking in the stands. Momentarily safe, she pressed one hand against her heart and waved to the audience.

As the crowd in the hall applauded, Coriolanus let his breath out in a huff and turned to acknowledge it. He'd done it. She'd done it. With her pockets full of poison, she'd made it to the final two. She must have sheltered the pink snake in her pocket, just as she had the green one at the reaping. Were there more? Or had Treech beaten the final survivor to death? No telling. But just the possibility of another reptilian weapon made Lucy Gray seem deadly.

While Lepidus ushered off Vipsania — who thanked the Gamemakers through gritted teeth — Coriolanus sank into his chair and watched Lucy Gray reclaim her feast. He leaned over to

Clemensia and whispered, "I'm glad it's us." She answered with a conspiratorial smile.

As Lucy Gray flattened the wrappings and spread all her food out in a pleasing fashion, Coriolanus thought of their picnic at the zoo. Was she restaging it now for his benefit? Something tugged at his heart, and the memory of the kiss hit him. Were there more in his future? For a minute, he drifted into a daydream of Lucy Gray winning, leaving the arena, and coming to live with him in the Snows' penthouse, which was somehow saved from taxes. He'd attend the University on his Plinth Prize while she headlined at Pluribus's newly reopened nightclub, because the Capitol would agree to let her stay and, well, he hadn't worked out all of the details, but the point was, he got to keep her. And he wanted to keep her. Safe and close at hand. Admired and admiring. Devoted. And entirely, unequivocally his. If what she'd said just before she kissed him — *"The only boy my heart has a sweet spot for now is you"* — was true, then wouldn't she want that, too?

Stop it! he thought. *No one has won anything yet!* She had polished off most of her food, so he ordered another round, a large one that she could squirrel away and live off for the next few days, in case she just decided to hunker down and wait for Reaper to die. It was a good plan, low risk to her and inevitable if he stayed on his current course of rejecting all sustenance. But what if he didn't? What if he regained his senses and decided to eat the nearly unlimited sponsor gifts that Clemensia could provide him with? Then it would come down to a physical matchup again, and Lucy Gray would be at a real disadvantage unless she was packing more snakes.

When the drones had delivered her supplies, Lucy Gray sorted them and stowed them in her pockets. They hadn't seemed spacious enough to hold all the food and drink along with another snake, but she was awfully clever. He hadn't even seen her remove the snake that killed Treech.

Festus brought Coriolanus and Clemensia sandwiches at lunch, but they were both too nervous to eat. The rest of the students ate in their seats, not wanting to miss a moment. Coriolanus could hear whispered yet passionate debates over who would win the day. He could never remember people caring in the past.

The beating sun began to dry out the arena, soaking up the shallow puddles and leaving only a few deep enough to drink from. Lucy Gray rested on a bit of rubble, her skirt spread out to catch the rays. The lull brought out Lucky, who gave a detailed weather forecast, including a heat advisory and tips to avoid related cramps, exhaustion, and stroke. The line at the lemonade stand outside the arena stretched long, and people hid under umbrellas or crammed into precious bits of shade. Even the dependable coolness of Heavensbee Hall failed, so students stripped off their jackets and fanned themselves with notebooks. By midafternoon, the school had made fruit punch available, which gave a festive feel to the event.

Lucy Gray kept Reaper in her sights, but he'd made no move to engage her. Suddenly, she rose as if impatient to get on with things, and retraced her steps to Treech's body. Taking hold of one ankle, she began to drag him over to Reaper's morgue. Reaper appeared to wake up the moment she touched the body. He leaned out and shouted something unintelligible, then hurried down from the stands. Lucy Gray let go of Treech and ran to a nearby tunnel. Reaper assumed the job of transporting Treech, placing him neatly in the row of dead tributes and covering him with the flag remnant. Satisfied, he made his way back to the stands, but he'd only just reached the wall when Lucy Gray ran out from a second tunnel, pulled one of the flag pieces off the bodies, and gave a holler. Reaper whipped around and ran at her. Lucy Gray wasted no time in vanishing behind the barricade. Reaper replaced the flag, tucking the fabric under the bodies to hold it more securely in place, and went to rest against a pole. After a few minutes, he seemed to drift off, his eyes closed against the sun. Lucy Gray darted out again, yanked one of the flag segments free, and this time ran off with it trailing behind her. By the time Reaper had come to realize her disruption, she'd put fifty yards between them. His indecision allowed her to widen her lead, and she dragged the flag to the dead center of the arena, where she left it in the dirt and made for the stands. Angry now, Reaper ran over and repossessed his flag. He took a few steps after her, but the exertion had taken a toll on him. Pressing his hands against his temples, he panted rapidly, although he didn't appear to be sweating. As Lucky's recent update had reminded them, that could be a sign of heatstroke.

She's trying to run him to death, thought Coriolanus. *And it might just work.*

Reaper staggered a bit, as though drunk. Flag in tow, he made his way to his puddle, one of the few that hadn't dried up during the afternoon. He dropped down on his knees and drank, slurping until only a muddy sludge remained on the bottom. As he sat back on his heels, a funny look crossed his face, and his fingers began to knead his ribs and chest. He vomited up a portion of the water, then retched for a while on his hands and knees before rising unsteadily. Still gripping the flag in one hand, he began to walk, in slow, uneven steps, back toward his morgue. Reaper had just made it when he collapsed on the ground, dragging himself in line next to Treech. One hand made an attempt to pull the flag over the group, but he managed only to cover himself partway before he drew in his limbs and went still.

Coriolanus sat frozen in anticipation. Was that it? Had he really won? The Hunger Games? The Plinth Prize? The girl? He studied Lucy Gray's face as she watched Reaper from the stands, but she had a distant look, as if she were far away from the action in the arena.

The audience in the hall began to murmur. Was Reaper dead? Shouldn't they be declaring a winner? Coriolanus and Clemensia waved Lepidus and his mic away as they awaited the outcome. Half an hour passed before Lucy Gray climbed down from the stands and approached Reaper. She placed her fingers on his neck, checking his pulse. Satisfied, she closed his eyelids and tenderly arranged the flag over the tributes, as if she were putting children to bed. Then she went over and sat against a pole to wait.

This seemed to convince the Gamemakers, because Lucky appeared, jumping up and down, announcing that Lucy Gray Baird, tribute of District 12, and her mentor, Coriolanus Snow, had won the Tenth Hunger Games.

Heavensbee Hall erupted around Coriolanus, and Festus organized a few classmates to lift his chair and parade him around the dais. When they finally set him down, Lepidus hounded him with questions, to which he could only reply that the experience had been both exhilarating and humbling. Then the entire student body was directed to the dining hall, where cake and posca had been provided for a celebration. Coriolanus sat in a place of honor, receiving congratulations and downing more posca than was good for him. So what? Right now, he felt invincible.

Satyria rescued him just as his head felt fuzzy, ushering him from the dining hall and directing him to the high biology lab. "I think they're bringing your girl over. Don't be surprised if they put you on camera together. Well done."

Coriolanus gave her a spontaneous hug and hurried for the lab, grateful for the moment of quiet. He felt his lips stretching into an insane grin. He had won. He'd won glory, and a future, and maybe love, too. Any minute now, he'd have Lucy Gray in his arms. *Oh, Snow lands on top; it most certainly does.* He forced his cheeks to relax as he got to the door, and straightened his jacket to help conceal the tipsy mess he actually was. It wouldn't do, somehow, to let Dr. Gaul see him like that.

When he opened the door to the high biology lab, he found only Dean Highbottom, sitting in his usual place at the table. "Close the door behind you." Coriolanus obliged. Perhaps the dean wanted to congratulate him in private. Or even apologize for abusing him. A falling star might one day have need of a rising one. But as he approached the dean, a cold dread washed over him. There, arranged on the table like lab specimens, were three items: an Academy napkin stained with grape punch, his mother's silver compact, and a dingy white handkerchief.

The meeting could not have lasted more than five minutes. Afterward, as agreed, Coriolanus headed directly to the Recruitment Center, where he became Panem's newest, if not shiniest, Peacekeeper.

PART III

"THE PEACEKEEPER"

Coriolanus leaned his temple against the glass window, trying to absorb any bit of coolness it might have retained. The stifling train car had just cleared when a half dozen of his fellow recruits piled out at District 9. Alone at last. He'd been on the train for twenty-four hours without a moment of privacy. Forward motion was often interrupted by long, unexplained waits. With the fitful travel and the jabbering of the other enlistees, he hadn't slept a wink. Instead he'd feigned sleep in an attempt to dissuade anyone from talking to him. Perhaps he could nap now, then awake from this nightmare that seemed, by its tenacity, to actually be his real life. He rubbed his scabby cheek with the stiff, scratchy cuff of his new Peacekeeper shirt, only reinforcing his hopelessness.

What an ugly place, he thought dully as the train chugged its way through District 9. The concrete buildings, flaking paint and misery, baked in the relentless afternoon sun. And how much uglier District 12 had the likelihood of being, with its additional coat of coal dust. He'd never really seen much of it, just the grainy coverage of the square on reaping day. It didn't look fit for human habitation.

When he'd asked to be assigned there, the officer's eyebrows had lifted in surprise. "Don't hear that much," he'd said, but stamped it through without further discussion. Apparently, not everyone had been following the Hunger Games, as he didn't seem to know who Coriolanus was or make mention of Lucy Gray. All the better. At the moment, anonymity was a condition greatly to be desired. Much of the shame of his situation came from bearing his last name. He burned as he remembered his encounter with Dean Highbottom. . . .

"Do you hear that, Coriolanus? It's the sound of Snow falling."

How he hated Dean Highbottom. His bloated face floating above the evidence. The tip of his pen poking at the items on the lab table. "This napkin. Confirmed with your DNA. Used to illegally smuggle food from the dining hall into the arena. We picked it up as evidence from the crime scene after the bombing. Ran a routine check, and there you were."

"You were starving her to death," Coriolanus had said, his voice cracking.

"Rather standard procedure in the Hunger Games. But it wasn't so much the feeding, which we overlooked for all the mentors, but the thieving from the Academy. Strictly forbidden," said Dean Highbottom. "I was all for exposing you then, presenting you with another demerit, and disqualifying you from the Games, but Dr. Gaul felt you were of more use as a martyr for the cause of the wounded Capitol. So instead we had your recording bellowing out the anthem while you recuperated in the hospital."

"Then why bring it up now?" Coriolanus asked.

"Only to establish a pattern of behavior." The pen tapped the silver rose next. "Now, this compact. How many times did I see your mother pull it from her handbag to check her face? Your pretty, vapid mother, who'd somehow convinced herself that your father would give her freedom and love. Out of the frying pan and into the fire, as they say."

"She wasn't" was all Coriolanus managed. Vapid, he meant.

"Only her youth excused her, and, really, she seemed fated to be a child forever. Just the opposite of your girl, Lucy Gray.

Sixteen going on thirty-five, and a hard thirty-five at that," observed Dean Highbottom.

"She gave you the compact?" Coriolanus's heart dropped at the thought.

"Oh, don't blame her. The Peacekeepers had to wrestle her to the ground to get the thing. Naturally, we do a thorough search of the victors when they leave the arena." The dean cocked his head and smiled. "So smart about how she poisoned Wovey and Reaper. Not really fair play, but what's to be done? Sending her back to District Twelve seems punishment enough. She said the rat poison was all her idea, that the compact had just been a token."

"It's true," said Coriolanus. "It was. A token of my affection. I don't know anything about any poison."

"Let's say I believe you, which I don't. But let's say I do. What, then, am I to make of this?" Dean Highbottom lifted the handkerchief with the tip of the pen. "One of the lab assistants found it in the snake tank yesterday morning. Everyone was baffled at first, checking their pockets to see if their own hankies had gone astray, because who else had been near the mutts? One young fellow actually claimed it, saying his allergies had been particularly bad and that he'd misplaced his handkerchief only a few days before. But just as he was offering his resignation, someone noticed the initials. Not yours. Your father's. So delicately stitched in the corner."

CXS. Stitched in the same white thread as the border. Part of the border pattern, really, so unassuming that you'd have to look carefully for it, but irrefutably there. Coriolanus never bothered to examine his daily handkerchief; he just stuffed one in his pocket as he headed out. There would've been a slim chance of denying the charge if the middle name hadn't been so distinctive. Xanthos. The only name Coriolanus even knew that began with an *X*, and the only person who carried it was his father. Crassus Xanthos Snow.

There was no need to ask about the DNA test, which Dean Highbottom had surely run, finding both his and Lucy Gray's signature. "So why haven't you made this public?"

"Oh, believe me, I was tempted. But the Academy, when expelling a student, has a tradition of offering them a lifeline," the dean explained. "As an alternative to public disgrace, you may join the Peacekeepers by the end of the day."

"But . . . why would I do that? I mean, why would I say I would do that? When I've just . . . won the Plinth Prize to the University?" he stammered.

"Who knows? Because you're that kind of patriot? Because you believe learning to defend your country is a better education than a lot of book knowledge?" Dean Highbottom began laughing. "Because the Hunger Games changed you, and you're going where you can best serve Panem? You're a clever young man, Coriolanus. I'm sure you'll think of something."

"But . . . but I . . . ?" His head swam with posca and adrenaline. "Why? Why do you hate me so much?" he blurted out. "I thought you were my father's friend!"

That sobered the dean. "I thought I was, too. Once. But it turned out I was only someone he liked because he could use them. Even now."

"But he's dead now! He's been dead for years!" cried Coriolanus.

"He deserves to be, but he seems very much alive in you." The dean made a shooing motion. "Better hurry. The office closes in twenty minutes. If you run, you can just make it."

And so he'd run, not knowing what else to do. After he'd enlisted, he made straight for the Citadel, hoping to throw himself on Dr. Gaul's mercy. He was denied entrance, even when he pleaded infected stitches. The Peacekeepers phoned down to the lab and were told to redirect him to the hospital. One of the guards took pity on him and agreed to try to get his final paper to Dr. Gaul. No promises. In the margin, he started to scribble a note begging for her to intercede but felt the pointlessness of the thing. He merely wrote *Thank you.* For what, he didn't know, but he refused to let her feed on his desperation.

On the walk home, the congratulations from neighbors went like daggers to his heart, but the real agony began when he entered the apartment to the sounds of tin horns and cheers. Tigris and the Grandma'am had gotten out the party favors they used to celebrate the new year and had bought a bakery cake for the occasion. He attempted a weak smile, then burst into tears. And then he told them everything. When he finished, they both became very calm and still, like a pair of marble statues.

"When do you leave?" asked Tigris.

"Tomorrow morning," he said.

"When will you be back?" asked the Grandma'am.

He couldn't bear to say twenty years. She would never last that long. If he saw her again, it would be in the mausoleum. "I don't know."

She nodded that she understood, then drew herself up in her chair. "Remember, Coriolanus, that wherever you go, you will always be a Snow. No one can ever take that from you."

He wondered if that wasn't the problem. The impossibility of being a Snow in this postwar world. What it had driven him to do. But he only said, "I'll try to one day be worthy of it."

Tigris rose. "Come on, Coryo. I'll help you pack." He followed her to his room. She hadn't cried. He knew she would try to hold in her tears until he left.

"Not much to pack. They said wear old clothes to throw out.

They provide all our uniforms, hygiene, everything. I can only bring personal items that fit in this." Coriolanus pulled a box, eight by twelve inches, about three inches deep, from his book bag. The cousins stared at it a long moment.

"What will you take?" asked Tigris. "You must make it count."

Photographs of his mother holding him as a toddler, of his father in uniform, of Tigris and the Grandma'am, of a few of his friends. An old compass with a brass body, which had been his father's. The disk of rose-scented powder that had once lived in his mother's silver compact, wrapped carefully in his orange silk scarf. Three handkerchiefs. Stationery with the Snow family seal. His Academy ID. A ticket stub from a childhood circus, stamped with an image of the arena. A chip of marble from the rubble of a bombing. He felt for all the world like Ma Plinth, with her handful of District 2 memories in her kitchen.

Neither of them slept. They went up to the roof and stared out at the Capitol until the sun began to rise. "You were set up to fail," said Tigris. "The Hunger Games are an unnatural, vicious punishment. How could a good person like you be expected to go along with them?"

"You mustn't say that to anyone but me. It isn't safe," Coriolanus warned her.

"I know," she said. "And that's wrong, too."

Coriolanus showered and dressed in a fraying pair of uniform pants, a threadbare T-shirt, and broken flip-flops, then drank a cup of tea in the kitchen. He kissed the Grandma'am good-bye and took one last look at his home before heading out.

In the hall, Tigris offered him an old sun hat and a pair of sunglasses that had been her father's. "For the trip."

Coriolanus recognized a disguise when he saw it and gratefully put them on, tucking his curls up under the hat. They remained silent as they walked through the largely deserted streets to the Recruitment Center. Then he turned to her, his voice raspy from emotion. "I've left you with everything to deal with. The apartment, the taxes, the Grandma'am. I'm so sorry. If you never forgive me, I'll understand."

"Nothing to forgive," she said. "Write as soon as you can?"

They hugged so tightly he felt several stitches pop on his arm. Then he marched into the Center, where three hundred or so of the Capitol's citizens milled around, waiting to embark on their new life. He felt a flicker of hope that he might fail his physical, then a flare of panic at the thought. What fate awaited him if he did? A public dressing-down? Prison? Dean Highbottom hadn't said, but he imagined the worst. He passed easily and they even took out his stitches without comment. The buzz cut that separated him from his signature curls left him feeling naked but looking so altered that the few curious glances he'd been receiving stopped entirely. He changed into spanking-new fatigues and received a duffel bag filled with additional clothing, a hygiene kit, a water bottle, and a packet of meat-spread sandwiches for the train trip. Then he signed a stack of forms, one of which directed them to send half of his small paycheck to Tigris and the Grandma'am. That provided him a scrap of consolation.

Shorn, costumed, and vaccinated, Coriolanus joined a busload of recruits going to the train station. It was a mix of boys and girls from the Capitol, mostly recent graduates from secondary schools whose commencements fell earlier than the Academy's. Burying himself in a corner of the station, he watched Capitol News, dreading a report on his predicament, but he saw only standard Saturday fare. Weather. Traffic rerouted for reconstruction.

A recipe for summer vegetable salad. It was as if the Hunger Games had never happened.

I'm being erased, he thought. *And to erase me, they must erase the Games.*

Who knew of his disgrace? The faculty? His friends? No one had contacted him. Perhaps word had not yet gotten out. But it would. People would speculate. Rumors would fly. A version of the truth, twisted and juicy, would win the day. Oh, how Livia Cardew would gloat. Clemensia would get the Plinth Prize at graduation. In the month of summer break, they would wonder about him. A few might even miss him. Festus. Lysistrata, maybe. In September, his classmates would begin university. And he would slowly be forgotten.

To erase the Games would be to erase Lucy Gray as well. Where was she? Had she really been sent back home? Was she at this moment returning to District 12, locked in the stinking cattle car that had brought her to the Capitol? That's what Dean Highbottom had indicated would happen, but the ultimate decision would be Dr. Gaul's, and she might not be so forgiving about their cheating. Under her direction, Lucy Gray might be imprisoned, or killed, or turned into an Avox. Or, even worse, sentenced to a life of experimentation in Dr. Gaul's lab of horrors.

Remembering he was on the train, Coriolanus shut his eyes, afraid tears might come. It would never do to be seen bawling like a baby, so he wrestled his emotions back under control. He calmed himself with the idea that returning Lucy Gray to District 12 might be the best strategy for the Capitol anyway. Perhaps, as time passed, Dr. Gaul might produce her again, especially if he was well out of the way. Have her come back and sing to kick off the Games. Her crimes, if there had been any, were minor compared to his. And the audience had loved her, hadn't they? Perhaps her charms would save her once again.

Every so often the train would stop and vomit out more recruits, either at their designated district or for transfer to transports headed north or south or wherever they'd been assigned. Sometimes he stared out the windows at the dead cities they passed, now abandoned to the elements, and wondered what the world had been like when they'd all been in their glory. Back when this had been North America, not Panem. It must have been fine. A land full of Capitols. Such a waste . . .

Around midnight, the compartment door slid open and two girls bound for District 8 fell in with a half gallon of posca they'd somehow smuggled onto the train. Times being what they were, he spent the night helping them consume it and then awoke, a full day later, to find the train pulling into District 12 as a sultry Tuesday morning dawned.

Coriolanus stumbled onto the platform with a throbbing head and sandpaper mouth. Following orders, he and three other recruits formed a line and waited an hour for a Peacekeeper who didn't look much older than them to lead them out of the station and through the gritty streets. The heat and humidity turned the air to some state halfway between a liquid and a gas, and he could not confirm if he was inhaling or exhaling. Moisture bathed his body with an unfamiliar sheen that defied wiping away. Sweat didn't dry, only deepened. His nose ran freely, the snot already tinged black with coal dust. His socks squished in his stiff boots. After an hour's trek down cinder and cracked-asphalt streets lined with hideous buildings, they arrived at the base that was to be his new home.

The security fence enclosing the base, as well as the armed

Peacekeepers at the gate, made him feel less exposed. The recruits followed their guide through an assortment of nondescript gray buildings. At the barracks, the two girls peeled off while he and the only other new male recruit, a tall, rail-thin boy named Junius, were directed to a room lined with four sets of bunk beds and eight lockers. Two of the bunks were neatly made, and two of the remaining, placed near a smeared window that looked out on a dumpster, had stacks of bedding on them. The boys clumsily followed instructions for making them up, Coriolanus taking the top bunk in deference to Junius's fear of heights. Then they were given the rest of the morning to shower, unpack, and review the Peacekeeper training manual before reporting to the mess for lunch at eleven.

Coriolanus stood in the shower, head back, gulping down the lukewarm water that flowed from the tap. He toweled off three times before he accepted the dampness of his skin as a perpetual state and dressed in clean fatigues. After unpacking his duffel and tucking his precious box on the top shelf of his locker, he climbed onto his bed and perused the Peacekeepers' manual — or pretended to — to avoid conversation with Junius, a nervous fellow who needed reassurance that Coriolanus was ill-positioned to give. What he wanted to say was, *Your life is over, young Junius; accept it.* But that seemed likely to bring on more confidences that he lacked the energy to field. The sudden absence of responsibility in his life — to his studies, his family, his very future — had sapped his strength. Even the tiniest of tasks seemed daunting.

A few minutes before eleven, their bunkmates — a talkative, round-faced boy named Smiley and his diminutive buddy, Bug — collected them. The quartet headed to the mess hall, which held long tables lined with cracked plastic chairs.

"Tuesday means hash!" announced Smiley. Although he'd been a Peacekeeper for barely a week, he seemed not only to know but to revel in the routine. Coriolanus collected a slotted tray featuring something that resembled dog food studded with potatoes. Hunger and the enthusiasm of his comrades emboldened him, so he tried a bite and found the stuff quite edible, if heavily salted. He also received two canned pear halves and a big mug of milk. Not elegant, but filling. He realized that, as a Peacekeeper, he was unlikely to starve. In fact, he'd be guaranteed more consistent food than he'd had access to at home.

Smiley declared them all fast friends, and by the end of lunch, Coriolanus and Junius had been dubbed Gent and Beanpole respectively, one by way of table manners, the other because of his frame. Coriolanus welcomed the nickname, because the last thing he wanted to hear was the name Snow. None of his bunkmates commented on it, though, or made any mention of the Hunger Games. It turned out the enlisted only had access to one television in the rec room, and the reception proved so poor it was rarely on. If Beanpole had seen Coriolanus in the Capitol, he hadn't made the connection between the Hunger Games mentor and the grunt beside him. Perhaps no one recognized him because no one expected him to be there. Or perhaps his celebrity had only extended to the Academy and a handful of unemployed in the Capitol who'd had time to follow the drama. Coriolanus relaxed enough to admit to a military father killed in the war, a grandmother and cousin back home, and school having ended the previous week.

To his surprise, he discovered that Smiley and Bug, as well as many of the other Peacekeepers, were not Capitol but district-born. "Oh, sure," said Smiley. "Peacekeeping's good work if you can get it. Better than mill work. Lots of food, and money enough to send back to my folks. Some people sneer at it, but I say the war's history and a job's a job."

"So you don't mind policing your own people?" Coriolanus couldn't help asking.

"Oh, these aren't my people. My people are in Eight. They don't leave you where you're born," said Smiley with a shrug. "'Sides, you're my family now, Gent."

Coriolanus got introduced to more of his new family that afternoon when he was assigned to kitchen detail. Under the guidance of Cookie, an old soldier who'd lost his left ear in the war, he stripped to the waist and stood over a sink of steaming water for four hours, scrubbing pots and hosing off meal trays. Then he was allowed fifteen minutes to eat another round of hash before he spent the next few hours mopping the mess hall and hallways. He had about half an hour back in the room before lights went out at nine and he collapsed into bed in his undershorts.

By five the next morning, he was dressed and on the field to begin training in earnest. The first stage was designed to bring the new troops up to an acceptable level of fitness. He squatted and sprinted and drilled until his clothes were sodden and his heels blistered. Professor Sickle's instruction served him well; she'd always insisted on rigorous exercise, and he'd been marching in formation since he was twelve. Beanpole, on the other hand, with his two left feet and concave chest, had the drill sergeant baiting and abusing him by turns. That night, as Coriolanus drifted off to sleep, he could hear the boy trying to stifle his sobs with his pillow.

Blocks of training, eating, cleaning, and sleeping made up his new life. He moved through them mechanically but with enough competence to avoid reproach. If he was lucky, he had a precious half hour to himself before lights-out at night. Not that he accomplished anything. It was all he could do to shower and climb into his bunk.

The thought of Lucy Gray tormented him, but it was tricky getting information about her. If he went around the base asking questions, someone might figure out his role in the Games, and he wanted to avoid that at all costs. The squad's designated day off was Sunday, and their duties ended Saturday at five. As new recruits, they were confined to base until the following weekend. Then Coriolanus planned to go into town and surreptitiously ask the locals about Lucy Gray. Smiley said the Peacekeepers hung out at an old coal warehouse called the Hob, where you could purchase homemade liquor and maybe buy yourself some company. District 12 had a town square as well, the same one used for the reaping, with a smattering of small shops and tradespeople, but that was more active in the daytime.

Except for Beanpole, who pulled latrine duty for his shortcomings, his bunkmates headed to the rec room to play poker after Saturday's dinner. Coriolanus lingered over his noodles and canned meat in the mess hall. Since Smiley was usually distracting them all with his prattle, it was the first time he had to really take stock of the other Peacekeepers. They ranged in age from late teens to one old man who looked to be the Grandma'am's contemporary. Some chatted among themselves, but most sat silent and depressed, sucking down their noodles. Was he looking, he wondered, at his future?

Coriolanus opted to spend his evening in the barrack. Having left his last coins with his family, he would have no money for gambling, not even pocket change, until he was paid on the first of the month. More importantly, he had received a letter from Tigris that he wanted to read in private. He soaked in his solitude, free of the sight, sound, and smell of his comrades. All the togetherness overwhelmed him, used as he was to ending his days alone. He climbed onto his bunk and carefully opened his letter.

My dearest Coryo,

It's Monday night now, and the apartment echoes with your absence. The Grandma'am doesn't quite seem to know what's going on, as twice today she asked when you'd be home and should we wait on dinner. Word of your situation has begun to spread. I went to see Pluribus, and he said he'd heard any number of rumors: that you'd followed Lucy Gray to Twelve out of love, that you'd gotten drunk celebrating and signed up on a dare, that you'd broken the rules and sent Lucy Gray gifts in the arena yourself, that you had some kind of falling out with Dean Highbottom. I tell people that you're doing your duty to your country, just as your father did.

Festus, Persephone, and Lysistrata came by this evening, all very concerned about you, and Mrs. Plinth called to get your address. I think she means to write you.

Our apartment is officially going on the market now, thanks to some help from the Dolittles. Pluribus says that, if we can't find a place immediately, he has a couple of spare rooms we can use above the club, and that maybe I can help out with the costumes if he reopens it. He's also placed several pieces of our furniture with buyers. He's been very kind and says to send his regards to you and Lucy Gray. Have you been able to see her? That's the one sweet spot in all this madness.

I'm sorry this is so short, but it's quite late, and I've so much to do. I just wanted to get something off to remind you how much you are loved and missed. I know how hard things must be, but don't lose hope. It has sustained us through the darkest of times and will do so now. Please write and tell us of your life in 12. It may not seem ideal, but who knows where it may lead?

SLOT,
Tigris

Coriolanus buried his face in his hands. The Capitol making a mockery of the Snow name? The Grandma'am losing her mind? Their home a pair of shabby rooms above a nightclub, where Tigris stitched sequined unitards? Was this the fate of the magnificent Snow family?

And what of him, Coriolanus Snow, future president of Panem? His life, tragic and pointless, unspooled before him. He saw himself in twenty years' time, grown stout and stupid, the breeding beaten out of him, his mind atrophied to the point where nothing but base, animal thoughts of hunger and sleep ever crossed it. Lucy Gray, having languished in Dr. Gaul's lab, would be long dead, and his heart dead with her. Twenty wasted years, and then what? When his time had been served? Why, he'd just reenlist, because even then the humiliation would be too great. And what would await him in the Capitol if he did return? The Grandma'am passed on. Tigris, middle-aged but seeming older, sewing away in servitude, her kindness transformed to insipidity, her existence a joke to those she had to please to earn her keep. No, he'd never return. He'd stay on in 12 like that old man in the mess hall had, because this was his life. No partner, no children, no address but the barrack. The other Peacekeepers, his family. Smiley, Bug, Beanpole, his band of brothers. And he would never see anyone from home again. Never, ever again.

A terrible pain clutched his chest as a toxic wave of homesickness and despair swamped him. He felt sure he was having a heart attack but made no attempt to call for help, instead curling into a ball and pressing his face against the wall. Perhaps it was for the best. Because there was no out. Nowhere to run. No hope of rescue. No future that was not a living death. What did he have to look forward to? Hash? A weekly cup of gin? A promotion from dish washing to dish scraping? Wasn't it better to die now, quickly, than to drag it out painfully for years?

Somewhere — it seemed very distant — he heard a door bang shut. Footsteps came down the hall, pausing for a minute and then continuing toward him. He gritted his teeth, willing his heart to stop at once, because the world and he had finished with each other and it was time to part ways. But the footsteps grew louder and came to a halt at his door. Was the person looking at him? Was it the patrol? Staring at him in this mortifying position? Lapping up his wretchedness? He waited for the laughter, the derision, and the latrine duty that was sure to follow.

Instead he heard a quiet voice say, "Is this bunk taken?" A quiet and familiar voice . . .

Coriolanus twisted around on the bed, his eyes flying open to confirm what his ears already knew. Standing in the doorway, looking oddly at home in a set of fatigues still creased from the package, stood Sejanus Plinth.

Coriolanus had never been so glad to see anyone in his life. "Sejanus!" he burst out. He launched off his bunk, landed shakily on the painted concrete floor, and flung his arms around the newcomer.

Sejanus embraced him. "This is a surprisingly warm welcome for the person who almost destroyed you!"

A slightly hysterical laugh left Coriolanus's lips, and for a moment he considered the accuracy of the claim. It was true, Sejanus had endangered his life by stealing into the arena, but it was too far a reach to blame him for all the rest. As aggravating as Sejanus could be, he'd had no hand in Dean Highbottom's vendetta against his father or in the handkerchief debacle. "No, no, quite the opposite." He released Sejanus and examined him. Dark circles shadowed his eyes and he must have lost at least fifteen pounds. But on the whole he had a lighter air, as if the great weight he'd carried in the Capitol had been lifted. "What are you doing here?"

"Hm. Let's see. Having defied the Capitol by entering the arena, I, too, was on the verge of expulsion. My father went before the board and said he'd pay for a new gymnasium for the Academy if they would let me graduate and sign up for the Peacekeepers. They agreed, but I said I wouldn't take the deal unless they'd let you graduate, too. Well, Professor Sickle really wanted a new gym, and she said what did it matter if we were both tied up for the next twenty years anyway?" Sejanus set his duffel on the floor and dug out his box of personal items.

"I got to graduate?" said Coriolanus.

Sejanus opened the box, removed a small leather folder with the school's emblem, and held it out with great ceremony. "Congratulations. You are no longer a dropout."

Coriolanus flipped open the cover and found a diploma with his name inscribed in curlicues. The thing must have been written out in advance, because it even credited him with *High Honors*. "Thank you. I guess it's stupid, but it still matters to me."

"You know, if you ever wanted to take the officer candidate test, it might matter. You need to have graduated secondary school. Dean Highbottom brought that up as something that should be denied you. He said you broke some rule in the Games to help Lucy Gray? Anyway, he got outvoted." Sejanus chuckled. "He's really wearing on people."

"So I'm not universally reviled?" said Coriolanus.

"For what? Falling in love? I think more people pity you. A lot of romantics among our teachers, come to find out," said Sejanus. "And Lucy Gray made quite a good impression."

Coriolanus grabbed his arm. "Where is she? Do you know what happened to her?"

Sejanus shook his head. "They usually send the victors back to their districts, don't they?"

"I'm afraid they've done something worse to her. Because we cheated in the Games," Coriolanus confessed. "I tampered with the snakes so they wouldn't bite her. But all she did was use rat poison."

"So that was it. Well, I haven't heard anything about that. Or about her being punished," Sejanus reassured him. "The truth is, she's so talented, they'll probably want to bring her back next year."

"I thought of that, too. Maybe Highbottom was right about

her being sent home." Coriolanus sat on Beanpole's bunk and stared down at the diploma. "You know, when you came in, I was weighing the merits of suicide."

"What? Now? When you're finally free from the clutches of Dean Highbottom and the evil Dr. Gaul? When the girl of your dreams is in reach? When my ma is, at this moment, packing a box the size of a truck full of baked goods for you?" exclaimed Sejanus. "My friend, your life has just begun!"

And then Coriolanus was laughing; they both were. "So this isn't our ruin?"

"I'd call it our salvation. Mine anyway. Oh, Coryo, if you only knew how glad I was to escape," said Sejanus, turning grave. "I never liked the Capitol, but after the Hunger Games, after what happened to Marcus . . . I don't know if you were kidding about suicide, but it was no joke to me. I had the whole thing worked out. . . ."

"No. No, Sejanus," said Coriolanus. "Let's not give them the satisfaction."

Sejanus nodded thoughtfully, then wiped his face on his sleeve. "My father says it won't be better here. I'll still be a Capitol boy as far as the districts are concerned. But I don't care. Anything would have to be an improvement. What's it like?"

"We're either marching or mopping," said Coriolanus. "It's mind-numbing."

"Good. My mind could stand a little numbing. I've been trapped in these endless debates with my father," said Sejanus. "At the moment, I don't want to have a serious discussion about anything."

"Then you'll love our roommates." The pain in Coriolanus's chest had retreated, and he felt a glimmer of hope. Lucy Gray had, at least publicly, been spared punishment. Just knowing that he still had allies in the Capitol buoyed Coriolanus's spirits, and Sejanus's mention of becoming an officer caught his attention. Perhaps there was a way out of his predicament after all? Another path to influence and power? It was solace enough, at the moment, to know this was something Dean Highbottom feared.

"I'm planning to," said Sejanus. "I'm planning to build a whole new beautiful life here. One where, in my own small way, I can make the world a better place."

"That's going to take some work," said Coriolanus. "I don't know what ever possessed me to ask for Twelve."

"Completely random, obviously," Sejanus teased.

Like a fool, Coriolanus felt himself blush. "I don't even know how to find her. Or if she'll still be interested in me, now that so much has changed."

"You're kidding, right? She's head over heels in love with you!" said Sejanus. "And don't worry, we'll find her."

As he helped Sejanus unpack and make his bed, Coriolanus got caught up on the Capitol news. His suspicions about the Hunger Games were right.

"By the next morning, there was no mention of it," said Sejanus. "When I went into the Academy for my review, I heard some of the faculty talking about what a mistake it'd been to involve the students, so I think that was a one-off. But I wouldn't be surprised if we see Lucky Flickerman back again next year, or the post office open for gifts and betting."

"Our legacy," said Coriolanus.

"So it seems," said Sejanus. "Satyria told Professor Sickle that Dr. Gaul is determined to keep it going somehow. A part of her eternal war, I guess. Instead of battles, we have the Hunger Games."

"Yes, to punish the districts and remind us what beasts we are," said Coriolanus, focused on lining up Sejanus's folded socks in the locker.

"What?" asked Sejanus, giving him a funny look.

"I don't know," said Coriolanus. "It's like . . . you know how she's always torturing that rabbit or melting the flesh off something?"

"Like she enjoys it?" asked Sejanus.

"Exactly. I think that's how she thinks we all are. Natural-born killers. Inherently violent," Coriolanus said. "The Hunger Games are a reminder of what monsters we are and how we need the Capitol to keep us from chaos."

"So, not only is the world a brutal place, but people enjoy its brutality? Like the essay on everything we loved about the war," said Sejanus. "As if it had been some big show." He shook his head. "So much for not thinking."

"Forget it," said Coriolanus. "Let's just be happy that she's out of our lives."

A downcast Beanpole appeared, reeking of urinals and bleach. Coriolanus introduced him to Sejanus, who, upon learning of his predicament, cheered him up by promising to help him with the drills. "It took me awhile to get it, too, back at school. But if I can master it, so can you."

Smiley and Bug rolled in shortly after and greeted Sejanus warmly. They'd been cleaned out at the poker table but were excited about the following Saturday's entertainment. "There's going to be a band at the Hob."

Coriolanus practically jumped on him. "A band? What band?"

Smiley shrugged. "Can't remember. But some girl will be singing. Supposed to be pretty good. Lucy somebody."

Lucy somebody. Coriolanus's heart leaped and a grin nearly split his face in two.

Sejanus grinned back at him. "Really? Well, that's something to look forward to."

After lights-out, Coriolanus lay beaming at the ceiling. Lucy Gray was not only alive, she was in 12, and he would reunite with her next weekend. His girl. His love. His Lucy Gray. They had survived the dean, the doctor, and the Games somehow. After all the weeks of fear and yearning and uncertainty, he would wrap her in his arms and never let her go. Wasn't that why he had come to 12?

But it wasn't just news of her. As ironic as it was, the appearance of that decade-long irritant, Sejanus, had helped bring him back to life as well. Not just with his diploma and promised cakes, or his reassurances that the Capitol did not scorn him, or even the hope of a career as an officer. Coriolanus was so relieved to have someone to talk to who knew his world and, more importantly, his true worth in that world. He felt heartened by the fact that Strabo Plinth had allowed Sejanus to insist his graduation be part of the deal for the gym, and took it as at least partial payment toward his having saved Sejanus's life. Old Plinth had not forgotten him, he felt sure of that, and might be willing to use his wealth and power to help him in the future. And, of course, Ma adored him. Perhaps things were not so dire after all.

With Sejanus, plus another few stragglers from the districts, they had enough recruits to form a full squad of twenty, and they began to train as such. There was no question, the Academy's regimen had given Coriolanus and Sejanus a decided edge in fitness and drilling, although they'd had no class in firearms as they did now. The standard Peacekeeper's rifle was a formidable thing, capable of firing a hundred rounds before reloading. To start out, the trainees focused on learning the weapon parts as they cleaned and assembled and disassembled their guns until they could do it in their sleep. Coriolanus had felt a little leery on the first day they did target practice, so bad were his memories of the war, but he found having his own weapon made him feel safer. More powerful. Sejanus turned out to be a natural marksman and soon earned the nickname Bull's Eye. Coriolanus could tell the name made him uncomfortable, but he accepted it.

The Monday after Sejanus's arrival, August 1st, had brought disappointment. The recruits discovered they had to be in service for a full month to collect their first payment. Smiley was particularly down, as he'd been counting on his pay to cover his weekend revelries. Coriolanus felt his heart drop as well. How could he hope to see Lucy Gray without the price of a ticket?

After three days of nothing but training, Thursday brought a bright spot. Ma's packages arrived, bursting with sugary delights. Beanpole's, Smiley's, and Bug's faces were something to behold as they watched the unpacking of the cherry tarts, caramel popcorn balls, and frosted chocolate cookies. Sejanus and Coriolanus made them common property in the room, cementing the brotherhood even further. "You know," said Smiley through a mouthful of tart, "if we wanted, I bet we could trade some of this on Saturday. For gin and all." It was agreed, and a certain amount of the bounty was set aside for the big event on Saturday night.

Juiced by the sugar, Coriolanus got off a thank-you note to Ma and a letter to Tigris reassuring her that he was fine. He tried to make light of the grueling routine and play up the officer angle. He'd picked up a dog-eared manual for the officer candidate test, which had a sampling of questions. It was designed to measure scholastic aptitude and consisted primarily of verbal, math, and spatial problems, although he'd need to learn some basic rules and regulations for the one military section. If he passed, he wouldn't be an officer, but he would get to begin training as one. He had a good feeling about his chances, if for no other reason than that many of the other recruits were barely literate. Their handful of classes on Peacekeeper values and traditions had made that clear. He told Tigris the regretful news about his pay but assured her that money should be coming in like clockwork as of September 1st. As his tongue dug the popcorn out of his teeth, he remembered to mention Sejanus's arrival and advised that if she ever had an emergency, Ma Plinth could probably be counted on to help.

On Friday morning, a tense mood infused the mess hall, and Smiley got the story out of a nurse he'd met at the clinic. About a month earlier, just around the time of the reaping, a Peacekeeper and two District 12 bosses had been killed by an explosion in the mines. A criminal investigation had led to the arrest of a man whose family had been known rebel leaders during the war. He was to be hanged at one that afternoon. The mines were shutting down for the event, and the workers were expected to attend.

Green as he was, Coriolanus couldn't see how this could involve him, and went about his schedule as usual. But during drill practice, the base commander himself, an old goat named Hoff, dropped by and observed for a short time. Before leaving, he exchanged a few words with their drill sergeant, who promptly called Coriolanus and Sejanus forward. "You two, you're to go to the hanging this afternoon. Commander wants more bodies there for show, and he's looking for recruits who can handle the drills. Report to transport at noon in uniform. Just follow orders, you'll be fine."

Coriolanus and Sejanus bolted their lunches and hurried back to the barrack to change. "So, was the murderer targeting the Peacekeeper in particular?" asked Coriolanus as he pulled on his crisp, white uniform for the first time.

"I heard he was trying to sabotage coal production and accidentally killed the three," said Sejanus.

"Sabotage production? To what end?" asked Coriolanus.

"I don't know," said Sejanus. "Hoping to get the rebellion going again?"

Coriolanus only shook his head. Why did these people think that all they needed to start a rebellion was anger? They had no army, weapons, or authority. At the Academy, they'd been taught that the recent war had been incited by rebels in District 13 who were able to access and disseminate arms and communications to their cohorts around Panem. But 13 had vanished in a nuclear puff of smoke, along with the Snow fortune. Nothing remained, and any thought of re-upping the rebellion was pure stupidity.

When they reported for duty, Coriolanus was surprised to be issued a gun, since his training was minimal at best. "Don't worry, the major said all we need to do is stand at attention," another recruit told him. They were loaded onto the bed of a truck, which rolled out of the base and down a road that ringed District 12. Coriolanus felt nervous, as this was his first real Peacekeeping assignment, but a little excited, too. A few weeks ago he was a schoolboy, but now he had the uniform, the weapon, the status of a man. And even the lowest-ranking Peacekeeper had power conveyed on him by his association with the Capitol. He stood up straighter at the thought.

As the truck drove around the perimeter of the district, the buildings went from dingy to squalid. The doors and windows of the decrepit houses gaped in the heat. Hollow-faced women sat on doorsteps, watching half-naked children with sharp rib cages playing listlessly in the dirt. In some yards, pumps attested to the lack of running water, and the sagging power lines suggested that electricity was not guaranteed.

It frightened Coriolanus, this level of want. He'd been broke most of his life, but the Snows had always worked hard to maintain decency. These people had given up, and some part of him blamed them for their plight. He shook his head. "We pour so much money into the districts," he said. It must be true. People always complained about it in the Capitol.

"We pour money into our industries, not into the districts themselves," said Sejanus. "The people are on their own."

The truck rattled off the cinders and onto a dirt road that curved around a large field of hard-packed earth and weeds, ending at a wood. The Capitol had small wooded areas in some of the parks, but even those were fairly well manicured. Coriolanus supposed this was what people meant by a forest, or even a wilderness. Thick trees, vines, and underbrush grew every which way. The disorder alone felt disturbing. And who knew what sort of creatures inhabited it? The medley of buzzing, humming, and rustling set him on edge. What a racket the birds here made!

A great tree stood at the edge of the wood, its branches stretching out like large, knotty arms. A noose dangled from one particularly horizontal appendage. Directly below it, a rough platform with two trapdoors had been erected. "They keep promising us a proper gallows," the middle-aged major in charge said. "Until then, some of us rigged this. We used to just string them up from the ground, but then they'd take forever to die, and who's got time for that?"

One of the female recruits Coriolanus recognized from his walk to the base raised her hand tentatively. "Who are we hanging, please?"

"Oh, some malcontent who tried to shut the mines down," said the major. "They're all malcontents, but this one's the ringleader. Name's Arlo Something-or-other. Still tracking down some of the others, although I don't know where they plan on running. Nowhere *to* run. Okay, everybody out!"

Coriolanus's and Sejanus's roles were largely decorative. They stood at parade rest in the back row of one of two squads of twenty that flanked the platform. Another sixty Peacekeepers spread along the edge of the field. Coriolanus did not like to have his back facing all the unkempt flora and fauna, but orders were orders. He stared straight ahead, across the field and into the district, from which a steady stream of people began to emerge. By the looks of them, many had come directly from the mines, for coal dust blackened their faces. They were joined by only slightly cleaner women and children as families formed in the field. Coriolanus began to feel anxious when scores became hundreds, and still more people arrived, pushing the crowd forward in an ominous fashion.

A trio of vehicles slowly made its way down the dirt road toward the gallows. Out of the first, an old car that would've been classified as luxury before the war, stepped District 12's Mayor Lipp, followed by a middle-aged woman with dyed blonde hair, and Mayfair, the girl Lucy Gray had targeted with the snake on the day of the reaping. They formed a tight knot at the side of the platform. Commander Hoff and a half dozen officers emerged from a second car, which sported a fluttering flag of Panem on the hood. A wave of distress went through the crowd as the back of the final vehicle, a white Peacekeepers' van, swung open. A pair of guards jumped to the ground, then turned to help the prisoner out. Heavily shackled, the tall, lean man managed to stay upright as they escorted him to the platform. With difficulty, he dragged his chains up the rickety steps, and the guards positioned him on one of the two trapdoors.

The major barked the order for attention, and Coriolanus's body snapped into position. Technically, his gaze should have been forward, but he could just see the action from the corner of his eye, and he felt concealed in the back row. He'd never seen an execution in real life, only on television, and somehow he couldn't look away.

The crowd fell silent, and a Peacekeeper read out the list of crimes the condemned, Arlo Chance, had been convicted of, including the murder of three men. Although he tried to project, his voice seemed puny in the hot, damp air. When he concluded, the commander gave a nod to the Peacekeepers on the platform. They offered the condemned a blindfold, which he refused, and then put the noose around his neck. The man stood stoically, staring into the distance as he awaited his end.

A drumroll began from the far side of the platform, triggering a cry from the front of the crowd. Coriolanus shifted his gaze to locate the source. A young woman with olive skin and long black hair rose above the mass into the air as a man tried to carry her off, but she desperately fought to move forward, shrieking, "Arlo! Arlo!" Already, Peacekeepers were closing in on her.

The voice had an electrifying effect on Arlo, as his face registered first surprise, then horror. "Run!" he screamed. "Run, Lil! Run! Ru — !" The clap of the trapdoor release and subsequent twang of the rope cut him off mid-word, drawing a gasp from the crowd. Arlo dropped fifteen feet and seemed to die instantly.

In the ominous silence that followed, Coriolanus could feel the sweat running down his ribs as he waited for the outcome. Would the people attack? Would he be expected to shoot them? Did he remember how the gun worked? He strained his ears for the order. Instead he heard the voice of the dead man ringing out eerily from the gently swaying corpse.

"Run! Run, Lil! Ru — !"

A shiver ran down Coriolanus's spine, and he could sense the rest of the recruits stirring.

"Run! Run, Lil! Ru — !"

The cry built and then seemed to engulf him, bouncing off the trees and attacking him from behind. For a moment, he thought he'd gone mad. He disobeyed orders and whipped his head around, almost expecting to see an army of Arlos breaking through the teeming woods behind him. Nothing. No one. Then the voice came again from a branch a few feet above him.

"Run! Run, Lil! Ru — !"

At the sight of the small, black bird, he flashed back to Dr. Gaul's lab, where he'd seen the same creatures, perched at the top of a cage. Jabberjays. Why, the woods must be full of the things, mimicking Arlo's death cry as they had the wails of the Avoxes in the lab.

"Run! Run, Lil! Ru — ! Run! Run, Lil! Ru — ! Run! Run, Lil! Ru — !"

As Coriolanus turned back to attention, he could see the disruption the birds had caused in the back row of recruits, although the rest of the Peacekeepers stood unaffected. *Used to it by now,* Coriolanus thought. He was not sure he'd ever be used to the refrain of someone's death cry. Even now it was transforming, changing from Arlo's speech into something almost melodic. A string of notes that mirrored the inflection of his voice, somehow more haunting than the words had been.

Out in the crowd, the Peacekeepers had the woman, Lil, and were carrying her away. She gave one last wail of despair, and the birds picked that up as well, first as a voice and then as part of the arrangement. Human speech had vanished, and what remained was a musical chorus of Arlo and Lil's exchange.

"Mockingjays," grumbled a soldier in front of him. "Stinking mutts."

Coriolanus remembered talking to Lucy Gray before the interview.

"Well, you know what they say. The show's not over until the mockingjay sings."

"The mockingjay? Really, I think you're just making these things up."

"Not that one. A mockingjay's a bona fide bird."

"And it sings in your show?"

"Not my show, sweetheart. Yours. The Capitol's anyway."

This must be what she'd meant. The Capitol's show was the hanging. The mockingjay some sort of bona fide bird. Not a jabberjay. Different somehow. A regional thing, he supposed. But that was strange, because the soldier had called them mutts. His eyes strained to try and isolate one in the foliage. Now that he knew what he was looking for, he found several jabberjays. Perhaps the mockingjays were identical . . . but no, wait, there! A little higher up. A black bird, slightly larger than the jabberjays, suddenly opened its wings to reveal two patches of dazzling white as it lifted its beak in song. Coriolanus felt sure he'd spotted his first mockingjay, and he disliked the thing on sight.

The birdsong unsettled the audience, and whispers turned to mutters, which turned to objections as the Peacekeepers shoved Lil into the van that had brought Arlo. Coriolanus felt afraid of this mob's potential. Were they about to turn on the soldiers? Unbidden, he felt his thumb release the safety on his gun.

A volley of bullets made him jump, and he looked for bleeding bodies but only saw one of the officers lowering his gun. The officer laughed and nodded to the commander, having just fired into the trees and caused the flock of birds to take flight. Among them, Coriolanus could make out dozens of pairs of flashing black-and-white wings. The gunfire subdued the crowd, and he could see the Peacekeepers waving them out, shouting, "Back to work!" and "Show's over!" As the field emptied, he continued to stand at attention, hoping no one had noticed his jumpiness.

When they'd all piled onto the truck to head back to the base, the major said, "I should've warned you about the birds."

"What are they, exactly?" asked Coriolanus.

The major snorted. "A mistake, if you ask me."

"A muttation?" Coriolanus persisted.

"Of a kind. Well, it's them and their offspring," the major said. "After the war, the Capitol let all the jabberjay mutts loose to die out, and they should've, too, all being male. But they had an eye for the local mockingbirds, and the birds seemed willing enough. Now we've got these mockingjay freaks to deal with. In a few years, all the jabberjays will be gone, and we'll see if the new ones can mate with one another."

Coriolanus did not want to spend the next twenty years listening to them serenade the local executions. Perhaps, if he ever did become an officer, he could organize a hunting party to clear the woods of them. But why wait? Why not suggest it now, for the recruits, as a form of target practice? Surely, no one liked the birds. The idea made him feel a bit better. He turned to Sejanus to tell him of his plan, but Sejanus's face was as gloomy as it'd been in the Capitol. "What's wrong?"

Sejanus kept his eyes on the woods as the truck pulled out. "I really didn't think this through."

"What do you mean?" asked Coriolanus. But Sejanus only shook his head.

Back on base, they returned their guns and were unexpectedly free until supper at five. As soon as they changed back into fatigues, Sejanus mumbled something about writing to Ma and disappeared. Coriolanus found a letter one of his bunkmates must've picked up for him. He recognized the fine, spidery hand of Pluribus Bell and boosted himself up onto his bed to read it. Much of it confirmed what Tigris had already told him: that Pluribus was at the Snows' service, both selling their goods and offering temporary lodgings while they figured out their situation. But one paragraph jumped out at Coriolanus.

> *I'm so sorry about how all this worked out for you. Casca Highbottom's punishment seems excessive, and it started me wondering. I think I mentioned that he and your father were as thick as thieves when they were at the University. But I do remember, toward the end there, a row of sorts. Very uncharacteristic of them. Casca was furious, saying he'd been drunk and the whole thing was meant to be a joke. And your father said he should be grateful. That he'd been doing him a favor. Your father left, but Casca stayed drinking until I closed. I asked what was wrong, but all he would say was "Like moths to a flame." He was quite drunk. I supposed they patched it up eventually, but maybe not. They both went on to jobs soon after, and I didn't see them much. People move on.*

This snatch of a story provided the closest explanation Coriolanus had gotten yet for Dean Highbottom hating him. A row. A falling out. He knew it hadn't been patched up, unless another had succeeded it, because of the bitter way the dean had spoken about his father. What a petty little man Dean Highbottom was, still nursing his wounds over some disagreement in school. Even now, when his imagined persecutor was long dead. *Let it go, can't you?* he thought. *How can it still be of consequence?*

At dinner, Smiley, Beanpole, and Bug wanted to hear all about the hanging, and Coriolanus tried his best to satisfy them. His idea of using mockingjays for target practice was met with enthusiasm, and his bunkmates encouraged him to pitch it to the higher-ups. The only damper was Sejanus, who sat silent and withdrawn, pushing his tray of noodles out for public consumption. Coriolanus felt a twinge of concern. The last time Sejanus had lost his appetite, he'd lost his sanity as well.

Later, as they mopped the mess hall, Coriolanus cornered him. "What's bothering you? And don't say nothing."

Sejanus sloshed his mop around the bucket of gray water. "I don't know. I keep wondering what would've happened today if the crowd had gotten physical. Would we have had to shoot them?"

"Oh, probably not," said Coriolanus, although he'd wondered the same thing. "Probably just fired a few rounds in the air."

"If I'm helping to kill people in the districts, how is it any better than helping to kill them in the Hunger Games?" asked Sejanus.

Coriolanus's instincts had been right. Sejanus was sliding into another ethical quagmire. "What did you think it was going to be? I mean, what did you think you'd signed up for?"

"I thought I could be a medic," confessed Sejanus.

"A medic," Coriolanus repeated. "Like a doctor?"

"No, that would require university training," Sejanus explained. "Something more basic. Something where I could help anyone who'd been injured, Capitol or district, when violence breaks out. At least I wouldn't do any harm. I just don't know if I could ever kill anyone, Coryo."

Coriolanus felt a stab of annoyance. Had Sejanus forgotten that it was his own reckless behavior that had led to Coriolanus killing Bobbin? That his selfishness had robbed his friend of the luxury of such a statement? Then he suppressed a laugh at the thought of old Strabo Plinth. A munitions giant with a pacifist heir. He could imagine the conversations that had transpired between father and son. *What a waste*, he thought. *What a waste of a dynasty.*

"What about in a war?" he asked Sejanus. "You're a soldier, you know."

"I know. A war would be different, I guess," said Sejanus. "But I would have to be fighting for something I believed in. I would have to believe it would make the world a better place. I'd still rather be a medic, but there isn't much demand for them at the moment, it turns out. Without a war. They've got a long waiting list of people who'd like to be trained to work at the clinic. But even for that, you need a recommendation, and the sergeant doesn't want to give me one."

"Why not? Sounds like a perfect fit," said Coriolanus.

"Because I'm too good with a gun," Sejanus told him. "It's true. I'm a crack shot. My father taught me from when I was tiny, and every week I had mandatory target practice. He considers it part of the family business."

Coriolanus tried to process the information. "Why didn't you hide it?"

"I thought I was. In reality, I shoot much better than I do in training. I tried not to stand out, but the rest of the squad is terrible." Sejanus caught himself. "Not you."

"Yes, me." Coriolanus laughed. "Look, I think you're making

too much of this. It's not like we have a hanging every day. And if it ever did come to it, just shoot to miss."

But the words only fueled Sejanus. "And what if that means you, or Beanpole, or Smiley, end up dead? Because I didn't protect you?"

"Oh, Sejanus!" Coriolanus burst out in exasperation. "You have to stop overthinking everything! Imagining every worst-case scenario. That isn't going to happen. We're all going to die right here, of old age or excessive mopping, whatever takes us first. In the meantime, quit hitting the target! Or invent a problem with your eyes! Or smash your hand in the door!"

"Stop being so self-indulgent, in other words," said Sejanus.

"Well, so dramatic anyway. That's how you ended up in the arena, remember?" asked Coriolanus.

Sejanus reacted as if Coriolanus had slapped him. After a moment, though, he nodded in recognition. "That's how I almost got us both killed. You're right, Coryo. Thanks. I'm going to think over what you said."

A thunderstorm ushered Saturday in, leaving behind a thick layer of mud and air so heavy Coriolanus felt he could wring it out like a sponge. He'd begun to crave the salty food Cookie favored and cleaned his plate at every meal. The effects of the daily training on his body left him stronger, more flexible, and confident. He'd be a match for the locals, even if they spent the day mining. Not that hand-to-hand combat seemed likely, not with the Peacekeepers' arsenal, but he'd be ready if it happened.

During target practice, he kept one eye on Sejanus, whose aim seemed a bit off. Good. A sudden reduction in his skills would draw attention. Another boy's estimation of his talent might be suspect, but he'd never known Sejanus to brag. If he said he was a crack shot, no doubt he was. Which meant he'd be a real asset in the mockingjay slaughter if he could be persuaded to try. At the end of practice, Coriolanus pitched the idea to the sergeant, and felt gratified by his answer: "That might not be a bad idea. Kill two birds with one stone."

"Oh, I hope more than two," Coriolanus joked, and the sergeant rewarded him with a grunt.

After a sweltering afternoon in the laundry, shuttling fatigues in and out of industrial washing machines and dryers, sorting and folding, Coriolanus bolted down dinner and made for the showers. Was it his imagination, or had his beard filled in? He admired it as he scraped a razor over his face. Another sign that he was leaving boyhood behind. He towel-dried his hair, relieved that his buzz had become less severe. Here and there he could coax a bit of wave.

The promise of a band at the Hob that night filled the bathroom with excitement. Apparently, none of the recruits had followed this year's Hunger Games.

"Some girl is going to be singing there."

"Yeah, from the Capitol."

"No, not from the Capitol. She went there for the Hunger Games."

"Oh. Guess she won."

Their faces shiny with heat and scrubbing, Coriolanus and his bunkmates headed out into the evening. The guard on duty told them to keep their heads up as they left the base.

"I guess the five of us could take on some miners," said Beanpole, glancing around.

"Hand-to-hand, sure," said Smiley. "But what if they had guns?"

"They can't have guns here, can they?" asked Beanpole.

"Not legally. But there's got to be some of them floating around out there after the war. Hidden under floorboards and in trees and things. You can get anything if you have money," Smiley said with a knowing nod.

"Which clearly none of them do," said Sejanus.

Being off the base on foot made Coriolanus edgy, too, but he put it down to the mess of emotions he was experiencing. He was by turns thrilled, terrified, cocksure, and madly insecure about seeing Lucy Gray. There were so many things he wanted to say to her, so many questions he wanted to ask, he didn't know where he'd begin. Maybe with just another of those long, slow kisses . . .

After about twenty minutes, they arrived at the Hob. A warehouse for coal in better days, reduced production had left it abandoned. Probably someone in the Capitol owned it, if not the Capitol itself, but no oversight or upkeep was apparent. Along the walls, a few makeshift stalls displayed odds and ends, much of them secondhand. Among the offerings, Coriolanus saw everything from candle stubs to dead rabbits, homemade woven sandals to cracked eyeglasses. He worried that in the wake of the hanging they would be treated with hostility, but no one seemed to give them a second glance, and much of the clientele had come from the base.

Smiley, who had wheeled and dealed in the black market back home, strategically sacrificed one cookie to sampling, breaking it into a dozen pieces and allowing tastes to people he deemed likely buyers. Ma's magic hit home, and between direct trade with the bootleggers and money from other interested parties, they ended up in possession of a quart bottle of clear liquid so potent the smell made their eyes water.

"That's good stuff!" Smiley promised. "They call it white liquor here, but it's your basic moonshine." They each took one swig, provoking a round of coughing and backslapping, and saved the rest for the show.

Still in possession of a half dozen popcorn balls, Coriolanus asked about tickets but people waved him off.

"They don't take their pay 'til after," said one man. "Better get a seat if you want a good one. Expecting a crowd. The girl's back."

Getting a seat involved grabbing an old crate, spool, or plastic bucket from a pile in the corner and staking out a spot where you could see the stage, which was no more than an arrangement of wooden pallets at one end of the Hob. Coriolanus chose one against the wall, about halfway back. In the dusky light, Lucy Gray would be hard-pressed to notice him, and he wanted that. He needed time to decide how to approach her. Had she heard he was here? Likely not, for who would have told her? Around the base he was merely Gent, and his exploits in the Hunger Games caused no mention.

Nightfall came and someone flipped a switch, kicking on a hodgepodge of lights strung together by an ancient cable and several suspicious-looking extension cords. Coriolanus looked for the nearest exit in anticipation of the inevitable fire. With the old wooden structure and the coal dust, a stray spark could turn it into an inferno in a flash. The Hob began to fill with a mix of Peacekeepers and locals, mostly men but with a fair number of women as well. There must've been close to two hundred assembled in all when a skinny boy of about twelve, in a hat adorned with colorful feathers, came out and set up a single microphone on the stage, running a cord to a black box off to the side. He dragged a wooden crate behind the mic and retreated to an area blocked with a raggedy blanket. His appearance had set off something in the crowd, and people began to clap in unison, in a manner that proved contagious. Even Coriolanus found his hands joining in. Voices called for the show to begin, and just when it seemed it never would, the side of the blanket flipped back, and out stepped a little girl in a pink swirl of a dress. She gave a curtsy.

The audience cheered as the girl began to beat on a drum that hung from a strap around her neck and to dance her way to the microphone. "Whoo, Maude Ivory!" hooted a Peacekeeper near Coriolanus, and he knew this was the cousin Lucy Gray had mentioned, the one who could remember every song she heard. It was a big claim for such a young thing; she couldn't be more than eight or nine.

She hopped up on the box set behind the microphone and gave the audience a wave. "Hey, everybody, thanks for coming out tonight! Is it hot enough for you?" she said in a sweet, squeaky voice, and the crowd laughed. "Well, we're planning on heating things up a sight more. My name's Maude Ivory, and I'm pleased to introduce the Covey!" The crowd applauded, and she bobbed curtsies until they quieted enough for her to start the introductions. "On mandolin, Tam Amber!" A tall, rawboned young man in a feathered hat came from behind the curtain, strumming an instrument similar to a guitar but with a body more like a teardrop. He walked straight to Maude Ivory's side, not acknowledging the audience in any way, his fingers moving easily over the strings. Next, the boy who'd set up the microphone appeared with a violin. "That's Clerk Carmine on fiddle!" announced Maude Ivory, as he played his way across the stage. "And Barb Azure on bass!" Hauling out an instrument that looked like a huge version of the fiddle, a willowy young woman in an ankle-length, checkered blue dress gave the crowd a shy wave as she joined the others. "And now, fresh from her engagement in the Capitol, the one and only Lucy Gray Baird!"

Coriolanus held his breath as she spun onto the stage, guitar in one hand, the ruffles of her acid-green dress flaring out around her, her features brightened with makeup. The crowd rose to their feet. She ran lightly over as Tam Amber scooted Maude Ivory's box back and took center stage before the mic. “Hey there, District Twelve, did you miss me?” She grinned as they roared in response. “I bet you never expected to lay eyes on me again, and that goes both ways. But I’m back. I sure am back.”

Encouraged by his mates, a Peacekeeper sheepishly approached the stage and handed her a half-filled bottle of white liquor.

“Well, what’s this? Is that for me?” she asked, receiving the bottle. The Peacekeeper made a gesture indicating it was from the group. “Now, you all know I stopped drinking when I was twelve!” A big laugh came from the audience. “What? I did! Of course, there’s no harm in having some on hand for medicinal purposes. Thank you kindly, I do appreciate it.” She considered the bottle, then shot the audience a knowing look and took a swig. “To clear my pipes!” she said innocently in response to the howls. “You know, as bad as you treat me, I don’t know why I keep coming back. But I do. Reminds me of that old song.”

Lucy Gray strummed her guitar once and looked around at the rest of the Covey, who were gathered in a close half circle around the mic. “Okay, pretty birds. A one, a two, a one two three and . . .” The music began, bright and upbeat. Coriolanus felt his heel tapping out the beat even before Lucy Gray leaned into the mic.

My heart’s stupid and that’s not maybe.
Can’t blame Cupid, he’s just a baby.
Shoot it, boot it, execute it,
Still comes a-crawling to you-hoo.

Heart’s gone funny, it won’t hear reason.
You’re like honey, you bring the bees in.
Sting it, wring it, give a fling, it
Still comes a-crawling to you.

I wish it mattered that
You chose to smash it up.
How come you shattered that
Thing I love with?

Did you feel flattered that
You could just trash it up?
That's why you battered that
Thing I love with.

Lucy Gray relinquished the mic, allowing Clerk Carmine to step up and do some fancy finger work on his fiddle, embellishing the melody, while the others backed him up. Coriolanus couldn't take his eyes off Lucy Gray's face, lit up like he'd never seen it before. *That's her when she's happy*, he thought. *She's beautiful!* Beautiful in a way anyone could see, not just him. That could be a problem. Jealousy pricked his heart. But no. She was his girl, wasn't she? He remembered the song she'd sung in the interview, about the guy who'd broken her heart, and examined the Covey for a likely suspect. There was only Tam Amber with the mandolin, but there were no sparks flying between them. One of the locals maybe?

The crowd applauded Clerk Carmine, and Lucy Gray took over again.

Trapped my ticker but haven't freed it.
People snicker at how you treat it.
Snare it, tear it, strip it bare, it
Still comes a-crawling to you-hoo.

Heart's been jumping just like a rabbit.
Blood keeps pumping but that's just habit.

Drain it, pain it, I'm insane, it
Still comes a-crawling to you.

Burn it, spurn it, don't return it,
Break it, bake it, overtake it,
Wreck it, deck it, what the heck, it
Still comes a-crawling to you.

After the applause and a fair amount of hollering, the audience settled down to listen some more.

As Coriolanus knew from helping Lucy Gray rehearse in the Capitol, the Covey had a wide and varied repertoire, and played straight instrumental numbers as well. At times, some of the members would exit, disappearing behind the blanket to leave the stage to a pair or a solo performer. Tam Amber proved something of a standout on his mandolin, riveting the crowd with his lightning-fast fingering while his face remained expressionless and distant. Maude Ivory, a crowd favorite, piped out a darkly funny song about a miner's daughter who drowned, and invited the audience members to join in the chorus, which, surprisingly, many of them did. Or maybe it was not that surprising, given that most were companionably drunk now.

Oh, my darling, oh, my darling,
Oh, my darling, Clementine,
You are lost and gone forever.
Dreadful sorry, Clementine.

Some of the numbers bordered on unintelligible, with unfamiliar words that Coriolanus struggled to get the gist of, and he remembered Lucy Gray saying that they were from another time.

During these in particular, the five Covey seemed to turn in on themselves, swaying and building complicated harmonies with their voices. Coriolanus didn't care for it; the sound unsettled him. He sat through at least three songs of this kind before he realized it reminded him of the mockingjays.

Fortunately, most of the songs were newer and more to his liking, and they finished up with the one he recognized from the reaping . . .

No, sir,
Nothing you can take from me is worth dirt.
Take it, 'cause I'd give it free. It won't hurt.
Nothing you can take from me was ever worth keeping!

. . . the irony of which was not lost on the audience. The Capitol had tried to take everything from Lucy Gray, and it had utterly failed.

When the applause died out, she gave Maude Ivory a nod. The girl ran behind the blanket and appeared carrying a basket woven with cheerful ribbons.

"Thank you kindly," said Lucy Gray. "Now, you all know how this works. We don't charge for tickets, because sometimes hungry people need music the most. But we get hungry, too. So if you'd like to contribute, Maude Ivory will be around with the basket. We thank you in advance."

The four older Covey softly played while Maude Ivory scampered around the crowd, collecting coins in her basket. Between the five of them, Coriolanus and his bunkmates only had a few coins, which didn't seem nearly enough, though Maude Ivory thanked them with a polite curtsy.

"Hold on," said Coriolanus. "Do you like sweets?" He lifted a flap of the brown paper package with the last of the popcorn balls so Maude Ivory could take a peek, and her eyes widened with delight. Coriolanus set them all in the basket, as they'd been earmarked for the tickets anyway. If he knew Ma, more boxes were on their way.

Maude Ivory did a little pirouette in thanks, hurried through the rest of the audience, and then ran up onstage to tug on Lucy Gray's skirt, showing her the treats in the basket. Coriolanus could see Lucy Gray's lips make an *ooh* sound and ask where they'd come from. He knew this was the moment, and he found himself taking a step out of the shadows. His body tingled in anticipation as Maude Ivory lifted her hand to point him out. What would Lucy Gray do? Would she acknowledge him? Ignore him? Would she even recognize him, made over as he was as a Peacekeeper?

Her eyes followed Maude Ivory's finger until they landed on him. A look of confusion crossed her face, then recognition, and then joy. She shook her head in disbelief and laughed. "Okay, okay, everybody. This is . . . this is maybe the best night of my life. Thanks to everybody here for showing up. How about one more song to send you off to sleep? You might've heard me do this before, but it took on a whole new meaning for me in the Capitol. Guess you'll figure out why."

Coriolanus moved back to his seat — she knew where to find him now — to listen and to savor their actual reunion, which was only a song away. His eyes teared up when she began the song from the zoo.

Down in the valley, valley so low,
Late in the evening, hear the train blow.
The train, love, hear the train blow.
Late in the evening, hear the train blow.

Coriolanus felt an elbow nudge his ribs and looked over to see Sejanus beaming at him. It was nice, after all, to have someone else who knew the significance of the song. Someone who knew what they'd been through.

Go build me a mansion, build it so high,
So I can see my true love go by.
See him go by, love, see him go by.
So I can see my true love go by.

That's me, Coriolanus wanted to tell people around him. *I'm her true love. And I saved her life.*

Go write me a letter, send it by mail.
Bake it and stamp it to the Capitol jail.
Capitol jail, love, to the Capitol jail.
Bake it and stamp it to the Capitol jail.

Should he say hello first? Or just kiss her?

Roses are red, love; violets are blue.
Birds in the heavens know I love you.

Kiss her. Definitely, just kiss her.

Know I love you, oh, know I love you,
Birds in the heavens know I love you.

"Good night, everybody. Hope we see you next week, and until then, keep singing your song," said Lucy Gray, and the whole Covey took one final bow. As the audience applauded, she smiled at Coriolanus. He began to move toward her, stepping around people collecting their makeshift seats to pile back in the corner. A few of the Peacekeepers had gathered around her, and she chatted with them, but he could see her eyes darting his way. He paused to give her time to extricate herself and just to bask in the sight of her, glowing and in love with him.

The Peacekeepers were bidding her good night, starting to back away. Coriolanus smoothed his hair and moved in. They were only about fifteen feet apart when a disturbance in the Hob, the sound of glass breaking and voices protesting, caused him to turn his head. A dark-haired young man around his age, dressed in a sleeveless shirt and pants ripped off at the knees, pushed through the thinning crowd. His face gleamed with sweat, and his movements suggested he'd exceeded his white liquor limit some time ago. Over one shoulder hung a boxy instrument with part of a piano keyboard along one side. Behind him trailed the mayor's daughter, Mayfair, taking care not to brush against the patrons, her mouth tight with disdain. Coriolanus shifted his gaze to the stage, where a cold, fixed stare had replaced Lucy Gray's eager expression. The other members of the band drew in around her protectively, their showtime levity draining away into a mix of raw anger and sadness.

It's him, Coriolanus thought with dead certainty, his stomach twisting unpleasantly. *It's the lover from the song.*

Maude Ivory planted her wispy frame squarely in front of Lucy Gray. She scrunched her face and balled her hands into fists. "You get out of here, Billy Taupe. None of us want you anymore."

Billy Taupe rocked slightly as he surveyed the group. "Less want than need, Maude Ivory."

"Don't need you neither. Go on and get. And take your weasel girl with you," ordered Maude Ivory. Lucy Gray encircled her with her arm, pressing her hand against the little girl's chest, either to soothe or restrain her.

"You're all sounding thin. You're sounding thin," slurred Billy Taupe, and one hand slapped his instrument.

"We can do without you, Billy Taupe. You made your choice. Now leave us be," said Barb Azure, her quiet voice underlaid with steel. Tam Amber said nothing but gave a small nod of assent.

Pain flashed across Billy Taupe's face. "Is that how you feel, CC?"

Clerk Carmine curled his fiddle in close to his body.

Although the Covey varied in complexion, hair, and features, Coriolanus noticed a distinct resemblance between these two. Brothers, maybe?

"You can come with me. We'd do all right, we two," Billy Taupe pleaded. But Clerk Carmine stood his ground. "All right, then. Don't need you. Never needed any of you anyway. Never will. Always did better on my own."

A couple of Peacekeepers began to close in on him. The one

who'd given Lucy Gray the bottle of white liquor laid a hand on his arm. "Come on, now, show's over."

Billy Taupe jerked away from his touch and then gave him a drunken shove. In an instant, the sociable mood in the Hob changed. Coriolanus could feel the tension, sharp as a knife. Miners who'd either ignored him or given him nods over their bottles became belligerent. The Peacekeepers straightened up, suddenly alert, and he found his own body almost standing at attention. As a half dozen Peacekeepers moved in on Billy Taupe, he felt the miners surge forward. He was readying himself for the brawl that was sure to follow, when someone pulled the plug on the lights, sending the Hob into blackness.

Everything froze for an instant, then chaos erupted. A fist caught Coriolanus's mouth, sending his own fists into action. He struck out arbitrarily, focused only on securing his own circle of safety. The same animal wildness he'd experienced when the tributes had hunted him down in the arena swept over him. Dr. Gaul's voice echoed in his ears. *"That's mankind in its natural state. That's humanity undressed."* And here was naked humanity again, and here again he was a part of it. Punching, kicking, his teeth bared in the darkness.

A horn outside the Hob blared repeatedly, and truck headlights flooded the area by the door. Whistles blew, and voices shouted for the dispersal of the crowd. People lurched toward the exit. Coriolanus fought the wave, trying to locate Lucy Gray, but then decided the best chance of finding her would be out front. He jostled his way through the bodies, still throwing the occasional punch, and spilled out into the night air, where the locals took flight and the Peacekeepers gathered in a loose bunch, making only a weak show of pursuit. Most of them had not even been on duty, and there was no organized unit to address the spontaneous eruption. In the dark, nobody was even sure who they'd been fighting. Better to let it lie. Coriolanus found it unnerving, though; unlike at the hanging, the miners had fought back.

Sucking on a split lip, he positioned himself to watch the door, but the last stragglers wandered out without any sign of Lucy Gray, the Covey, or even Billy Taupe. He felt frustrated at having been so close but unable to talk to her. Was there another exit to the Hob? Yes, he remembered a door by the stage, which must have allowed them to slip out. Mayfair Lipp had not been so fortunate. She stood flanked by Peacekeepers, not under arrest but not free to go either.

"I've done nothing wrong. You've no right to hold me," she spat at the soldiers.

"Sorry, miss," said a Peacekeeper. "For your own protection, we can't let you go home alone. Either you let us escort you or we call your father for further instructions."

The mention of her father shut Mayfair up but did not improve her attitude. She seethed, her lips pressed into a thin, mean line that said someone would pay, just give her time.

There did not seem to be much enthusiasm for the task of taking her home, and Coriolanus and Sejanus found themselves recruited for the job, either because they'd made a good showing at the hanging or because they were both relatively sober. Two officers and three other Peacekeepers made up the rest of the party. "At this hour, what with the climate, it's probably better to be on the safe side," one officer said. "It's not far."

As they wove through the streets, their boots grinding against the grit, Coriolanus squinted into the darkness. Streetlights illuminated the Capitol, but here he had to rely on the sporadic flickers from windows and the pale beams of the moon. Unarmed, without even the protection of his white uniform, he felt vulnerable and stuck close to the group. The officers had guns; hopefully, that would keep assailants at bay. He remembered the Grandma'am's words. *"Your own father used to say those people only drank water because it didn't rain blood. You ignore that at your own peril, Coriolanus."* Were they out there now, watching and waiting for a chance to quench their thirst? He missed the safety of the base.

Fortunately, after only a few short blocks, the streets opened up onto a deserted square, which he realized was the location of the annual reaping. A few unevenly spaced floodlights helped him navigate the cobblestones under his feet.

"I can get home fine from here," said Mayfair.

"We're in no hurry," one of the officers told her.

"Why don't you just leave me alone?" snapped Mayfair.

"Why don't you stop running around with that good-for-nothing?" suggested the officer. "Trust me, that won't end well."

"Oh, mind your own business," she retorted.

They made a diagonal cross, left the square, and followed a freshly paved road to the next street over. The party drew to a halt at a large house that might count for a mansion in District 12 but would be unremarkable in the Capitol. Through the windows, wide open in the August heat, Coriolanus caught glimpses of well-lit, furnished rooms in which humming electric fans fluttered the curtains. His nose picked up a whiff of the evening's dinner — ham, he thought — causing his mouth to water slightly and thinning out the bloody taste from his lip. Maybe it was just as well he'd missed Lucy Gray; his lips were in no shape for a kiss.

As one of the officers laid a hand on the gate, Mayfair pushed past him, darted up the path, and slipped into the house.

"Should we tell her parents?" asked the other.

"What's the point?" said the first. "You know how the mayor is. Somehow her traipsing around at night will be our fault. I can do without a lecture."

The other muttered agreement, and the party headed back across the square. As Coriolanus followed, a soft, mechanical wheeze caught his attention, and he turned to the shadowy bushes that lined the side of the house. He could just make out a figure standing motionless in the gloom, back pressed against the wall. A light on the second floor flipped on, and the yellow glow extending down revealed Billy Taupe, nose bloodied, scowling directly at him. He held his instrument, the source of the wheeze, against his chest.

Coriolanus's lips parted to alert the others, but something held his tongue. What was it? Fear? Indifference? Uncertainty as to how Lucy Gray would react? The band had made their position clear when it came to his rival, and yet he didn't know how they would take Coriolanus's ratting him out, possibly landing him in jail. What if it made Billy Taupe a sympathetic character, someone they would rally around and forgive? He could tell that the Covey loyalties ran deep. Then again, perhaps they would welcome it? Particularly Lucy Gray, who might be very interested to know that her old flame had run to the mayor's daughter's house for solace. What had he done to be ousted from all things Covey, band and home? He remembered the final words to her song, her ballad, from the interview.

Too bad I'm the bet that you lost in the reaping.
Now what will you do when I go to my grave?

Surely, the answer lay there.

Mayfair appeared and closed the window. Then she drew

the curtain, blocking the light and concealing Billy Taupe. The bushes rustled, and the moment had passed.

"Coryo?" Sejanus had returned for him. "You coming?"

"Sorry, just lost in thought," said Coriolanus.

Sejanus nodded to the house. "It reminds me of the Capitol."

"You don't say home," Coriolanus pointed out.

"No. For me, that will always be District Two," Sejanus confirmed. "But it doesn't matter. I'll probably never see either place again."

As they walked back, Coriolanus wondered about his own odds of seeing the Capitol again. Before Sejanus came, he'd thought they were zero. But if he could return as an officer, maybe even a war hero, things might be different. Of course, then he'd need a war to excel in, just as Sejanus needed one in order to be a medic.

Coriolanus's shoulders relaxed when the gates of the base closed behind him. He washed his face and crawled into his bunk above Beanpole's inebriated snores. His pulse beat in his swollen lip as he replayed the evening. It had all gone like a dream — seeing Lucy Gray, hearing her sing, her joy at the sight of him — until Billy Taupe had showed up and spoiled the reunion. It was just another reason to hate Billy Taupe, although seeing the Covey's rejection of him was deeply satisfying. It confirmed that Lucy Gray belonged to him.

Sunday breakfast brought the bad news that, because of the previous evening's altercation, no soldier was to leave the base alone. The higher-ups were even considering placing the Hob off-limits. Smiley, Bug, and Beanpole, although hungover and bruised from the night before, bemoaned the state of things, having nothing to look forward to if their Saturday outings were canceled. Sejanus only cared because Coriolanus cared, recognizing that this was just one more hurdle to seeing Lucy Gray.

"Maybe she'll visit you here?" he suggested as they cleared their trays.

"Can she do that?" Coriolanus asked, but then hoped she wouldn't, even if she could. He had little unscheduled time, and where would they even be allowed to talk? Through the fence? How would that be viewed? Caught up as he had been in the romance of the previous evening, he'd been planning to greet her publicly with a kiss, but in hindsight, that would've brought on a barrage of questions from his bunkmates, and doubtless raised a few eyebrows among the officers. Their whole history, including his forced enlistment, would come out, and with it his cheating in the Games. In addition, given the troubles between the locals and the Peacekeepers, it would be wise to keep the relationship private. Whispering through the fence might encourage rumors that he was a rebel sympathizer or, even worse, a spy. No, if they were going to meet, he would have to go to her. Secretly. Today would be a rare opportunity to track her down, but he'd need a buddy to leave the base.

"I think we'd better keep things between us a secret. She might get in trouble if she came here. Sejanus, did you have plans today, or —" he began.

"She lives in a place called the Seam," said Sejanus. "Near the woods."

"What?" said Coriolanus.

"I asked one of the miners last night. Very casually." Sejanus smiled. "Don't worry, he was too drunk to remember. And yes, I'd be happy to go with you."

Sejanus told their bunkmates they were heading into town to see if they could swap a pack of Capitol chewing gum for letter paper, but the ruse proved unnecessary, as all the mates took their abused bodies back to their bunks right after breakfast. Coriolanus wished he had money for a gift of some kind, but he had nary a cent. As they passed the mess hall on the way out, his eyes fell on the ice machine, and he had an idea. In this hot weather, the soldiers were permitted to take the ice freely for their drinks, or to cool off. Rubbing cubes over their bodies provided a little relief in the sauna of a kitchen.

Cookie, who he'd won over with his diligent dish washing, gave Coriolanus an old plastic bag. The day being so hot, he agreed it would be all right to take some ice on their outing to ward off heatstroke. Coriolanus didn't know if the Covey had a freezer, but by the looks of the houses he'd passed on his way to the hanging, he thought that might be a luxury few could afford. Anyway, the ice was free, and he didn't want to go empty-handed.

They signed out at the gate, where the guard cautioned them to be careful, and walked off in what they remembered to be the general direction of the town square. Coriolanus felt apprehensive. With the mines shut down for the day, though, a hush lay over the district, and the few people they passed ignored them. Only a small bakery stood open in the town square, its doors propped wide to allow a breeze to temper the heat of the ovens. The owner, a beet-faced woman, had little interest in providing directions to nonpaying customers, so Sejanus bartered his fancy chewing gum for a loaf of bread. Relenting, she took them out on the square and pointed at the street they were to follow to the Seam.

Beyond the town center, the Seam sprawled out for miles, the regular streets quickly dissolving into a web of smaller, unmarked lanes that rose up and then petered out for no discernible reason. Some boasted rows of worn, identical houses; others had makeshift structures it would be generous to call shacks. Many homes were so shored up, patched up, or broken down that their original framework was nothing but a memory. Many others had been abandoned and scavenged for their parts.

With no grid, no landmark of note, Coriolanus lost his bearings almost immediately, and his unease returned. Once in a while, they'd pass someone sitting on their stoop or in the shade of their homes. None of them looked the least bit friendly. The only sociable creatures were the gnats, whose fascination with his injured lip required constant shooing. As the sun beat down on them, condensation from the melting bag of ice left a splotch on his pant leg. Coriolanus's enthusiasm began dissolving as well. The intoxication he'd experienced the night before in the Hob, the heady mix of liquor and yearning, seemed like a feverish dream now. "Maybe this was a bad idea."

"Really?" asked Sejanus. "I'm pretty sure we're headed in the right direction. See the trees over there?"

Coriolanus made out a fringe of green in the distance. He trudged along thinking with fondness of his bunk and remembering that Sunday meant fried baloney and potatoes. Maybe he was not cut out to be a lover. Maybe he was more of a loner at heart. Coriolanus Snow, more loner than lover. One thing about Billy Taupe, he reeked of passionate feelings. Is that what Lucy Gray wanted? Passion, music, liquor, moonlight, and a wild boy who embraced them all? Not a perspiring Peacekeeper showing up at her door on a Sunday morning with a split lip and a sagging bag of ice.

He gave over the lead to Sejanus, following him up and down cinder paths without comment. Eventually, his companion would grow tired, and they could go back and catch up on their letter writing. Sejanus, Tigris, his friends, the faculty, all of them had been dead wrong about him. He'd never been motivated by love or ambition, only a desire to get his prize and a nice, quiet bureaucratic job pushing papers around and leaving him plenty of time to attend tea parties. Cowardly and . . . what had Dean Highbottom called her? Oh, yes, vapid. Vapid, like his mother. What a disappointment he'd have been to Crassus Xanthos Snow.

"Listen," said Sejanus, catching his arm.

Coriolanus paused and lifted his head. A high-pitched voice pierced the morning air with a melancholy tune. Maude Ivory? They made for the source of the music. At the end of a path at the edge of the Seam, a small wooden house tilted at a precarious angle, like a tree in a stiff wind. The dirt patch of a front yard was deserted, so they picked their way around the clumps of wildflowers, in various states of bloom and decay, that appeared to have been transplanted without much rhyme or reason. When they reached the back of the house, they discovered Maude Ivory sitting on a makeshift stoop in an old dress two sizes too big for her. She was cracking nuts on a cinder block with a rock, beating time to her song.

"Oh, my darling" — *crack* — "Oh, my darling" — *crack* — "Oh, my darling, Clementine!" — *crack.* She looked up and grinned when she saw them. "I know you!" Brushing the stray nutshells from her frock, she ran into the house.

Coriolanus wiped his face on his sleeve, hoping his lip wouldn't look too bad when Lucy Gray appeared. Instead Maude Ivory came out with a sleepy Barb Azure, who had twisted her hair up in a hasty knot. Like Maude Ivory, she'd changed her costume for a dress you might see on anyone in District 12. "Good morning," she said. "You looking for Lucy Gray?"

"He's her friend from the Capitol," Maude Ivory reminded her. "The one who introduced her on the television, only he's near bald now. He gave me the popcorn balls."

"Well, we certainly enjoyed those and appreciate all you did for

Lucy Gray," said Barb Azure. "I expect you'll find her down in the Meadow. That's where she goes early to work, so as not to disturb the neighbors."

"I'll show you. Let me!" Maude Ivory hopped off the porch and took Coriolanus's hand, as if they were old friends. "It's this way."

With no younger siblings or other relatives, Coriolanus had little experience with kids, but it made him feel special, the way she'd attached herself to him, the cool little hand pressed trustingly in his. "So, you saw me on the television?"

"Just the one night. It was clear and Tam Amber used a lot of foil. Usually, we can't get anything but static, but it's special we even have a television," explained Maude Ivory. "Most don't. Not that there's much to watch but that boring old news anyway."

Dr. Gaul could go on all she wanted about engaging people in the Hunger Games, but if practically no one in the districts had a working television, the impact would be confined to the reaping, when everyone gathered in public.

While they walked toward the woods, Maude Ivory rattled on about their show the night before and the fight that followed. "Sorry you got punched," she said, pointing to his lip. "That's Billy Taupe, though. Where he goes, trouble follows."

"Is he your brother?" asked Sejanus.

"Oh, no, he's a Clade. Him and Clerk Carmine are brothers. The rest of us are all Baird cousins. The girls, I mean. And Tam Amber's a lost soul," said Maude Ivory matter-of-factly.

So Lucy Gray didn't have a monopoly on the strange manner of talking. It must be a Covey thing. "A lost soul?" asked Coriolanus.

"Sure. The Covey found Tam Amber when he was just a baby. Somebody left him in a cardboard box on the side of the road, so he's ours. Joke's on them, too, because he's the finest picker alive," Maude Ivory declared. "Not much of a talker, though. Is that ice?"

Coriolanus swung the diminishing clump of cubes. "What's left of it."

"Oh, Lucy Gray will like that. We've got a fridge, but the freezer's long broke," said Maude Ivory. "Seems fancy to have ice in summertime. Like flowers in wintertime. Rare."

Coriolanus agreed. "My grandmother grows roses in winter. People make a big fuss over them."

"Lucy Gray said you smelled like roses," said Maude Ivory. "Is your whole house full of them?"

"She grows them on the roof," Coriolanus told her.

"The roof?" giggled Maude Ivory. "That's a silly place for flowers. Don't they slide off?"

"It's a flat roof, up very high. With lots of sunlight," he said. "You can see the whole Capitol from there."

"Lucy Gray didn't like the Capitol. They tried to kill her," said Maude Ivory.

"Yes," he acknowledged. "It couldn't have been very nice for her."

"She said you were the only good thing about it, and now you're here." Maude Ivory gave his hand a tug. "You're going to stay here, right?"

"That's the plan," said Coriolanus.

"I'm glad. I like you, and that will make her happy," she said.

By this time, the three had reached the edge of a large field that dipped down to the woods. Unlike the weedy expanse in front of the hanging tree, this one had clean, fresh, high grass and swaths of bright wildflowers. "There she is, with Shamus." Maude Ivory pointed to a lone figure on a rock. Wearing a dress of her namesake color, Lucy Gray sat with her back to them, her head bent over her guitar.

Shamus? Who was Shamus? Another member of the Covey? Or had he misread Billy Taupe's role in her life, and Shamus was the lover? Coriolanus put a hand above his eyes to shield them from the sunlight but could make out only her figure. "Shamus?"

"She's our goat. Don't be fooled by the boy's name; she can give a gallon a day when she's fresh," said Maude Ivory. "We're trying to skim enough cream for butter, but it takes forever."

"Oh, I love butter," said Sejanus. "That reminds me, I forgot to give you this bread. Did you have your breakfast already?"

"It's a fact, I didn't," said Maude Ivory, eyeing the loaf with interest.

Sejanus handed it over. "What do you say we head back to the house and break into this now?"

Maude Ivory tucked the bread under her arm. "What about Lucy Gray and this one?" she asked, nodding at Coriolanus.

"They can join us after they've caught up," said Sejanus.

"Okay," she agreed, transferring her hand to Sejanus's. "Barb Azure might make us wait for them. You could help me shell nuts first, if you want. They're last year's, but nobody's gotten sick yet."

"Well, that's the best offer I've had in a long time." Sejanus turned to Coriolanus. "We'll see you later?"

Coriolanus felt self-conscious. "Do I look okay?"

"Gorgeous. Trust me, that lip's working for you, soldier," said Sejanus, and he headed back toward the house with Maude Ivory.

Coriolanus gave his hair a swipe and waded into the Meadow. He'd never walked in such high grass, and the sensation of it tickling his fingertips added to his nervousness. It far exceeded his hopes, getting to meet up with her in private, in a flower-filled field, with the whole day ahead. Just the opposite of what the rushed encounter in the filthy Hob would've been. This was, for lack of a better word, romantic. He moved forward as quietly as possible. As a rule, she mystified him, and he welcomed the chance to observe her without her usual defenses in place.

Drawing close, he took in the song she sang as she quietly strummed her guitar.

Are you, are you
Coming to the tree
Where they strung up a man they say murdered three?
Strange things did happen here
No stranger would it be
If we met up at midnight in the hanging tree.

He didn't recognize it, but it brought to mind the hanging of the rebel two days before. Had she been there? Had it prompted this?

Are you, are you
Coming to the tree
Where the dead man called out for his love to flee?
Strange things did happen here
No stranger would it be
If we met up at midnight in the hanging tree.

Ah, yes. It *was* Arlo's hanging, because where else would a dead man call out for his love to flee? *"Run! Run, Lil! Ru — !"* You'd need those unnatural mockingjays for that. But who was she inviting to meet her in the tree? Could it be him? Maybe she planned to sing this next Saturday as a secret message for him to meet her at midnight in the hanging tree? Not that he could, as he'd never be allowed off base at that hour. But she probably didn't know that.

Lucy Gray hummed now, testing out different chords behind the melody, while he admired the curve of her neck, the fineness of her skin. As he drew nearer, his foot landed on an old branch, which broke with a sharp snap. She sprang from the rock, twisting her body as she rose, her eyes wide with fear and the guitar held out as if to block a blow. For a moment, he thought she'd flee, but her alarm shifted to relief at the sight of him. She shook her head, as close as he'd ever seen her to embarrassed, as she propped her guitar against the rock. "Sorry. Still got one foot in the arena."

If his brief foray in the Games had left him nervous and nightmarish, he could only imagine how damaged she was. The last month had upended their lives and changed them irrevocably. Sad, really, as they were both rather exceptional people, for whom the world had reserved its harshest treatment.

"Yes, it leaves quite an impression," he said. They stood for a moment, drinking each other in, before they moved together. The bag of ice slid from his hand as she wrapped her arms around him, melting her body into his. He locked her in an embrace, remembering how scared he'd been for her, for himself, and how he hadn't dared fantasize about this moment as it had seemed so unattainable. But here they were, safe in a beautiful meadow. Two thousand miles away from the arena. Awash in daylight, but none between them.

"You found me," she said.

In District 12? In Panem? In the world itself? Never mind, it didn't matter. "You knew I would."

"Hoped you would. Didn't know. The odds didn't seem in my favor." She leaned back enough to free a hand and brushed his lips with her fingers. He felt the calluses from her guitar strings, the soft surrounding skin, as she examined the previous night's injury. Then, almost shyly, she kissed him, sending shock waves through his body. Ignoring the pain in his lips, he responded, hungry and curious, every nerve in his body awake. He kissed her until his lip started to bleed a little, and would have kept going had she not pulled away.

"Here," she said. "Come in the shade."

The remaining ice cracked under his foot, and he retrieved it. "For you."

"Why thank you." Lucy Gray drew him over to sit at the base of the rock. Taking the bag, she bit off a corner of the plastic to make a tiny hole and lifted it high to let the melted ice water drip into her mouth. "Ah. This must be the only cold thing this side of November." Her hand squeezed the bag, sending a light spray over her face. "It's wonderful; lean back." He tilted his head back and felt the stuff drizzle over his lips, licking it off just in time for another long kiss. Then she drew up her knees and said, "So, Coriolanus Snow, what are you doing in my meadow?"

What, indeed? "Just spending some time with my girl," he answered.

"I can hardly believe it." Lucy Gray surveyed the Meadow. "Nothing since the reaping has seemed very real. And the Games were just a nightmare."

"For me, too," he said. "But I want to hear what happened to you. Off camera."

They sat side by side, shoulders, ribs, hips pressed together, hands entwined, exchanging stories as they shared the ice water. Lucy Gray began with an account of the opening days of the

Games, when she'd hidden with a progressively more rabid Jessup. "We kept moving from spot to spot in those tunnels. It's like a maze down there. And poor Jessup getting sicker and crazier by the minute. That first night, we bedded down near the entrance. That was you, wasn't it? Who came to move Marcus?"

"It was me and Sejanus. He snuck in to . . . well, I'm not even sure what, to make some sort of statement. They sent me in to retrieve him," Coriolanus explained.

"Was it you killed Bobbin?" she asked quietly.

He nodded. "Didn't have a choice. And then three of the others tried to kill me."

Her face darkened. "I know. I could hear them boasting when they came back from the turnstiles. I thought you might be dead. Scared me, the thought of losing you. I didn't draw breath until you sent in the water."

"Then you know what every moment was like for me," Coriolanus said. "You were all I could think about."

"You, too." She flexed her fingers. "I clutched that compact so hard you could see the imprint of the rose on my palm."

He caught her hand and kissed the palm. "I wanted so badly to help, and I felt so useless."

She caressed his cheek. "Oh, no. I could feel you looking out for me. With the water, and the food, and believe me, taking out Bobbin was major, even though I know it must have been awful for you. It sure was for me." Lucy Gray admitted to three of her own kills. First Wovey, although that had not been targeted. She'd merely positioned a bottle of water with a few swallows and a bit of powder as if it had been dropped accidentally in the tunnels, and Wovey had been the one to find it. "I was gunning for Coral." She claimed Reaper, whose puddle she'd poisoned, had contracted rabies when Jessup spat in his eye in the zoo. "So that was really a mercy killing. I spared him what Jessup went through. And taking out Treech with that viper was self-defense. Still not sure why those snakes loved me so. Not convinced it was my singing. Snakes don't even hear well."

So he told her. About the lab, and Clemensia, and Dr. Gaul's plan to release the snakes into the arena, and how he'd secretly dropped his handkerchief, his father's handkerchief, into the tank so they could become accustomed to her scent. "But they found it, loaded with DNA from both of us."

"And that's why you're here? Not the rat poison in the compact?" she asked.

"Yes," he said. "You covered beautifully for me on that one."

"Did my best." She considered things for a minute. "Well, that's it, then. I saved you from the fire, and you saved me from the snakes. We're responsible for each other's lives now."

"Are we?" he asked.

"Sure," she said. "You're mine and I'm yours. It's written in the stars."

"No escaping that." He leaned over and kissed her, flushed with happiness, because although he did not believe in celestial writings, she did, and that would be enough to guarantee her loyalty. Not that his own loyalty was in question. If he hadn't fallen in love with any of the girls in the Capitol, it was unlikely District 12 could offer much else in the way of temptation.

A strange sensation at his neck called for attention, and he found Shamus sampling his collar. "Oh, hello. Can I help you, madam?"

Lucy Gray laughed. "Happens you can, if you've a mind to. She needs milking."

"Milking. Hm. I'm not sure where to begin," he said.

"With a bucket. Up at the house." She squirted a bit of ice

water in Shamus's direction, and the goat released the collar. Tearing the bag, she took out the last couple of cubes, popping one in Coriolanus's mouth and one in her own. "Sure is nice to have ice this time of year. A luxury in summer and a curse in winter."

"Can't you just ignore it?" asked Coriolanus.

"Not around here. In January, our pipes froze, and we had to melt down ice chunks for water on the stove. For six people and a goat? You'd be surprised how much work that takes. It was better once the snow came; that melts pretty quick." Lucy Gray took Shamus's lead rope and picked up her guitar.

"I got it." Coriolanus reached for the instrument. Then he wondered if she trusted him with it.

Lucy Gray easily handed it over. "Not as nice as the one Pluribus loaned us, but it pays for our keep. Only thing is, we're running low on strings, and the homemade ones don't cut it. Do you think, if I wrote to him, he could send me a few? I bet he has some leftover from when he ran his club. I can pay. I've still got most of the money Dean Highbottom gave me."

Coriolanus stopped in his tracks. "Dean Highbottom? Dean Highbottom gave you money?"

"He did, but it was kind of on the quiet. First, he apologized for what I'd been through, then he stuffed a wad of cash into my pocket. Glad to have it. The Covey didn't perform while I was gone. Too shook up over losing me," she said. "Anyway, I can pay for those strings if he's of a mind to help."

Coriolanus promised to ask in his next letter, but the news of Dean Highbottom's covert generosity threw him. Why would evil incarnate help his girlfriend? Respect? Pity? Guilt? Morphling-induced whimsy? He mulled it over as they made their way to her front porch, where she hitched Shamus to a post.

"Come on in. Meet the family." Lucy Gray took his hand and led him to the door. "How's Tigris? I sure wish I could've thanked her in person for the soap and my dress. Now that I'm home, I mean to send her a letter, and maybe a song if I come up with something good enough."

"She'd like that," said Coriolanus. "Things aren't going so well at home."

"I'm sure they miss you. Is it more than that?" she asked.

Before he could answer, they'd entered the house. It consisted of one large, open room and what seemed to be a sleeping area up in a loft. Along the back, a coal stove, a sink, a shelf of dishware, and an ancient refrigerator designated the kitchen. A rack of costumes lined the right wall, their collection of instruments to the left. An old television with an oversized antenna that branched out like antlers, rigged with twisted pieces of aluminum foil, sat on a crate. Other than some chairs and a table, the place was bare of furniture.

Tam Amber leaned back in one of the chairs, holding his mandolin on his lap but not playing. Clerk Carmine hung his head off the loft, gazing unhappily at Barb Azure and Maude Ivory, who seemed to have worked herself into a state of indignation. At the sight of them, she shot across the floor and started pulling Lucy Gray toward the window that looked out over the backyard. "Lucy Gray, he's making trouble again!"

"You let him in?" Lucy Gray asked, seeming to know who she meant.

"No. Said he just wanted the rest of his stuff. We threw it out back," said Barb Azure, her arms crossed in disapproval.

"So, what's the problem?" Lucy Gray spoke calmly, but Coriolanus could feel her grip tighten.

"That," said Barb Azure, nodding out the back window.

Still in tow, Coriolanus followed Lucy Gray and looked into the backyard. Maude Ivory wriggled in between them. "Sejanus is supposed to be helping me with the nuts."

Billy Taupe knelt on the ground, a pile of clothes and a few books beside him. He was talking rapidly as he scraped out some kind of picture in the dirt. Periodically, he'd gesture, pointing this way and that. Across from him, down on one knee, Sejanus listened intently, nodding in understanding and occasionally throwing in a question. While the sight of Billy Taupe in what he now considered his territory annoyed him, Coriolanus did not see much cause for concern. He could not imagine what he and Sejanus had to discuss. Perhaps they'd found some mutual grievance — like how their families didn't understand them — to whine about?

"Are you worried about Sejanus? He's fine. He talks to anybody." Coriolanus tried but failed to make out Billy Taupe's picture in the dirt. "What's he drawing?"

"Looks like he's giving some sort of directions," said Barb Azure, relieving him of the guitar. "And if I'm right, your friend needs to go home."

"I'll take care of it." Lucy Gray started to release Coriolanus's hand, but he hung on. "Thanks, but you don't have to deal with all my baggage."

"It's in the stars, I guess," Coriolanus said with a smile. It was time anyway that he confronted Billy Taupe and laid down a few rules. Billy Taupe had to accept that Lucy Gray was no longer his, but belonged firmly, and for always, to Coriolanus.

Lucy Gray didn't answer, but she stopped trying to free her hand. As they walked quietly through the open back door, the brightness of the August sun, now climbing high in the sky, made him squint. So engrossed was the pair that it was not until he and Lucy Gray stood directly over them that Billy Taupe reacted, swiping the picture from the dirt with his hand.

Without Barb Azure's tip-off, Coriolanus might have been clueless, but as it was, he recognized the image almost immediately. It was a map of the base.

Sejanus startled in what Coriolanus couldn't help thinking was a guilty manner, getting rapidly to his feet as he brushed the dust from his uniform. Billy Taupe, on the other hand, rose slowly, almost lazily, to confront them.

"Well, look who's decided to talk to me," he said, grinning uneasily at Lucy Gray. Was this the first time they'd spoken since the Hunger Games?

"Sejanus, Maude Ivory's all bent out of shape about you bailing on those nuts," she said.

"Yes, I've been shirking my duties." Sejanus held out his hand to Billy Taupe, who didn't hesitate to give it a shake. "Nice meeting you."

"Sure, you, too. You can find me around the Hob some days, if you want to talk more," Billy Taupe replied.

"I'll keep it in mind," said Sejanus, making for the house.

Lucy Gray released Coriolanus's hand and squared her shoulders with Billy Taupe's. "Go away, Billy Taupe. And don't come back."

"Or what, Lucy Gray? You'll sic your Peacekeepers on me?" He laughed.

"If need be," she said.

Billy Taupe glanced over at Coriolanus. "Seem like a pretty tame pair."

"You don't get it. There's no walking this back," said Lucy Gray.

Billy Taupe turned angry. "You know I didn't try and kill you."

"I know you're still running with the girl that did," Lucy Gray shot back. "Hear you've made yourself right at home at the mayor's."

"And who sent me over there in the first place, I wonder? Makes me sick how you're playing the kids. Poor Lucy Gray. Poor lamb," he sneered.

"They're not stupid. They want you gone, too," she spat out.

Billy Taupe's hand whipped out, grabbing her wrist and pulling her up against him. "Where, exactly, am I supposed to go?"

Before Coriolanus could intervene, Lucy Gray sank her teeth into Billy Taupe's hand, causing him to yelp and release her. He glared at Coriolanus, who'd stepped up protectively beside her. "Doesn't look like you're so lonely yourself. This your fancy man from the Capitol? Chased all this way after you? He's got a few surprises waiting for him."

"I already know all about you." Coriolanus didn't, really. But it made him feel at less of a disadvantage.

Billy Taupe gave a disbelieving laugh. "Me? I'm the rosebud in that dung heap."

"Why don't you go, like she asked?" said Coriolanus coldly.

"Fine. You'll learn." Billy Taupe gathered his possessions into his arms. "You'll learn soon enough." He strode off into the hot morning.

Lucy Gray watched him go, rubbing the wrist he'd grabbed. "If you want to run, now's the time."

"I don't want to run," said Coriolanus, although the exchange had been unsettling.

"He's a liar and a louse. Sure, I flirt with anybody. It's part of my job. But what he's implying, that just isn't true." Lucy Gray looked over at the window. "And what if it was? What if it was that or letting Maude Ivory starve? Neither of us would have let that happen, no matter what it took. Only, he's got a different set of rules for him than for me. Like always. What makes him a victim makes me trash."

This brought back disturbing memories of his conversation with Tigris, and Coriolanus changed the subject quickly. "He's seeing the mayor's daughter now?"

"That's how it is. I sent him over there to pick up some cash teaching piano lessons, and the next thing I know, her daddy's calling out my name in the reaping," said Lucy Gray. "Not sure what she told him. He'd go nuts if he knew she was running around with Billy Taupe. Well, I survived the Capitol, but not to come back for more of the same."

Something in her manner, the raw distress, convinced Coriolanus. He touched her arm. "Make a new life, then."

She entwined her fingers with his. "A new life. With you." But a cloud hung over her.

Coriolanus gave her a nudge. "Don't we have a goat to milk?"

Her face relaxed. "We do." She led him back into the house, only to find Maude Ivory had taken Sejanus out to teach him to milk Shamus.

"He couldn't say no. He's in the doghouse for talking to the enemy," said Barb Azure. She took a pan of chilled milk from the old refrigerator, set it on the table, and examined it. From a shelf, Clerk Carmine retrieved a glass jar with some sort of contraption on the top. A crank attached to the lid appeared to move small paddles within the jar.

"What are you doing there?" asked Coriolanus.

"A fool's errand." Barb Azure laughed. "Trying to get enough cream so as we can make butter. Only goat's milk doesn't separate like cow's."

"Maybe if we gave it another day?" Clerk Carmine said.

"Well, maybe." Barb Azure returned the pan to the refrigerator.

"We promised Maude Ivory we'd try. She's crazy for butter. Tam Amber fashioned the churn for her birthday. Guess we'll see," said Lucy Gray.

Coriolanus fiddled with the crank. "So you . . . ?"

"Theoretically, when we get enough cream, we turn the handle, and the paddles churn it into butter," Lucy Gray explained. "Well, that's what someone told us anyway."

"Seems like a lot of work." Coriolanus thought of the beautiful, uniform pats he'd helped himself to from the buffet on reaping day, never giving a moment's thought as to where they came from.

"It is. But it'll be worth it if it works. Maude Ivory doesn't sleep well since they took me away. Seems fine during the day, then wakes up screaming at night," confided Lucy Gray. "Trying to get some happy in her head."

Barb Azure strained the fresh milk Sejanus and Maude Ivory brought in and poured it into mugs while Lucy Gray portioned out the bread. Coriolanus had never had goat's milk, but Sejanus smacked his lips, saying it reminded him of his childhood in District 2.

"Did I ever go to District Two?" Maude Ivory asked.

"No, baby, that's out west. The Covey stayed more east," Barb Azure told her.

"Sometimes we went north," said Tam Amber, and Coriolanus realized it was the first time he'd heard him speak.

"To what district?" asked Coriolanus.

"No district, really," said Barb Azure. "Up where the Capitol didn't care about."

Coriolanus felt embarrassed for them. No such place existed. At least not anymore. The Capitol controlled the known world.

For a moment, he imagined a group of people in wild animal furs scraping out an existence in a cave somewhere. He supposed such a thing could happen, but that life would be a big step down from even the districts. Barely human.

"Probably rounded up like we were," said Clerk Carmine.

Barb Azure gave a sad smile. "Doubt we'll ever know."

"Is there any more? I'm still hungry," Maude Ivory complained, but the bread was gone.

"Eat a handful of your nuts," Barb Azure said. "They'll feed us at the wedding."

To Coriolanus's dismay, it turned out that the Covey had a job that afternoon, playing for a wedding in town. He had hoped to get Lucy Gray off alone again for a more in-depth conversation about Billy Taupe, her history with him, and exactly why he might be drawing a map of the base in the dirt. But it would all have to wait, since the Covey began to prepare for their gig as soon as the dishes were washed.

"Sorry to run you off so soon, but this is how we earn our bread." Lucy Gray saw Coriolanus and Sejanus to the door. "The butcher's daughter's getting hitched, and we need to make a good impression. People with money to hire us will be there. You could wait and walk us over, I guess, but that might . . ."

"Start people gossiping," he finished for her, glad she had been the first to suggest it. "Probably best if we keep it between us. When can I see you again?"

"Anytime you like," she said. "I have a feeling your schedule's a little more demanding than mine."

"Do you play at the Hob next Saturday?" he asked.

"If they let us. After the trouble last night." They agreed he would come as early as he could to share a few precious minutes with her before the show. "There's a shed we use, just behind the Hob. You can meet us there. If there's no show, just come to the house."

Coriolanus waited until he and Sejanus reached the deserted backstreets near the base before he broached the subject of Billy Taupe. "So, what did you two have to talk about?"

"Nothing, really," said Sejanus uncomfortably. "Just some local gossip."

"And that required a map of the base?" asked Coriolanus.

Sejanus pulled up short. "You never miss a beat, do you? I remember that from school. Watching you watch other people. Pretending you weren't. And choosing the moments you weighed in so carefully."

"I'm weighing in now, Sejanus. Why were you in deep discussion with him over a map of the base? What is he? A rebel sympathizer?" Sejanus averted his gaze, so Coriolanus continued. "What possible interest can he have in a Capitol base?"

Sejanus stared at the ground for a minute, then said, "It's the girl. From the hanging. The one they arrested the other day. Lil. She's locked up there."

"And the rebels want to rescue her?" pressed Coriolanus.

"No. They just want to communicate with her. Make sure she's all right," explained Sejanus.

Coriolanus tried to keep his temper in check. "And you said you would help."

"No, I made no promises. But if I can, if I'm near the guardhouse, perhaps I can find something out. Her family's frantic," said Sejanus.

"Oh, wonderful. Fantastic. So now you're a rebel informant." Coriolanus took off down the road. "I thought you were letting the whole rebel thing go!"

Sejanus followed on his heels. "I can't, all right? It's part of who I am. And you're the one who said I could help the people in the districts if I agreed to leave the arena."

"I believe I said you could fight for the tributes, meaning you might be able to procure more humane conditions for them," Coriolanus corrected him.

"Humane conditions!" Sejanus burst out. "They're being forced to murder each other! And the tributes are from the districts, too, so I don't really see a distinction. It's a tiny thing, Coryo, to check up on this girl."

"Clearly, it isn't," said Coriolanus. "Not to Billy Taupe, anyway. Or why did he wipe out that map so fast? Because he knows what he's asking. He knows he's making you a collaborator. And do you know what happens to collaborators?"

"I just thought —" began Sejanus.

"No, Sejanus, you're not thinking at all!" steamed Coriolanus. "And, even worse, you're falling in with people who barely seem capable of thought. Billy Taupe? What's his stake in this anyway? Money? Because to hear Lucy Gray talk, the Covey aren't rebels. Or Capitol. They're pretty much set on hanging on to their own identity, whatever that is."

"I don't know. He said he . . . he was asking for a friend," stammered Sejanus.

"A friend?" Coriolanus realized he was shouting and dropped his voice to a hush. "A friend of old Arlo, who set the explosions in the mines? There was a piece of brilliant plotting. What possible result could he have been hoping for? They have no resources, nothing at all that would allow them to reengage in a war. And in the meantime, they're biting the hand that feeds them, because how will they eat here in Twelve without those mines? They're not exactly bubbling over with options. What sort of strategy was that?"

"A desperate one. But look around!" Sejanus grabbed his arm, forcing him to stop. "How long can you expect them to go on like this?"

Coriolanus felt a surge of hatred as he remembered the war, the devastation the rebels had brought to his own life. He yanked his arm free. "They lost the war. A war they started. They took that risk. This is the price they pay."

Sejanus looked about, as if unsure which direction to go, and then slumped down on a broken wall along the road. Coriolanus had the unpleasant feeling that he was somehow taking old Strabo Plinth's role in the endless discussion over where Sejanus's loyalties lay. He had not signed up for this. On the other hand, if Sejanus went rogue out here, there was no telling where it would end.

Coriolanus sat down beside him. "Look, I think things will improve, really, but not like this. As it gets better overall, it will get better here, but not if they keep blowing up the mines. All that does is add to the body count."

Sejanus nodded, and they sat there as a few raggedy children went by, kicking an old tin can down the road. "Do you think I've committed treason?"

"Not quite yet," said Coriolanus with a half smile.

Sejanus tugged at some weeds growing out of the wall. "Dr. Gaul does. My father went to see her, before he went to Dean Highbottom and the board. Everyone knows she's really the one in charge. He went to ask if I might be given the chance you were, to sign up for the Peacekeepers."

"I thought that would be automatic," said Coriolanus. "If you were expelled like me."

"That was my father's hope. But she said, 'Don't conflate the boys' actions. A piece of faulty strategy is not commensurate with a treasonous act of rebel support.'" Bitterness crept into his voice.

"And so a check appeared for a new lab for her mutts. It must have been the priciest ticket to District Twelve in history."

Coriolanus gave a low whistle. "A gymnasium *and* a lab?"

"Say what you will, I've done more for Capitol reconstruction than the president himself," Sejanus joked halfheartedly. "You're right, Coriolanus. I've been stupid. Again. I'll be more careful in the future. Whatever that holds."

"Probably some fried baloney," Coriolanus said.

"Well, then, lead on," said Sejanus, and they resumed their trek to the base.

Their bunkmates were just rolling out of bed when they returned. Sejanus took Beanpole out to work on his drills, and Smiley and Bug went over to see what was happening in the rec room. Coriolanus planned to use the hours until dinner studying for the officer candidate test, but his conversation with Sejanus had planted an idea in his brain. It grew rapidly until it wiped out everything else. Dr. Gaul had defended him. Well, not defended him. But made sure Strabo Plinth understood that Coriolanus was in an entirely different class than his delinquent son. Coriolanus's crime had been only "a piece of faulty strategy," which didn't sound like much of a crime at all. Perhaps she hadn't written him off entirely? She'd seemed to take special pains with his education during the Games. Singled him out. Would it be worth writing to her now, just to . . . just to . . . well, he didn't know what he hoped to achieve. But who knew, up the road, when he might be an officer of some consequence, if their paths might not cross again. It couldn't hurt to write her. He'd already been stripped of everything of value. The worst she could do was ignore him.

Coriolanus chewed on his pen as he tried to compose his thoughts. Should he start with an apology? Why? She would know he wasn't sorry for trying to win, only for being caught.

Better to bypass the apology entirely. He could tell her of his life here on the base, but it seemed too mundane. Their conversations had been, if nothing else, elevated. An ongoing lesson, exclusively for his benefit. And then it struck him. The thing to do was to continue the lesson. Where had they left off? His one-pager on chaos, control, and — what was that third one? He always had trouble remembering. Oh, yes, contract. The one it took the might of the Capitol to enforce. And so he began. . . .

> *Dear Dr. Gaul,*
>
> *So much has occurred since our last conversation, but every day I am informed by it. District Twelve provides an excellent stage upon which to watch the battle between chaos and control play out, and, as a Peacekeeper, I have a front-row seat.*

He went on to discuss the things he'd been privy to since his arrival. The palpable tension between the citizens and the Capitol forces, how it threatened to spill over into violence at the hanging, how it had overflowed into a brawl at the Hob.

> *It reminded me of my stint in the arena. It's one thing to speak of humans' essential nature theoretically, another to consider it when a fist is smashing into your mouth. Only this time I felt more prepared. I'm not convinced that we are all as inherently violent as you say, but it takes very little to bring the beast to the surface, at least under the cover of darkness. I wonder how many of those miners would have thrown a punch if the Capitol could have seen their faces?*

In the midday sun of the hanging, they grumbled but didn't dare to fight.

Well, it's something to think over while my lip heals.

He added that he did not expect she would reply but wished her well. Two pages. Short and sweet. Not overly demanding of attention. Not asking for anything. Not apologizing. He folded the letter crisply, sealed the envelope, and addressed it to her at the Citadel. To avoid questions, especially from Sejanus, he went over directly and dropped it in the mail. *There goes nothing*, he thought.

At dinner, the fried baloney came with applesauce and greasy chunks of potatoes, and he ate every bite on his heaping tray with relish. After supper, Sejanus helped him study for the test, being noncommittal as to his own interest in it.

"They only offer it three times a year, and one's this Wednesday afternoon," said Coriolanus. "We should both take it. If only for practice."

"No, I don't have a handle on this military stuff yet. I think you'll get through it, though," Sejanus replied. "Even if you're a little shaky, you'll ace the rest of it, and your overall score might be high enough to pass. Go ahead, take it before you forget all your math." He had a point. Already some of Coriolanus's geometry seemed a bit rusty.

"If you were an officer, perhaps they'd let you train to be a doctor. You were awfully good in science," said Coriolanus, trying to feel out where Sejanus's head might be after their conversation. He definitely needed something new to focus on. "And then you could, like you said, help people."

"That's true." Sejanus thought it over. "Maybe I'll talk to the doctors over at the clinic and find out how they got there."

The following morning, after a night of strange dreams that vacillated between him kissing Lucy Gray and feeding Dr. Gaul's snakelets, Coriolanus added his name to the list to take the test. The officer in charge told him that he'd be officially excused from training, and that in itself seemed incentive to sign up, for the week promised to be broiling. It was more than that, really. The heat, yes, but also the boredom of his day-to-day life had begun to wear on him. If he could become an officer, Coriolanus would be given more challenging tasks.

The day brought two alterations to the regular schedule. The first, that they would begin serving on guard duty, caused little excitement, as the job was widely known for its tedium. Still, Coriolanus reasoned, he'd rather be manning the desk at the front of the barracks than scrubbing pans. Perhaps he could sneak in a bit of reading or writing.

The second change unnerved him. When they reported for marksmanship, they were informed that Coriolanus's suggestion to shoot the birds around the gallows had been approved. Beforehand, however, the Citadel wanted them to trap a hundred or so jabberjays and mockingjays and return them to the lab, unharmed, for study. His squad had been tapped to help position cages in the trees that afternoon, which meant he'd be working with scientists from Dr. Gaul's lab. A team had arrived by hovercraft that morning. He'd only ever seen a handful of people at the Citadel, but the idea of encountering anyone from the lab, where no doubt everyone knew the details of his trickery with the snakes and subsequent disgrace, set him on edge. And then a terrible thought hit him: Surely, Dr. Gaul wouldn't oversee the bird roundup herself? Sending her a letter across the expanse of Panem had seemed almost like a lark, but it made him tremble to think of meeting her face-to-face for the first time since his banishment.

As Coriolanus bounced along in the back of the truck, unarmed and perhaps soon to be unmasked, his optimism from the weekend vanished. The other recruits, happy to be on what they seemed to view as a field trip, chattered around him as he sank into silence.

Sejanus, however, understood his trepidation. "Dr. Gaul won't be here, you know," he whispered. "This is strictly lackey work if we're involved." Coriolanus nodded but was not convinced.

When the truck pulled up under the hanging tree, he hid in the back of the squad while he surveyed the four Capitol scientists, all of whom were ridiculously dressed in their white lab coats, as if they might be about to discover the secret to immortality instead of trapping a bunch of insipid birds in hundred-degree heat. He examined each face, but none looked even remotely familiar, and he relaxed a bit. The cavernous lab had contained hundreds of scientists, and these were bird, not reptile, specialists. They greeted the soldiers good-naturedly, directing everyone to grab one of the wire mesh traps, which looked like cages, while they explained the setup. The recruits obliged, collected their traps, and took seats at the edge of the woods near the gallows.

Sejanus gave him a thumbs-up at Dr. Gaul's absence, and he was about to return it when he noticed a figure in a clearing deeper in the woods. A woman in a lab coat stood motionless, her back to them, head tipped sideways as she listened to the cacophony of birdsong. The other scientists waited respectfully until she finished and made her way back through the trees. As she pushed a branch aside, Coriolanus got a clear look at her face, which might have been forgettable had it not been for the large, pink glasses perched on her nose. He recognized her at once. She was the one who'd chewed him out for upsetting her birds when he'd been flailing around, trying to escape the lab after watching Clemensia collapse in a rainbow of pus. The question was, would she remember him? He slouched down even farther behind Smiley's back and developed a fascination with his bird trap.

The rosily bespectacled woman, who one of the scientists affectionately introduced as "Our Dr. Kay," greeted them in a friendly manner, explaining their mission — to collect fifty each of the jabberjays and mockingjays — and laying out the plan for achieving it. They were to help seed the forest with the traps, which would be baited with food, water, and decoy birds to draw in the prey. The traps would be open for two days so that the birds could freely come and go. On Wednesday, they would return, refresh the bait, and set the traps to capture the birds.

Eager to please, the recruits divided into five groups of four, each of which followed one of the scientists into a different part of the woods. Coriolanus swerved into a clump with the man who'd introduced Dr. Kay and concealed himself in the foliage as soon as possible. In addition to the traps, they carried backpacks containing various types of bait. They hiked a hundred yards until they reached a red mark on one of the trunks indicating their ground zero. Under the scientist's direction, they spread out concentrically from the spot, working in teams of two to bait the traps and position them high in the trees.

Coriolanus found himself paired with Bug, who turned out to be a first-class climber, having been raised in District 11, where the children helped to tend the orchards. They spent a sweaty but productive couple of hours working, with Coriolanus baiting and Bug hauling the traps into the branches. When they reconvened,

Coriolanus ducked out and sat on the truck bed, examining his multiple bug bites until they'd put some distance between him and Dr. Kay. She had paid him no special attention at all. *Don't be paranoid*, he thought. *She doesn't remember you.*

Tuesday was back to business as usual, though Coriolanus reviewed for the test over meals and in the brief time before lights-out. He was itching to get back to Lucy Gray, and she kept drifting into his thoughts, but he did his best to push her out, promising himself he could revel in daydreams when the test was over. On Wednesday, he muscled his way through the morning workout, sat alone during lunch with the manual for a final cram, and then went over to the classroom in which they did their tactical lessons. Two other Peacekeepers had signed up, one in his late twenties who claimed to have taken the test five times already and another who must have been pushing fifty, which seemed ancient for a life change.

Test-taking ranked among Coriolanus's greatest talents, and he felt the familiar rush of excitement as he opened the cover of his booklet. He loved the challenge, and his obsessive nature meant almost instant absorption into the mental obstacle course. Three hours later, sweat-soaked, exhausted, and happy, he handed in his booklet and went to the mess hall for ice. He sat in the strip of shade his barrack provided, rubbing the cubes over his body and reviewing the questions in his head. The ache of losing his university career returned briefly, but he pushed it away with thoughts of becoming a legendary military leader like his father. Maybe this had been his destiny all along.

The rest of his squad was still out with the Citadel scientists, climbing trees and activating the traps, so he wandered over to collect the mail for his room. Two giant boxes from Ma Plinth greeted him, promising another wild night at the Hob. He carried them back but decided to wait to open them until the others returned. Ma had also sent him a separate letter, thanking him for all he had done for Sejanus and asking him to continue to keep an eye on her boy.

Coriolanus put down the letter and sighed at the thought of being Sejanus's keeper. Escaping the Capitol may have temporarily relieved his torment, but he'd already worked himself into a state about the rebels. Conspiring with Billy Taupe. Agonizing over the girl in the guardhouse. How long would it be before he pulled another stunt like sneaking into the arena? Then, once again, people would look to Coriolanus to get him out of the mess.

The thing was, he didn't believe Sejanus would ever really change. Perhaps he was incapable of it, but, more to the point, he didn't want to. Already he had rejected what the Peacekeeping life offered: pretending he couldn't shoot, refusing to take the officer candidate test, making it clear he had no desire to excel on behalf of the Capitol. District 2 would always be home. District people would always be family. District rebels would always have a just cause on their side . . . and it would be Sejanus's moral duty to help them.

Coriolanus felt a new sense of threat rising up inside him. He'd tried to shrug off Sejanus's misguided behavior in the Capitol, but here it was different. Here he was viewed as an adult, and the consequences of his actions could be life or death. If he helped the rebels, he could find himself in front of a firing squad. What was going on in Sejanus's head anyway?

On impulse, Coriolanus opened Sejanus's locker, removed his box, and slid the contents onto the floor carefully. They included a stack of mementos, a pack of gum, and three medicine bottles prescribed by a Capitol doctor. Two appeared to be sleeping capsules and the third a bottle of morphling with a dropper built into the lid, much like the one he'd seen Dean Highbottom use on occasion. He knew Sejanus had been medicated during his breakdown, Ma had told him as much, but why had he brought these here? Had Ma slipped them in as a precaution? He flipped through the rest of the contents. A scrap of fabric, stationery, pens, a small chunk of marble crudely carved into something that might be a heart, and a pile of photos. The Plinths had annual portraits taken, and he could map Sejanus's growth from infant to this past new year. All the pictures were of family, except an old photo of a group of schoolchildren. Coriolanus took it to be one of their class, but no one looked familiar, and a lot of the kids were dressed in rather ill-fitting, shabby clothing. He spotted Sejanus, in a neat suit, smiling pensively from the second row. Behind him towered a boy who he took to be much older. On closer inspection, though, the pieces fell together. It was Marcus. In a school photo from Sejanus's last year in District 2. There was no record of his Capitol classmates at all, not even Coriolanus. For some reason, this seemed the greatest confirmation of where Sejanus's loyalties lay.

At the bottom of the pile, he found a thick silver frame holding, of all things, Sejanus's diploma. It had been removed from its fine leather folder and transferred to the frame, as if for display. But why? Sejanus would not in a million years hang it on the wall, even if he had a wall to hang it on. Coriolanus fingered the frame, tracing the tarnished metal, and flipped it over. The back panel seemed slightly askew, and a tiny corner of pale green paper peeked from the side. *That's not just paper*, he thought grimly, and slid the fasteners to free the panel. As it popped off, a stack of freshly minted bills spilled to the floor.

Money. And quite a lot of it. Why would Sejanus have brought so much cash to his new life as a Peacekeeper? Would Ma have insisted? No, not Ma. She seemed to feel money was at the root of their misery. Strabo, then? Thinking that whatever his son encountered, the money would shield him from harm? Possibly, but Strabo usually handled the payoffs himself. Was it something Sejanus had done on his own, without his parents' knowledge? That was more worrisome to think of. Was this a lifetime of allowances carefully squirreled away for a rainy day? Withdrawn from the bank the day before his departure and hidden in his picture frame? Sejanus always complained about his father's habit of buying his way out of trouble, but had it been ingrained from birth? The Plinth method of solving problems. Passed down from father to son. Distasteful but efficient.

Coriolanus scooped up the cash, tapped it into a neat stack, and flipped through the bills. There were hundreds, thousands of dollars here. But what use would it be in District 12, where there was nothing to buy? Nothing, anyway, that a Peacekeeper's salary wouldn't cover. Most of the recruits were sending half their paychecks home, as the Capitol provided almost everything they needed, short of stationery and a night at the Hob. He supposed the Hob had the black market, but he hadn't seen much to tempt a Peacekeeper once the booze had been bought. They didn't need dead rabbits, or shoelaces, or homemade soap. And even if they did, they could easily afford it. Of course, there were other things you could buy. Like information, and access, and silence. There were bribes. There was power.

Coriolanus heard the voices of his returning squad. He swiftly concealed the cash in the silver frame, being careful to leave one tiny corner of green visible. He repacked the box and stored it in Sejanus's locker. By the time his bunkmates rolled in, he was standing over Ma's boxes with his arms spread wide, wearing a big grin and asking, "Who's free on Saturday?"

As Smiley, Beanpole, and Bug tore open the boxes and unpacked the treasures within, Sejanus sat on a bed and watched with amusement.

Coriolanus leaned on the bunk above him. "Thank goodness for your ma. Otherwise we'd all be flat broke."

"Yes, not a penny between us," Sejanus agreed.

The one thing Coriolanus had never questioned was Sejanus's honesty. If anything, he'd have welcomed a little less of it. But this was a bald-faced lie, delivered as naturally as the truth. Which meant that now anything he said was suspect.

Sejanus smacked himself on the forehead. "Oh! How did the test go?"

"We'll see, I guess," said Coriolanus. "They're sending it to the Capitol for grading. They said it could take awhile before I get the results."

"You'll pass," Sejanus assured him. "You deserve to."

So supportive. So duplicitous. So self-destructive. Like a moth to a flame. Coriolanus started a bit, remembering Pluribus's letter. Wasn't that what Dean Highbottom had kept muttering after his fight with Coriolanus's father all those years ago? Almost. He'd used the plural. *"Like moths to a flame."* As if an entire flock of moths were flying straight into an inferno. A whole group bent on self-destruction. Who was he referring to? Oh, who cared? Drugged, hate-fueled, old High-as-a-Kite-Bottom. Better not to even wonder.

After dinner, Coriolanus put in his first hour of guard duty at an air hangar on the far side of the base. Paired with an old-timer who immediately dozed off after instructing him to keep an eye out, he found his thoughts fixating on Lucy Gray, wishing he could see her, or at least talk to her. It seemed a waste to be on guard, where clearly nothing ever happened, when he could be holding her in his arms. He felt trapped here on base, while she could freely roam the night. In some ways, it had been better to have her locked up in the Capitol, where he always had a general idea of what she was doing. For all he knew, Billy Taupe was trying to worm his way back into her heart at this very moment. Why pretend he wasn't at least a little jealous? Perhaps he should have had him arrested after all. . . .

Back in the barrack, he penned a quick note to Ma, praising the treats, and another to Pluribus to thank him for his help, then to ask him about getting strings for Lucy Gray. His brain tired from the test, Coriolanus slept deeply and awoke already sweating in the hot August morning. When did the weather break? September? October? By lunchtime, the line from the ice machine extended halfway around the mess hall. Slated for kitchen detail, Coriolanus braced himself for the worst but found that he'd been upgraded from dishes to chopping. This would've been a welcome change had he not been assigned the onions. The tears he could live with, but he became increasingly concerned about the smell that radiated from his hands. Even after an evening of mopping, it still drew comment in the barrack, and no amount of scrubbing erased it. Would he be reeking when he saw Lucy Gray again?

Friday morning, despite the heat and his unease around the Citadel scientists, he felt a certain relief that he'd be dealing with birds that afternoon. Though unlikable, they left no noticeable odor. When Beanpole collapsed during drills, the sergeant had his bunkmates haul him to the clinic, where Coriolanus took the opportunity to get a metal can of powder for a heat rash that extended across his chest and under his right arm. "Keep it dry," the medic advised. He had to suppress the impulse to roll his eyes. He'd not been dry, not one moment, since he'd arrived in the steam bath of District 12.

After a lunch of cold meat-spread sandwiches, they bounced along in the truck to the woods, where the scientists, still sporting their white lab coats, awaited them. Just as they teamed up, Coriolanus learned that Bug, lacking a partner on Wednesday, had been working in tandem with Dr. Kay. She'd been so impressed with his agility in the branches, she'd requested him again. It was too late to switch partners, so Coriolanus followed her group into the trees, hanging as far back as he could.

It was no use. As he watched Bug carry a newly baited cage up into the first tree and swap it with one holding a captured jabberjay, Dr. Kay came up behind him. "So, what do you think of the districts, Private Snow?"

He was trapped like a bird. Trapped like the tributes in the zoo. Fleeing into the trees was not an option. He remembered Lucy Gray's advice that had saved him in the monkey house. *Own it.*

He turned to her with a smile sheepish enough to acknowledge her nailing him but amused enough to show he didn't care. "You know, I think I learned more about Panem in one day as a Peacekeeper than I did in thirteen years of school."

Dr. Kay laughed. "Yes. There's a world of education to be had out here. I was assigned to Twelve during the war. Lived on your base. Worked in these woods."

"You were part of the jabberjay project, then?" asked Coriolanus. At least they'd both had public failures.

"I headed it," said Dr. Kay significantly.

A *major* public failure. Coriolanus felt more comfortable. He'd only embarrassed himself in the Hunger Games, not a nation-wide war. Perhaps she would be sympathetic and give a favorable report to Dr. Gaul on her return if he made a good impression. Making an effort to engage her might pay off. He remembered that the jabberjays were all male and couldn't reproduce with one another. "So these jabberjays, they were the actual birds you used for surveillance during the war?"

"Mm-hmm. These were my babies. Never thought I'd see them again. The general consensus was they wouldn't last the winter. The genetically engineered often struggle in the wild. But they were strong, my birds, and nature has a mind of its own," she said.

Bug reached the lowest branch and handed down the cage holding the jabberjay. "We should leave them in the traps for now." It wasn't a question, just a remark.

"Yes. It may help reduce the stress of the transition," agreed Dr. Kay.

Bug nodded, slid to the ground, and accepted another fresh trap from Coriolanus. Without asking, he made for a second tree. Dr. Kay watched approvingly. "Some people just understand birds."

Coriolanus felt, unequivocally, that he would never be one of those people, but surely he could pretend to be for a few hours. He squatted down beside the trap and examined the jabberjay, which chattered away. "You know, I never quite grasped how these worked." Not that he'd made any effort to find out. "I know they recorded conversations, but how did you control them?"

"They're trained to respond to audio commands. If we're lucky, I can show you." Dr. Kay pulled a small rectangular device from her pocket. Several colored buttons protruded from it, none of which were marked, but maybe age and use had worn the markings away. She knelt down across the cage from him and studied the bird with more affection than Coriolanus felt befitted a scientist. "Isn't he beautiful?"

Coriolanus tried to sound convincing. "Very."

"So, what you hear now, this chatter, it's his own. He can mimic the other birds, or us, or say whatever he likes. He's in neutral," she said.

"In neutral?" Coriolanus asked.

"In neutral?" He heard his voice echo from the bird's beak. *"In neutral?"*

Even creepier when it's your own voice, he thought, but he gave a delighted laugh. "That was me!"

"That was me!" the jabberjay said in his voice, and then began to mimic a nearby bird.

"It was indeed," said Dr. Kay. "But in neutral, he'll move on to something else quickly. Another voice. Usually, just a short phrase. Or a snatch of birdsong. Whatever catches his fancy. For surveillance, we needed to put him in record mode. Fingers crossed." She pressed one of the buttons on her remote control.

Coriolanus heard nothing. "Oh, no. I guess it's too old."

Dr. Kay's face, however, wore a smile. "Not necessarily. The command tones are inaudible to human beings but easily registered by the birds. Notice how quiet he is?"

The jabberjay had fallen silent. It hopped around in its trap, cocking its head, pecking at things, the same in all ways except its verbalizing.

"Is it working?" asked Coriolanus.

"We'll see." Dr. Kay hit another button on her control, and the bird resumed its normal chirping. "Neutral again. Now let's see what he's retained." She pressed a third button.

After a brief pause, the bird began to speak.

"Oh, no. I guess it's too old."

"Not necessarily. The command tones are inaudible to human beings but easily registered by the birds. Notice how quiet he is?"

"Is it working?"

"We'll see."

An exact replica. But no. The rustling of the trees, the buzzing of the insects, the other birds, none of that had been recorded. Only the pure sound of the human voices.

"Huh," said Coriolanus, somewhat impressed. "How long can they record for?"

"An hour or so, on a good day," Dr. Kay told him. "They're designed to seek out forested areas and then are attracted to human voices. We'd release them into the woods in record mode, then retrieve them with a homing signal back at the base, where we'd analyze the recordings. Not just here, but in Districts Eleven, Nine, wherever we thought they'd be of value."

"You couldn't just set microphones in the trees?" Coriolanus asked.

"You can bug buildings, but the forest is too large. The rebels knew the terrain well; we didn't. They moved from place to place. The jabberjay is an organic, mobile recording device and, unlike a microphone, it's undetectable. The rebels could catch one, kill it, eat it even, and all they would find is an ordinary bird," explained Dr. Kay. "They are perfect, in theory."

"But in practice, the rebels figured out what they were," said Coriolanus. "How did they manage that?"

"Not entirely sure. Some thought they saw the birds returning to base, but we only recalled them in the dead of night, in which they're virtually impossible to detect, and only a few at a time. More likely we didn't cover our tracks. Didn't make sure that the information we acted on could have had a source other than a recording in the woods. That would've brought suspicion, and even though their black feathers are an excellent camouflage at night, their activity after hours would be a clue. Then, I think, they just started experimenting with them, feeding us false information and seeing how we reacted." She shrugged. "Or maybe they had a spy on the base. I doubt we'll ever really know."

"Why don't you just use the homing device to call them back to the base now? Instead of —" Coriolanus stopped himself, not wanting to seem like a whiner.

"Instead of dragging you out in this heat to be eaten alive by mosquitoes?" She laughed. "The whole transmission system was dismantled, and our old aviary seems to store supplies now. Besides, I'd rather have my hands on them. We don't want them to fly off and never come back, do we?"

"Of course not," Coriolanus lied. "Would they do that?"

"I'm not sure what they'll do, now that they've gone native. At the end of the war, I released them on neutral. It would have been cruel otherwise. A mute bird would have faced too many challenges. They not only survived but mated successfully with the mockingbirds. So now we have a whole new species." Dr. Kay pointed up at a mockingjay in the foliage. "Mockingjays, the locals call them."

"And what can they do?" asked Coriolanus.

"Not sure. I've been watching them for the last few days. They've no ability to mimic speech. But they have a better, more sustained ability to repeat music than their mothers," she said. "Sing something."

Coriolanus only had one song in his repertoire.

Gem of Panem,
Mighty city,
Through the ages, you shine anew.

The mockingjay cocked its head and then sang back. No words, but an exact replica of the melody, in a voice that seemed half human, half bird. A few other birds in the area picked it up and wove it into a harmonic fabric, which again reminded him of the Covey with their old songs.

"We should kill them all." The words slipped out before he could stop them.

"Kill them all? Why?" said Dr. Kay in surprise.

"They're unnatural." He tried to twist the comment so it sounded like it came from a bird lover. "Perhaps they'll hurt the other species."

"They appear to be rather compatible. And they're all over Panem, wherever jabberjays and mockingbirds cohabited. We'll take some back and see if they can reproduce, mockingjay with mockingjay. If they can't, they'll all be gone in a few years anyway. If they can, what's one more songbird?" she said.

Coriolanus agreed they were probably harmless. He spent the rest of the afternoon asking questions and treating the birds gently to make up for his callous suggestion. He didn't mind the jabberjays so much — they seemed rather interesting from a military standpoint — but something about the mockingjays repelled him. He distrusted their spontaneous creation. Nature running amok. They should die out, and die out soon.

At the end of the day, though they found themselves in possession of over thirty jabberjays, not one mockingjay had been caught in the traps.

"Perhaps the jabberjays are less suspicious, given that the traps are more familiar to them. They were raised in cages, after all," mused Dr. Kay. "No matter. We'll give them a few more days and, if needed, we'll bring out the nets."

Or the guns, thought Coriolanus.

Back at the base, he and Bug were chosen to unload the cages and help the scientists position them in an old hangar that was to be the birds' temporary home. "Would you like to help us care for them until we take them back to the Capitol?" Dr. Kay asked them. Bug gave one of his rare smiles in assent, and Coriolanus accepted with enthusiasm. Besides wanting to make a good impression, it was cooler in the hangar, with its industrial fans.

That seemed better for his heat rash, which had flared up impressively in the woods. At least it made for a change.

Before lights-out, the bunkmates laid out Ma's treats and made a plan for the next two Hob weekends, in case she didn't send boxes regularly. By virtue of his trading skills, Smiley became their treasurer, carefully setting aside enough for two rounds of white liquor and donations into the Covey bucket after the show. What remained they divided five ways. For his share, Coriolanus took another six popcorn balls, of which he allowed himself only one. The rest he would save for the Covey.

On Saturday morning, Coriolanus awoke to a hailstorm drumming away at the roof of the barrack. On the way to breakfast, the bunkmates pelted each other with ice balls the size of oranges, but by midmorning the sun came out, stronger than ever. He and Bug were assigned to care for the jabberjays in the afternoon. They cleaned cages, then fed and watered the birds under the direction of two of the Citadel scientists. Although some had been trapped in pairs or threesomes, each bird now resided in its own cage. During the latter part of their shift, they carefully carried the birds, one at a time, to an area of the hangar where a makeshift lab had been set up. The jabberjays were numbered, tagged, and run through basic drills to see if they still responded to the audio commands from the remote controls. All appeared to have retained the ability to record and play the human voice.

Out of earshot of the scientists, Bug shook his head. "Is that good for them?"

"I don't know. It's what they're built to do," said Coriolanus.

"They'd be happier if we just left them in the woods," said Bug.

Coriolanus wasn't sure Bug was right. For all he knew, they'd wake up in the Citadel lab in a few days, wondering what that atrocious ten-year nightmare in District 12 had been. Maybe they'd be happier in a controlled environment, where so many threats had been removed. "I'm sure the scientists will take good care of them."

After supper, he tried not to show his impatience as he waited for his bunkmates to ready themselves. As he'd decided to keep his romance secret, he planned to slip away once they'd arrived at the Hob. That left the problem of Sejanus. He'd lied about the money, but maybe he was just trying to fit in with the rest of his penniless bunkmates. After the incident with the map, he'd seemed genuinely contrite, so hopefully he'd recognized the danger of acting as a go-between with Lil. But would Billy Taupe or the rebels try to approach him again, since he'd initially expressed a willingness to help them? He was such a sitting duck. The easiest thing would be to take him along to see the Covey once they'd given the others the slip.

"Want to come backstage with me?" he asked Sejanus quietly when they'd reached the Hob.

"Am I invited?" asked Sejanus.

"Of course," said Coriolanus, although really only he had been. Maybe it was good, though. If Sejanus could keep Maude Ivory entertained, then Coriolanus might get a few moments alone with Lucy Gray. "But we'll need to shake the rest of the crew."

This proved to be simple, since the crowd had grown from the previous week, and the new batch of white liquor was particularly strong. Leaving Smiley, Bug, and Beanpole to haggle, they found the door near the stage and exited onto a narrow, empty backstreet.

What Lucy Gray had referred to as the shed turned out to be some sort of old garage that could hold about eight cars. The large doors used for vehicle entry were chained shut, but a smaller door in the corner of the building directly across from the stage door was held open with a cinder block. When Coriolanus heard chatter and instruments tuning, he knew they had the right place.

They entered and found the Covey had commandeered the space, making themselves at home on old tires and odd bits of furniture, their instrument cases and equipment scattered everywhere. Even with a second door in the far back corner propped open, the place felt like an oven. The evening light poured in through a few cracked windows, catching the dust that floated thick in the air.

When she saw them, Maude Ivory ran over, dressed in her pink frock. "Hey there!"

"Good evening." Coriolanus bowed and then presented her with the packet of popcorn balls. "Sweets to the sweet."

Maude Ivory pulled back the paper and gave a little hop on one foot before she dipped into a curtsy. "Thank you kindly. I'll sing you a special song tonight!"

"I came with no other hope," said Coriolanus. It was funny how the society talk of the Capitol seemed natural with the Covey.

"Okay, but I can't say your name, because you're a secret," she giggled.

Maude Ivory ran over to Lucy Gray, who sat cross-legged on an old desk, tuning her guitar. She smiled down at the child's excited face but said sternly, "Save them for after." Maude Ivory skipped over to show her treasure to the rest of the band. Sejanus joined them while Coriolanus waved in passing and headed for Lucy Gray. "You didn't need to do that. You're going to spoil her."

"Just trying to get some happy in her head," he said.

"How about my head?" teased Lucy Gray. Coriolanus leaned over and kissed her. "Okay, that's a start." She scooted over and patted the desk beside her.

Coriolanus sat and checked out the shed. "What's this place?"

"Right now it's our break room. We come here before and after the show and when we go offstage between numbers," she told him.

"But who owns it?" He hoped they weren't trespassing.

Lucy Gray seemed unconcerned. "No idea. We'll just perch here until they shoo us off."

Birds. Always birds with her, when it came to the Covey. Singing, perching, feathers in their hats. Pretty birds all. He told her about his assignment with the jabberjays, thinking she might be impressed that he'd been singled out to work with them, but it only seemed to make her sad.

"I hate to think of them caged up, when they've had a taste of freedom," Lucy Gray said. "What do they expect to find back in their labs?"

"I don't know. If their weapons still work?" he guessed.

"Sounds like torture, having someone controlling your voice like that." Her hand reached up to touch her throat.

Coriolanus thought that a bit dramatic but tried to sound comforting. "I don't think there's a human equivalent."

"Really? Do you always feel free to speak your mind, Coriolanus Snow?" she asked, giving him a quizzical look.

Free to speak his mind? Of course, he did. Well, within reason. He didn't go around shooting his mouth off about every little thing. What did she mean? She meant what he thought about the Capitol. And the Hunger Games. And the districts. The truth was, most of what the Capitol did, he supported, and the rest rarely concerned him. But if it came to it, he'd speak out. Wouldn't he? Against the Capitol? Like Sejanus had? Even if it meant repercussions? He didn't know, but he felt on the defensive. "I do. I think you should say what you think."

"That's what my daddy thought, too. And he ended up with more bullet holes than I could count on my fingers," she said.

What was she implying? Even if she didn't say so, he'd bet those bullets came from a Peacekeeper's gun. Perhaps from someone dressed exactly as Coriolanus was now. "And my father was killed by a rebel sniper."

Lucy Gray sighed. "Now you're mad."

"No." But he was. He tried to swallow his anger. "I'm just tired. I've been looking forward to seeing you all week. And I'm sorry about your father — I'm sorry about *my* father — but I don't run Panem."

"Lucy Gray!" Maude Ivory called across the shed. "It's time!" The Covey had begun to assemble by the door, instruments in hand.

"I better go." Coriolanus slid off the desk. "Have a good show."

"Will I see you after?" she asked.

He brushed off his uniform. "I have to get back for curfew."

Lucy Gray rose and swung her guitar strap over her head. "I see. Well, tomorrow we're planning a trip to the lake, if you're free."

"The lake?" Were there actually pleasurable destinations in this miserable place?

"It's in the woods. A bit of a hike, but the water's fine for swimming," she said. "Sure would like you to come along. Bring Sejanus, too. We'd have the whole day."

He wanted to go. To be with her for a whole day. He was still upset, but it was stupid. She hadn't accused him of anything, really. The conversation had just gotten off track. It was all on account of those stupid birds. She was reaching out; did he really want to push her away? He saw her so little he could not afford moodiness. "All right. We'll come after breakfast."

"Okay, then." She planted a kiss on his cheek and joined the rest of the Covey as they left the shed.

Back in the Hob, he and Sejanus pushed their way through the dim interior, the air heavy with sweat and liquor. They found their bunkmates in the same spot as the week before. Bug had secured crates for them, and Coriolanus and Sejanus settled in on either side of him, each taking a swig from the communal bottle.

Maude Ivory scampered out to introduce the band. The music began as soon as the Covey had taken the stage.

Coriolanus leaned against the wall and made up for lost time with the white liquor. He wasn't going to see Lucy Gray after, so why not get a little drunk? The knot of anger in his chest began to unwind as he stared at her. So attractive, so engaging, so alive. He began to feel bad about losing his temper, and had trouble even remembering what she'd said to set him off. Maybe nothing at all. It'd been a long, stressful week, with the test, and the birds, and Sejanus's foolishness. He deserved to enjoy himself.

He knocked back several more swallows and felt friendlier toward the world. Tunes, familiar and new, washed over him. Once he caught himself singing along with the audience and stopped self-consciously before he realized no one cared, or was sober enough to remember much if they did.

At some point, Barb Azure, Tam Amber, and Clerk Carmine left the stage, apparently to take a break in the shed, leaving Maude Ivory up on her box at the mic with Lucy Gray strumming beside her.

"I promised a friend I'd sing him something special tonight, so this is it," Maude Ivory chirped. "Every one of us Covey owes our name to a ballad, and this one belongs to this pretty lady right here!" She held out a hand to Lucy Gray, who curtsied to scattered applause. "It's a really old one by some man named Wordsworth.

We mixed it up a little, so it makes better sense, but you still need to listen close." She pressed her finger to her lips, and the audience settled down.

Coriolanus gave his head a shake and tried to focus. If this was Lucy Gray's song, he wanted to pay careful attention so he could say something nice about it tomorrow.

Maude Ivory nodded to Lucy Gray for her intro and began to sing in a solemn voice:

Oft I had heard of Lucy Gray:
And, when I crossed the wild,
I chanced to see at break of day
The solitary child.

No mate, no comrade Lucy knew;
She dwelt where none abide,
— The sweetest thing that ever grew
Upon the mountainside!

Okay, so there was a little girl who lived on a mountain. And apparently had trouble making friends.

You yet may spy the fawn at play
The hare among the green;
But the sweet face of Lucy Gray
Will never more be seen.

And she died. How? He had a feeling he was about to find out.

"To-night will be a stormy night —
You to the town must go;

And take a lantern, Child, to light
Your mother through the snow."

"That, Father! Will I gladly do:
'Tis scarcely afternoon —
The village clock has just struck two,
And yonder is the moon!"

At this the Father turned his hook,
To kindling for the day;
He plied his work; — and Lucy took
The lantern on her way.

As carefree as a mountain doe:
A fresh, new path she broke
Her feet dispersed the powdery snow,
That rose up just like smoke.

The storm came on before its time:
She wandered up and down;
And many a hill did Lucy climb:
But never reached the town.

Ah. Lots of nonsense words, but she got lost in the snow. Well, no wonder, if they sent her out into a snowstorm. And then she probably froze to death.

The wretched parents all that night
Went shouting far and wide;
But there was neither sound nor sight
To serve them as a guide.

At daybreak on a hill they stood
That overlooked the scene;
And thence they saw the bridge of wood,
That spanned a deep ravine.

They wept — and, turning homeward, cried,
"In heaven we all shall meet";
— When in the snow the mother spied
The print of Lucy's feet.

Oh, good. They found her footprints. Happy ending. It was one of those silly things, like that song Lucy Gray sung about a man they thought had frozen to death. They tried to cremate him in an oven, but he only thawed out and was fine. Sam Somebody.

Then downwards from the steep hill's edge
They tracked the footmarks small;
And through the broken hawthorn hedge,
And by the long stone-wall;

And then an open field they crossed:
The marks were still the same;
They tracked them on, not ever lost;
And to the bridge they came.

They followed from the snowy bank
Those footmarks, one by one,
Into the middle of the plank;
And further there were none!

Wait? What? She vanished into thin air?

— Yet some maintain that to this day
She is a living child;
That you may see sweet Lucy Gray
Upon the lonesome wild.

O'er rough and smooth she trips along,
And never looks behind;
And sings a solitary song
That whistles in the wind.

Oh, a ghost story. Ugh. Boo. So ridiculous. Well, he'd try hard to love it when he saw the Covey tomorrow. But, really, who named their child after a ghost girl? Although, if the girl was a ghost, where was her body? Maybe she got tired of her negligent parents sending her into blizzards and ran off to live in the wild. But then, why didn't she grow up? He couldn't make sense of it, and the white liquor wasn't helping. It reminded him of the time he hadn't understood the poem in rhetoric class and Livia Cardew had humiliated him in front of everyone. What a dreadful song. Maybe no one would mention it. . . . No, they would. Maude Ivory would expect a response. So he'd say it was brilliant and leave it at that. What if she wanted to talk about it?

Coriolanus decided to put it to Sejanus, who'd always been good at rhetoric, just to see if he had any thoughts.

But when he leaned across Bug, he found Sejanus's crate was empty.

Coriolanus scanned the area, trying to hide his growing anxiety. Where was Sejanus? Adrenaline fought with the white liquor for control of his brain. He'd been so steeped in music and alcohol that he really didn't know when Sejanus had disappeared. What if he hadn't had a change of heart about Lil? Was he out there in the crowd, conspiring with the rebels at this very moment?

He waited for the audience to finish applauding Maude Ivory and Lucy Gray before he rose to his feet. Just as he began to make his way to the door, he saw Sejanus returning in the hazy light.

"Where've you been?" Coriolanus asked.

"Outside. That white liquor runs right through me." Sejanus sat on his crate and turned his attention to the stage.

Coriolanus resumed his seat as well, his eyes on the entertainment, his thoughts anywhere but. White liquor didn't run through anyone. It was too strong, the amount consumed too small. Another lie. What did that mean? That he couldn't let Sejanus out of his sight for one second now? Throughout the rest of the show, he kept shooting sideways glances at him to make sure he didn't sneak off again. He stayed close after Maude Ivory collected money in her beribboned basket, but Sejanus seemed focused on helping Bug steer a drunken Beanpole back to the base. No opportunity presented itself for further discussion. If, in fact, Sejanus had slipped away to plot with the rebels, Coriolanus's directly confronting him after the Billy Taupe incident had obviously failed. A new strategy was clearly called for.

Sunday dawned too brightly for Coriolanus's throbbing head. He threw up the white liquor and stood in the shower until his eyes focused properly again. The greasy eggs at the mess hall were unthinkable, so he nibbled on his toast while Sejanus finished both of their helpings, only confirming Coriolanus's suspicions that he'd consumed next to no alcohol the night before, certainly not enough to have it run through him. Their three bunkmates had not even managed to get up for breakfast. Until he thought of a better approach, he'd have to watch him like a hawk, especially when they left the base. Today, anyway, he'd need a companion to go to the lake.

Although Coriolanus's own enthusiasm had waned, Sejanus cheerfully accepted the invitation. "Sure, it sounds like a holiday. Let's take some ice!" While Sejanus talked Cookie out of another plastic bag, Coriolanus went to the clinic for an aspirin. They met up at the guardhouse and then set out.

Not knowing a shortcut to the Seam, they returned to the town square and retraced their steps from the previous week. Coriolanus considered attempting another heart-to-heart with Sejanus, but if the threat of being found guilty of treason didn't move him, what would? And he didn't know for sure that he'd been conspiring with the rebels. Maybe he really had just needed to take a piss last night, in which case accusing him would only make him defensive. The only real evidence he had was the hidden money, and maybe Strabo had insisted he take it but Sejanus was determined never to use it. He didn't value money, and munitions money was probably burdensome to him. It might be a point of honor with him, to make it on his own.

If Lucy Gray was still upset about their tiff, she didn't show it. She greeted him at the back door with a kiss and a glass of cold water to tide him over until they reached the lake. "It's two to three hours, depending on the briars, but it's worth it."

For once, the Covey left their instruments behind. Barb Azure stayed at home, too, to keep an eye on things. She sent them off with a bucket containing a jug of water, a loaf of bread, and an old blanket.

"She just started seeing a gal down the road," confided Lucy Gray when they were out of earshot of the house. "Probably glad to have the place to themselves for the day."

Tam Amber led the rest of them across the Meadow and into the woods. Clerk Carmine, Maude Ivory, and Sejanus formed a line behind him, leaving Lucy Gray and Coriolanus to bring up the rear. There was no path. They followed single file, stepping over fallen trees, pushing aside branches, trying to skirt the prickly bushes that popped up in the undergrowth. Within ten minutes, nothing remained of District 12 but the acrid smell from the mines. Within twenty, even that had been cloaked by vegetation. The canopy of trees provided shade from the sun but little respite from the heat. The hum of insects, chatter of squirrels, and birdsong filled the air, undisturbed by their presence.

Even with two days of bird duty under his belt, Coriolanus felt increasingly wary the farther away they got from what passed for civilization out here. He wondered what other creatures — larger, more powerful, and fanged — might be lurking in the trees. He had no weapon of any kind. After that realization, he pretended to need a walking stick and stopped a moment to strip a sturdy fallen branch of its excess limbs.

"How does he know the way?" he asked Lucy Gray, nodding ahead to Tam Amber.

"We all know the way," she said. "It's our second home."

As no one else acted concerned, he trooped along for what

seemed like an eternity, happy when Tam Amber pulled the group up. But he only said, "About halfway." They passed around the bag of ice, drinking what had melted and sucking on the remaining cubes.

Maude Ivory complained of a pain in her foot and pulled off her cracked, brown shoe to show a good-sized blister. "These shoes don't walk right."

"They're an old pair of Clerk Carmine's. We're trying to make them last the summer," said Lucy Gray, examining the little foot with a frown.

"They're too tight," said Maude Ivory. "I want herring boxes like in the song."

Sejanus crouched, offering her his back. "How about a ride instead?"

Maude Ivory scampered aboard. "Watch out for my head!"

Once the precedent was set, they took turns carrying the little girl. No longer needing to exert herself, she used her lungs for singing.

In a cavern, in a canyon,
Excavating for a mine,
Dwelt a miner, forty-niner
And his daughter, Clementine.

Light she was and like a fairy,
And her shoes were number nine.
Herring boxes, without topses,
Sandals were for Clementine.

To Coriolanus's dismay, a mockingjay chorus picked up the melody from high in the branches. He'd not expected them to be out this far — the things were positively infesting the woods. But

Maude Ivory was delighted and kept the racket going. Coriolanus carried her the final leg and distracted her by thanking her for the Lucy Gray song the night before.

"What'd you make of it?" she asked.

He dodged the question. "I liked it very much. You were fantastic."

"Thanks, but I meant the song. Do you think people really see Lucy Gray, or they're just dreaming her?" she said. "Because I think they really see her. Only now, she flies like a bird."

"Does she?" Coriolanus felt better that the cryptic song was at least subject to debate, and he wasn't too dim to grasp the one erudite interpretation.

"Well, how else can she not make footprints?" she said. "I think she flies around and tries not to meet people, because they'd kill her because she's different."

"Yeah, she's different. She's a ghost, bonehead," said Clerk Carmine. "Ghosts don't leave footprints, because they're like air."

"Then where's her body?" asked Coriolanus, feeling that at least Maude Ivory's version made some sense.

"She fell off the bridge and died, only it's so far down, no one could see her. Or maybe there was a river and it washed her away," said Clerk Carmine. "Anyway, she's dead and she's haunting the place. How can she fly without wings?"

"She didn't fall off the bridge! The snow would look different where she was standing!" Maude Ivory insisted. "Lucy Gray, which is it?"

"It's a mystery, sweetheart. Just like me. That's why it's my song," Lucy Gray answered.

By the time they arrived at the lake, Coriolanus was panting and parched, and his rash burned from his sweat. When the Covey stripped down to their undergarments and plunged into the water, he lost no time in following suit. He waded out, and the cold water embraced him, clearing the cobwebs from his head and soothing his rash. He swam well, having been taught from an early age in school, but had never tried it anywhere but a pool. The muddy lake floor dropped off quickly, and he had a sense of deep water. He cruised out to the middle of the lake and floated on his back, taking in the scenery. The woods rose up all around, and although there seemed to be no access road, small, broken houses dotted the banks. Most were beyond repair, but a solid-looking concrete structure still had a roof, and a door shut tight against the wild. A family of ducks swam by a few feet away, and he could spot fish down below his toes. Concern over what else might be swimming around him prompted him to head back to shore, where the Covey had already pulled Sejanus into some kind of keep-away game, using a large pinecone for the ball. Coriolanus joined in, glad to be doing something just for fun. The strain of being a full-fledged adult every day had grown tiresome.

After a brief rest, Tam Amber made a couple of fishing poles, trimming down tree branches and attaching thread and homemade hooks. While Clerk Carmine dug for worms, Maude Ivory enlisted Sejanus to pick berries.

"Stay away from that patch near the rocks," warned Lucy Gray. "Snakes like it there."

"She always knows where they'll be," Maude Ivory told Sejanus as she led him away. "She catches them in her hands, but they scare me."

That left Coriolanus with Lucy Gray to collect dry wood for a fire. It all excited him a little, the swimming half-naked among wild creatures, the building of the fire in the open air, the unorchestrated time with Lucy Gray. She had a box of matches, but they were dear and she said she had to make do with just one. When the flame caught in a pile of dry leaves, he sat close to her on the ground as they fed it first the twigs, then larger scraps of wood, feeling happier to be alive than he had in weeks.

Lucy Gray leaned into his shoulder. "Listen, I'm sorry if I upset you last night. I wasn't laying my daddy's death on you. We were both just kids when that happened."

"I know. I'm sorry if I overreacted. It's just, I can't pretend I'm someone I'm not. I don't agree with everything the Capitol does, but I am Capitol, and on the whole I think we're right about needing order," said Coriolanus.

"The Covey believe you're put on earth to reduce the misery, not add to it. Do you think the Hunger Games are right?" she asked.

"I'm not even sure why we do them, to be honest. But I do think people are forgetting the war too fast. What we did to each other. What we're capable of. Districts and Capitol both. I know the Capitol must seem hard-line out here, but we're just trying to keep things under control. Otherwise, there'd be chaos and people running around killing each other, like in the arena." This was the first time he'd tried to put these thoughts into words with anyone other than Dr. Gaul. He felt a little unsteady, like a toddler learning to walk, but he felt the independence of getting on his feet as well.

Lucy Gray drew back a bit. "That's what you think people would do?"

"I do. Unless there's law, and someone enforcing it, I think we might as well be animals," he said with more assurance. "Like it or not, the Capitol is the only thing keeping anyone safe."

"Hm. So they keep me safe. And what do I give up for that?" she asked.

Coriolanus poked at the fire with a stick. "Give up? Why, nothing."

"The Covey did," she said. "Can't travel. Can't perform

without their say-so. Can only sing certain types of songs. Fight getting round up, and you get shot dead like my daddy. Try to keep your family together, and you get your head broken like my mama. What if I think that price is too high to pay? Maybe my freedom's worth the risk."

"So, your family were rebels after all." Coriolanus wasn't really surprised.

"My family were Covey, first and last," Lucy Gray asserted. "Not district, not Capitol, not rebel, not Peacekeeper, just us. And you're like us. You want to think for yourself. You push back. I know because of what you did for me in the Games."

Well, she had him there. If the Hunger Games were thought necessary by the Capitol, and if he had tried to thwart them, had he not refuted the Capitol's authority? Pushed back, as she said? Not like Sejanus, in outright defiance. But in a quieter, subtler way of his own? "Here's what I believe. If the Capitol wasn't in charge, we wouldn't even be having this conversation, because we'd have destroyed ourselves by now."

"People have been around a long time without the Capitol. I expect they'll be here a long time after," she concluded.

Coriolanus thought of the dead cities he'd passed on the journey to District 12. She claimed the Covey had traveled, so she must have seen them as well. "Not many of them. Panem used to be magnificent. Look at it now."

Clerk Carmine brought Lucy Gray a plant he'd uprooted from the lake, with pointy leaves and small white flowers. "Hey, you found some katniss. Good work, CC." Coriolanus wondered if he meant it to be decorative, like the Grandma'am's roses, but she immediately examined the roots, from which small tubers hung. "Little too early yet."

"Yeah," Clerk Carmine agreed.

"For what?" asked Coriolanus.

"For eating. In a few weeks, these will grow into decent-sized potatoes, and we can roast them," said Lucy Gray. "Some people call them swamp potatoes, but I like katniss better. Has a nice ring to it."

Tam Amber appeared with several fish that he cleaned, gutted, and cut up into pieces. He wrapped the fish in leaves and sprigs of some kind of herb he'd picked, and Lucy Gray arranged them in the embers of the fire. By the time Maude Ivory and Sejanus arrived with their bucket loaded with blackberries, the fish were cooked through. With the hike and the swimming, Coriolanus's appetite had returned. He ate every morsel of his share of the fish, bread, and berries. Then Sejanus brought out a surprise — a half dozen of Ma's sugar cookies he'd saved as his share of the box.

After lunch they spread out the blanket under the trees, half lying on it, half propped against the trunks, and stared up at the fleecy clouds in the brilliant sky.

"I've never seen a sky quite that color," said Sejanus.

"It's azure," Maude Ivory told him. "Like Barb Azure. That's her color."

"Her color?" asked Coriolanus.

"Sure. We each get our first name from a ballad and our second from a color." She popped up to explain. "Barb is from 'Barbara Allen' and azure blue like the sky. Me, I'm 'Maude Clare' and ivory like piano keys. And Lucy Gray is special, because her whole name came right from her ballad. Lucy and Gray."

"That's right. Gray like a winter day," Lucy Gray said with a smile.

Coriolanus had not really noticed the connection before; he'd just thought they had odd Covey names. Ivory and amber brought to mind old ornaments in the Grandma'am's jewelry box. And azure, taupe, and carmine weren't colors he recognized. As to their ballads, who knew where those had come from? It all seemed a strange way to name your child.

Maude Ivory poked him in the stomach. "Your name sounds Covey."

"How so?" he said with a laugh.

"Because of the snow part. White as snow. Snow white," giggled Maude Ivory. "Is there a ballad with Coriolanus in it?"

"Not that I know of. Why don't you write one about me?" he said, poking her back. "'The Ballad of Coriolanus Snow.'"

Maude Ivory sat down on his stomach. "Lucy Gray's the writer. Why don't you ask her?"

"Stop pestering him, you." Lucy Gray pulled Maude Ivory beside her. "You should probably take a nap before we head home."

"People will carry me," said Maude Ivory, wriggling to get free. "And I'll sing for them!"

Oh, my darling, oh, my darling —

"Oh, pipe down," said Clerk Carmine.

"Come on, try to lie down," said Lucy Gray.

"Well, I will if you sing to me. Sing me the one from when I had croup." She flattened out with her head on Lucy Gray's lap.

"Okay, but only if you hush." Lucy Gray stroked Maude Ivory's hair back behind her ear and waited for her to settle down before she began to sing soothingly.

Deep in the meadow, under the willow
A bed of grass, a soft green pillow

Lay down your head, and close your sleepy eyes
And when again they open, the sun will rise.

Here it's safe, here it's warm
Here the daisies guard you from every harm
Here your dreams are sweet and tomorrow brings
them true
Here is the place where I love you.

The song quieted Maude Ivory, and Coriolanus felt his anxieties melt away. Full of fresh food, shaded by the trees, Lucy Gray singing softly beside him, he began to appreciate nature. It really was beautiful out here. The crystal clean air. The lush colors. He felt so relaxed and free. What if this was his life: rising whenever, catching his food for the day, and hanging out with Lucy Gray by the lake? Who needed wealth and success and power when they had love? Didn't it conquer all?

Deep in the meadow, hidden far away
A cloak of leaves, a moonbeam ray
Forget your woes and let your troubles lay
And when again it's morning, they'll wash away.

Here it's safe, here it's warm
Here the daisies guard you from every harm
Here your dreams are sweet and tomorrow brings
them true
Here is the place where I love you.

Coriolanus was on the verge of dozing off when the mockingjays, who'd listened quite respectfully to Lucy Gray's rendition, began one of their own. He felt his body tense and the pleasant drowsiness drain away. But the Covey were all smiles as the birds ran off with the song.

"Like sandstones to diamonds, that's what we are to them," said Tam Amber.

"Well . . . they practice more," said Clerk Carmine, and the others laughed.

Listening to the birds, Coriolanus noticed the absence of jabberjays. The only explanation he could think of was that the mockingjays had begun to reproduce without them, either with one another or with the local mockingbirds. This elimination of the Capitol birds from the equation deeply disturbed him. Here they were, multiplying like rabbits, completely unchecked. Unauthorized. Co-opting Capitol technology. He didn't like it one bit.

Maude Ivory finally napped, curling up against Lucy Gray, her bare feet twisted in the blanket. Coriolanus stayed with them while the others headed back into the lake for another dip. After a while, Clerk Carmine brought over a bright blue feather he'd found along the bank and set it on the blanket for Maude Ivory, gruffly saying, "Don't tell her where it came from."

"Okay. That's sweet, CC," said Lucy Gray. "She'll love it." When he'd run back to the water, she shook her head. "I worry about him. He misses Billy Taupe."

"Do you?" Coriolanus propped himself up on his elbow to watch her face.

She didn't hesitate. "No. Not since the reaping."

The reaping. He remembered the ballad she'd sung for the interview. "What did it mean when you said you were the bet he lost in the reaping?"

"He bet he could have us both, me and Mayfair," she said. "It was a gamble. Mayfair found out about me, I found out about her. She had her pa call my name in the reaping. I don't know what she told him. Certainly not that Billy Taupe was her flame. Something else. We're outsiders here, so it's easy to lie about us."

"I'm surprised they're together," said Coriolanus.

"Well, Billy Taupe's always going on about how he's happiest alone, but what he really wants is some girl to take care of him. I guess Mayfair seemed a likely candidate for the job, so he went after her. No one can pour on the charm like Billy Taupe. That girl didn't stand a chance. Besides, she's got to be lonely. No brothers or sisters. No friends. Miners hate her family. Driving up in their flashy car to watch the hangings." Maude Ivory stirred, and Lucy Gray smoothed her hair. "People are suspicious of us, but they despise them."

He didn't like the way her rage against Billy Taupe had faded. "Is he trying to get back with you?"

She picked up the feather and twirled it between her thumb and forefinger before she answered. "Oh, sure. Came to my meadow yesterday. Big plans. Wants me to meet him at the hanging tree and run off."

"The hanging tree?" Coriolanus thought of Arlo swinging while the birds mocked his final words. "Why there?"

"That's where we used to go. It's the one place in District Twelve you're guaranteed some privacy," she said. "Wants us to go north. He thinks there's people up there. Free people. Says we'll find them and then come back for the others. He's piling up supplies, not sure with what. But what does it matter? I can't ever trust him again."

Coriolanus felt jealousy tighten his throat. He thought she'd banished Billy Taupe, and here she was casually telling him about some chance meeting in the Meadow. Only it hadn't been chance.

He'd known where to find her. How long had they been there, with him pouring on the charm, tempting her to run away? Why had she stayed to listen? "Trust is important."

"I think it's more important than love. I mean, I love all kinds of things I don't trust. Thunderstorms . . . white liquor . . . snakes. Sometimes I think I love them because I can't trust them, and how mixed up is that?" Lucy Gray took a deep breath. "I trust you, though."

He sensed this was a difficult admission for her to make, perhaps harder than a declaration of love, but it didn't erase the image of Billy Taupe wooing her in the Meadow. "Why?"

"Why? Well, I'll have to give that one some thought." When she kissed him, he kissed her back, but without much conviction. These new developments upset him. Maybe it was a mistake to be getting so attached to her. And something else bothered him, too. It was the song she'd been playing in the Meadow that first day. About the hanging, he'd thought then, but it had mentioned meeting up at the hanging tree as well. If that was their old place, why was she still singing about it? Maybe she was only using him to get Billy Taupe back. Playing the two of them off each other.

Maude Ivory awoke and admired her feather, which she had Lucy Gray fix in her hair. They readied themselves to go back, collecting the blanket, the jug, and the bucket. Coriolanus volunteered to carry the little girl for the first leg of the trip. When they'd left the lake, he dropped back behind the others to ask her, "So, do you see Billy Taupe these days?"

"Oh, no," she said. "He's not one of us anymore." That pleased him, but it also suggested that Lucy Gray had kept her meeting with him a secret from the Covey, which made him suspicious again. Maude Ivory bent over his ear and whispered, "Don't let him around Sejanus. He's sweet, and Billy Taupe feeds on sweet."

Coriolanus bet he fed on money, too. Just how was he paying for supplies for his escape?

Tam Amber took a slightly different route, detouring to berry patches so they could fill the bucket along the way. When they'd almost reached the town, Clerk Carmine spotted a tree loaded with apples just beginning to ripen. Tam Amber and Sejanus went on, carrying Maude Ivory and the gear between them. Clerk Carmine climbed the tree and threw down apples, and Coriolanus piled them into Lucy Gray's skirt. It was early evening by the time they reached the house. Coriolanus felt exhausted and ready to return to the base, but Barb Azure sat alone at the kitchen table, picking through berries. "Tam Amber took Maude Ivory to the Hob to see if they could trade some berries for some shoes. I told them to go ahead and get warm ones, it'll be cold before you know it."

"And Sejanus?" Coriolanus looked into the backyard.

"He left a few minutes after. Said he'd meet you there, too," she said.

The Hob. Coriolanus said his good-byes immediately. "I've got to go. If they see Sejanus there without another Peacekeeper, he'll get written up. So will I, for that matter. We have to stay in pairs. He knows that — I don't know what he's thinking." But in truth, he thought he knew exactly what Sejanus was thinking. What a great opportunity to visit the Hob without Coriolanus policing him. He pulled Lucy Gray in for a kiss. "Today was wonderful. Thank you for it. I'll see you next Saturday at the shed?" He shot out the door before she could reply.

He walked, double time, straight to the Hob, and looked in the open door. A dozen or so people wandered around, turning over merchandise at the stalls. Maude Ivory sat on a barrel while Tam Amber laced up a boot for her. At the far end of the warehouse, Sejanus stood at a counter, engaged in conversation with a woman.

As Coriolanus approached, he made note of her wares. Miners' lamps. Picks. Axes. Knives. Suddenly, he realized what Sejanus could buy with all that Capitol money. Weapons. And not just the ones laid out before him. He could buy guns. As if to confirm shady dealings, the woman broke off talking when he came into earshot. Sejanus joined him directly.

"Shopping?" Coriolanus asked.

"I was thinking of getting a pocketknife," said Sejanus. "But she's out at the moment."

Perfect. A lot of the soldiers carried them. There was even a game they played when they were off duty, where they bet money on who could hit a target. "I was thinking of getting one myself. Once we get paid."

"Of course, once we get paid," agreed Sejanus, as if that had been understood.

Suppressing an impulse to strike him, Coriolanus strode out of the Hob without acknowledging Maude Ivory and Tam Amber. He barely spoke on the way back as he revised his strategy. He had to find out what Sejanus was mixed up in. Logic had failed to induce a confidence. Would intimacy work? It wouldn't hurt to try. A few blocks from the base, he laid a hand on Sejanus's shoulder, bringing them both to a stop. "You know, Sejanus, I'm your friend. More than a friend. You're the closest thing I'll ever have to a brother. And there are special rules for family. If you need help . . . I mean, if you get into something you can't handle . . . I'm here."

Tears welled up in Sejanus's eyes. "Thank you, Coryo. That means a lot. You may be the only person in the world who I actually trust."

Ah, trust again. The air was full of it.

"Come here." He pulled Sejanus into an embrace. "Just

promise not to do anything stupid, okay?" He felt him nod in assent but knew the likelihood of his keeping that promise was almost nil.

At least their busy schedule kept Sejanus under constant supervision, even when they left the base. Monday afternoon, they retrieved the traps from the trees again. Although they'd been undisturbed for the entire weekend, not one contained a mockingjay. Contrary to expectations, Dr. Kay seemed pleased by the birds. "It seems they've inherited more than advanced mimicry. They've evolved their survival skills as well. Forget replacing the cages; we have plenty of jabberjays. Tomorrow we'll try the mist nets."

By the time the soldiers got out of the trucks on Tuesday afternoon, the scientists had chosen locations with heavy mockingjay traffic. They broke into groups — Coriolanus and Bug were with Dr. Kay again — and helped erect sets of poles. Between each was stretched a finely woven mist net designed to capture the mockingjays. Nearly invisible, the nets began to yield results almost immediately, entangling the birds and dropping them into horizontal rows of pockets in their mesh surfaces. Dr. Kay had given instructions that the nets were never to be left unsupervised and that the birds were to be removed immediately, to keep them from becoming too snarled and to make the experience as trauma-free as possible. She personally removed the first three mockingjays from their nets, carefully freeing the birds while holding them securely in her hand. When given the go-ahead, Bug proved to be a natural, gently untangling his mockingjay and placing it in a waiting cage. Coriolanus's bird began a tortured screaming the minute he touched it, and when he gave it a squeeze designed to dissuade it, it drove its beak into his palm. He reflexively dropped it, and in moments it had vanished into the foliage.

Noxious creature. Dr. Kay cleaned and bandaged his hand, which reminded him of how Tigris had done the same on reaping day when the thorn on the Grandma'am's rose had punctured him. Not even two months ago. What hopes he'd had that day, and now look at him. Rounding up mutt spawn in the districts. He spent the rest of the afternoon carrying the caged birds to the truck. The hand didn't excuse him from bird duty, though, and he resumed cleaning cages back at the hangar.

Coriolanus began to warm up to the jabberjays. They really were impressive pieces of engineering. A few of the remotes lay around the lab, and the scientists allowed him to play with the birds once they'd been cataloged. "It won't hurt anything," one said. "In fact, they seem to enjoy the interaction." Bug wouldn't participate, but when he grew bored, Coriolanus made them record silly phrases and sing bits of the anthem, seeing how many he could operate with one remote click. Up to four sometimes, if their cages were close together. He always took care to erase them by doing a final quick recording in which he was silent, ensuring his voice would not end up back in the Citadel lab. He stopped with the singing entirely when the mockingjays began to pick it up, even if there was a certain satisfaction in hearing them pipe out praise for the Capitol. He had no way to silence them, and they could string one melody out endlessly.

On the whole, he was beginning to weary of the infusion of music into his life. *Invasion* might be a better word. It seemed to be everywhere these days: birdsong, Covey song, bird-and-Covey song. Perhaps he did not share his mother's love of music after all. At least, such a quantity of it. It consumed his attention greedily, demanding to be listened to and making it hard to think.

By midafternoon Wednesday, they'd collected fifty mockingjays in total, enough to satisfy Dr. Kay. Coriolanus and Bug spent the rest of the day attending to the birds and shuttling the new mockingjays over to the lab table to be numbered and tagged. They finished before dinner and returned after to prepare the birds for travel to the Capitol. The scientists showed Coriolanus and Bug how to fasten the cloth covers on the cages, and then they relocated to the hovercraft, trusting the pair to take care of it. Coriolanus volunteered to do the covers while Bug carried the birds to the hovercraft and helped settle them in for their journey.

Coriolanus started with the mockingjays, happy to see them go. He moved the cages one at a time to his work table, snapped on their covers, wrote the letter *M* and the bird's number in chalk on the cloth, and handed them off. Bug was just leaving with the fiftieth cage, which contained a madly chirping mockingjay, when Sejanus bounced in the door, sounding a bit hyper. "Good news! Another delivery from my ma!"

Bug, who'd been down about the birds leaving, cheered up a bit. "She's the best."

"I'll tell her you said so." Sejanus watched Bug move off and turned to Coriolanus, who'd just collected the jabberjay tagged with the number *1*. The bird twittered away in its cage, still imitating the last mockingjay. Sejanus's grin had vanished, and an anguished expression had taken its place. His eyes swept the hangar to ensure they were alone, and he spoke in a hushed voice. "Listen, we've only got a few minutes. I know you won't approve of what I'm going to do, but I need you to at least understand it. After what you said the other day, about us being like brothers, well, I feel I owe you an explanation. Please, just hear me out."

This was it, then. The confession. Coriolanus's entreaties for sanity and caution had been weighed and found insufficient. Misguided passion had won the day. Now was the time for the pieces to be explained. The money. The guns. The base map. The moment the whole treasonous rebel plot would be revealed. Once Coriolanus heard it, he'd be as good as a rebel himself. A traitor to the Capitol. He should panic, or run, or at least try to shut Sejanus up. But he did none of these things.

Instead his hands acted on their own. Like the time he'd dropped the handkerchief into the tank of snakes before he'd been aware of deciding to do it. Now his left hand adjusted the cover of the jabberjay cage while his right, concealed from Sejanus's view by his body, dropped to the counter, where a remote sat. Coriolanus pressed RECORD, and the jabberjay fell silent.

Coriolanus turned his back to the cage, leaning on the table with his hands, waiting.

"It's like this," said Sejanus, his voice rising with emotion. "Some of the rebels are leaving District Twelve for good. Heading north to start a life away from Panem. They said if I help them with Lil, I can go, too."

As if questioning the claim, Coriolanus raised his eyebrows.

Sejanus's words tumbled out. "I know, I know, but they need me. The thing is, they're determined to free Lil and take her with them. If they don't, the Capitol will hang her with the next lot of rebels they bring in. The plan is simple, really. The prison guards work in four-hour shifts. I'm going to drug a couple of my ma's treats and give them to the outside guards. This medicine they gave me in the Capitol, it knocks you out like that —" Sejanus snapped his fingers. "I'll take one of their guns. The inside guards are unarmed, so I can force them into the interrogation room at gunpoint. It's soundproof, so no one can hear them yell. Then I'll get Lil. Her brother can get us through the fence. We'll head north immediately. We should have hours before they discover the guards. Since we're not going through the gate, they'll assume we're hiding on base, so they'll lock it down and search here first. By the time they figure it out, we'll be long gone. No one hurt. And no one the wiser."

Coriolanus dropped his head and rubbed his brow with his

fingertips, as if trying to collect his thoughts, unsure how long he could refrain from talking without seeming suspicious.

But Sejanus hurried on. "I couldn't go without telling you. You're as good to me as any brother could be. I'll never forget what you did for me in the arena. I'll try to figure out some way to let Ma know what happened to me. And my father, I suppose. Let him know the Plinth name lives on, if only in obscurity."

There it was. The Plinth name. It was enough. His left hand found the remote and he pressed the NEUTRAL button with his thumb. The jabberjay resumed the song it had been singing earlier.

Something caught Coriolanus's eye. "Here comes Bug."

"Here comes Bug," the bird repeated in his voice.

"Hush, you silly thing," he told the bird, inwardly pleased it had resumed its normal, neutral pattern. Nothing to alert Sejanus there. He quickly snapped the cloth in place and marked it with *J1*.

"We need another water bottle. One broke," said Bug as he entered the hangar.

"One broke," said the bird in Bug's voice, and then it began to imitate a passing crow.

"I'll find one." Coriolanus handed him the cage. As Bug left, Coriolanus crossed over to a bin where they kept supplies and began to dig around. Better to stay away from the other jabberjays while the conversation continued. If they started mimicking too much, Sejanus might wonder why the first bird had been so silent. Not that he really knew how the birds worked. Dr. Kay had not explained that to the group at large.

"It sounds crazy, Sejanus. So many things could go wrong." Coriolanus rattled off a list. "What if the guards don't want your ma's treats? Or one does, and collapses with the other watching?

What if the inside guards call for help before you get them in the room? What if you can't find the key to Lil's cell? And what do you mean, her brother will get you through the fence? No one's going to notice him, what, cutting through it?"

"No, there's a weak spot in the fence behind the generator. It's already loose or something. Look, I know a lot of things have to go right, but I think they will." Sejanus sounded as if he was trying to convince himself. "They have to. And if they don't, then they'll arrest me now instead of later, right? When I'm wrapped up in something worse?"

Coriolanus shook his head unhappily. "I can't change your mind?"

Sejanus was adamant. "No, I've decided. I can't stay here. We both know it. Sooner or later I'll snap. I can't do the Peacekeeping work in good conscience, and I can't keep endangering you with my crazy plans."

"But how will you live out there?" Coriolanus found a box with a new water bottle.

"We have some supplies. I'm a good shot," said Sejanus.

He had not mentioned the rebels having guns, but apparently they did. "And when the bullets run out?"

"We'll figure something out. Fish, net birds. They say there are people in the north," Sejanus told him.

Coriolanus thought of Billy Taupe luring Lucy Gray to that imaginary outpost in the wilderness. Had he heard about it from the rebels, or had they heard about it from him?

"But even if there aren't, there's no Capitol," Sejanus continued. "And that's the main thing for me, isn't it? Not this district or that. Not student or Peacekeeper. It's living in a place where they can't control my life. I know it seems cowardly running away, but I'm hoping that once I'm out of here, maybe I can think straighter and come up with some way I can help the districts."

Fat chance, thought Coriolanus. *It will be amazing if you survive the winter.* He pulled the water bottle from its packaging. "Well, I guess all there is to say is I'll miss you. And good luck." He felt Sejanus moving in for an embrace when Bug came through the door. He held up the bottle. "Found one."

"I'll let you get back to your work." Sejanus gave a wave and left.

Coriolanus went on mechanically covering and marking cages while his mind raced. What should he do? Part of him wanted to run to the hovercraft and erase jabberjay number 1. Put it on PLAY, then NEUTRAL, then RECORD, then NEUTRAL again in swift succession so that it would have nothing memorized but the distant shouts of the soldiers on the tarmac. But then what would his options be? To try to dissuade Sejanus from his plan? He had no confidence that he could, and even if he did, it was only a matter of time before Sejanus came up with another scheme. To rat him out to the base commander? He would likely deny it, and as the only proof lay in the jabberjay's memory bank, Coriolanus would have nothing to back up his accusation. He didn't even know the time of the breakout, so no trap could be set. And where would that leave him with Sejanus? Or if it got out, the entire base? As a snitch, an unreliable one at that, and a troublemaker?

He'd taken care not to speak while the jabberjay was recording so as not to incriminate himself in any way. But Dr. Gaul would get the reference to the arena, and she would understand the taping had been intentional. If he sent the bird to the Citadel, she could decide how best to handle the matter. Probably she'd put in a call to Strabo Plinth, discharge Sejanus, and send him home before he did any damage. Yes, that would be best for everybody. He dropped the remote into the bin of bird supplies. If all went well, Sejanus Plinth would be out of his hair in a matter of days.

The calm proved short-lived. Coriolanus awoke after a few hours' sleep from a terrible dream. He'd been in the stands of the arena, looking down at Sejanus, who knelt beside Marcus's wrecked body. He was sprinkling it with bread crumbs, unaware that a multicolored army of snakes was closing in on him from all sides. Coriolanus screamed at him over and over, to get up, to run, but Sejanus didn't seem to hear. When the snakes reached him, he had plenty of screaming of his own to do.

Guilt-ridden and slick with sweat, Coriolanus realized he had not thought through the ramifications of sending the jabberjay. Sejanus could be in real trouble. He leaned over the side of his bunk and was reassured for a moment by the sight of Sejanus sleeping peacefully across the barrack from him. He was overreacting. Most likely, the scientists would never even hear the recording, let alone pass it on to Dr. Gaul. Why would they bother to put the bird on PLAY? There was no reason to, really. The jabberjays had been tested at the hangar already. It had been a questionable act, but it would not result in Sejanus's death, by snakes or otherwise.

That thought soothed him until he realized that, in that case, he was back to square one and in great danger for knowing about the rebel plan. Lil's rescue, the escape, even the weak spot in the fence behind the generator weighed on him. That chink in the Capitol armor. The whole idea of the rebels having secret access to the base. It frightened and infuriated him. This breaking of the contract. This invitation to chaos and all that could follow. Didn't these people understand that the whole system would collapse without the Capitol's control? That they all might as well run away to the north and live like animals, because that's what they'd be reduced to?

It made him hope the jabberjay delivered its message after all. But if the Capitol officials did, by chance, hear Sejanus's confession, what would they do to him? Would buying rebel guns to use against the Peacekeepers be cause for execution? No, wait, he hadn't recorded anything about the illegal guns. Only the part about Sejanus stealing the Peacekeeper's . . . but that was bad enough.

Maybe he was doing Sejanus a favor. If they caught him before he had a chance to act, maybe he could get prison time instead of a more severe sentence. Or, most likely, Old Plinth would buy him out of whatever trouble he faced. Foot the bill for a new base for District 12. Sejanus would get kicked out of the Peacekeepers, which would make him happy, and probably end up with a desk job in his father's munitions empire, which would not. Miserable, but alive. And, most importantly, someone else's problem.

Sleep evaded Coriolanus for the rest of the night, and his thoughts turned to Lucy Gray. What would she think about him if she knew what he'd done to Sejanus? She'd hate him, of course. Her and her love of freedom for the mockingjays, for the jabberjays, for the Covey, for everybody. She'd probably support Sejanus's escape plan entirely, especially since she'd been locked in the arena herself. He'd be a Capitol monster, and she'd run back to Billy Taupe, taking with her what little happiness he had left.

In the morning, he climbed down from his bunk tired and irritable. The scientists had flown home to the Capitol the night before, leaving his squad to its dull routines. He dragged through the day, trying not to think about how, in a couple of weeks, he should be starting an education at the University with a full ride. Choosing his classes. Touring the campus. Buying his books. As to the Sejanus dilemma, he'd accepted that no one would ever hear the jabberjay's dispatch, and he should just corner him and throttle some sense into him. Threaten to report him to both the commander and his father and carry through on that threat if he persisted. He'd had enough of the whole idiotic thing. Unfortunately, the day offered no opportunity to present his ultimatum.

To make matters worse, Friday brought a letter from Tigris, chock-full of bad news. Prospective buyers and a lot of nosy people had been touring the Snows' apartment. They'd received two offers, both far below the amount they'd need to move to the most modest apartments Tigris had seen. The visitors distressed the Grandma'am, who camped among her rosebushes in a great show of denial when they appeared. However, she overheard one couple, who were inspecting the roof, discussing how they could replace her beloved garden with a goldfish pond. The idea that the roses, the very symbol of the Snow dynasty, were to be demolished precipitated her downward spiral into even greater agitation and confusion. It was worrisome to leave her alone now. Tigris was at her wit's end and asking for advice, but what advice could he give? He had failed them in every possible way and could think of no road out of their despair. Anger, impotence, humiliation — those were all he had to offer.

By Saturday, he almost looked forward to confronting Sejanus. He hoped it would come to blows. Someone should pay for the indignities of the Snow family, and who better than a Plinth?

Smiley, Bug, and Beanpole were as eager to go to the Hob as ever, although they were getting tired of spending Sundays recuperating. As they dressed for the evening out, the bunkmates decided to forgo the white liquor for some fermented apple cider, which didn't pack as much punch but still gave the drinker a nice buzz. The question was academic for Coriolanus, who had no intention of imbibing at all. He wanted a clear head when he dealt with Sejanus.

As they were leaving the barracks, they got roped into an extra detail by Cookie, and spent half an hour unloading a hovercraft full of crates. "You'll be glad about it next weekend. Commander's birthday party," he said, and slipped them a quart bottle of what turned out to be cheap whiskey. It was a big improvement over the local brew.

When they arrived at the Hob, they barely had time to grab some crates and squeeze into a spot against the back wall before Maude Ivory danced onstage to introduce the Covey. Not great seats, but between Cookie's whiskey and the fact that they could enjoy some of Ma's treats instead of trading them, no one felt the need to complain, although Coriolanus privately regretted missing his time with Lucy Gray in the shed. He placed his crate practically on top of Sejanus's so he would know if he tried to disappear again. Sure enough, about an hour into the show, he felt Sejanus rise and watched him move off toward the main door. Coriolanus counted to ten before he followed, trying to attract as little attention as possible, but they were near the exit and no one seemed to notice.

Lucy Gray began a downbeat number, and the Covey played mournfully behind her.

You come home late,
Fall on your cot.
You smell like something that money bought.
We don't have cash, or so you say.
So where did you get it and how'd you pay?

The sun don't rise and set for you.
You think so, but you're wrong.
You tell me lies, I can't stay true —
I'll sell you for a song.

The song grated on him. It sounded like another Billy Taupe–inspired number. Why didn't she write something about him instead of dwelling on that nobody? He was the one who'd saved her life after Billy Taupe had bought her a ticket to the arena.

Coriolanus stepped outside just in time to see Sejanus rounding the corner of the Hob. Lucy Gray's voice poured out into the night air as he skirted along the side of the building.

You get up late,
Won't say a word.
You been with her, that's what I've heard.
I don't own you, so I've been told.
But what do I do when the nights get cold?

The moon don't wane and wax for you.
You think so, but you're wrong.
You cause me pain, you make me blue —
I'll sell you for a song.

Coriolanus paused in the shadows at the back of the Hob as he watched Sejanus hurry through the open door of the shed. All five of the Covey were onstage, so who would he be looking for? Was this a prearranged meeting with the rebels to lock down their escape plans? He had no desire to walk in on a whole nest of them, and he had just resolved to wait it out, when the woman from the Hob, the one Sejanus had supposedly seen about the pocketknife, came out the door stuffing a wad of bills into her pocket. She disappeared down an alley, leaving the Hob behind.

So that was it. Sejanus had come to give her money for weapons, most likely those guns he was planning to hunt with in the north. This seemed as good a time as any to confront him, while the contraband was still hot in his hands. He crept over to the shed, not wanting to startle Sejanus if he was handling a gun, his footsteps masked by the music.

You're here, you're not.
It's more than me,
It's more than you, it's more like we.
They're young and soft, they worry so.
You coming or going, they need to know.

The stars don't shine and shoot for you.
You think so, but you're wrong.
You mess with mine, I'll hurt you, too —
I'll sell you for a song.

During the applause that followed, Coriolanus peered around the shed's open doorway. The only light came from a small lantern, the type he'd seen some of the coal miners holding at Arlo's hanging, positioned on a crate in the back of the shed. In its glow, he could make out Sejanus and Billy Taupe crouched over a burlap sack, out of which protruded several weapons. As he took a step in, he froze, suddenly aware of the barrel of a shotgun positioned inches from the side of his rib cage.

He drew in his breath and was beginning to raise his hands slowly when he heard the quick tap of shoes behind him and Lucy Gray's laughter. Her hands landed on his shoulders with a "Hey!

Saw you slip out. Barb Azure said if you —" Then she tensed, aware of the gunman.

"Inside" was all he said. Coriolanus moved toward the lamp with Lucy Gray holding tightly to his arm. He heard the cinder block scrape on the cement floor and the door shut behind them.

Sejanus leaped to his feet. "No. It's all right, Spruce. He's with me. They're both with me."

Spruce moved into the lamplight. Coriolanus recognized him as the man who had restrained Lil the day of the hanging. The brother Sejanus had mentioned, no doubt.

The rebel looked them over. "Thought we agreed this was between us."

"He's like my brother," said Sejanus. "He'll cover for me when we run. Buy us more time."

Coriolanus had promised to do no such thing, but he nodded.

Spruce redirected his barrel to Lucy Gray. "What about this one?"

"I told you about her," said Billy Taupe. "She's going north with us. She's my girl."

Coriolanus could feel Lucy Gray clench his arm, then drop it. "If you'll take me," she said.

"You two aren't together?" said Spruce, his gray eyes moving from Coriolanus to Lucy Gray. Coriolanus had been wondering this as well. Was she really going with Billy Taupe? Had she been using him, as he'd suspected?

"He's seeing my cousin. Barb Azure. She sent me to tell him where to meet up tonight is all," said Lucy Gray.

So she'd just lied to defuse the moment. Was that it? Still unsure, Coriolanus played along. "That's right."

Spruce considered it, then shrugged and lowered the gun, releasing Lucy Gray from its hold. "I guess you'll be company for Lil."

Coriolanus's eyes fell to the cache of weapons. Two more shotguns, a standard Peacekeeper rifle like the ones they used in target practice. Some sort of heavy piece that appeared to launch grenades. Several knives. "That's quite a haul."

"Not for five people," Spruce replied. "It's the ammo I'm concerned about. Be helpful if you could get us some more of that from the base."

Sejanus nodded. "Maybe. We don't really have access to the armory. But I can look around."

"Sure. Stock up."

Everyone's head snapped toward the sound. A female voice, coming from the far corner of the shed. Coriolanus had forgotten about the second door, since no one ever seemed to use it. In the pitch-blackness outside the lamp's circle of light, he could not say if it was open or shut, or make out the intruder. How long had she been hiding there in the gloom?

"Who's there?" said Spruce.

"Guns, ammo," mocked the voice. "You can't make more of that, can you? Up north?"

The nastiness helped Coriolanus place it from the night of the brawl in the Hob. "It's Mayfair Lipp, the mayor's daughter."

"Trailing after Billy Taupe like a hound in heat," said Lucy Gray under her breath.

"Always keep that last bullet somewhere safe. So as you can blow your brains out before they catch you," said Mayfair.

"Get home," ordered Billy Taupe. "I'll explain this later. It's not how it sounded."

"No, no. Come in and join us, Mayfair," invited Spruce. "We've got no quarrel with you. You can't choose your pa."

"We won't hurt you," said Sejanus.

Mayfair gave an ugly laugh. "'Course you won't."

"What's going on?" Spruce asked Billy Taupe.

"Nothing. She's just talking," he said. "She won't do anything."

"That's me. All talk, no action. Right, Lucy Gray? How'd you enjoy the Capitol, by the way?" The door gave a small creak, and Coriolanus had the sense Mayfair was backing away, about to flee. With her would go his entire future. No, more than that, his very life. If she reported what she'd heard, the whole lot of them would be as good as dead.

In a flash, Spruce lifted his shotgun to shoot her, but Billy Taupe knocked the barrel toward the floor. Coriolanus reflexively reached for the Peacekeeper rifle and fired toward Mayfair's voice. She gave a cry, and there was the sound of her collapsing to the floor.

"Mayfair!" Billy Taupe bolted across the shed to where she lay in the doorway. He staggered back into the light, his hand shiny with blood, spitting at Coriolanus like a rabid animal. "What'd you do?"

Lucy Gray began to shake, the way she had in the zoo when Arachne Crane's throat had been slit.

Coriolanus gave her a push, and her feet started moving toward the door. "Go back. Get onstage. That's your alibi. Go!"

"Oh, no. If I swing, she's swinging with me!" Billy Taupe charged after her.

Without hesitating, Spruce shot Billy Taupe through the chest. The blast carried him backward, and he crumpled to the floor.

In the stillness that followed, Coriolanus registered the music coming from the Hob for the first time since Lucy Gray had finished her number. Maude Ivory had the entire warehouse caught up in a sing-along.

Keep on the sunny side, always the sunny side,

"You better do like he said," Spruce told Lucy Gray. "Before they miss you and someone comes looking."

Keep on the sunny side of life.

Lucy Gray couldn't take her eyes off Billy Taupe's body. Coriolanus grabbed her by the shoulders, forcing her to look at him. "Go. I'll take care of this." He propelled her to the door.

It will help us every day, it will brighten all the way,

She opened it, and they both looked out. The coast was clear.

If we keep on the sunny side of life.
Yessir, keep on the sunny side of life.

The whole Hob broke into drunken cheers, signifying the end of Maude Ivory's song. They were just in time. "You were never here," Coriolanus whispered in Lucy Gray's ear as he let her go. She stumbled across the pavement and into the Hob. He slid the door shut with his foot.

Sejanus checked Billy Taupe's pulse.

Spruce stuffed the weapons back into the burlap bag. "Don't bother. They're dead. I'm planning to keep this to myself. What about you two?"

"The same. Obviously," said Coriolanus. Sejanus stared at them, still in shock. "Him, too. I'll make sure."

"You might think about coming with us. Someone's going to

pay for this," said Spruce. He retrieved the lamp and vanished out the back door, throwing the shed into darkness.

Coriolanus fumbled forward until he found Sejanus and pulled him out after Spruce. He forced Mayfair's body into the shed with his boot and firmly closed the door on the murder scene with his shoulder. There. He'd successfully made it in and out of the shed without touching anything with his skin. Except the gun he'd killed Mayfair with, of course, no doubt covered in his fingerprints and DNA — but Spruce would take that when he left District 12, never to return. The last thing he needed was a repeat of the handkerchief scenario. He could still hear Dean Highbottom taunting him. . . .

"Do you hear that, Coriolanus? It's the sound of Snow falling."

For a moment he inhaled the night air. Music, some sort of instrumental piece, floated over to them. He guessed Lucy Gray had made it onto the stage but had not yet reclaimed her voice. Grabbing Sejanus by the elbow, he steered him around the shed and checked the passage between the buildings. Empty. He hurried them down the side of the Hob, pausing before they turned the corner. "Not a word," he hissed.

Sejanus, pupils wide, sweat staining his collar, repeated, "Not a word."

Inside the Hob, they took their seats. Next to them, Beanpole sat propped against the wall, apparently blacked out. On the other side of him, Smiley chatted up a girl while Bug killed the whiskey. No one seemed to have missed them.

The instrumental ended and Lucy Gray had pulled herself together enough to sing again, choosing a number that required all the Covey to back her up. Smart girl. They would likely be the ones to discover the bodies, since the shed was their break room. The longer she kept them all together up there, the better their alibi would be, the more time Spruce would have to get those murder weapons out of the area, and the harder it would be for the audience to place anything in time.

Coriolanus's heart pounded in his chest as he tried to assess the damage. He thought no one would much care about Billy Taupe, except Clerk Carmine maybe. But Mayfair? The only child of the mayor? Spruce was right; someone was going to pay for her.

Lucy Gray opened the floor to requests and managed to keep all five of the Covey onstage for the rest of the program. Maude Ivory collected money from the audience as usual. Lucy Gray thanked everybody, the Covey took a final bow, and the audience began to shuffle toward the door.

"We need to head straight back," Coriolanus said quietly to Sejanus. They each threw one of Beanpole's arms over their shoulders and headed out with Bug and Smiley trailing behind. They'd traveled about twenty yards down the road when Maude Ivory's hysterical screams cut through the night air, causing everyone to turn back. Since it would have been suspicious to keep going, Coriolanus and Sejanus swung Beanpole around as well. Then, very quickly, Peacekeeper whistles blew, and a couple of officers were waving them back to the base. They lost themselves in the herd and did not speak to each other again until they'd reached the barrack, heard their bunkmates snoring, and snuck into the bathroom.

"We know nothing. That's the whole story," Coriolanus whispered. "We left the Hob briefly to piss. The rest of the night, we were at the show."

"All right," said Sejanus. "What about the others?"

"Spruce is long gone and Lucy Gray won't tell a soul, not even the Covey. She won't want to put them in danger," he said.

"Tomorrow, we'll both be hungover and spend the day on the base."

"Yes. Yes. Day on the base." Sejanus seemed distracted to the point of incoherence.

Coriolanus grasped his face between his hands. "Sejanus, this is life or death. You have to hold it together." Sejanus agreed, but Coriolanus knew he didn't sleep a wink after that. He could hear him shifting around the whole night through. In his own mind, he replayed the shooting again and again. He'd killed for the second time. If Bobbin's death had been self-defense, what was Mayfair's? Not premeditated murder. Not murder at all, really. Just another form of self-defense. The law might not see it that way, but he did. Mayfair may not have had a knife, but she had the power to get him hanged. Not to mention what she'd do to Lucy Gray and the others. Perhaps because he hadn't actually seen her die, or even had a good look at the body, he felt less emotional than when he'd killed Bobbin. Or perhaps the second killing was just easier than the first. At any rate, he knew that he'd shoot her again if he had it all to do over, and somehow that supported the rightness of his actions.

The next morning, even the hungover bunkmates made it to the mess hall for breakfast. Smiley got the scoop from his nurse friend, who'd been on duty at the clinic the night before, when they'd brought in the bodies. "They're both locals, but one of them is the mayor's daughter. The other one's a musician or something, but not one that we've seen. They were shot dead in that garage behind the Hob. Right during the show! Only none of us heard it because of the music."

"Did they find who did it?" asked Beanpole.

"Not yet. These people aren't even supposed to have guns, but like I told you, they're floating around out there," Smiley said. "Killed by one of their own, though."

"How do they know that?" asked Sejanus.

Shut up! thought Coriolanus. Knowing Sejanus, he could be one step away from confessing to a crime he didn't even commit.

"Well, she said they think the girl was shot with a Peacekeeper's rifle, probably an old one that got stolen during the war. And the musician was killed by some sort of shotgun the locals used for hunting. Probably two shooters," Smiley reported. "They searched the surrounding area and couldn't find the weapons. Long gone with the murderers, if you ask me."

Coriolanus's nerves unwound a bit, and he ate a forkful of pancakes. "Who found the bodies?"

"That little girl singer — you know, the one in the pink dress," said Smiley.

"Maude Ivory," said Sejanus.

"I think that's it. Anyway, she freaked out. They questioned the band, but when would they have had time to do it? They barely leave the stage, and anyway no guns were found," Smiley told them. "Shook them up pretty good, though. I guess they knew the musician guy somehow or other."

Coriolanus stabbed a link of sausage with his fork, feeling much improved. The investigation was off to a good start. Even so, it could still be bad for Lucy Gray, having the double motive of Billy Taupe being her old flame and Mayfair having sent her into the arena. And once the arena was brought into it, could he be implicated? No one from 12 knew he was her new love except the Covey, and Lucy Gray would keep them quiet. Anyway, if she had a new love, why would either of them care about Billy Taupe? They might want to kill Mayfair, though, as a form of revenge, and Billy Taupe might try to defend her. Actually, that was not far from what had happened. But hundreds of witnesses could swear that Lucy Gray had been onstage for all but a brief period of the show. No guns had been found. It would be tough to prove her guilty. He would have to have patience, give things time to simmer down, but then they could be together again. In many ways, he felt closer to her than ever now that they had this new and unbreakable bond.

In view of the past night's events, the commander locked down the base for the day. Not that Coriolanus had plans anyway — he would have to steer clear of the Covey for a while. He and Sejanus floated around, trying to look normal. Playing cards, writing letters, cleaning their boots. As they knocked the mud from the treads, Coriolanus whispered, "What about the escape plan? Is it still on?"

"I've no idea," Sejanus said. "The commander's birthday isn't until next weekend. That was the night we were supposed to go. Coryo, what if they arrest an innocent person for the murders?"

Then our troubles are over, thought Coriolanus, but he only said, "I think it's highly unlikely, with no guns. But let's cross that bridge when we come to it."

Coriolanus slept better that night. Monday the lockdown ended, and the rumor mill claimed that the murders had to do with rebel infighting. If they wanted to kill each other, let them. The mayor came on base and pitched a fit to the commander about his daughter, but since he'd spoiled Mayfair rotten and let her run loose like a wildcat, the feeling was he had no one to blame but himself if she had been keeping time with a rebel.

By Tuesday afternoon, the interest in the murders had died down to the extent that Coriolanus began to make plans for the future as he peeled potatoes for the next day's breakfast. The first thing was to ensure that Sejanus had given up on the escape plan. Hopefully, the events at the shed had convinced him he was playing with fire. Tomorrow night they would have mopping detail together, so that would be the best time to confront him. If he didn't agree to abandon the breakout, Coriolanus would have no choice but to report him to the commander. Feeling resolved, he peeled with such zeal that he finished early, and Cookie let him off for the last half hour of his shift. He checked the mail and found a box from Pluribus, loaded with packets of strings for assorted musical instruments and a kind note saying there was no charge. He put them in his locker, happy at the thought of how happy the Covey would be when it was safe enough to see them again. Maybe in a week or two, if things continued to settle down.

Coriolanus began to feel like his old self as he headed to the mess hall. Tuesday meant hash. He had a few extra minutes and went to pick up another can of powder for his rash, which had finally begun to heal. But as he came out of the clinic, a base ambulance pulled up, the back doors swung open, and two medics pulled a man on a stretcher from the back. His blood-soaked shirt suggested he might be dead, but as they carried him inside, he turned his head. A pair of gray eyes landed on Coriolanus, who could not suppress a gasp. Spruce. Then the doors swung shut, blocking him from view.

Coriolanus got word to Sejanus after hours, but neither knew what it meant. Spruce had clearly mixed it up with the Peacekeepers, but why? Had they connected him with the murders? Did they know about the escape plan? Had they found out about the gun purchase? What would he tell them now that they'd captured him?

Wednesday breakfast, Smiley's reliable nurse let him know

that Spruce had died from his wounds during the night. She didn't really know, but most people thought he'd been involved with the murders. Coriolanus went through the morning on autopilot, waiting for the other shoe to drop. At lunch, it did. A pair of military police officers came to their table in the mess and arrested Sejanus, who went without a word. Coriolanus tried to mirror his bunkmates' shocked faces. Obviously, he parroted, there had been a mistake.

Led by Smiley, they confronted the sergeant at target practice. "We'd just like to say that there's no way Sejanus committed those murders. He was with us all night."

"We never were apart," ventured Beanpole. As if he could have possibly known, blacked out as he'd been against the wall, but all of them backed him up.

"I appreciate your loyalty," said the sergeant, "but I think this is about something else."

A chill went through Coriolanus. Something else, like the escape plan? Spruce didn't seem like he'd have spilled the news, especially because it could have affected his sister. No, Coriolanus felt certain his jabberjay had made it through to Dr. Gaul, and this was the fallout. First Spruce's arrest, then Sejanus's.

For the next two days, everything seemed to tumble forward, as he tried to reassure himself that this was in Sejanus's best interest, as the bunkmates' pleas to see their friend were denied, as the detention stretched on. He kept waiting for Strabo Plinth to descend in a private hovercraft, negotiate a discharge, offer to upgrade the entire air fleet for free, and whisk his errant son back home. But did his father even know about Sejanus's predicament? This wasn't the Academy, where they called your parents if you messed up.

As casually as possible, Coriolanus asked an older soldier if they were ever allowed to call home. Yes, everyone was allowed a biannual call, but only once they'd put in six months. All other correspondence had to be by mail. Not knowing how long Sejanus might be in lockup, Coriolanus scribbled a short note to Ma, generally informing her that Sejanus was in trouble and suggesting Strabo might want to make a few calls. He hurried over to mail it Friday morning but was waylaid by a base-wide announcement calling all but essential personnel to the auditorium. There, the commander informed them that one of their own was to be hanged for treason that afternoon. One Sejanus Plinth.

It was so surreal, like a waking nightmare. In drill practice, his body felt like a marionette being jerked here and there by invisible strings. When it ended, the sergeant called him forward, and everyone — his fellow recruits, Smiley, Bug, and Beanpole — watched while Coriolanus was given the order to attend the hanging to fill out the ranks.

Back at the barrack, his fingers were so stiff he could hardly manipulate the uniform buttons, each one carrying the impression of the Capitol seal on its silver face. His legs had the same lack of coordination he associated with bomb time, but somehow he wobbled to the armory to collect his rifle. The other Peacekeepers, none of whom he knew by name, gave him a wide berth in the truck bed. He was certain he was tainted by association with the condemned.

As with Arlo's hanging, Coriolanus was instructed to stand in a squad flanking the hanging tree. The size and volatility of the crowd confused him — surely, Sejanus had not garnered this sort of support in a few weeks — until the Peacekeeper van arrived and both Sejanus and Lil stumbled out in their chains. At the sight of the girl, many in the crowd began to wail her name.

Arlo, an ex-soldier toughened by years in the mines, had

managed a fairly restrained end, at least until he'd heard Lil in the crowd. But Sejanus and Lil, weak with terror, looked far younger than their years and only reinforced the impression that two innocent children were being dragged to the gallows. Lil, her shaking legs unable to bear her weight, was hauled forward by a pair of grim-faced Peacekeepers who would probably spend the following night trying to obliterate this memory with white liquor.

As they passed him, Coriolanus locked eyes with Sejanus, and all he could see was the eight-year-old boy on the playground, the bag of gumdrops clenched in his fist. Only this boy was much, much more frightened. Sejanus's lips formed his name, *Coryo*, and his face contorted in pain. But whether it was a plea for help or an accusation of his betrayal he couldn't tell.

The Peacekeepers positioned the condemned side by side on the trapdoors. Another tried to read out the list of charges over the shrieks of the crowd, but all Coriolanus could catch was the word *treason*. He averted his eyes as the Peacekeepers moved in with the nooses, and he found himself looking at Lucy Gray's stricken face. She stood near the front in an old gray dress, her hair hidden in a black scarf, tears running down her cheeks as she stared up at Sejanus.

As the drumroll began, Coriolanus squeezed his eyes shut, wishing he could block out the sound as well. But he could not, and he heard it all. Sejanus's cry, the bang of the trapdoors, and the jabberjays picking up Sejanus's last word, screaming it over and over into the dazzling sun.

"Ma! Ma! Ma! Ma! Ma!"

Coriolanus soldiered his way through the aftermath, remaining stone-faced and speechless as he traveled back to the base, returned his gun, and walked to the barrack. He knew people were staring at him; Sejanus was known to be his friend, or at least a member of his squad. They wanted to see him crack, but he refused to give them the satisfaction. Alone in his room, he slowly removed his uniform, hanging each piece with precision, smoothing the creases with his fingers. Away from prying eyes, he allowed his body to deflate, his shoulders to droop in fatigue. All he'd managed to get down today had been a few swallows of apple juice. He felt too debilitated to rejoin his squad for target practice, to face Bug and Beanpole and Smiley. His hands shook too badly to hold a rifle anyway. Instead he sat on Beanpole's bunk in his underwear in the stifling room, waiting for whatever was to come.

It was only a matter of time. Maybe he should just give himself up. Before they came to arrest him because Spruce had confessed to, or — more likely — Sejanus had divulged the details of the murders. Even if they had not, the Peacekeeper's rifle was still out there, covered in his DNA. Spruce had not fled to freedom, probably lying low until he could rescue Lil, and if he had remained in District 12, so had the murder weapons. They could be testing his gun right at this minute, looking for confirmation that Spruce had used it to kill Mayfair and discovering that the shooter was their own Private Snow. The one who'd ratted out his best friend and sent him to the gallows.

Coriolanus buried his face in his hands. He had killed Sejanus as surely as if he'd bludgeoned him to death like Bobbin or gunned him down like Mayfair. He'd killed the person who considered him his brother. But even as the vileness of the act threatened to drown him, a tiny voice kept asking, *What choice did you have?* What choice? No choice. Sejanus had been bent on self-destruction, and Coriolanus had been swept along in his wake, only to be deposited at the foot of the hanging tree himself.

He tried to think rationally about it. Without him, Sejanus would have died in the arena, prey to the pack of tributes who had tried to kill them as they fled. Technically, Coriolanus had given him a few more weeks of life and a second chance, an opportunity to mend his ways. But he hadn't. Couldn't. Didn't care to. He was what he was. Maybe the wilderness would have been best for him. Poor Sejanus. Poor sensitive, foolish, dead Sejanus.

Coriolanus crossed to Sejanus's locker, removed his box of personal items, and sat on the floor, spreading the contents in front of him. The only additions since his first search were a couple of homemade cookies, covered in a bit of tissue. Coriolanus unwrapped one and took a bite. Why not? The sweetness spread across his tongue, and images flashed in his brain — Sejanus holding out a sandwich at the zoo, Sejanus standing up to Dr. Gaul, Sejanus embracing him on the road back to the base, Sejanus swinging from the rope —

"Ma! Ma! Ma! Ma! Ma!"

He gagged on the cookie, bringing up a splash of apple juice, sour and acidic, along with the crumbs. Sweat poured off his body and he began to cry. Leaning back against the lockers, he curled his legs into his chest and let the ugly, violent sobs shake him. He wept for Sejanus, and for poor old Ma, and for sweet, devoted Tigris and his feeble, delusional Grandma'am, who would soon be losing him in such a sordid way. And for himself, because any day now, he would be dead. He started gasping for air in terror, as if the rope already choked the life from his body. He did not want to die! Especially not in that field, with those mutant birds echoing his last utterance. Who knew what crazy thing you'd say in a moment like that? And him dead and the birds screaming it all out until the mockingjays turned it into some macabre song!

After about five minutes, the outburst ended, and he calmed himself, rubbing his thumb over the cool marble heart from Sejanus's box. There was nothing to do except try to face his death like a man. Like a soldier. Like a Snow. Having accepted his fate, he felt the need to get his affairs in order. He had to make what small amends he could to those he loved. Unfastening the back of the silver picture frame, he found quite a bit of cash still remained after Sejanus's gun purchase. He took one of the creamy, fancy envelopes Sejanus had brought from the Capitol, stuffed the money in, sealed it, and addressed it to Tigris. After tidying Sejanus's keepsakes, he returned the box to his locker. What else? He found himself thinking of Lucy Gray, the one and now only love of his life. He would like to leave her a remembrance of him. He dug through his own box and decided on the orange scarf, since the Covey loved color, and her more than most. He was unsure of how he'd get it to her, but if he made it to Sunday, maybe he could sneak off the base and see her one last time. He placed the neatly folded scarf with the strings Pluribus had sent. After rinsing the snot and tears from his face, he dressed and walked over to the post office to mail the money home.

At dinner, he whispered an account of the hanging to his miserable bunkmates, trying to soften it. "I think he died immediately. He couldn't have felt any pain."

"I still can't believe he did it," said Smiley.

Beanpole's voice quavered. "I hope they don't think we were all involved."

"Bug and I are the only ones who'd be suspected of being rebel sympathizers, being from the districts," said Smiley. "What are you worried about? You guys are Capitol."

"So was Sejanus," Beanpole reminded him.

"But not really, right? The way he always talked about District Two?" said Bug.

"No, not really," agreed Coriolanus.

Coriolanus spent the evening on guard duty at the empty prison. He slept like the dead, which made sense since it was only a matter of hours before he joined them.

He went through the motions during morning drills and almost felt relief when, at the end of lunch, Commander Hoff's aide appeared and requested that he follow him. Not as dramatic as the military police, but as they were trying to reinstate a sense of normalcy among the troops, it was the right way to proceed. Sure that he would be taken straight from the commander's office to the prison, Coriolanus regretted not placing some bit of home in his pocket to hang on to in his last hours. His mother's powder would've been the thing, something to soothe him while he waited for the rope.

While not grand, the commander's office proved nicer than any other space he'd seen on base, and he sank into the leather seat across the desk from Hoff, grateful that he could receive his death sentence with a little class. *Remember, you're a Snow,* he told himself. *Let's go out with some dignity.*

The commander excused his aide, who left the office and closed the door behind him. Hoff leaned back in his chair and considered Coriolanus for a long moment. "Quite a week for you."

"Yes, sir." He wished the man would just get on with the interrogation. He was too tired to play some cat-and-mouse game.

"Quite a week," repeated Hoff. "I understand you were a stellar student back in the Capitol."

Coriolanus had no idea who he'd heard that from, and wondered if it could have been Sejanus. Not that it mattered. "That's a generous assessment."

The commander smiled. "And modest, too."

Oh, just arrest me, thought Coriolanus. He didn't need some long windup to what a disappointment he'd turned out to be.

"I'm told you were close friends with Sejanus Plinth," said Hoff.

Ah, here we go, thought Coriolanus. Why not speed the thing along instead of dragging it out with denials? "We were more than friends. We were like brothers."

Hoff gave him a sympathetic look. "Then all I can do is express the Capitol's sincerest gratitude for your sacrifice."

Wait. What? Coriolanus stared at him in confusion. "Sir?"

"Dr. Gaul received your message from the jabberjay," Hoff reported. "She said sending it couldn't have been an easy choice for you to make. Your loyalty to the Capitol came at a great personal cost."

So, a reprieve. Apparently, the gun with his DNA had not yet surfaced. They viewed him as a conflicted Capitol hero. He adopted a suffering look, as befitted a man who grieved for his wayward friend. "Sejanus wasn't bad, just . . . confused."

"I agree. But conspiring with the enemy crosses a line we can't afford to ignore, I'm afraid." Hoff paused in thought. "Do you think he could've been mixed up in the murders?"

Coriolanus's eyes widened, as if the idea had never crossed his mind. "The murders? You mean at the Hob?"

"The mayor's daughter and . . ." The commander flipped

through some papers, then he decided not to bother. "That other fellow."

"Oh . . . I don't think so. Do you think they're connected?" asked Coriolanus, as if mystified.

"I don't know. Don't care much," Hoff told him. "The young man was running with the rebels, and she was running with him. Whoever killed them probably saved me a lot of trouble up the road."

"It doesn't sound like Sejanus," said Coriolanus. "He never wanted to hurt anyone. He wanted to be a medic."

"Yes, that's what your sergeant said," Hoff agreed. "So he didn't mention getting them guns?"

"Guns? Not that I know of. How would he get guns?" Coriolanus was beginning to enjoy himself a bit.

"Buy them on the black market? He's from a rich family, I hear," said Hoff. "Well, never mind. It's likely to remain a mystery unless the weapons turn up. I've got Peacekeepers searching the Seam over the next few days. In the meantime, Dr. Gaul and I have decided to keep your help with Sejanus quiet for your safety. Don't want the rebels targeting you, do we?"

"That's what I would prefer anyway," said Coriolanus. "It's hard enough dealing with my decision privately."

"I understand. But when the dust settles, remember you did a real service for your country. Try to put it behind you." Then, as if as an afterthought, he added, "It's my birthday today."

"Yes, I helped unload some whiskey for the party," said Coriolanus.

"Usually a good time. Try and enjoy yourself." Hoff stood up and extended his hand.

Coriolanus rose and shook it. "I'll do my best. And happy birthday, sir."

The bunkmates greeted him with delight when he returned,

ambushing him with questions about the commander's calling him in.

"He knew Sejanus and I had a history together, and he just wanted to make sure I was all right," Coriolanus told them.

The news improved everyone's spirits, and the update to their afternoon schedule gave Coriolanus some satisfaction. Instead of shooting at targets, they were cleared to take out the jabberjays and mockingjays at the hanging tree. Their chorus following Sejanus's final outcry had been the last straw.

Coriolanus felt giddy as he blasted the mockingjays off the branches, managing to kill three. *Not so clever now, are you!* he thought. Unfortunately, most of the birds flew out of range after a short while. But they'd be back. He'd be back, too, if he didn't hang first.

In honor of the commander's birthday, they all showered, then dressed in fresh fatigues before heading over to the mess hall. Cookie had laid out a surprisingly elegant meal, serving up steak, mashed potatoes and gravy, and fresh, not canned, peas. Each soldier got a big mug of beer, and Hoff was on hand to cut an enormous frosted cake. After dinner, they all assembled at the gymnasium, which had been decorated with banners and flags for the occasion. Whiskey flowed freely, and many impromptu toasts were made over the mic brought out for this purpose. But Coriolanus didn't realize there would be entertainment until some of the soldiers started setting up chairs.

"Sure," an officer told him. "We hired that band from the Hob. The commander gets a kick out of them."

Lucy Gray. This would be his chance, probably his only chance, to see her again. He ran to the barrack, retrieved the box from Pluribus with the instrument strings and his scarf, and hurried back to the party. He could see that his bunkmates had saved a chair for him about halfway up, but he stood at the back of the audience. If an opportunity came, he didn't want to make a scene getting out. The lights flickered off in the main part of the gym, leaving only the area by the mic illuminated, and the crowd grew quiet. All eyes were on the locker room, which had been hung with the blanket the Covey used in the Hob.

Maude Ivory scampered out in a buttercup yellow dress with a wide skirt and hopped up on a crate someone had set in front of the mic. "Hey there, everybody! Tonight is a special night, and you know why! It's somebody's birthday!"

The Peacekeepers broke into raucous applause. Maude Ivory began to sing the old, standby birthday song, and everyone joined in:

Happy birthday
To someone special!
And we wish you many more!
Once a year
We give a cheer
To you, Commander Hoff!
Happy birthday!

It was the only verse, but they sang it three times while the Covey, one by one, took their places onstage.

Coriolanus drew in a sharp breath when Lucy Gray appeared in the rainbow dress from the arena. Most people would think it was for the commander's birthday, but he felt certain that it was for him. A way to communicate, to bridge the chasm that circumstance had dug between them. An overwhelming flush of love ran through him at her reminder that he was not alone in this tragedy. They were back in the arena, fighting for survival, just the two of them against the world. He felt a bittersweet pang at the thought of her watching him die, but gratitude that she would survive. He was the only one left who could place her at the murders. She hadn't touched the weapons. Whatever happened to him, there was comfort in knowing she would live on for the both of them.

For the first half hour, he didn't take his eyes off her as the Covey ran through some of their regular numbers. Then the rest of the band cleared out, leaving her alone in the light. She settled in on a high stool and then — had he imagined it? — patted the pocket of her dress as she had in the arena. It was her signal that she was thinking of him. That even if they were separated by space, they were together in time. Every nerve tingling, he listened intently as she began an unfamiliar song:

Everyone's born as clean as a whistle —
As fresh as a daisy
And not a bit crazy.
Staying that way's a hard row for hoeing —
As rough as a briar,
Like walking through fire.

This world, it's dark,
And this world, it's scary.
I've taken some hits, so
No wonder I'm wary.
It's why I
Need you —
You're pure as the driven snow.

Oh, no. He had not imagined anything. The mention of snow confirmed it. She'd written this song for him.

Everyone wants to be like a hero —
The cake with the cream, or
The doer not dreamer.
Doing's hard work,
It takes some to change things —
Like goat's milk to butter,
Like ice blocks to water.

This world goes blind
When children are dying.
I turn into dust, but
You never stop trying.
It's why I
Love you —
You're pure as the driven snow.

His eyes filled with tears. They would hang him, but she would be there, knowing he was still a genuinely good person. Not a monster who'd cheated or betrayed his friend, but someone who'd really tried to be noble in impossible circumstances. Someone who had risked everything to save her in the Games. Someone who'd risked it all again to save her from Mayfair. The hero of her life.

Cold and clean,
Swirling over my skin,
You cloak me.
You soak right in,
Down to my heart.

To her heart.

Everyone thinks they know all about me.
They slap me with labels.
They spit out their fables.
You came along, you knew it was lying.
You saw the ideal me,
And yes, that's the real me.

This world, it's cruel,
With troubles aplenty.
You asked for a reason —
I've got three and twenty
For why I
Trust you —
You're pure as the driven snow.

Had there been any doubt, this confirmed it. Three and twenty. Twenty-three. The number of tributes she'd survived in the Games. All because of him.

That's why I
Trust you —
You're pure as the driven snow.

The mention of trust. Before need, before love, came trust. The thing she valued most. And he, Coriolanus Snow, was the one she trusted.

As the audience applauded, he stood still, clutching his box, too moved even to join in. The rest of the Covey ran onstage while Lucy Gray disappeared behind the blanket. Maude Ivory got her crate back in place and a twangy tune began.

Well, there's a dark and a troubled side of life.
There's a bright and a sunny side, too.

Coriolanus recognized the tune. The song about the sunny side. The one she'd been singing during the murders. This was his chance. He maneuvered his way out the nearby door as inconspicuously as possible. With everyone safely inside, he sprinted around the gymnasium to the locker room and tapped on the outside door. It flew open immediately, as if she'd been waiting for him, and Lucy Gray flung herself into his arms.

For a while, they just stood there, clinging to each other, but time was precious.

"I'm so sorry about Sejanus. Are you okay?" she asked breathlessly.

Of course, she knew nothing about his role in that. "Not really. But I'm still here, for the moment."

She drew back to look at his face. "What happened? How did they find out about him helping to get Lil out?"

"I don't know. Someone betrayed him, I guess," he said.

Lucy Gray didn't hesitate. "Spruce."

"Probably." Coriolanus touched her cheek. "What about you? Are you all right?"

"I'm awful. It's been just awful. Watching him die like that. And then, everything after that night. I know you killed Mayfair to protect me. Me and the rest of the Covey." She rested her forehead on his chest. "I'll never be able to thank you for that."

He stroked her hair. "Well, she's gone for good now. You're safe."

"Not really. Not really." Distraught, Lucy Gray twisted away and began to pace. "The mayor, he's . . . He won't leave me alone.

He's sure I killed her. Killed them both. He drives that awful car down to our house and sits in front of it for hours. The Peacekeepers, they've questioned us all three times now. Anyway, they say he's on them night and day to arrest me. And if they don't make me pay, he will."

That was scary. "What did they say to do?"

"Avoid him. But how can I, when he's sitting ten feet from my house?" she cried. "Mayfair was all that mattered to him. I don't think he'll rest until I'm dead. Now he's starting to threaten the rest of the Covey. I — I'm going to run away."

"What?" asked Coriolanus. "Where?"

"North, I guess. Like Billy Taupe and the others talked about. If I stay here, I know he'll find a way to kill me. I've been setting some supplies by. Out there, I might survive." Lucy Gray rushed back into his arms. "I'm glad I got to tell you good-bye."

Run away. She was really going to do it. Head into the wilderness and take her chances. He knew only the prospect of certain death could drive her to do such a thing. For the first time in days, he saw a way to escape the noose. "Not good-bye. I'm going with you."

"You can't. I won't let you. You'd be risking your life," she warned him.

Coriolanus laughed. "My life? My life consists of wondering how long it will be until they find those guns and connect me to Mayfair's murder. They're searching the Seam now. It could be any moment. We'll go together."

Her brow creased with disbelief. "Do you mean it?"

"We go tomorrow," he said. "One step ahead of the executioner."

"And the mayor," she added. "We'll finally be free of him, of District Twelve, of the Capitol, all of it. Tomorrow. At dawn."

"Tomorrow at dawn," he confirmed. He thrust the box into her hands. "From Pluribus. Except the scarf — that's from me. I better run before someone realizes I'm gone and gets suspicious." He pulled her in for a passionate kiss. "It's just us again."

"Just us," she said, her face shining with joy.

Coriolanus flew out of the locker room with wings on his heels.

Let us greet with a song of hope each day,
Though the moments be cloudy or fair.

He was not just going to live; he was going to live with her, as they had that day at the lake. He thought of the taste of the fresh fish, the sweet air, and the freedom to act however he wanted, as nature had intended. To answer to no one. To truly be rid of the world's oppressive expectations forever.

Let us trust in tomorrow always
To keep us, one and all, in its care.

He made it back to the gymnasium and slipped into his place in time to join in the last chorus.

Keep on the sunny side, always the sunny side,
Keep on the sunny side of life.
It will help us every day, it will brighten all the way
If we keep on the sunny side of life.
Yessir, keep on the sunny side of life.

Coriolanus's mind was in a whirl. Lucy Gray rejoined the Covey for one of those harmonious things with unintelligible words, and he tuned them out as he tried to ride the curve life had just thrown him. He and Lucy Gray, running away into the wilderness. Madness. But then again, why not? It was the only lifeline in his reach, and he meant to grasp it and hold on tightly. Tomorrow was Sunday, so he had the day off. He'd leave as early as possible. Grab breakfast, possibly his last meal in civilization, when the mess opened at six, then hit the road. His bunkmates would be sleeping off the whiskey. He would have to sneak off the base. . . . The fence! He hoped Spruce had had good information about the weak spot behind the generator. And then he'd make his way to Lucy Gray and run as fast and as far as he could.

But wait. Should he go to her house? With the Covey all there? And possibly the mayor? Or did she mean to meet in the Meadow? He was mulling it over when the number ended and she slid back up on her stool with her guitar.

"I almost forgot. I promised to sing this for one of you," she said. And there it was again, ever so casually, her hand on her pocket. She began the song she'd been working on when he'd come up behind her in the Meadow.

Are you, are you
Coming to the tree
Where they strung up a man they say murdered three?
Strange things did happen here
No stranger would it be
If we met up at midnight in the hanging tree.

The hanging tree. Her old meeting spot with Billy Taupe. That's where she wanted him to meet her.

Are you, are you
Coming to the tree

Where the dead man called out for his love to flee?
Strange things did happen here
No stranger would it be
If we met up at midnight in the hanging tree.

He would have preferred not to meet up at her old lover's rendezvous spot, but it was certainly much safer than meeting at her house. Who would be there on a Sunday morning? Anyway, Billy Taupe was no longer a concern. She took another breath. She must have written more. . . .

Are you, are you
Coming to the tree
Where I told you to run, so we'd both be free?
Strange things did happen here
No stranger would it be
If we met up at midnight in the hanging tree.

Who did she mean? Billy Taupe telling her to come there so they'd be free? Her telling him tonight that they'd be free?

Are you, are you
Coming to the tree?
Wear a necklace of rope, side by side with me.
Strange things did happen here
No stranger would it be
If we met up at midnight in the hanging tree.

Now he got it. The song, the speaker in the song, was Billy Taupe, and he was singing it to Lucy Gray. He'd witnessed Arlo's death, heard the birds call out his last words, begged Lucy Gray to run away to freedom with him, and when she'd rejected him, he'd wanted her to hang with him rather than get to live without him. Coriolanus hoped this was the final Billy Taupe song. What else could be said, really? Not that it mattered. This might be his song, but she was singing it to Coriolanus. Snow lands on top.

The Covey performed a few more numbers, then Lucy Gray said, "Well, as my daddy used to say, you have to go to bed with the birds if you want to greet them at dawn. Thanks for having us tonight. And how about one more round of wishes for Commander Hoff!" The whole drunken gymnasium slurred out one more "Happy Birthday" chorus for the commander.

The Covey took their final bow and exited the stage. Coriolanus waited in the back to help Bug get Beanpole back to the barrack. Before they knew it, it was lights-out and they had to climb into bed in the dark. His bunkmates lost consciousness almost immediately, but he lay awake, going over the escape plan in his head. It didn't require much. Just him, the clothes on his back, a couple of mementos in his pockets, and a lot of luck.

Coriolanus rose at dawn, dressed in fresh fatigues, and tucked a couple of clean changes of underclothes and socks into his pockets. He chose three photos of his family, the circle of his mother's powder, and his father's compass, and hid them among his clothes as well. Last, he made the most convincing form of himself he could with his pillow and blanket and arranged the sheet over it. As his bunkmates snored on, he gave the room one final look and wondered if he would miss them.

He joined a handful of early risers for a breakfast of bread pudding, which seemed a positive omen for the trip, as it was Lucy Gray's favorite. He wished he could take her some, but his pockets were full to bursting, and they didn't have napkins in the mess. Draining his cup of apple juice, he wiped his mouth on the back of his hand, dropped off his tray for the dish washers, and headed outside, planning to make a beeline for the generator.

As he stepped into the sunlight, a pair of guards descended on him. Armed guards, not aides. "Private Snow," said one. "You're wanted in the commander's office."

A jolt of adrenaline shot through him. His blood pounded in his temples. This couldn't be happening. They couldn't be coming to arrest him just when he was on the verge of freedom. Of a new life with Lucy Gray. His eyes darted to the generator, about a hundred yards from the mess hall. Even with his recent training, he'd never make it. He never would. *I just need five more minutes*, he pleaded with the universe. *Even two will do.* The universe ignored him.

Flanked by the guards, he drew back his shoulders and marched straight to the commander's office, prepared to face his doom. As he entered, Commander Hoff rose from his desk, snapped to attention, and gave him a salute. "Private Snow," he said. "Let me be the first to congratulate you. You leave for officers' school tomorrow."

Coriolanus stood stunned as the guards slapped him on the back, laughing. "I — I —"

"You're the youngest person ever to pass the test." The commander beamed. "Ordinarily, we'd train you here, but your scores recommend you for an elite program in District Two. We'll be sorry to see you go."

Oh, how he wished he could go! To District Two, which was not really that far from his home in the Capitol. To officers' school, *elite* officers' school, where he could distinguish himself and find a way back to a life worth living. This might be an even better road to power than the University had offered. But there was still a murder weapon with his name on it out there. His DNA would condemn him, just as it had on the handkerchief. Sadly, tragically, it was too dangerous to stay. It hurt to play along.

"What time do I leave?" he asked.

"There's a hovercraft headed that way early tomorrow morning, and you'll be on it. You're off today, I think. Use the time to pack up and say your good-byes." The commander shook his hand for the second time in two days. "We expect great things from you."

Coriolanus thanked the commander and headed outside, where he stood a moment, weighing his options. It was no use. There were no options. Hating himself, and hating Sejanus Plinth even more, he walked toward the building that housed the generator, almost not caring if he was apprehended. What a bitter disappointment, to have a second chance at a bright future so irrevocably stripped away. He had to remind himself of the rope, and the gallows, and the jabberjays mimicking his last words to renew his focus. He was about to desert the Peacekeepers; he needed to snap out of it.

When he reached the building, he took a quick look over his shoulder, but the base still slept, and he slunk around to the back without witnesses. He examined the fence and could find no opening at first. He wound his fingers in the links and gave them a shake of frustration. Sure enough, the mesh pulled free of a supporting pole, leaving a break in the fence he could just squeeze through. Outside, his natural wariness reinstated itself. He skirted around the rear of the base and through a wooded area, eventually making his way to the road that led to the hanging tree. Once there, he simply followed the path the truck had taken on previous trips, walking briskly, but not so fast as to attract attention. There was precious little to attract anyway on a hot Sunday shortly after dawn. Most miners and Peacekeepers would not rise for hours.

After a few miles, he reached the depressing field and broke into a run for the hanging tree, eager to conceal himself in the woods. There was no sign of Lucy Gray, and as he passed under the branches, he wondered if in fact he'd misinterpreted her message and should have headed to the Seam instead. Then he caught a glimpse of orange and tracked it to a clearing. There she stood, unloading a stack of bundles from a small wagon, his scarf wound in a fetching manner around her head. She ran over and hugged him, and he responded even though it felt too hot for an embrace. The kiss that followed put him in a better mood.

His hand went to the orange scarf in her hair. "This seems very bright for fugitives."

Lucy Gray smiled. "Well, I don't want you to lose me. You still up for this?"

"I have no choice." Realizing that sounded halfhearted, he added, "You're all that matters to me now."

"You, too. You're my life now. Sitting here, waiting for you to show up, I realized I'd never really be brave enough to do this without you," she admitted. "It's not just how hard it will be. It's too lonely. I might've made it for a few days, but then I'd have come home to the Covey."

"I know. I didn't even consider running until you brought it up. It's so . . . daunting." He ran a hand over her bundles. "I'm sorry, I couldn't risk bringing anything much."

"I didn't think you could. I've been collecting all this, and I raided our storeroom, too. It's okay. I left the Covey the rest of the money." As if convincing herself, she said, "They'll be okay." She hoisted up a pack and threw it over her shoulder.

He gathered some of the supplies. "What will they do? I mean, the band. Without you."

"Oh, they'll get by. They can all carry a tune, and Maude Ivory's just a few years from replacing me as lead singer anyway," said Lucy Gray. "Besides, the way trouble seems to find me, I may be wearing out my welcome in District Twelve. Last night the commander told me not to sing 'The Hanging Tree' anymore. Too dark, he said. Too rebellious, more like it. I promised he'd never hear it from my lips again."

"It's a strange song," offered Coriolanus.

Lucy Gray laughed. "Well, Maude Ivory likes it. She says it has real authority."

"Like my voice. When I sang the anthem in the Capitol," Coriolanus remembered.

"That's it," said Lucy Gray. "You ready?"

They'd divided everything between them. It took him a moment to realize what was missing. "Your guitar. You're not taking it?"

"I'm leaving it for Maude Ivory. That and my mama's dresses." She struggled to make light of it. "What will I need them for? Tam Amber thinks there's still people in the north, but I'm not convinced. I think it's just going to be us."

For a moment, he realized that he wasn't the only one leaving his dreams behind. "We'll get new dreams out there," Coriolanus promised, with more conviction than he felt. He pulled out his father's compass, consulted it, and pointed. "North is this way."

"I thought we'd head to the lake first. It's mostly north. I'd kind of like to see it one more time," she said.

It seemed as good a plan as any, so he didn't object. Soon they'd just be adrift in the wilderness, never to return. Why not indulge her? He tucked in a bit of scarf that had come loose. "The lake it is."

Lucy Gray gazed back at the town, although the only thing Coriolanus could make out was the gallows. "Good-bye, District Twelve. Good-bye, hanging tree and Hunger Games and Mayor Lipp. Someday something will kill me, but it won't be you." She turned and headed deeper into the woods.

"Not much to miss," agreed Coriolanus.

"I'll miss the music and my pretty birds," said Lucy Gray with a catch in her voice. "I'm hoping one day they can follow me, though."

"You know what I won't miss? People," Coriolanus replied. "Except for a handful. They're mostly awful, if you think about it."

"People aren't so bad, really," she said. "It's what the world does to them. Like us, in the arena. We did things in there we'd never have considered if they'd just left us alone."

"I don't know. I killed Mayfair, and there was no arena in sight," he said.

"But only to save me." She thought it over. "I think there's a natural goodness built into human beings. You know when you've stepped across the line into evil, and it's your life's challenge to try and stay on the right side of that line."

"Sometimes there are tough decisions." He'd been making them all summer.

"I know that. Of course, I do. I'm a victor," she said ruefully. "It'd be nice, in my new life, not to have to kill anyone else."

"I'm with you there. Three seems enough for one lifetime. And certainly enough for one summer." A feral cry came from nearby, reminding him of his lack of a weapon. "I'm going to make a walking stick. Do you want one?"

She pulled up. "Sure. That could come in handy in more ways than one."

They found a couple of stout branches, and she steadied them while he snapped off their limbs. "Who's the third?"

"What?" She was giving him a funny look. His hand slipped, driving a piece of bark under his nail. "Ow."

She ignored his injury. "Person you killed. You said you killed three people this summer."

Coriolanus bit at the end of the splinter to pull it out with his teeth, buying a moment of time. Who, indeed? The answer was Sejanus, of course, but he couldn't admit to that.

"Can you get this out?" He held out his hand, wiggling the compromised fingernail, hoping to distract her.

"Let me see." She examined his splinter. "So, Bobbin, Mayfair . . . who's the third?"

His mind raced for a plausible explanation. Could he have been involved in a freak accident? A training death? He was cleaning a weapon, and it went off by mistake? He decided it was best to make a joke of it. "Myself. I killed the old me so I could come with you."

She plucked the splinter free. "There. Well, I hope old you doesn't haunt new you. We've already got enough ghosts between us."

The moment passed, but it had killed the conversation. Neither of them spoke again until the halfway point, where they stopped for a breather.

Lucy Gray unscrewed the plastic jug and offered it to him. "Will they miss you yet?"

"Probably not until dinner. You?" He took a deep drink of water.

"Only one up when I left was Tam Amber. I told him I was going to find out about a goat. We've been talking about building a herd. Sell the milk as a sideline," she said. "I've probably got a few more hours before they start looking. Might be night before they think about the hanging tree and find the wagon. They'll put it together."

He handed her the jug. "Will they try to follow you?"

"Maybe. But we'll be too far gone." She took a swig and wiped her mouth with the back of her hand. "Will they hunt you?"

He doubted the Peacekeepers would be concerned anytime soon. Why would he desert with elite officers' school waiting? If anyone even noticed he was missing, they'd probably think he'd gone into town with another Peacekeeper. Unless they found the gun, of course. He didn't want to go into all the school stuff now while the wound was still fresh. "I don't know. Even when they realize I've run, they won't know where to look."

They hiked on toward the lake, each lost in their own thoughts. It all seemed unreal to him, as if this were just a pleasure outing, as the one two Sundays ago had been. As if they were going for a picnic, and he must be sure to get back in time for fried baloney and curfew. But no. When they reached the lake, they'd move on into the wilderness, to a life consumed with the most basic type of survival. How would they eat? Where would they live? And what on earth would they do with themselves, when the challenges of obtaining food and shelter had been met? Her with no music. Him with no school, or military, or anything. Have a family? It seemed too bleak an existence to condemn a child to. Any child, let alone one of his own. What was there to aspire to once wealth, fame, and power had been eliminated? Was the goal of survival further survival and nothing more?

Preoccupied as he was with these questions, the second leg of the journey to the lake passed quickly. They set down their loads on the shore, and Lucy Gray went directly to find branches for fishing poles. "We don't know what lies ahead, so we better fill up here," she said. She showed him how to attach the heavy thread and hooks to their poles. Clawing through the soft mud for worms disgusted him, and he wondered if this would be a daily activity. It would, if they were hungry enough. They baited the hooks and sat silently on the bank, waiting for a strike as the birds chattered around them. She caught two. He caught nothing.

Heavy, dark clouds rolled in, providing some relief from the beating sun but adding to his oppression. This was his life now. Digging for worms and being at the mercy of the weather. Elemental. Like an animal. He knew this would be easier if he wasn't such an exceptional person. The best and the brightest humanity had to offer. The youngest to pass the officer candidate test. If he'd been useless and stupid, the loss of civilization would not have hollowed out his insides in this manner. He'd have taken it in stride. Thick, cold raindrops began to plop down on him, leaving wet marks on his fatigues.

"Never be able to cook in this," Lucy Gray said. "Better go inside. There's a fireplace in there we can use."

She could only mean the one lake house that still had a roof. Probably his last roof, until he built one himself. How did you build a roof anyway? It had not been a question on the officer candidate test.

After she'd quickly cleaned the fish and wrapped them in leaves, they gathered up their bundles and hurried to the house as the rain pelted them. It might've been fun, if it hadn't been his real life. Just an adventure for a few hours, with a charming girl and a fulfilling future elsewhere. The door was jammed, but Lucy Gray bumped it with her hip and it swung open. They scrambled in out of the wet and dropped their belongings. It was only one room, with concrete walls, ceiling, and floor. There was no sign of electricity, but light came through the windows on four sides and the single door. His eyes lit on the fireplace, full of old ashes, with a neat pile of dried wood stacked beside it. At least they wouldn't have to forage for that.

Lucy Gray crossed to the fireplace, laid the fish down on the little concrete hearth, and began to arrange layers of wood and twigs on an old metal grate. "We keep some wood in here so there's always some dry."

Coriolanus considered the possibility of just staying in the sturdy little house, with plenty of wood around and the lake to fish in. But no, it would be too dangerous to put down roots this close to District 12. If the Covey knew of this spot, surely other people did, too. He had to deny himself even this last shred of protection. Would he end up in a cave after all? He thought of the beautiful Snow penthouse, with its marble floors and crystal chandeliers. His home. His rightful home. The wind blew a splatter of rain in, peppering his pants with icy drops. He swung the door shut behind him and froze. The door had concealed something. A long burlap bag. From the opening poked the barrel of a shotgun.

It couldn't be. Unable to breathe, he nudged the bag open with his boot, revealing the shotgun and a Peacekeeper's rifle. A little more and he could recognize the grenade launcher. Beyond question, these were the black market guns Sejanus had bought in the shed. And among them the murder weapons.

Lucy Gray lit the fire. "I brought along an old metal can thinking maybe we could carry live coals from place to place. I don't have many matches, and it's hard to get a fire going from flint."

"Uh-huh," said Coriolanus. "Good idea." How had the weapons gotten here? It made sense, really. Billy Taupe could have brought Spruce to the lake, or maybe Spruce had simply known about it anyway. It would have been useful to the rebels during the war, to have as a hideout. And Spruce had been smart enough to know he couldn't risk hiding the evidence in District 12.

"Hey, what'd you find there?" Lucy Gray joined him and leaned down, pulling the burlap from the weapons. "Oh. Are these the ones they had in the shed?"

"I think they must be," he said. "Should we take the guns along?"

Lucy Gray drew back, rose to her feet, and considered them for a long moment. "Rather not. I don't trust them. This will come in handy, though." She pulled out a long knife, turning the blade over in her hand. "I think I'll go dig up some katniss, since we got the fire going anyway. There's a good patch by the lake."

"I thought they weren't ready," he said.

"Two weeks can make a lot of difference," she said.

"It's still raining," he objected. "You'll get soaked."

She laughed. "Well, I'm not made of sugar."

In truth, he was happy for a minute alone to think. After she left, he lifted the bottom of the burlap bag, and the weapons slid out onto the floor. Kneeling beside the pile, he picked up the Peacekeeper's rifle he'd killed Mayfair with and cradled it in his arms. Here it was. The murder weapon. Not in a Capitol forensic lab, but here, in his hands, in the middle of the wilderness, where it posed no threat at all. All he had to do was destroy it, and he would be free from the hangman's noose. Free to go back to the base. Free to go forward to District 2. Free to rejoin the human race without fear. Tears of relief flooded his eyes, and he began to laugh out of sheer joy. How would he do it? Burn it in a bonfire? Disassemble it and scatter the parts to the four winds? Throw it into the lake? Once the gun was gone, there'd be nothing to connect him to the murders. Absolutely nothing.

No, wait. There would be one thing. Lucy Gray.

Well, no matter. She would never tell. She wouldn't be thrilled, obviously, when he told her there'd been a change of plans. That he was returning to the Peacekeepers and heading to District 2 tomorrow at dawn, essentially leaving her to her fate. Still, she'd never rat him out. It wasn't her style, and it would implicate her in the murders as well. It would mean she could wind up dead, and as the Hunger Games had shown, Lucy Gray possessed an extraordinary talent for self-preservation. Plus, she loved him. She'd said so last night in the song. Even more, she trusted him. Although, if he ditched her in the woods to claw out an existence alone, no doubt she would consider that a breach of faith. He had to think of just the right way to break the news. But what would that be? "I love you deeply, but I love officers' school more?" That wasn't going to go over well.

And he did love her! He did! It was just that, only a few hours into his new life in the wilderness, he knew he hated it. The heat, and the worms, and those birds yakking nonstop . . .

She was certainly taking a long time with those potatoes.

Coriolanus glanced out the window. The rain had diminished to a sprinkle.

She hadn't wanted to go by herself. Too lonely. Her song said that she needed, loved, and trusted him, but would she forgive him? Even if he deserted her? Billy Taupe had crossed her, and he'd ended up dead. He could hear him now . . .

"Makes me sick how you're playing the kids. Poor Lucy Gray. Poor lamb."

. . . and see her sinking her teeth into his hand. He thought about how coolly she'd killed in the arena. First that frail little Wovey; that was a cold-blooded move if he'd ever seen one. Then the calculated way she'd taken out Treech, baiting him to attack her, really, so she could whip that snake out of her pocket. And she claimed that Reaper had rabies, that it was a mercy kill, but who knew?

No, Lucy Gray was no lamb. She was not made of sugar. She was a victor.

He checked to see that the Peacekeeper's rifle was loaded, then opened the door wide. She was nowhere in sight. He walked down to the lake, trying to remember where Clerk Carmine had been digging before he brought them the katniss plant. It didn't matter. The swampy area around the lake was deserted, and the bank undisturbed.

"Lucy Gray?" The only response came from a lone mockingjay on a nearby branch, who made an effort to mimic his voice but failed, as his words were not particularly musical. "Give it up," he muttered to the thing. "You're no jabberjay."

No question, she was hiding from him. But why? There could only be one answer. Because she'd figured it out. All of it. That destroying the guns would wash away all physical evidence of his connection to the murders. That he no longer wanted to run away. That she was the last witness to tie him to the crime. But they'd always had each other's backs, so why would she suddenly think he might harm her? Why, when only yesterday, he'd been pure as the driven snow?

Sejanus. She must have figured out that Sejanus was the third person Coriolanus had killed. She wouldn't have to know anything about the stunt with the jabberjays, only that he'd been Sejanus's confidant, and that Sejanus was a rebel, while Coriolanus was a defender of the Capitol. Still, to think he'd kill her? He looked down at the loaded gun in his hands. Maybe he should've left it in the shed. It looked bad coming after her armed. As if he was hunting her. But he wasn't really going to kill her. Just talk to her and make sure she saw sense.

Put down the gun, he told himself, but his hands refused to cooperate. *All she has is a knife.* A big knife. The best he could manage was to sling the gun onto his back. "Lucy Gray! Are you okay? You're scaring me! Where are you?"

All she'd have to say was "I understand, I'll go on alone, like I was planning to all along." But just this morning she'd admitted she didn't think she could make it on her own, that she'd return to the Covey after a few days. She knew he wouldn't believe her.

"Lucy Gray, please, I just want to talk to you!" he shouted. What was her plan here? To hide until he grew tired and went back to the base? And then sneak back home tonight? That didn't work for him. Even with the murder weapon gone, she'd still be dangerous. What if she went back to District 12 now and the mayor succeeded in getting her arrested? What if they interrogated or even tortured her? The story would come out. She hadn't killed anyone. He had. His word against hers. Even if they didn't believe her, his reputation would be destroyed. Their romance would be revealed, along with the details of how he'd cheated in the Hunger Games. Dean Highbottom might be brought in as a character witness. He couldn't risk it.

Still no sign of her. She was giving him no choice but to hunt her down in the woods. The rain had stopped now, leaving the air humid and the earth muddy. He went back to the house and scanned the ground until he found the slight imprint of her shoes, then followed her tracks until he reached the brush where the woods began again in earnest and quietly made his way into the dripping trees.

Bird chatter filled his ears, and the overcast sky made visibility poor. The underbrush concealed her footprints, but somehow he felt he was on the right track. Adrenaline sharpened his senses, and he noticed a snapped branch here, a scuff mark in the moss there. He felt a bit guilty, frightening her this way. What was she doing, quivering in the bushes while she tried to suppress her sobs? The idea of life without him must be breaking her heart.

A patch of orange caught his eye, and he smiled. "I don't want you to lose me," she'd said. And he hadn't. He pushed through the branches and into a small clearing canopied by trees. The orange scarf lay across some briars, where it had apparently blown loose and snagged as she fled. Oh, well. It confirmed he was on the right track. He went to retrieve it — maybe he'd keep it after all — when a faint rustle in the leaves pulled him up short. He'd just registered the snake when it struck, uncoiling like a spring and digging its teeth into the forearm extended toward the scarf.

"Aa!" he screamed in pain. It released him immediately and

slithered into the brush before he even had a chance to get a good look at it. Panic set in as he stared at the red, arched bite mark on his forearm. Panic and disbelief. Lucy Gray had tried to kill him! This was no coincidence. The trailing scarf. The poised snake. Maude Ivory had said she always knew where to find them. This was a booby trap, and he'd walked straight into it! Poor lamb, indeed! He was beginning to sympathize with Billy Taupe.

Coriolanus knew nothing about snakes, other than the rainbow ones in the arena. Feet rooted to the ground, heart racing, he expected to die on the spot, but while the wound hurt, he was still standing. He didn't know how long he might have, but by all things Snow, she was going to pay for this. Should he tie off the arm with a tourniquet? Suck out the venom? They hadn't done survival training yet. Afraid his first aid treatments might only spread the poison more swiftly through his system, he yanked his sleeve down over his forearm, pulled his rifle off his shoulder, and started after her. If he'd felt better, he'd have laughed at the irony of how quickly their relationship had deteriorated into their own private Hunger Games.

She wasn't so easy to track now, and he realized the earlier clues had been left to lead him directly to the snake. But she couldn't be that far away. She'd want to know if the thing killed him, or if she should form another plan of attack. Maybe she hoped he'd pass out so she could cut his throat with the long knife. Trying to quiet his panting, he moved deeper into the woods, gently pushing the branches back with the nose of his rifle, but it was impossible to discern her whereabouts.

Think, he told himself. *Where would she go?* The answer hit him like a ton of bricks. She would not want to battle him, armed with a rifle, when she had only a knife. She'd return to the lake house to get a gun herself. Perhaps she'd circled around him and was headed there right now. He strained his ears and yes. Yes! He thought he could hear someone moving off to his right, retreating to the lake. He started running toward the sound and then stopped abruptly. Sure enough, having heard him, she was flying through the underbrush, realizing what he had realized, no longer caring if he heard her. He estimated her to be about ten yards away, lifted the rifle to his shoulder, and released a spray of bullets in her direction. A flock of birds squawked as they took to the air, and he heard a faint cry. *Got you*, he thought. He crashed through the woods after her, branches and thorns catching his clothes and scratching his face, ignoring all of it until he came to the spot where he'd guessed her to be. There was no trace of her. No matter. She would have to move again, and when she moved, he'd find her.

"Lucy Gray," he said in his normal voice. "Lucy Gray. It's not too late to work something out." Of course, it was, but he owed her nothing. Certainly not the truth. "Lucy Gray, won't you talk to me?"

Her voice surprised him, lifting suddenly and sweetly into the air.

> *Are you, are you*
> *Coming to the tree?*
> *Wear a necklace of rope, side by side with me.*
> *Strange things did happen here*
> *No stranger would it be*
> *If we met up at midnight in the hanging tree.*

Yes, I get it, he thought. *You know about Sejanus. "Necklace of rope" and all that.*

He took a step in her direction just as a mockingjay picked up her song. Then a second. Then a third. The woods came alive with their melody as dozens joined in. He dove through the trees and then opened fire on the spot the voice had come from. Had he hit her? He couldn't tell, because the birdsong filled his ears, disorienting him. Little black specks swam in his field of vision, and his arm began to throb. "Lucy Gray!" he bellowed in frustration. Clever, devious, deadly girl. She knew they'd cover for her. He lifted the rifle and machine-gunned the trees, trying to wipe out the birds. Many fluttered into the sky, but the song had spread, and the woods were alive with it. "Lucy Gray! Lucy Gray!" Furious, he turned this way and that and finally blasted the woods in a full circle, going around and around until his bullets were spent. He collapsed on the ground, dizzy and nauseous, as the woods exploded, every bird of every kind screaming its head off while the mockingjays continued their rendition of "The Hanging Tree." Nature gone mad. Genes gone bad. Chaos.

He had to get out of there. His arm had begun to swell. He had to get back to the base. Forcing himself to his feet, he tramped back to the lake. Everything in the house remained as he had left it. At least he'd prevented her from getting back. Using a pair of his socks as gloves, he wiped off the murder weapon, crammed all the weapons back in the burlap bag, hoisted it over his shoulder, and ran to the lake. Judging it heavy enough to sink without being weighted down with rocks, he plunged into the lake and towed it out into deeper water. He submerged the bag and watched it spiral slowly down into the gloom.

An alarming tingling enveloped his arm. A clumsy dog paddle carried him back to shore, and he staggered back to the house. What of the supplies? Should he drown those as well? No point. Either she was dead and the Covey would find them, or she was alive and she would hopefully use them to escape. He threw the fish into the fire to burn and left, closing the door tightly behind him.

The rain began again, a real downpour. He expected it would wash away any trace of his visit. The guns were gone. The supplies were Lucy Gray's. The only thing that remained were his footprints, and those were melting before his eyes. The clouds seemed to be infiltrating his brain. He struggled to think. *Get back. You must get back to base.* But where was it? He pulled his father's compass from his pocket, amazed it still worked after the dunking in the lake. Crassus Snow was still out there somewhere, still protecting him.

Coriolanus clung to the compass, a lifeline in the storm, as he headed south. He stumbled through the woods, terrified and alone but feeling his father's presence beside him. Crassus might not have thought much of him, but he'd have wanted his legacy to live on, and perhaps Coriolanus had redeemed himself somewhat today? None of it would matter if the venom killed him. He stopped to vomit, wishing he'd brought along the jug of water. He vaguely realized that his DNA would be on that, too, but who cared? The jug was not a murder weapon. It didn't matter. He was safe. If the Covey found Lucy Gray's body, they wouldn't report it. They wouldn't want the attention it brought. It might connect them to the rebels or reveal their hideout. If there was a body. He could not even confirm he'd hit her.

Coriolanus made it back. Not to the hanging tree, exactly, but to District 12, wandering out of a stretch of trees into a clump of miners' hovels and somehow finding the road. The ground shook with thunder, and lightning slashed the sky as he reached the town square. He saw no one as he made it to the base and climbed back through the fence. He went straight to the clinic, claiming he'd stopped to tie his shoe on his way to the gym, when a snake had appeared out of nowhere to bite him.

The doctor nodded. "The rain brings them out."

"Does it?" Coriolanus thought his story would have been challenged, or at least met with skepticism.

The doctor did not seem suspicious. "Did you get a look at it?"

"Not really. It was raining, and it moved fast," he answered. "Am I going to die?"

"Hardly," the doctor chuckled. "It wasn't even venomous. See the teeth marks? No fangs. Going to be sore for a few days, though."

"Are you sure? I threw up, and I couldn't think straight," he said.

"Well, panic can do that." She cleaned the wound. "Probably leave a scar."

Good, thought Coriolanus. *It will remind me to be more careful.*

She gave him several shots and a bottle of pills. "Come by tomorrow, and we'll check it again."

"Tomorrow I'm being reassigned to District Two," replied Coriolanus.

"Visit the clinic there, then," she said. "Good luck, soldier."

Coriolanus went back to his room, shocked to find it was only midafternoon. Between the booze and the rain, his bunkmates had never even risen. He went to the bathroom and emptied his pockets. The lake water had reduced his mother's rose-scented powder to a nasty paste, and he threw the whole thing in the trash. The photos stuck together and shredded when he tried to separate them, so they went the way of the powder. Only the compass had survived the outing. He peeled off his clothes and scrubbed off the last bits of the lake. When he'd dressed, he took down his duffel and began to pack, returning the compass to his box of personal items and stowing it deep in the bag. On reflection, he opened Sejanus's locker and took his box as well. When he got to District 2, he'd mail it to the Plinths with a note of condolence. That would be appropriate as Sejanus's best friend. And who knew? Maybe the cookies would keep coming.

The following morning, after a tearful good-bye from his bunkmates, he boarded the hovercraft for District Two. Things improved immediately. The plush seat. The attendant. The beverage selection. Not luxurious, by any means, but a far cry from the recruit train. Comforted by comfort, he leaned his temple against the window, hoping to get in a nap. All night, while the rain had drummed on the barrack's roof, he'd wondered where Lucy Gray was. Dead in the rain? Curled up by the fire in the lake house? If she'd survived, surely she'd abandoned the idea of returning to District 12. He dozed off with the melody to "The Hanging Tree" humming in his brain, and awoke hours later as the hovercraft touched down.

"Welcome to the Capitol," the attendant said.

Coriolanus's eyes popped open. "What? No. Did I miss my stop? I have to report to District Two."

"This craft goes on to Two, but we have orders to drop you here," said the attendant, checking a list. "I'm afraid you need to disembark. We have a schedule to keep."

He found himself on the tarmac of a small, unfamiliar airport. A Peacekeepers' truck pulled up, and he was ordered into the back. As he rattled along, unable to get any information from the driver, dread seeped into him. There had been a mistake. Or had there? What if they had somehow linked him to the murders? Maybe Lucy Gray had returned and accused him, and they needed to question him? Would they drag the lake for the weapons? His heart gave a little jump as they turned onto Scholars

Road and drove past the Academy, quiet and still on a summer afternoon. There was the park where they'd sometimes hung out at after school. And the bakery with those cupcakes he loved. At least he'd been granted one more glimpse of his hometown. Nostalgia faded as the truck made a sharp turn and he realized they were heading up the drive to the Citadel.

Inside, the guards waved him right through to the elevator. "She's expecting you in the lab."

He held on to the thin hope that "she" meant Dr. Kay, not Dr. Gaul, but his old nemesis waved to him from across the lab as he stepped off the elevator. Why was he here? Was he going to end up in one of her cages? As he crossed to her, he saw her drop a live baby mouse into a tank of golden snakes.

"So the victor returns. Here, hold these." Dr. Gaul pushed a metal bowl filled with squirming, pink rodents into his hands.

Coriolanus suppressed a gag. "Hello, Dr. Gaul."

"I got your letter," she said. "And your jabberjay. Too bad about young Plinth. Although, is it, really? Anyway, I was pleased to see you were continuing your studies in Twelve. Developing your worldview."

He felt himself pulled right back into the old tutorial with her, as if nothing had happened. "Yes, it was eye-opening. I thought about all the things we'd discussed. Chaos, control, the contract. The three *C*'s."

"Did you think about the Hunger Games?" she asked. "The day we met, Casca asked you what their purpose was, and you gave the stock answer. To punish the districts. Would you change that now?"

Coriolanus remembered the conversation he'd had with Sejanus as they'd unpacked his duffel. "I'd elaborate on it. They're not just to punish the districts, they're part of the eternal war.

Each one is its own battle. One we can hold in the palm of our hand, instead of waging a real war that could get out of our control."

"Hm." She swung a mouse away from a gaping mouth. "You there, don't be greedy."

"And they're a reminder of what we did to each other, what we have the potential to do again, because of who we are," he continued.

"And who are we, did you determine?" she asked.

"Creatures who need the Capitol to survive." He couldn't help getting in a dig. "It's all pointless, though, you know. The Hunger Games. No one in Twelve even watches it. Except for the reaping. We didn't even have a working television on base."

"While that could be a problem in the future, it's a blessing this year, given that I've had to erase the whole mess," said Dr. Gaul. "It was a mistake getting the students mixed up in it. Especially when they started dropping like flies. Presented the Capitol as far too vulnerable."

"You erased it?" he asked.

"Every last copy gone, never to be aired again." She grinned. "I've a master in the vault, of course, but that's just for my own amusement."

He was glad about the erasure. It was just one more way to eliminate Lucy Gray from the world. The Capitol would forget her, the districts barely knew her, and District 12 had never accepted her as one of their own. In a few years, there would be a vague memory that a girl had once sung in the arena. And then that would be forgotten, too. Good-bye, Lucy Gray, we hardly knew you.

"Not a total loss. I think we'll bring Flickerman back next year. And your idea about the betting is a keeper," she said.

"You need to somehow make the viewing mandatory. No one in Twelve will tune in to something that depressing by choice," he told her. "They spend what little free time they have drinking to forget the rest of their lives."

Dr. Gaul chuckled. "It seems you've learned a lot on your summer vacation, Mr. Snow."

"Vacation?" he said, perplexed.

"Well, what were you going to do here? Laze around the Capitol, combing out your curls? I thought a summer with the Peacekeepers would be far more educational." She took in the confusion on his face. "You don't think I've invested all this time in you to hand you off to those imbeciles in the districts, do you?"

"I don't understand, I was told —" he began.

She cut him off. "I've ordered you an honorable discharge, effective immediately. You're to study under me at the University."

"The University? Here in the Capitol?" he said in surprise.

She dropped one last mouse into the tank. "Classes start Thursday."

EPILOGUE

On a brilliant October afternoon halfway into fall term, Snow descended the marble steps of the University Science Center, modestly ignoring the turning heads. He looked gorgeous in his new suit, especially with the return of his curls, and his stint as a Peacekeeper had given him a certain cachet that drove his rivals wild.

He'd just finished a special honors class in military strategy with Dr. Gaul, after a morning at the Citadel, where he'd reported for his Gamemaker internship. If you wanted to call it that — really the others treated him as a full-fledged member of the team. They were already working on ideas to engage the districts, as well as the Capitol, in next year's Hunger Games. Snow had been the one to point out that, other than the life of two tributes they might not even know, the people in the districts had no stake in the Games. A tribute's win needed to be a win for the whole district. They'd come up with the idea that everyone in the district would receive a parcel of food if their tribute took the crown. And to tempt a better class of tributes to possibly volunteer, Snow suggested that the victor should be given a house in a special area of town, tentatively called the Victor's Village, which would be the envy of all those people in the hovels. That, and a token monetary prize, should go a long way toward bringing in a decent crop of performers.

His fingers stroked his butter-soft leather satchel, a back-to-school gift from the Plinths. He still tripped over what to call them. "Ma" was easy enough, but it didn't suit to call Strabo Plinth his father, so he used "sir" a lot. It wasn't as if they'd adopted him; he'd been too old at eighteen. Being designated an heir worked better for him anyway. He'd never give up the name Snow, not even for a munitions empire.

It had all happened very naturally. His homecoming. Their grief. The merging of the families. Sejanus's death had totaled the Plinths. Strabo had put it simply: "My wife needs something to live for. So do I, for that matter. You've lost your parents. We've lost our son. I was thinking perhaps we could work something out." He'd bought the Snows' apartment so they didn't have to move, and the Dolittles' below it for himself and Ma. There was talk of renovating, of building a spiral staircase and perhaps a private elevator to connect the two, but there was no rush. Ma already came by daily to help with the Grandma'am, who'd resigned herself to having a new "maid," and she and Tigris got on swimmingly. The Plinths paid for everything now: the taxes on the apartment, his tuition, the cook. They gave him a generous allowance as well. This was helpful because, although he'd intercepted and pocketed the envelope of money he'd sent Tigris from District 12, university life was expensive when done right. Strabo never questioned his expenditures or nitpicked over a few new additions to his wardrobe, and he seemed pleased when Snow asked for advice. They were surprisingly compatible. At times, he almost forgot old Plinth was district. Almost.

Tonight would've been Sejanus's nineteenth birthday, and they were gathering for a quiet dinner to remember him. Snow had invited Festus and Lysistrata to join the party, as they'd liked Sejanus better than most of his classmates and could be counted on to say nice things. He planned to present the Plinths with the box from Sejanus's locker, but first he had one more thing to do.

The fresh air on the walk to the Academy left his mind razor sharp. He hadn't bothered to make an appointment, preferring to drop in unexpectedly. The students had been let out an hour ago, and his footsteps rang in the hallways. Dean Highbottom's secretary's desk was empty, so he crossed to the dean's office and tapped on the door. Dean Highbottom bid him enter. Between the weight loss and the tremor, he looked worse than ever, slumped over his desk.

"Well, to what do I owe this honor?" he asked.

"I was hoping to recover my mother's compact, since you should have no further need of it," Snow replied.

Dean Highbottom reached into a drawer and slapped the compact on the desk. "Is that all?"

"No." He removed Sejanus's box from his satchel. "I'm returning Sejanus's personal effects to his parents tonight. I'm not sure what to do with this." He emptied the contents onto the desk and picked up the framed diploma. "I didn't think you'd want it floating around out there. An Academy diploma. Awarded to a traitor."

"You're very conscientious," said Dean Highbottom.

"That's my Peacekeeper training." Snow loosened the back of the frame and slipped out the diploma. Then, as if on impulse, he replaced it with a photo of the Plinth family. "I think his parents will prefer this anyway." They both stared at the remains of Sejanus's life. Then he swept the three medicine bottles into Dean Highbottom's trash can. "The fewer bad memories, the better."

Dean Highbottom eyed him. "So, you grew a heart in the districts?"

"Not in the districts. In the Hunger Games," Snow corrected him. "I have you to thank for that. After all, you're responsible for them."

"Oh, I think half the credit for that goes to your father," said the dean.

Snow frowned. "How do you mean? I thought the Hunger Games were your idea. Something you came up with at the University?"

"For Dr. Gaul's class. Which I was failing, since my loathing of her made participation impossible. We paired off for the final project, so I was with my best friend — Crassus, of course. The assignment was to create a punishment for one's enemies so extreme that they would never be allowed to forget how they had wronged you. It was like a puzzle, which I excel at, and like all good creations, absurdly simple at its core. The Hunger Games. The evilest impulse, cleverly packaged into a sporting event. An entertainment. I was drunk and your father got me drunker still, playing on my vanity as I fleshed the thing out, assuring me it was just a private joke. The next morning, I awoke, horrified by what I'd made, meaning to rip it to shreds, but it was too late. Without my permission, your father had given it to Dr. Gaul. He wanted the grade, you see. I never forgave him."

"He's dead," said Snow.

"But she isn't," Dean Highbottom shot back. "It was never meant to be anything more than theoretical. And who but the vilest monster would stage it? After the war, she pulled my proposal out, and me with it, introducing me to Panem as the architect of the Hunger Games. That night, I tried morphling for the first time. I thought the thing would die out, it was so ghastly. It didn't. Dr. Gaul took it and ran, and she has dragged me along with it for the last ten years."

"It certainly supports her view of humanity," said Snow. "Especially using the children."

"And why is that?" asked Dean Highbottom.

"Because we credit them with innocence. And if even the most innocent among us turn to killers in the Hunger Games, what does that say? That our essential nature is violent," Snow explained.

"Self-destructive," Dean Highbottom murmured.

Snow remembered Pluribus's account of his father's falling out with Dean Highbottom and quoted the letter. "Like moths to a flame." The dean's eyes narrowed, but Snow only smiled and said, "But, of course, you're testing me. You know her far better than I do."

"I'm not so sure." Dean Highbottom traced the silver rose on the compact with a finger. "So, what did she say when you told her you were leaving?"

"Dr. Gaul?" Snow asked.

"Your little songbird," the dean said. "When you left Twelve. Was she sad to see you go?"

"I expect it made us both a little sad." Snow pocketed the compact and gathered Sejanus's things. "I'd better go. We have a new living room set being delivered, and I promised my cousin I'd be there to oversee the movers."

"Off you go, then," said Dean Highbottom. "Back to the penthouse."

Snow did not care to talk about Lucy Gray with anyone, particularly not Dean Highbottom. Smiley had sent him a letter at the Plinths' old address, mentioning her disappearance. Everybody thought the mayor had killed her, but they couldn't prove it. As to the Covey, a new commander had replaced Hoff, and his first move had been to outlaw shows at the Hob, because music caused trouble.

Yes, thought Snow. *It certainly does.*

Lucy Gray's fate was a mystery, then, just like the little girl who shared her name in that maddening song. Was she alive, dead, a ghost who haunted the wilderness? Perhaps no one would ever really know. No matter — snow had been the ruination of them both. Poor Lucy Gray. Poor ghost girl singing away with her birds.

Are you, are you
Coming to the tree
Where I told you to run, so we'd both be free?

She could fly around District 12 all she liked, but she and her mockingjays could never harm him again.

Sometimes he would remember a moment of sweetness and almost wish things had ended differently. But it would never have worked out between them, even if he'd stayed. They were simply too different. And he didn't like love, the way it had made him feel stupid and vulnerable. If he ever married, he'd choose someone incapable of swaying his heart. Someone he hated, even, so they could never manipulate him the way Lucy Gray had. Never make him feel jealous. Or weak. Livia Cardew would be perfect. He imagined the two of them, the president and his first lady, presiding over the Hunger Games a few years from now. He'd continue the Games, of course, when he ruled Panem. People would call him a tyrant, ironfisted and cruel. But at least he would ensure survival for survival's sake, giving them a chance to evolve. What else could humanity hope for? Really, it should thank him.

He passed Pluribus's nightclub and allowed himself a small smile. A person could get rat poison at any number of places, but he'd surreptitiously scooped up a pinch of it from the back alley last week and taken it home. It'd been tricky getting it into the morphling bottle, especially using gloves, but eventually he'd squeezed what he judged to be a sufficient dose through the opening. He'd taken the precaution of making sure the bottle was wiped clean. There was nothing to make Dean Highbottom suspicious of it when he pulled it from the trash and slipped it into his pocket. Nothing when he unscrewed the dropper and dripped the morphling onto his tongue. Although he couldn't help hoping that, as the dean drew his final breath, he'd realize what so many others had realized when they'd challenged him. What all of Panem would know one day. What was inevitable.

Snow lands on top.

THE END

ACKNOWLEDGMENTS

I'd like to thank my parents for their love and for always supporting my writing: my dad, for teaching me about the Enlightenment thinkers and the state of nature debate from an early age; and my mom, the English major, for nurturing the reader in me and for all those happy hours around the piano.

My husband, Cap Pryor, and my literary agent, Rosemary Stimola, have long been my first readers. Their input on the early drafts of this novel was invaluable in the development of young Coriolanus Snow and his postwar world and no doubt saved my editors all kinds of headaches. And speaking of editors, never did an author have such a deep and talented bench. This time, they arrived in waves, starting with the amazing Kate Egan, who has so skillfully guided me through ten books, along with David Levithan, my most excellent editorial director, who was everywhere at once — forging that title, trimming those unwieldy passages, and arranging clandestine manuscript handoffs at (where else?) the Shakespeare in the Park production of *Coriolanus*. The second wave brought the gifted and insightful pair of Jen Rees and Emily Seife, followed by my eagle-eyed copy editors, Rachel Stark and Joy Simpkins, who left no stone unturned. I am deeply grateful to you all for helping me shape this story with your beautiful brains and hearts.

Such a pleasure to be back in the hands of the terrific team at Scholastic Press. Rachel Coun, Lizette Serrano, Tracy van Straaten, Ellie Berger, Dick Robinson, Mark Seidenfeld, Leslie Garych, Josh Berlowitz, Erin O'Connor, Maeve Norton, Stephanie Jones, JoAnne Mojica, Andrea Davis Pinkney, Billy DiMichele, and the entire Scholastic sales force — a big thanks to you all.

A special shout-out goes to Elizabeth B. Parisi and Tim O'Brien, who have dazzled me once again with their fabulous cover, consistent with their Hunger Games trilogy visions, but unique to this new book as well.

Much admiration and gratitude goes to all the artists who created songs that appear in the world of Panem. Three of the songs are classics in the public domain: "Down in the Valley," "Oh, My Darling, Clementine," and "Keep on the Sunny Side," which was written by Ada Blenkhorn and J. Howard Entwisle. The poem "Lucy Gray" was penned in 1799 by William Wordsworth and appeared in his *Lyrical Ballads*. The words in the above songs have been tweaked to fit the Covey. The rest of the lyrics are original. "The Ballad of Lucy Gray Baird" is meant to be sung to a variation of a traditional ballad tune that has long accompanied tales of the unfortunate ends of rakes, bards, soldiers, cowboys, and the like. Two other numbers first appeared in the Hunger Games trilogy. In the film version, the music for "Deep in the Meadow" was composed by T Bone Burnett and Simone Burnett, and "The Hanging Tree" music was composed by Jeremiah Caleb Fraites and Wesley Keith Schultz of The Lumineers and arranged by James Newton Howard.

Ongoing thanks to my wonderful agents, the aforementioned Rosemary Stimola and my entertainment representative, Jason Dravis, on whom I rely completely to help me navigate the publishing and film worlds with the aid of our legal eagles, Janis C. Nelson, Eleanor Lackman, and Diane Golden.

I'd like to send love to my friends and family, particularly Richard Register, who is always one text away, and to Cap, Charlie, and Izzy, who have ridden this ride with perspective, patience, and humor.

And finally, to all the readers who have invested in first Katniss's and now Coriolanus's tales: I sincerely thank you for traveling this road with me.

About the Author

Suzanne Collins is the author of the bestselling Underland Chronicles series, which started with *Gregor the Overlander*. Her groundbreaking young adult novels, *The Hunger Games*, *Catching Fire*, and *Mockingjay*, were *New York Times* bestsellers, received wide praise, and were the basis for four popular films. *Year of the Jungle*, her picture book based on the year her father was deployed in Vietnam, was published in 2013 to great critical acclaim. To date, her books have been published in fifty-three languages around the world.